By E.C. Deacon

For Jules

The sons of God saw that they were fair;
and they took wives for themselves
of all that they chose.

Genesis 6.1–4

Number sixteen

He was watching her through a pair of gun metal grey reading glasses. He owned a number of different designs, half long distance and half 4:5 readers, for the more intimate work. He bought them at Poundland, because you were required to pay in cash. She described herself on her profile as having chestnut hair, but an unkind person, he mused, would describe her as ginger. But, on closer examination, her pale skin intrigued him. He detected a hint of freckles beneath her foundation and wondered if they blighted the rest of her body.

She sat in a candlelit alcove of The Botanist. A bar that, considering its prime position outside the gates of Kew Gardens, was curiously always empty. Even in the summer, when the picture-postcard Green was full of cricketers and St. Anne's Church Hall was doing a roaring trade in home-made cakes and, being Kew, specialist teas, the Botanist and its tapas menu remained for some reason persona non grata.

Nephilim knew none of this. He'd made his recce on a windswept October night, and was immediately drawn to the bars recalcitrant staff and dimly lit nooks and crannies. In his mind, it was perfect. Perfect for watching and not being watched.

His mobile warbled a text warning. He ignored it. The ginger had caught his eye, it was time for work. He returned her smile. She was expecting him to make the first move – they were always so predictable – but he didn't. He knew he didn't match the photo of the "mature single" she'd agreed to meet, because he'd uploaded a stock image from the Internet and created a fake profile. He waited, enjoying her confusion…

"Excuse me. Are you Mark? Mark Knowles?"

For a moment, he actually felt sorry for her. She stood marooned in her faux-fur gilet, hiding behind her handbag like she was trying to protect her long-gone virginity. He pretended not to hear. Took out his cucumber hand gel, cleansed his hands – and his mind of human kindness.

The ginger flushed, cleared her throat, and tried again. "Excuse me?"

He turned, full of effusive apologies, and said, "Oh. Sorry. Were you talking to me?"

"Yes. Sorry. I didn't mean to interrupt you. It's Tessa? Tessa Hayes? Match.com?" Behind her middle-class veneer of confidence, she was faltering already. "You're not Mark?"

He shook his head and affected a look of disappointment. He'd rehearsed it numerous times, usually whilst shaving his head before taking his twice-daily shower. He never bathed; it was bad for his condition and the dirty water risked further infection.

"Sorry. I was waiting for someone. I thought... Sorry. I didn't mean to embarrass you."

He assured her she hadn't. Which was true. He enjoyed watching her squirm. It amused him. Besides, she'd brought it on herself. Desperation was unflattering in a woman, especially one on the wrong side of middle-age trying too hard to look like she wasn't.

He finally put her out of her misery, introducing himself as Robin Holt – a name stolen from *The Times* obituaries – a surveyor from Oxshott in Surrey. He was hanging on for a call from a potential client in Kew about a meeting, so he could sympathise with how she felt. Perhaps he could buy her a drink and they could wait together? He could see her weighing up her options. She'd been stood up; what had she to lose? He smiled sheepishly, already knowing the outcome.

Tessa Hayes didn't. If she had, she would never have accepted his offer. She'd have run screaming out of The Botanist on pretty Kew Green and away from the horror awaiting her.

* * *

2

Three-point-eight Google miles away, a Tube train grumbled beside platform four in Earls Court station. It had been stranded for twenty minutes and even with the doors open it reeked of sweat and frustration. Finally, the guard explained over the intercom that someone had "found themselves under a train" at West Brompton. A few commuters let out an audible moan. Not for the fate of the suicide but for the delay to their homeward journeys.

Gina Lewis suspected it must have been a man. Throwing yourself under a moving train seemed to her an unnecessarily macho thing to do and left a lot to chance. What if death wasn't instant? You'd be left with multiple fractures, amputated limbs… brain damage?

The pervert still hadn't answered her text, so she idled away some time by checking the stats on her iPhone. She found a site called Loss of All Hope and tapped it. It made for fascinating reading. She'd had no idea that in the United Kingdom, train incidents accounted for 3.5 per cent of all suicides. Or that there was a ninety per cent mortality rate for jumping in front of a high-speed train and only sixty-seven per cent for an underground train. Or that Wimbledon, her home station, was one of the UK's suicide hotspots.

A sudden swell of movement by the carriage doors interrupted her. She looked up and saw them file in two by two and fill their District line ark. She counted twenty of them, all dressed in navy and grey. She wasn't good with ages, never having had or wanted kids of her own, but guessed the oldest girls couldn't have been more than six or seven. Corralling the flock were three harassed teachers and in the middle of them were two young boys. Gina watched them from her seat, looking for any sign of embarrassment, but the boys seemed blissfully unaware of the sexual imbalance. She smiled ruefully to herself and wondered how long that innocence would last.

"Are those your real eyes?" A little blonde girl had stepped in front of Gina, staring quizzically at her. Gina could smell her sweet Orangeade breath as she leaned in for a closer look. "Or lenses?"

Gina swiftly dropped her eyes back down to her iPhone in an effort to ignore her.

"They're pretty. I've got amblyopia." She pulled down her lower lid to reveal her left iris, which was the palest of hazel and twisted down and slightly inward like a misplaced contact lens. It was curiously beautiful and leant her face an unearthly quality, like an angel hiding a dark secret.

"It's called Lazy Eye but we're not allowed to say that," said a tiny Indian girl with plaits down to her waist.

"I don't mind," said the little blonde girl.

"So," said Gina, warming to the girl's lack of self-pity, "will you have to have an operation?"

"Yes. Or she'll go blind," explained a seriously freckle-faced girl who had joined the clutch now encircling Gina. "We've been to a concert for her charity."

"Oh. That's nice. Who was playing?"

"We were," she announced to anyone who would listen. "We're a choir."

And on cue – albeit unasked for – the little troupe suddenly launched into "You Can't Always Get What You Want".

Gina was stunned. Not because it was bad; on the contrary, it was breath-taking. The purity of the children's voices counterpointed the cynical lyrics of The Rolling Stones' song perfectly, and utterly transformed the meaning. She sat there, mesmerised, as the other kids joined in and their voices swelled in innocent pleasure until they filled the whole carriage.

Thirty minutes later, Gina pulled up the hood on her Whistles parka and trotted down the steps of Wimbledon station, still thinking about the magical event she'd unwittingly become part of, and that if she hadn't looked up it never would have happened. She felt proud of herself, because her fellow commuters, mothers and fathers amongst them, had kept their heads steadfastly buried in their papers until the choir had safely disembarked at East Putney.

Gina stepped out into the sleeting rain, manoeuvred her way through another weary tide of commuters, parting like the Red

Sea around the wheelchair-bound *Big Issue* seller, and turned left onto Queens Road. She loved the long, arrow-straight walk past the police station on the right and the Everyday Church, offering tea, Zumba and spiritual solace, on the left. A fox loped out of a gateway ahead of her and sat on the pavement, watching her as she approached. She stopped in front of it. It eyed her, king of its patch, then shivered the rain from its fur and ambled past and into the next gate.

The rain was getting heavier now but she didn't care. "You can't always get what you want," she hummed to herself as she crossed to the south side of the road. The neon streetlights threw oval pools onto the path ahead of her like giant's footprints. She silently counted her own between them, feeling like a femme fatale in a movie making her way to some clandestine meeting, where her fate would finally be decided.

Which, in a sense, she was.

* * *

Christ, thought Tessa Hayes. *What's wrong with me?* She felt queasy, thought she might throw up. How could she be so drunk? She'd only had two small glasses of Merlot. One minute she'd been fine and the next she was slurring her words and could barely form a sentence.

"Wake up," Nephilim instructed as he pinched her nipple. "Come along. Open your eyes."

She should have been outraged but somehow it didn't seem to matter. Her shit of an ex-husband had shagged everything with a pulse and blamed *her* lack of sex drive. Why shouldn't she have some fun?

She hauled open her eyes and grinned lopsidedly up at him. But somehow the words wouldn't come. Something was choking them back. Blinking up at a strip light that hung from the corrugated metal ceiling, she saw pipes running like giant veins and disappearing into some shadowy void beyond. Perched on them, silhouetted against the grey metal, were birds. White birds, with bead-black eyes, staring implacably down at her... and it smelt of... meat? Raw meat. She tried to call out. But there was something in her mouth, something soft pressing down on her tongue. Panic rose like bile in her throat and she gagged.

Nephilim watched her choke, thinking about the demise of his first model. She'd been his Night Sister. After his operation, he contracted bacterial MRSA. Not from the wound itself but from the endotracheal tube that was inserted into his throat to aid his breathing. Within hours, sepsis had set in and he'd become delirious, lost consciousness, and nearly died. Something positive had come out of it though. His "angel of the night" – an ebullient, fifty-five-year-old night nurse. He'd kept her cadaver for three months to practice on and in retrospect realised that she'd help his work to grow in stature and depth. He was actually thankful for her shortcomings because they'd taught him to become more selective in his choice of future models. They now had to fulfil a number of criteria, not just physically but psychologically and sexually.

And the ginger lying at his feet appeared to.

* * *

Caxton Road was labelled as being on the "other side of the tracks" by those who care about such things. Gina Lewis didn't. Situated within walking distance of St. George's Hospital, which was handy for her appointments, she loved the road immediately. It felt authentic, democratic. Two rows of identical semis reflecting each other across the narrow street, but each somehow individual and populated by real, working people. The antithesis of the village with its designer boutiques, empty but for Wimbledon fortnight.

Her psychotherapist, Leonard, was less enthusiastic. But then, she reasoned, caution was part of his job description. Grey of hair and temperament, Len, as he preferred to be called, was concerned about her making an impulse buy, especially something as large as a house, so soon after coming off her lithium. But Gina's mind was made up. She finally knew who she really was. Had met someone who understood and loved her for who she was. She was going to stop picking at the scabs of the past and start making new memories. She sealed her electronic bid and, hey presto, won the auction. She was ecstatic. In all her thirty-eight years, she'd never won a thing. It was an omen. She was finally starting a new life.

Number sixteen was a freshly painted white semi, with racing green shutters, situated midway down on the left. She unlocked the Chubb and the mortise, switched on the light and made her way into the kitchen, eased off her Office brogues and black tights, and dumped them both in the pedal bin.

The pervert who'd ruined her life was still ignoring her texts – revenge was going to be so fucking sweet – but Laura Fell had left a message on the answerphone offering to pick her up on her way to the Chill Out. Gina toyed with the idea of ringing her. They'd grown up together – shared flats, holidays, even the occasional boyfriend. But she couldn't share this. She replaced the phone in its cradle and looked around her perfect lounge, drawing comfort from all her hard work. Her mother hated her calling it the lounge but it was *her* house and her favourite room. The Victorian fireplace she'd had sandblasted to reveal the original cast iron. Its antique tiles she'd restored herself. The floor-to-ceiling brocade curtains she'd found in the Curtain Exchange, the matching tapestry cushions online. She didn't care if her mother thought it might be more fashionable to have the whole thing knocked through into one modern living space. It was her home. *Hers.*

She strode back into the kitchen, yanked open a drawer, grabbed one of the neatly folded brown paper bags, unfolded it, held it over her mouth and nose, and began to count backwards from twenty as she slowly and methodically inhaled and exhaled.

Ten minutes later, she sat in her Victorian roll-top bath, shaving her legs with a disposable razor. She used smooth practised strokes, always following the direction of the growth. She had sensitive skin and didn't need any nicks, especially today. The water made her jet-coloured hair look indecently dark against the pale skin of her shoulders. The rest of her body was hairless. She washed the remains of the shaving gel off, stepped out onto the travertine tiles and wrapped herself in a towel. Then lowered the soft-close seat on the lavatory and sat on it to paint her toe nails.

She always wore the same colour on her hands and feet: Plum Wine. She loved the name. It made her feel sexy, even a little tarty, and she smiled to herself, remembering the first time she'd worn it. She'd met a guy on a singles holiday to Tenerife and they'd gone on a guided tour to Mount Teide, a dormant volcano. They slipped away from the party to have sex behind an outcrop of boulders. But afterwards when they lay nude sunbathing, she opened her eyes and found her toenails covered in tiny blue butterflies. And when they landed on her ink-black pubic hair she laughed and began posing like a living statue. But the idiot guy had thought she was being disgusting and demanded she brush them off before she caught something.

Hair and make-up flawless, she walked back into the lounge carrying a loop of blue-nylon clothes line. Putting it to one side, she checked her reflection in the mantle mirror, and smiled to herself as she adjusted the cowl neck of her vermillion dress. She looked good. Bloody good. Finally satisfied, she drew the curtains and stood back to admire her perfect lounge for the last time. Above her, the primrose chandelier, a joint moving-in present from her friends but obviously chosen by Laura Fell, hung like a promise of better things to come. Perhaps there were.

It took her three attempts to lasso the clothes line around the chandelier. The rococo design made it frustratingly difficult to completely encircle, but, she reflected grimly, it was better than a train. She gently tightened the slip knot and tested the weight, picked up her mobile and climbed carefully onto the pine coffee table.

Now all she had to do was tie the noose.

* * *

Tessa Hayes swam back up through the darkness and forced herself to breach the surface. Willing her throbbing head to lift, she saw to her horror that she was naked and lying on a plastic sheet. And that her hands and feet were bound by ropes to metal rings screwed into the scrubbed plank floor.

Nephilim heard her groan and turned from his metal workbench with a syringe in his left hand. Then knelt beside her and pulled her panties from her mouth with his right. Tessa gasped for air, but before she could scream, he squirted something into her throat, pinching her nose to make sure it went down. She tried to kick out but she couldn't; he was sitting astride her, his other hand on her throat, daring her to continue.

He felt her submit, pushed the gag back into place, eased himself off her and walked back to arrange the scalpels, scissors and forceps, that lay on his workbench.

"I've just given you another sixty milligrams of Rohypnol. I won't bore you with the details but, put simply, it binds with your brain's benzodiazepine receptor and shuts down your neurological functions. Don't worry, I'm not going to rape you, I just need you calm for my work." His voice had the professional detachment of a surgeon reassuring a fearful patient; benign but authoritative. "My name is Nephilim and my work is my vocation. It's a gift and I am going to share it with you. I'm going to make you whole again. For Him."

Him?

She thought she saw him smiling to himself, as if he were savouring a private joke, but it may have just been her raging imagination.

He swapped spectacles, blinking behind thick brown lashes as his eyes readjusted to the stronger reading glasses, picked up an SLR camera and fired off a couple of test shots. The flash blinded her for a moment. When her vision cleared, he was standing over her holding a pair of chrome pinking shears.

"I don't want to cut you so lay still." He knelt beside her and grabbed a fistful of her auburn hair, twisting it like a coil until it tugged at her scalp. "Shall we begin?"

He lifted the shears, placed them flat against her scalp and began to scissor. Tessa felt the hair fall across her face and for some inexplicable reason began to fret about the expensive home visit of her hair stylist prior to her date. *What a waste*, she thought as she sank slowly back into the darkness.

Her hair lay like a red halo around her. Nephilim was pleased, not a nick or scratch, he'd done his preliminary work well. He wished she'd have been conscious to see it and toyed with the idea of adjusting the dose next time. He placed the Bic razor aside and wiped the remaining smears of shaving foam from her bald head. Picked up his cordless trimmers, replaced its long comb with a shorter one, and repositioned himself to work on her lower body. He switched on the trimmer and began his work, then stopped, alert, listening. The skylark was calling again.

Eleven hours later, when Tessa Hayes staggered naked and traumatised from the River Wandle in Mitcham, she had no recollection of what had happened to her or that she'd been saved by an MMS, video message, from a dead woman.

The coven

A single woman living on the top-floor Victorian conversion of a terraced house in the hinterland of Kew, Laura Fell had learnt to be cautious of builders – and men in general. So, she gritted her teeth as she stepped under the shower.

"Shit!"

The water was *still* scalding. Her Polish plumber was supposed to have fixed the thermostatic mixer but had given her a lot of guff about problems with the loft overflow tank, which was rubbish because as far as she knew she didn't have one.

Her landline rang. She paused, listening, as the answerphone clicked on. It wasn't Gina Lewis but Megan Howell's insistent voice she heard, rechecking the travel arrangements for the evening. It was Megan, a relative newcomer to South West London, who'd suggested they set up their own Chill Out group within FrontRow, a social club for forty-somethings interested in the arts, and since then had become its driving force. Laura ignored it.

After her shower, Laura stretched out on her bed, swathed in her dusty-pink dressing gown, checking through the holiday photographs on her laptop as she waited for her expensively streaked blonde hair – one of the few indulgences she allowed herself – to dry.

Ibiza had been fun. It was supposed to have been a walking holiday, staying in pensions on the north of the island. But Gina had a cousin working at Lio, the famous club in Ibiza Old Town, and got them free passes to their Season Finale Party. The other ladies of Chill Out found the idea of clubbing at their age "faintly embarrassing" and declined the offer. Gina could not have cared less and told Laura they'd have a better time without them. Which they did. It was a blast. They may have been ten years older than anyone else but they'd partied as hard, dancing on their chairs and table, even stripping down to their underwear and jumping in the pool to join the bubble bath finale. Later, on their way back to the pension, Gina confided that she'd finally found the courage to stop taking her medication. Laura was concerned but Gina reassured her, telling her for the first time in years she felt truly happy and at peace with herself.

Laura sighed at the memory and stretched back onto the fresh cotton duvet. She liked the bed. It was big enough for sex but not overly comfortable for two people to sleep in. Perfect for her, since she was wary of that kind of intimacy. Even as a child she'd been uncomfortable with overt shows of emotion and instinctively mistrusted their proponents. Growing up in Kenya at the fag-end of British colonial rule, her magistrate father had epitomised everything she longed for in a partner: strength and integrity. She remembered him locking her in a Malindi jail, with nothing but a mattress and a slop bucket, for stealing a melon from a market vendor. She was seven years old and terrified. But it was only for a half an hour and afterwards she respected and loved him more for it.

She reached for her mobile on the shabby-chic bedside table, one of her better purchases from eBay. She didn't care if it was described as pine but in reality, was painted MDF; it looked beautiful and matched the old lace colour of the walls perfectly. Even though they would have to be redecorated if the ugly cracks fracturing the plaster below the sash window were confirmed as subsidence. Shunting the concern to the back of her mind, she dialled Gina Lewis' number again. It rang and rang, unanswered. Finally, she gave up and texted her instead.

She tossed the mobile on the bed, slipped out of her dressing gown and stood naked in front of the Cheval mirror. Her twice-weekly Spinning and Aerotone workouts showed. Perhaps an inch or two taller than she'd have preferred, and with wide swimmer's shoulders, she still looked lean and fit. She massaged her breasts and stomach with cucumber aloe vera body lotion and thought about how she'd love to have a family of her own. Be like her mother and father and live her life through her children. But she was thirty-nine and that dream was long gone, along with her parents…

And her closest friend in the world, Gina Lewis.

* * *

It had taken Nephilim over an hour to dump Tessa Hayes – too long he knew – and now the traffic was backed up along Wimbledon Parkside and he didn't know an alternative route to Gina's. He wanted to scream, to smash something, *someone*. He bit down on the leathery weal on the back of his hand until the urge subsided into the pain. It was a trick he'd learnt from his childhood to help him cope with the dark nights in the coop.

There was a road fifty metres ahead on the left. God knows where it went but anything was better than this. He inched the Mercedes out for a better look. The rain and the headlamps of the cars bearing down on him made it impossible to judge the distance, but he had no other option. He went for broke.

The driver of the Ford Fiesta heard the screaming engine, looked back in alarm, and literally stood on his brakes as a madman slewed in front of him, narrowly missing an oncoming bus before disappearing down Queensmere Road.

But hitting the T-junction at the end of the road, Nephilim realised he was lost. A sign pointed to the Wimbledon Tennis Museum but he had no idea where the stadium was in relation to Haydons Road. He pulled over to check Google Maps on his mobile and gasped as the screen glowed again with Gina's MMS video. He knew he should have deleted it earlier, but he was drawn again, moth-like, to it.

His eyes brimmed as he watched Gina tighten the nylon ligature around her neck, stare into her iPhone camera as she positioned herself, then jerk violently back as she stepped off the table, her puce face contorting as she held grimly onto the mobile.

A car horn sounded behind him. He couldn't hear it. He couldn't hear or feel anything but his own agony. She'd done it to hurt him. Sent it to him to hurt him. *Why?* He loved her. She'd taught him what love was. Real love. Not slut love, doled out like a bargaining chip–

"Hello?"

The SUV driver tapped on the window with the heel of his golf umbrella and mimed for him to open up. He slid down the glass. The driver pointed to a sign on his electronic gates.

"Is that not big enough for you?"

It read:

DO NOT BLOCK THIS DRIVEWAY

"Move. Now. Please."

He was a city type in a nice suit, confident and authoritative. Nephilim wanted to get out and kill him. Kick him to death on his precious driveway. Make him suffer like he was suffering. But he didn't have the time. Gina, his dove, was the priority.

"Are you deaf or–?"

He wasn't expecting the punch. He toppled forward onto the car, leaving a slurry of blood on the door as he disappeared from view.

* * *

Only a few hundred metres away, Laura Fell and five members of Chill Out were meeting in a snug upstairs room of The Telegraph, a large country-style pub loved by the locals, hidden in the heart of Putney Heath, although tonight the atmosphere was anything but cosy.

Megan Howell sat ramrod, in a green cashmere twin-set, at the top of the table, fixing the diners with a mile-long stare, unhappy that the meal had started without her and her driver, Laura.

"You should have phoned," chided Frieda Cole, whose grey hair and sensible clothes belied her bone-dry sense of humour. "You were the one that insisted we eat early."

"I couldn't get a signal."

Frieda smiled solicitously and shovelled another portion of mushroom risotto into her mouth, signalling an end to her part in the discussion. But Megan, bridling at what she perceived as a challenge to her authority, felt obligated to have the final word.

"And I wasn't late, although I'm not blaming Lolly."

Lolly? groaned Laura to herself. *Christ. Why does she have to make everyone sound like a character out of a Victorian bloody novel? Even her dogs are called Bathsheba and Gabriel Oak.*

"She was waiting for the elusive Mr Hart," continued Megan.

Solicitous smiles were offered. Laura tried to ignore them. She'd met Don Hart at Rendezvous, a dating club for "mature singles" run by his ex-wife, which she always thought a bit strange. But ever the pragmatist, and good-looking and available men in their forties being in short supply, Laura had let it go. Sometimes she wished she hadn't. Don had grown jealous of her friends, calling them "the coven" and Megan "Akela" – although he'd never dare say it to her face.

"So, where is he?" whispered Frieda from behind her large glass of Chilean Sauvignon Blanc.

"God knows." Laura shrugged. "I expect he'll phone later with some lame excuse."

In the past, she'd endured Don's erratic temperament, since berating him never seemed to change anything and she wasn't looking for a long-term relationship. On the surface, he appeared an easy-going and charming man, but underneath lurked a well of resentment. Once, she'd made a jokey enquiry about how he ended up living in "leafy Mitcham" and he nearly bit her head off: "Because, Laura, when you've been screwed over by women twice, you can't afford leafy fucking Kew!"

"What happened to Colin?" Laura said, attempting to change the subject.

"He cried off because he thought Don was coming," explained Frieda, who rather liked Colin Gould, having known him for years and accepted him for what he was. A serious man, muted in every way. A man who chose his words as carefully as he chose his clothes and friends – of which Don Hart was definitely not one.

"Did you have a row? Has he spoken to Gina?" interjected Megan. "I mean, it's a bit odd, both of them just not turning up?"

"Megan. You're not suggesting they're having a fling?" Frieda grinned wickedly.

Megan pursed her fecund lips into a small O of indignation and replied, "Of course not. Gina's Laura's friend. She'd never do something like that. It's just that I phoned them both before I booked the table and they confirmed they were coming."

Megan had never really trusted Gina Lewis, thinking of her as flaky, and her absence tonight was a prime example. But it was more than that. Gina's capriciousness reminded her of someone. Someone who had ruined her life, who she'd moved to London to forget, and was now stalking "Miss Kitty Licker" by phone and online.

"Anyone want another drink?" Megan enquired, putting an end to the conversation.

"Just a small Sauvignon. Chilean," said Frieda, who was already on her second.

"No one else?"

Barely waiting for a response, Megan disappeared back down the stairs into the lounge. It was a quiet night, with only a few of the well-to-do locals occupying the comfortably battered sofas around the open fire. The young barman, with the fashionably lop-sided haircut, dragged his attention from the Sky TV football and turned towards her with a well-worn smile as she approached. She ignored him. Made her way into the Ladies, locked the door behind her and threw up violently into the lavatory.

There was blood in her vomit.

* * *

Nephilim parked on Garfield Road and walked up the path, bordering the empty windswept park. An old guy, walking an even older dog, was taking a fag break on one of the swings in the playground but never looked up as he passed. He turned left onto Caxton Road. The street looked quiet. Most of the commuters had already made their way home and, it being Monday, settled in for a quiet night in front of the television. He pulled the hood of his windcheater further down over his face and made his way towards number sixteen. Pushed open the gate and walked purposefully towards the racing green door. But, in his haste, he'd forgotten the infrared security lamp. He slipped out of its amber spill and, pulling on a pair of latex gloves, picked his way down the gravel path towards the back garden. Reaching over the wooden gate, he slid the bolt and eased inside, shutting and bolting it quietly behind him.

The garden backed onto the railway siding, but the feather-edge fence adjoining the next garden was barely five feet high, forcing him to creep in the shadows to the back door. The wooden hedgehog boot brush, his present to Gina, was still there, as was the key hidden beneath it. He unlocked the door, removed his shoes, left them on the mat outside and let himself into the kitchen. Every surface gleamed. Every utensil, ornament and piece of crockery was perfectly arranged. The room was, like Gina, immaculate, and gave no clue to the horror that he knew awaited him next door. In his mind, he could smell her as he forced himself towards the lounge. He'd smelt death before in the battery on killing days; that faint, sickly sweet aroma of raw meat. But as he opened the door there was no odour, only his beautiful Gina, hanging like a Christmas turkey in a butcher's shop.

He began to cry. He wanted to cut her down and make her perfect for whoever found her. But he knew he couldn't. He couldn't touch her or leave any trace of himself. He knelt below her, retrieved her mobile phone and slipped it into his jacket pocket. He took a moment to composed himself, then stood, scanning the lounge for any other incriminating evidence. There was none. He walked out of the room and shut the door quietly behind him, as if not to disturb her sleep.

* * *

Laura Fell made her excuses and left The Telegraph early. Half the group, including her so-called partner, Don Hart, hadn't turned up, and those that had spent the evening sniping at one another. She was relieved to be out of it and not to have to ferry Megan home. Who, feeling impelled to make a statement, even at a cost to herself, had decided she'd "get some air" and walk back to her Upper Richmond Road flat.

Laura was checking her texts as she drove down Wildcroft Road towards Putney Hill – still nothing from Don – when she heard the sound of an approaching siren. An ambulance screamed up Putney Hill, blazing blue light and yelping sirens, and straight through the red traffic lights ahead of her. Laura jumped her light as it turned amber, praying there wasn't a camera. The ambulance, a hundred metres head of her, careered around Tibbets Corner and disappeared down Parkside. And for some inexplicable reason, she'd later call fate, she thought of Gina, and instead of turning right onto the A3 and heading home to Kew, she followed the siren's call.

The ambulance turned off Parkside and onto Queensmere Road; not the route to Gina's. Laura drove past feeling foolish. Why had she panicked about Gina? Was it what Megan had insinuated about her and Don Hart? No, that was ridiculous. Still, she reasoned, she'd come this far… She made her way through the village and down Wimbledon Hill. Passed the ugly sixties facade of Elys department store and the smokers huddled for warmth in the pub doorways of the town centre. The New Wimbledon Theatre billboards proudly announced Sinderella, their pre-Christmas adult pantomime starring Jim Davidson. *One to miss*, she thought, and swung a left in the direction of Haydons Road.

* * *

Nephilim had begun to breathe a little easier. He'd found Gina's iMac and discovered nothing else incriminating apart from a pink latex vibrator under her bed. Which he'd taken, not for sexual gratification but to protect her dignity and reputation. But where was their photo album? He'd given it to her on her birthday and she'd cried with joy and kissed him gently on the lips in thanks. It was then they felt the frisson between them. Not born out of lust but something deeper, purer, something he'd never felt before. Love.

He found the album in her leather shoulder bag hanging on the inside of the wardrobe door. It still smelt of roses. Of her. A small downy white feather floated from between its leaves as he flicked through the photographs, and landed on his trouser leg. He barely noticed it. His mind was on happier times – now all gone. He blinked the bitter thought away and closed the album. He was safe. That was all that mattered for now. He could grieve later. He tucked the album and laptop under his jacket and made his way swiftly out onto the landing and down the stairs. Halfway down he froze.

The security light had flared on outside. He could see the top of a woman's streaked blonde hair through the doors fanlight glass. She began rapping the brass knocker.

"Gina. It's me. Laura. Are you home? Gina!"

He was holding his breath, praying she didn't look through the top of the door and see him. He crouched down on the stairs, out of her line of sight.

"Gina! Are you in there?"

She was knocking louder now. The bitch wasn't going to leave. She was going to do something stupid, he knew it, and he'd be caught like a rat in a trap. He bit the back of his hand and waited.

He was right. Laura was getting increasingly concerned. Why wasn't Gina answering the door? She couldn't be in bed at ten thirty; she was a real night owl. Besides, it looked like all the downstairs lights were on. It was *odd*. She decided to ring Gina's mobile.

Abba started up in his trouser pocket. He scrambled for Gina's mobile, desperate to smother its ringtone, to switch it off.

Outside, Laura could hear it too – and then the connection suddenly went dead. Someone was in there! She lifted the brass letter box and leaned down to look inside.

"Jesus!"

A shape crash-wiped the letter box frame inches from her face. Panicking, she dropped the flap and staggered back.

Nephilim could hear her calling for help as he raced out through the kitchen. He re-locked the back door and replaced the key. Threw his shoes over the fence onto the railway siding, scrambled after them and ran.

Everton Bowe

Police Constable Everton Bowe was standing with a skin-and-bones girl, watching her boyfriend bleeding from his nose into the gutter below his Nike trainers.

"He's fucking nuts! Look what he did to Richie and me!" She couldn't have been more than sixteen and was missing a front tooth, which gave her a slightly comic piratical look. "Go on, Richie. Show him. Go on. He could have fucking killed us."

Bowe ignored her. His mind was on something else. Richie's blood dribbling down into the gutter struck him as a metaphor for his miserable career. He'd applied for Sergeant. Failed. Reapplied a year later. Failed again. Tried Heathrow – passed the firearms test, and didn't even make the shortlist. And now, at forty-five, he knew it wasn't going to happen. His career had disappeared, like Richie's blood, down the drain.

"Oi! You listening to me?"

Bowe pulled his dark thoughts back to the more immediate problem at hand. Not only the irate girl but the wiry Rasta guy standing opposite him. "You admit you hit them?"

"Yeah, man. They were trying to jack my Galaxy."

"Liar! We never did nothing! He's a fucking psycho! Needs locking up!" The girl's voice was like a buzz saw.

Bowe was finding it hard to concentrate. His tinnitus was playing up and her shrill whine wasn't helping. "So, let me get this straight. You say you hit her twice?"

"No, man. I hit him twice and her once. When she done bit me."

"Liar! You attacked me, you black prick! Don't just stand there, do something!"

Bowe wasn't sure who she was talking to – him or the other "black prick". He popped a piece of calming Nicorette gum and waited for her to run out of steam. She didn't, and the mosquito inside his head began shifting from ear to ear, like the Doppler effect of a passing train. He knew it wasn't there. That it was the tinnitus. His brain compensating for his loss of hearing, but it was getting worse, driving him crazy.

"Well don't just fucking stand there! You're a copper, do something!" the youth bellowed, his indignation fuelled by Bowe's lack of interest and the dregs of a bottle of Tesco value range vodka that lay smashed on the pavement.

Bowe did. He pulled out a handkerchief. He always kept a couple on him; one for wiping drunken gob off his uniform and one for personal use. He handed the youth the soiled one. Took the assailant's arm and directed him under the awning of Headmasters, one of the plethora of expensive hair salons in Wimbledon Village, sheltering them from the November rain and the youth's invective.

"Hold on," complained the Rasta, "They tried to mug me. It was self-defence–"

"Liar!" crowed the youth, jabbing an accusing finger inches from the Rasta guy's face. "Why'd we phone the cops then, eh? Eh? Come on! Why? Come on…?"

Bowe took the man's arm and eased him further away, feeling his biceps contract and then, thankfully, ease in submission. "Okay. Listen. They called 999. There's no CCTV. No witnesses. And there's two of them and one of you–"

"And I'm black."

Bowe held up his hands in weary surrender and said, "And I'm not Nelson Mandela trying to change the world. Do yourself a favour and walk away."

"They tried to mug me!"

"And you beat the crap out of them. Good for you. Walk away. You were never here. I never saw you. Go."

The man hesitated, wisely abandoned his principles and walked away. The youth was apoplectic.

"*What*? No fucking way! You ain't letting him go?"

Bowe waited until the man had disappeared around the corner and turned back to the youth, sporting a look of confusion. "Whoa. Calm down. What are you talking about? I'm letting who go?"

"Him! That black fucker that did this to me and her!"

"Where?" said Bowe, indicating the now empty Ridgway. "What black fucker?"

The youth went berserk. Bowe allowed himself a moment to savour the small victory, and excused himself to answer the burglary-in-progress shout on his personal radio.

And at that precise moment, his life changed for ever.

* * *

Specials, or "hobby bobbies" as they are referred to by the rank and file of the Met, are universally mistrusted, seen as a cheap alternative to real coppers. So, Bowe's heart sank as he slewed his patrol car to a halt outside 16 Caxton Road and saw one engrossed in an animated conversation with an attractive, middle-aged blonde woman in a trench coat.

The bright-eyed eager beaver was infected by the sort of enthusiasm that brought streetwise cynics like Bowe out in a rash. He was forced to listen as the Special breathlessly reported that he'd had no response to his calls or banging the front door so had proceeded to the rear of the property, where he found the back gate still bolted. He finally gained access through a neighbour's back garden, whereupon he found no sign of disturbance or forced entry… blah de blah de blah… Bowe turned away and strolled over to the lounge window.

Laura Fell couldn't believe his laissez-faire attitude. "Look. Someone was inside! Someone answered my phone call!"

The big cop didn't even look back at her as he trampled through Gina's flower beds to get a look inside.

Laura called indignantly after him, "Excuse me! You're ruining the–"

"Wait by the gate! Do not move."

"What? Why? I haven't done anything," she protested, misinterpreting his sudden change of demeanour as doubt in her story.

Bowe turned, grabbed her by the arm and manhandled her over to the Special, barking, "Put her in the back of the car and radio for an ambulance. Do it!" Then turned, took a run at the front door and kicked it in.

It felt like a weird out-of-body experience; Laura sat in the rear of the police car watching her life unravel, powerless to play any part in it or affect it. She watched in horror as the Special followed the surly black cop inside and moments later re-emerge, ashen-faced, and throw up in the flower bed. The medics push their way through the gaggle of inquisitive neighbours who'd congregated outside the gate. A uniformed sergeant glanced in at her as if she were a criminal, as he strode past shouting instructions to a PC. But still no-one told her what was happening. Who or what they'd found inside. She'd been abandoned to her imagination and it was terrifying. She just wanted to go home and sleep. Sleep and wake up from the nightmare she was in.

Her mobile jerked her out of her reverie. It was Don Hart. "It's me. I just wanted to say sorry about not making the, uh, get-together."

"Chill Out," she corrected.

He waited for her to speak. But the expected reprimand didn't come. "What's the matter? Laura? Are you alright?"

"No." She cut the connection, watching with growing apprehension as the black cop made his way out of the house with the female PC and over to the car. He opened the door and squatted down beside her.

"I'm sorry. I'm afraid I have some bad news."

She suddenly felt very vulnerable, like a lost child frightened to ask a stranger for help. "Is she... dead?"

"Yes. I'm sorry." He offered her his clean handkerchief, expecting – hoping – she'd break down, that her grief would fill the terrible silence. That she wouldn't ask.

"How?"

But they always did. He had himself when his brother had OD'd on ketamine, crashed a stolen car and drowned in his own blood.

"She took her own life. I'm sorry. I know it must be a terrible shock for you." He was running out of words. Why didn't the bloody PC do something, *say something*? He flashed her a warning look and said, "PC Carter will take a statement from you. Okay?"

Laura grabbed his arm as he started to rise and said, "What about the other person I saw?"

"There was no other person. There was no one else there."

He could see her confusion and felt for her. But what could he do? It was the truth. Everything else was a platitude. He handed her his card and turned away, thinking, *Christ, I have to get out of this job.*

Laura watched him trudge wearily back into the house and a terrible thought welled in her mind. If there had been no one else, it had to be Gina that she'd seen; which meant she was still alive and she could have stopped her.

She lowered her face into her hands and screamed.

Chinese whispers

DC Helen Lake swung left out of the Queens Road Police Station in her unmarked Ford Focus heading towards South Wimbledon and into "bandit country" – Mitcham. She knew the area well – every copper in Merton did – but she also had a more personal reason. Her father, Frank, had been an inpatient at the Wilson Hospital for over a year, suffering from Alzheimer's. Helen and her sister hadn't been able to cope with his violent mood swings and finally agreed to put him into care. A somewhat ironic term, considering what Helen had witnessed of her father's treatment. She'd have liked to have visited him whilst she was in the vicinity, but she didn't really have the time. In truth, his condition had deteriorated so rapidly that he no longer recognised her, often confusing Helen with her mother, who he blamed for abandoning him, which made it doubly distressing. She shut it from her mind and headed into Mitcham.

Statistically, Merton has one of the highest crime rates in London. Not because it's a particularly dangerous place, but because Mitcham and the notorious Phipps Bridge Estate are counted as within its boundaries, and they account for over seventy per cent of all crime in the borough. However, you'd never have thought that approaching the Hurst's house.

Helen walked past the for sale sign and under the pergola still spattered with late-blooming white roses and stopped in her tracks. The house was like something out of a Constable painting. Flowers tumbled from the stone urns and troughs in the walled front garden and a wisteria clung to the clapperboard walls. There was even a dovecot.

"Hello. Are you the police?"

The man was in his sixties, with a neatly trimmed white beard and contrasting thick coffee-coloured hair. Helen wondered if he dyed it, and how he knew she was a cop. She prided herself on her dress sense; today she was wearing a fashionable grey Boho trouser suit and Doc Martens.

"Yes. DC Lake," she said, flashing her warrant card. "We spoke on the phone."

"Eric Hurst. My wife, Anne, is inside." He looked relaxed, which was surprising considering he'd found a traumatised naked woman in his garden only a few hours earlier.

"I'm with the Missing Persons Unit, Mr Hurst."

Helen had been seconded to the unit after three women had gone missing in fourteen months from South West London. The number wasn't significant, but their ages were; the majority of missing people being in their teens or early twenties, whilst these women were all middle-aged. Mature women with homes, jobs and friendships don't normally just disappear. Plus, they had something else in common: like Tessa Hayes, they'd all been using online dating sites.

The interior of the Hurst's cottage was, if possible, even more beautiful than the exterior. It was full of antiques and objet d'art, which Eric explained they'd collected during their years as antiques dealers. Anne, despite Helen's protestations, insisted on making tea and busied herself in the kitchen. Eric conducted Helen to a drop-end Chesterfield facing the large French windows that allowed light to flood into the room.

"You have a really beautiful home, Mr. Hurst."

"Thank you."

"We're trying to sell it if you're interested," Anne chimed in from the kitchen.

"On my salary, I'm not sure I could afford it. Has it been on the market long?"

"Five months. Three viewings. No offers," Anne cheerily replied. "What do they say? Location. Location. Location."

Helen hoped she wasn't right because she lived next to the main Waterloo train line, but nodded along in polite agreement.

"Anyway, I'm glad you like it," interjected Eric, moving the conversation on to a happier topic. "It's seventeenth century. It used to be an old watermill."

"Really? How long have you lived here, Mr. Hurst?"

"Eighteen years—"

"Sixteen," Anne said from the kitchen.

"I stand corrected," said Eric good-naturedly. "And please call me Eric."

"And me Anne or Annie if you prefer. I answer to both."

They were like a double act. Happily correcting and answering the other's questions. Helen realised that they weren't frightened at all, but rather enjoying the excitement of being the centre of a police investigation.

Eric caught her quizzical look. "One of the perks of old age, Detective, is that you stop worrying about what other people think of you and become more concerned about what you think of yourself."

It was the gentlest of rebukes but a rebuke nevertheless. Helen made a mental note of it. "Can you please show me where you found the woman, sir?" she enquired, reverting to formality to demonstrate her respect.

"Of course. If you'll follow me into the garden, I'll show you."

There was no back garden as such, only a long wooden balcony that ran the length of the cottage and hung six feet above the bank of the River Wandle. Perhaps twenty feet wide, the river formed a natural barrier between the cottage and the parkland opposite. This was fortunate because, though pleasant during daylight, at night the park took on a more sinister character, populated by gangs and dealers.

But as she looked at it now, Helen could only marvel at its beauty. The water was crystal clear, no more than three feet deep and looked more like a trout stream than a London river. Moorhens and coots busied themselves between the reeds and a young cygnet swan sashayed through them and honed in on Eric like an old friend.

"Eric feeds them," explained Anne, who'd joined them, carrying a tray of tea and home-made cakes, which she placed on a small wicker table. "That's when we knew something was wrong. There weren't any. No birds. None." She handed Helen a porcelain cup and saucer and filled it from a silver teapot. "It's Lapsang Souchong. I do hope that's alright?"

Helen couldn't remember ever having had Chinese tea, let alone drinking it out of a bone china cup. She took a sip. It was so weak she could barely taste it.

"It's delicious," she lied. "So, you sensed something was wrong? What time was this?"

"Seven forty-five," said Eric. "I remember because Annie was making breakfast–"

"We always have it on the terrace. Summer, winter, rain or shine. It's a bit of a ritual."

"I was listening to Radio Four and Thought for the Day had just started, which I hate."

"He's an agnostic," apologised Anne. "Hates being preached at."

The double act had come on for an encore. Helen put down her tea and tried to steer them back to the question. "What exactly did you see?"

"Well, nothing to start with. It was what I heard," said Eric, pointing to a bed of tall broken reeds on the far side of the riverbank. "There was this terrible splashing and grunting noise, like an injured animal. I thought a fox had got one of the swans. But then I saw her thrashing about in the weeds."

"Did she say anything to you? Call for help?"

"No. She was incoherent – definitely on something. Annie had to help me pull her out."

"She was covered in bruises and cuts from falling. It was a miracle she hadn't drowned," Annie added, offering Helen a warm scone.

Helen shook her head in refusal, turned back to Eric and asked, "Did you see or hear anyone else?"

"No, nothing, and the park gate would have still been locked."

"So how do you think she got into the river?"

"The nearest road is a hundred metres upstream. It's possible she could have got in there."

"Or been dumped in by someone else?"

Eric looked shocked. Fishing a naked junkie out of a river was one thing, but the thought that someone might have tried to murder a woman was quite another. "Are you saying she's not a drug addict?"

"Her name is Tessa Hayes. She's a middle-aged, middle-class woman, Mr Hurst. Not the normal profile of a junkie. And someone shaved her hair off, she didn't do it to herself." Helen's mobile cut the interview short. "Excuse me," she said, and turned to answer it.

It was her DCI, Malcolm Teal, brief to the point of rudeness as usual.

Helen's hackles rose despite herself. "With respect, sir, 16 Caxton Road isn't a missing person's enquiry…"

Annie could sense from the tone of his barked reply, that Helen's boss wasn't taking no for an answer. She shot a quizzical look across at Eric. He shrugged, picked out a blueberry from the muffin and fed it to the swan.

* * *

Hounslow Council's quality assurance department did not, as the name suggested, deal with PR and complaints, but child protection. Laura Fell had been employed there for over eight months on a short-term secretarial contract, and she hated it.

Some of the cases were beyond belief. She actually felt physically sick whilst transcribing them. But much as she desperately wanted to leave, she knew that work for women of her age was in short supply, so had been forced to stick it out.

Which was the reason she'd put on her navy suit and driven into work the morning after her best friend had committed suicide, and sat at her shared desk as if nothing had happened. That and the fact she found it easier typing the case notes of a tragedy that wasn't her own, rather than remain in her flat and drown in phone calls from the press and Gina's horrified friends.

It had been 3am by the time she'd finally got to bed. The PC had taken for ever to write up her statement and then had the gall to suggest she give her a lift home, since she could smell alcohol on her breath. Laura was still fuming when she got back to her flat and had barely slept.

She was speed-typing on automatic. Her mind wasn't on an eighteen-year-old single mother accused of selling herself to feed her habit and her ten-month-old baby, but on a pretty semi-detached house in SW19 and the horror hanging inside it. Her thumbs were aching – repetitive strain injury, her doctor had told her – so she picked up her handbag and fished around in the clutter until she found her tube of Voltaren gel. She sat back in her chair and looked around the office as she applied it.

It was described as open plan but to the untrained eye there was little that was open and even less planned. Six large desks supported the eighteen Investigative Research Officers, four Safeguarding Advisors, and two Minute-Takers. It was supposedly run by the Business Support Manager, who'd introduced hot-desking to speed up the backlog of investigations but ignored the real problem, which was understaffing. With only two Minute-Takers, keeping on top of new cases was physically impossible, even when working through lunch. But it wasn't in Laura's nature to be a quitter; she had her father's integrity and her mother's work ethic.

"The McClaren minutes."

"I'm sorry?"

Laura's boss was looming above her, loudly invading her personal space; a favourite trick of hers to assert her authority. "It gets boring having to continually repeat myself, Laura. The Mc–"

"McClaren minutes. Yes, I heard that bit. The bit I didn't hear was "excuse me" or "please", or are they not in your vocabulary?"

The riposte was out before she could stop it, propelled as much by her grief as by her anger. Not that her bully boss knew that. She cleared her throat, not used to being publicly challenged, and said, "Excuse me?"

Laura could feel her eyes brimming with tears. She blinked them back and found herself standing face to face with her tormentor. "It's getting a bit boring having to repeat myself. What bit of that didn't you understand?"

The room fell silent. Heads turned. The manager was in a quandary, not wanting to be seen to back down but sensing something irrational in Laura's sudden anger. She eased back, lowering her voice, speaking slowly, attempting to defuse the situation. "Are you alright, Laura? You seem upset."

"I wonder why that is. Could it be that I object to being spoken to like an idiot?"

"If you have a problem, we can talk about it," her manager replied, as if reasoning with a recalcitrant teenager.

"What, am I a child now?" mimicked Laura.

Laura's mobile punctured the gruelling silence. She saw the Caller ID DON, said in a strong, clear voice, "And you can fuck off, too," picked up her bag and walked out of the room.

* * *

Fuck her, Don Hart said to himself, and tossed his mobile aside. Besides, he had more pressing problems than Laura you're-not-meeting-my-needs Fell. The previous night had been a disaster and his mind was still reeling with the possible repercussions.

It was about to get worse.

"We got any aspirin?" grunted his son, Richie, as he trundled into the kitchen, wearing only a pair of tracksuit bottoms and a black DC baseball cap.

"Christ. What happened to you?"

Richie's right eye was swollen shut and the colour of an angry boil. "Nothing," he replied, ramming a couple of pieces of bread into the toaster. "Some Rasta dude tried to jack my mobile. I sorted it. Aspirin?"

"Did you call the cops?"

"Yeah. He was another black bastard. Didn't do nothing."

"Where was this?"

"Wimbledon. Up on the Ridgway."

"Wimbledon?" Warning signals flashed in Don's mind. "What the hell were you doing in Wimbledon?"

"Going for a drink," said Richie, yanking open the fridge door, retrieving a packet of frozen peas from the freezer and holding it gingerly to his eye.

"You've got an exclusion order."

"It expired Saturday. We got any aspirin?" He began searching the kitchen cabinets, spilling the frozen peas from the open bag. "Anyway, I didn't do nothing–"

"*Anything.* I didn't do anything – and you're spilling the peas!"

Richie banged the cabinet door shut and slouched out. Soon he was venting his anger by committing a drive-by shooting on Grand Theft Auto.

Don opened his laptop and immersed himself in the possibilities of another virtual assignation on PlentyMoreFish. com. He'd normally ignore his mobile but, checking the Caller ID, found it was Iris the social secretary of the Chill Out group, and he remembered her adventurous tongue when he'd once given her a lift home.

"Don."

"Iris. What's wrong?"

He prided himself on his intuition – in his business you needed it – and knew already that it was more bad news.

* * *

Everton Bowe had a Homedics sound machine next to his bed. It was supposed to lull him to sleep with sounds from the seashore or rainforest. It didn't work. His tinnitus was worse at night, like a high-pitched tuning fork in his head, and he needed more than nature to stop it. He'd taken a Zolpidem at 6am and it hadn't touched his tiredness. Then another along with his Propananol at eight thirty which had done the trick but given him bad dreams.

He was having a heart attack, lying under a kidney-shaped dressing table and calling his wife for help. She entered the bedroom with another man and stared down at him. He tried to reach out to her but his arms wouldn't move. He was panicking. His chest was constricting, crushing the life out of him, and still she did nothing, just stood and watched. He felt himself falling and heard another voice calling him.

"Everton! Are you in there?"

Now there was a different ringing in his ears. He groaned, realising it was his doorbell, and muttered, "Yeah, yeah, I'm coming."

He hauled himself up and out of bed, pulled on his towelling dressing gown and Uggs – his feet were like ice and never really thawed – and shuffled into the lounge. The remains of his post-work dawn snack lay on the Ikea coffee table: a half-eaten bacon sandwich, a cold mug of tea and the roach of a spliff.

"Are you going to open up or what?" Her finger was permanently glued on the bell and it was beginning to irritate Bowe.

"Stop doing that!" he bellowed as he pocketed the spliff, shoved the sandwich into his mouth and made his way out into the tiny vestibule that constituted his hall to open the front door. "I heard you. Okay?" he grunted and turned back into the flat.

Helen followed him inside the boxy new-build lounge. "Well, look who got out of bed the wrong side," she said, ignoring another grunted response. "Are those my Uggs you're wearing?"

"They're not Uggs. They're fake Uggs. And they're not yours – they're your present to me."

"Ooh, grumpy." She grinned, opening the double-glazed windows and letting in a blast of cold air. "Dope will do that to you."

"Do you want something, DC Lake or is this just a social call to annoy me?"

"A bit of both," she replied. "Tea?"

Bowe watched her as she made her way into the galley kitchen. Even through a headache, she looked good, and she moved like she

34

knew it. She'd pulled her brambly hair back in a simple ponytail, exposing her long slender neck… He scrubbed his face with his palms, washing away the memory, and walked into the bathroom.

"Your milk's off."

"I like my coffee black," he said, shutting the door on her and the conversation.

Helen glugged the coagulated milk down the sink, made two cups of black coffee, then carried them back into the lounge to wait for Everton. She disliked what he'd done to his flat; it reminded her of an Ikea-inspired minimalist painting. It was neat and tidy but had no heart. And Everton, beneath all his sarky bullshit, did. It was what had attracted her to him in the first place. He was slightly damaged goods and so was she. And being a detective made her feel more in control of their brief relationship. He'd been her booty call first, and become her friend only after they'd mutually finished it.

She took a sip of her coffee, burnt her lip on the mug, grimaced and called, "I heard you had a suicide last night?"

"Can't talk. I'm shitting," came the terse reply.

She let it go, knowing that Everton and his ailing body were slow starters in the morning. She idled away the time by mentally listing his ailments from the head down. Tinnitus: He'd been prescribed hearing aids but given up on them because it would have meant him joining the ranks of the shiny arses, and although he hated being a copper, he hated pushing papers even more. Uveitis and/or iritis: She was never quite sure which one it was, but it was excruciatingly painful. Like a migraine inside your eyeball was how he'd described it, and it made you hypersensitive to light. High blood pressure: 140/95, which added to his ear and eye problems and caused occasional bouts of vertigo.

She'd urged him to jump on the bandwagon and sue the Met, claim his medical conditions were all stress related. But he'd refused, insisting his health problems were symptoms of his own private failures rather than the job. It was another thing, despite herself, that she admired him for: his brutal honesty.

Everton yanked open the bathroom door and walked, naked and dripping, across the lounge and into the bedroom.

Helen picked up his coffee and followed him. "You've put on weight."

"Do you mind? I'm trying to get dressed."

"If you didn't want me to look you should have put some clothes on," she said, handing him the coffee and making her way back into the lounge. "Does the name Celia Lewis mean anything to you?"

"Should it?"

"She's the mother of your suicide."

"So?"

"The new government enquiry into child abuse in London – she's chairing it."

Bowe buttoned up his 501s and digested the implications.

"The press is all over it like a rash."

"Flies like shit. What can you do?"

"You should know. You married one."

"We're getting divorced. You want to get to the point?"

"Mrs Lewis. She wants to speak to the cop who found her daughter ASAP."

"Sorry. Going to see my son play football," said Everton, who spent every Tuesday he could sitting in his car, secretly watching his estranged son, who blamed him for the breakdown of the marriage, playing for his school team.

"That's an order from the DCI – put your uniform on."

Bowe groaned and unbuttoned his jeans.

* * *

The news of Gina Lewis' suicide spread like a gruesome Chinese whisper through the Chill Out group, gaining momentum as each new recipient struggled to acquire the information they needed to dispel their disbelief. Within hours, Gina's death became a feeding frenzy – not only fed by the press but by her friends.

Megan Howell came home from work during her lunch break to feed and walk her two King Charles Spaniels. She always gave them identical bowls of Bob and Lush kibble to stop any squabbling; a dry food containing no artificial sweeteners. Perfect for King Charles Spaniels since they were prone to weight gain.

They knew she was going back to work and were sulking, lying dolefully beside the kitchen radiator on their quilted blankets. Megan ignored them; a trick she learnt at a very early age to bring her parents to heel when they refused to bow to her wishes.

She wasn't a particularly precocious child but had an extraordinary sense of self-worth and demanded it be recognised. Despite her veneer of privately educated, middle-class respectability, she'd been brought up in a working-class home. Her father, a bus driver in Cardiff, met her mother over the counter in the company canteen. He was a member of the UNISON, like his father before him, and proud of his working-class Welsh heritage. Their only daughter was not. She had aspirations far above the smell of stale chip fat that clung to her mother's clothes and hair.

Her father finally bowed to her ferocious teenage ambition and agreed to let her try for university. When she was later offered a place at Bristol to read English Literature, he'd applied and won a maintenance grant from the TUC. Megan gratefully accepted the money but never acknowledged it had come from a Trade Union.

Her parents were thrilled with her 2:1, but she was disappointed and asked for her final dissertation to be re-marked. Her request was to her mind unfairly rejected and from that day on her CV read that she'd been awarded a first-class-honours. And amazingly, few employers had ever questioned it.

It reinforced her belief in herself, added to her self-confidence. She practised never asking questions, only making statements, not following but being seen to lead and, above all, not caring if she was disliked as long as she was respected. It became her mantra, and until three years ago it had served her well in her career and her personal life.

She walked out of the kitchen and into the sitting room. She loved her mansion flat's understated elegance. It might be only rented, but it had high ceilings and its own terrace accessed through the French windows, which was a boon. Especially with Bathsheba and Gabriel Oak. She'd taught the dogs to use the litter trays hidden behind some pots containing rosemary to mask the occasional smell. It took her weeks to train them, but she firmly believed that anything or anyone was trainable.

It was what had made her successful as a teacher – and, in the end, was the cause of her fall from grace. But now she was resurrecting herself and her career and letting go of the past. Even if part of her past refused to let go of her.

The phone rang as if to remind her. She picked up the receiver, listened for a second and quickly cut the connection. Her mobile vibrated on the oak mantelpiece. She checked the Caller ID – Iris Costa – and, relieved it was the secretary of Chill Out, answered it.

"Iris. Why are you – *what?*"

* * *

Colin Gould, was a lecturer in Modern European Cinema at St. Mary's University, an attractive Gothic pile within a stone's throw of the Thames at Twickenham. He loved his subject, but was an uninspiring teacher and immune to the indifference of his students.

Colin came late to teaching, after retiring from HMRC as a tax inspector. He'd always loved the arts and thought of himself even then as creative. Crafting a narrative for each of his investigations, he pursued his prey mercilessly and each success felt like a warm kill. During his career, he'd been punched, throttled and once nearly had his eye gouged out, which was why he now wore glasses.

He was supposed to be meeting Frieda Cole, one of the Chill Out group, for lunch. He rarely went to the staff canteen since some egalitarian had suggested it be opened to the post-grads to allow them to keep in touch with their tutors, whatever that meant. Every day at twelve fifty-five he'd pull on his ten-year-old camel coat and make the five-minute jog over to the river to sequester one of the benches. But today Frieda was disappointingly late and he'd been finally forced to surrender her place to a hugely pregnant woman and her garrulous mother. Unwilling to give up the bench entirely, he retreated into his head, thinking about how his life had so radically changed since meeting Frieda.

He met her whilst working at the tax office and bumped into her four years later at a Sunday matinee of the Red Balloon at the Curzon in Richmond. Afterwards, they had coffee and chatted, and she told him about Chill Out, confiding that the group was short of eligible, intelligent, men, which had fed his ego and interest.

Frieda wasn't possessive – she wasn't interested in him in that way – so he got a considerable amount of attention from the other women in the group. Iris Costa asked him to share traditional Greek meze at her Twickenham cottage and made a pass at him. It was the first time he'd been kissed by a woman in years, and her wet, garlicky tongue in his mouth made him ejaculate in his pants, which he found acutely embarrassing, although, thank God, she never knew. A few weeks later, Gina Lewis, who loved the cinema and his knowledge of it, asked him to Arthur's, a pretty bistro on The Green in Twickenham, which themed dinners to match the films they screened on Sunday evenings.

It was the start of their secret relationship, shared with no one and even more special because of it. He began to believe there might actually be attractive, intelligent women who liked him for who he was and what he knew, not what he looked like: a geeky guy in wire-rimmed glasses. His Monday nights at The Telegraph soon became sacrosanct.

But Don Hart's arrival put all that at risk. Within a couple of weeks, he was ruling the roost, swapping risqué jokes with Gina and Iris, hogging the conversation with his too-easy wit and interminable stories. Only Megan Howell remained aloof from his charm. He sought her out as an ally. But she refused to take him seriously, laughing that jealousy was unbecoming in a man his age. He felt humiliated and began to hate her as much as he hated Don Hart.

"Your mobile's ringing," the chattering mother prompted as she nudged him back to the present. He forced a polite smile, picked up his lunch box and thermos and walked away to answer it. The Caller ID displayed the name Iris Costa, and a flashing signal below it indicated '3 MISSED CALLS', all from her.

* * *

Wheatley was within the Thames Valley Police jurisdiction, but a phone call had been made and an exception granted for Everton Bowe due to the unusual circumstances and high profile of the suicide case. The easy commute from London made the pretty village an increasingly popular and expensive place to live. Over half the properties were owned, much to the local's disapproval, by the "enders" from London, which made the village almost a ghost town during the week.

Helen followed her satnav directions from the M40, entered the village on the Upper Road and missed the sign to Stadhampton. Five minutes and a matching number of expletives later, they were approaching the outskirts of Oxford.

"I was following the bloody GPS."

"Like a lemming, Helen, and it's wrong."

Bowe needed a cigarette desperately, but Helen, a reformed-again non-smoker, was having none of it, even with the window open. He'd been chewing a piece of Nicorette gum to death for twenty minutes and was not in the best of moods.

"Do you want me to turn around?"

"What, and upset your satnav?"

"Oh, fuck off, smartarse. Check the address again," Helen ordered, handing Bowe her notepad. "I could have got it wrong."

"Great Leys Farm, Stadhampton. Have you got a map?"

"Why would I need a map when I've got a bloody satnav?"

Everton opened his mouth to tell her but, seeing her cautionary look, thought better of it. "Okay. Do you by any chance have her phone number?"

"No! Look, I was just told to escort you. Okay?"

"What, are they frightened I might say something inappropriate? Like how come the recently appointed head of the Met's child abuse enquiry failed to recognise that her own daughter was suicidal?"

"Jesus, Everton. You can be a cynical bastard sometimes."

"Yeah. Tell me I'm wrong."

Helen couldn't hold the quizzical look in his coal-coloured eyes, and merely said, "Shall I turn around or what?"

* * *

Frieda Cole missed Colin's lunch after being phoned by a journalist, who had somehow got her number and wanted a comment on the "tragedy".

She'd been drinking steadily since and was now watching an interview on the London Lunchtime News with one of Gina's neighbours, who admitted hearing a woman calling for help but, thinking it was a domestic dispute, ignored it. Gina was hardly featured apart from a still photograph of her graduation day with her politician mother, Celia, who was the main focus of attention. Megan Howell phoned to ask if she was watching.

"Yes," Frieda replied. "Where did they get that photograph from? It must be years old."

"They keep libraries of stuff. Have you spoken to her mother?"

"It just goes straight through to voicemail."

"I'm not surprised. She's probably too ashamed to answer."

"Megan! Her daughter just died."

"She didn't die, she committed suicide, and if her mother had been more caring, less controlling and concerned about her own career, it may never have happened."

"Look. Gina was ill. We all loved her, but she was ill."

"She should never have been on those drugs. Her new GP told her so."

"She told you that?"

"She invited me round to see her new house and told me the whole story. How her mother got some tame psychiatrist to prescribe her drugs to 'calm' her–"

"That sounds highly unlikely." Frieda prickled. She'd known Gina nine years, infinitely longer than Megan, and wasn't going to be browbeaten.

"She cried when she told me, Frieda…"

Frieda switched her mobile to speakerphone, placed it on the table, and topped up her tea with a large splash of Scotch.

* * *

Celia and Angus Lewis lived outside Wheatley village on the road to Stadhampton. They bought the large converted barn five years ago from a local builder, intending to sell their Fulham Palace house and move permanently when Angus retired. But his car accident flung their plans and their lives into turmoil.

Celia hid behind the floor-length curtain of her bedroom window, staring out at the posse of press huddled outside her locked gates, thinking it had taken two years to forgive her husband, and now their daughter had re-opened the wound, and, worse, risked throwing her career away.

"Are they still there?" Angus called from his bedroom.

"Yes. The police will be here any minute. I'm going down."

She checked her immaculate reflection in the floor-to-ceiling wardrobe mirrors. She wasn't a tall woman but had a certain practised presence – common in politicians. Her ash-grey hair was swept back from her face in a lacquer-hard bob. Her pearl earrings were discreet but expensive, as was the diamond solitaire ring that complimented her white-platinum wedding band. She brushed a piece of lint from her Max Mara linen jacket and made her way out onto the spacious landing.

"Shave, please," she ordered as she passed Angus' bedroom. She pressed the RISE button on the stairlift and made her way down the carpeted stairs, ignoring it as it glided past her on its way up.

High heels clicking on the polished flagstone floors, she entered her office. The MESSAGE WAITING light was pulsing on the answerphone on her mahogany desk. She pressed PLAY.

"You have nine new messages," it advised brightly. She switched it off, knowing that few, if any, would be from her friends, and slumped into her chair. She felt sick with worry and knew it was only going to get worse. And that as desperate as she felt, she had to control it – and herself. She removed a brass key from a zip pocket inside her handbag and unlocked one of the desk drawers. She took out a small green bottle, that could easily be mistaken for eye drops, and drew a precise amount of liquid into the dispenser before dropping it into her mouth, not her eyes.

Gina smiled radiantly up at her from one of the silver framed photos on the desk. Celia's eyes brimmed as she stared at it. Then she shook her head and, in a futile gesture, removed the object of her pain from view, and placed it in the drawer alongside the green lithium bottle. The same drug that she suspected had killed her daughter.

The video entryphone began chiming a warning. She stood, and walked out into the hall to answer it. Pressing the RECEIVE button, she watched the tiny screen flicker to life. An attractive raven-haired woman was leaning close to the monitor.

"Mrs Lewis? DC Lake. I have Constable Bowe with me."

"Come in," Celia said, and hit ENTER.

Bowe was impressed. Unlike most of the people he dealt with on the street, Celia Lewis appeared to be a woman totally in control of her emotions. She accepted their condolences, thanked them for making the long journey from London and even offered them tea and Duchy shortbread. But there was an elephant in the room and they all knew it. Bowe felt obligated to broach the subject.

"Mrs Lewis, I understand you have some questions about last night, if I can help at all?"

"Yes. Thank you, I do. Would you mind?"

Helen thought she was still talking to Everton, and then realised that she'd been asked to leave. "Oh. Of course," she said, and made her way out into the hall.

"The door. Would you?"

Helen nodded, closed the polished mahogany door, and stood admiring the huge Georgian grandfather clock that dominated the hall.

"Are you the police?"

Helen swivelled around and saw a grey cadaver of a man descending sedately towards her in the stairlift.

"Yes, sir. DC Lake," Helen replied, not totally sure who she was speaking to.

"Ah." His voice sounded hoarse and he continually licked the tip of his tongue across his cracked lips, as if trying to lubricate them. "Is my wife in there with the black chap that found her?"

"Yes," replied Helen, a little surprised by his politically incorrect choice of words.

Angus pulled out a handkerchief and loudly blew his nose. "I suppose I should go in."

The stairlift had stopped but he didn't move. Helen wondered if he were waiting for her to help. "Do you need a hand, sir?"

"No," he said, adding, "Thank you," as an afterthought. "Do you have children?"

"I'm not married, sir. But I hope to one day."

"They can be like love," he said. "A blessing and a burden."

Helen waited for him to continue. He didn't. He just sat sideways on the grey plastic chair, adrift in his own dark thoughts.

"May I offer my sincere condolences, sir."

"Why do people always say that?"

"Excuse me?"

"Sincere condolences. Shouldn't any form of condolence be sincere?"

Helen thought she'd offended him, then realised he was merely speaking his thoughts out loud.

"It's like people saying 'with respect' when they don't respect you at all." A wry smile briefly twisted the corner of his cracked lips and died just as quickly. He looked apologetically over at Helen. "Please excuse me. I have a habit of speaking to myself. I didn't mean to embarrass you. There's been quite enough embarrassment in this house for one day."

On the other side of the mahogany door, Bowe was feeling uneasy too. He assumed their conversation was going to be about the circumstances of Gina's death but Mrs Lewis seemed to accept the fact her daughter had committed suicide, even though, somewhat unusually, she left no suicide note. She merely smiled and said, a little wearily, "Gina had... issues... She'd been on medication..." As if that were explanation enough.

She was, however, concerned about Laura Fell, asking question after question about her involvement. What she was doing there late at night? Why did she assume someone had broken in when they hadn't? Why had she phoned the police? Had she been drinking? Had her daughter been drinking? He tried to reassure her that Laura was just an innocent bystander and that things would become clearer after the post-mortem, but he wasn't sure if she was really listening to him. Something else, something as yet unspoken, was clearly bothering her.

"Is there anything else I can help you with, Mrs Lewis? Would you like me to speak to your husband?"

"No. That won't be necessary," she said, too quickly. "But there is, unfortunately, another issue: the press." She paused, choosing her words carefully. "We are a very private family, Constable, and as you can see," she said, waving a manicured hand towards the window and the journalists lurking outside. "The jackals are already gathering."

"If you need security, I can ask Thames Valley Police to send someone out."

"That is already in hand, thank you. I assume you're aware of my present position?"

"As a government minister, yes," replied Bowe, waiting to see where the conversation was leading.

"Junior minister," Celia corrected. "The circumstances of my daughter's death and my position as chair of the Childhood Abuse

Enquiry is going to put myself and my family under considerable scrutiny."

Bowe marvelled at her iron composure, but thought he noticed the slightest tremble in her fingers as she pulled an electronic cigarette from her bag.

"Forgive me. I'm trying to quit, but under the circumstances..." She left the rest of the sentence unsaid and drew gratefully on the comforting fake smoke.

"I've been trying for years. Believe me, I understand."

She nodded and for a brief moment he felt they'd made a connection. But then the shutter came down and her voice reclaimed its brittle authority. "I'd prefer you say nothing of last night to anyone, least of all the press."

"Mrs Lewis, I'm no great fan of the press."

"Your wife is a journalist, is she not?"

Bowe was stunned. So that's what their interview was really about. But how did she know, and so soon? He didn't attempt to hide the irony in his reply. "We're in the process of getting divorced. I'm surprised whoever you asked didn't tell you that as well."

"Be that as it may, Gina's friends and associates are likely to be approached and offered an inducement."

"I don't take bribes, ma'am. I do my job to the best of my ability and go home at night with a clear conscience." *Unlike some politicians*, he felt like saying.

"Can I assume that no one has been in touch with you yet?"

"Apart from you, no."

She registered the rebuff, took out an embossed business card and handed it to him.

"If anyone does, please contact me through this number."

"I'm assuming you've cleared this—"

"With your Borough Commander? Of course. Now if you'll excuse me." She was already opening the door, dismissing him. "As you can imagine, it's been extremely" – she paused, searching for the least emotive word – "distressing trying to cope with the last few hours and I haven't had much sleep."

Bowe nodded, thinking how well she disguised it, wondering if she really felt anything at all. He didn't see her, as the door closed behind him, reach again for the comfort of the little green bottle.

* * *

Frieda Cole was drunk, although at first glance you'd never know it. She'd been drinking heavily since the death of her wealthy alcoholic husband eight years ago and knew how to disguise it. She was a proud woman and didn't need advice or sympathy. She'd stayed faithfully married for nineteen years to a man she had very little in common with when he was sober and made the decision to support him and his addiction rather than divorce him. Now, she was free to live her life and drink herself to death if she wanted to.

"Christ, not now," she groaned as she heard the knock at her front door.

She took another sip of Scotch from the bottle and replaced it in the cupboard. Then she composed herself and walked out into the Victorian tiled hall to open the front door. Laura was on the doorstep, clutching a bottle of champagne.

Soon, Laura was drunk too. Not badly, but enough to take the panic out of her pain.

"Do you think it was coming off the tablets, the lithium, too quickly?" she asked, as much to herself as Frieda. "She told me that she'd been misdiagnosed by the psychologist."

"Psychiatrist," Frieda corrected, and immediately wished she hadn't. It was developing into a habit.

"What's the difference?" said Laura, topping up their glasses with the last of the champagne and mopping up the frothy spillage with the sleeve of her suit jacket.

"A psychiatrist is a medical doctor who specialises in disorders of the mind. A psychologist studies the way we the think."

They sat in silence. Isolated in their own grief, until Frieda whispered, "Megan said Gina was frightened of her mother's reaction when she found out."

"Do you think that's true?" Laura replied, not convinced.

Frieda shrugged. "Women like Megan always need someone to blame. She and Iris have been phoning around. They're arranging a memorial dinner to honour Gina."

"Isn't it a bit early for that?"

"I told her that. Besides, there's sure to be an inquest. We don't need to start our own. Has anyone from the press phoned you?"

"I didn't answer it."

"Don't. They got short thrift from me, I can tell you."

"I suppose people are just trying to make sense of it.'

Laura shook her head, feeling weary as the booze and the stress hit her. "I quit my job today."

"What? Laura, do you think that was sensible?"

"Probably not."

"Do they know about Gina? Did you tell them?"

"I haven't spoken to anyone but you all day. You and the police."

"What did they say?"

"That I was mistaken, there was no one else in the house. But I know there was."

"Hold on. What are you saying? That there was someone with Gina last night?"

"She wasn't answering the door so I rang her mobile. I heard it ringing inside and suddenly it cut off. I saw them through the letter box."

"You mean someone inside cut the connection?"

"Yes.

"Are you sure?"

"Yes! I just told you, I saw them!"

"Who? Who was it?"

"I don't know. It was just a blur, a shadow… flashing past."

"Are you sure it wasn't Gina?"

"That's what the police said. They said there was no sign of a break-in."

Frieda leant forward and took Laura's hands in hers. "Listen to me. You're in shock. She was your best friend and you found her–"

"I know what I saw!" Laura shouted, trying to pull her hands free.

Frieda gripped them tighter. "There was no one there, Laura. You have nothing to feel guilty about. You couldn't have done any more."

"So how come they never found her mobile? Or did I imagine that ringing too?"

Frieda daren't answer. She'd already lost one friend and felt in danger of losing another.

* * *

Nephilim's mind was reeling. He stared down at the four missed calls on Gina's mobile and could see from the Caller ID that they'd all come from Laura Fell. Why did she keep ringing when she knew Gina was dead? Maybe it wasn't her? Maybe it was the police trying to pinpoint the mobile's position? Could they really do that? It had been a mistake to keep it; he should have destroyed it. What was there to see anyway? The only person he'd ever loved hanging on the end of a nylon rope?

He gnawed at the back of his hand, eating away at his self-disgust. He picked up a hammer and smashed the mobile again and again until it was in pieces. Hundreds of heads turned like clockwork from their feeding trays, bead-eyes alert, watching him. "Like little feathered Marie Antoinette's waiting for the chopper," his mother used to laugh and say. He knelt on the concrete floor amongst the rows of cages and their doomed occupants and picked up the SIM card. Then walked out of Battery 1 and into the chill night air.

His coop was at the rear of the two corrugated iron hangars. Shielded by tall willow cladding that he'd bound to the wire-mesh fence, and backing onto a pine wood, it was completely hidden from the industrial killing machines fifty metres away. Far enough to muffle the chicken's screams but near enough to make collecting their feathers easy for his work. Since it housed doves and tumbler pigeons, it wasn't technically a coop. But he'd always thought it too large to be called a dovecote. He built it himself from reclaimed timber and it contained his prize creations. Not just the birds that soared and tumbled above it like fallen angels, but his artwork.

You entered the enclosure through a padlocked gate. There were two separate roosts, one at each end of the fifteen-metre long wooden structure. It had chicken-wire sides but he'd added hinged wooden flaps that could be lowered over them at night to keep the birds warm. Connecting the two roosts was a large windowless studio lit by a strip light. One key fitted both locks and was hidden under a loose floorboard by the entrance to the dove roost.

Nephilim let himself in and stood, arms outstretched, palms upwards, like a messiah, a demigod, allowing the doves to settle on his arms and shoulders. Gently shaking them, he knelt and lifted the loose floorboard, carefully placed the SIM card inside and replaced the plank.

Satisfied, he made his way back outside. Downy white feathers stuck to his mud-and-bird-shit encrusted boots. He hosed them off with a rusty standpipe in the yard, then crunched up the gravel path to his late mother's farmhouse.

The place was a mess. He left it that way partly to spite her, but also because the farm held no interest for him, apart from the coop. He wasn't living there but he couldn't rent it out and risk people interfering with his projects. For a while, he kept on a couple of farmhands to keep the place ticking over but now he needed privacy for his sacred work.

He was tired and dirty. He'd had to drive back from Wimbledon to clean up after the ginger slut. Another mistake, and one he still worried could be costly. Still, he reasoned, as he made his way up the narrow stairs to the bathroom, what could she tell them even if she did remember something – which she wouldn't. She didn't know who he was or where she'd been. And he'd already removed his false profile from the dating website and destroyed his pay-as-you-go mobile. No, he was safe. He smiled as a more pleasant thought struck him: maybe, subliminally, letting Tessa Hayes live was his farewell gift to Gina?

He tugged the cord and switched on the bathroom light. Pulled off his clothes and stared at his hairless body in the mirror above the sink. A ten-inch scar ran like a puce zip from his chest down through his navel. Another gift from his mother. He gently dabbed at the puckered flesh. He could still feel the marks left by the staples that had held his skin and stomach together. He turned on the taps above the grey-stained porcelain sink. The water complained its way through the pipes and burst into the bowl. He couldn't find a plug so he stuffed the hole with lavatory paper and washed himself. The water was freezing but soft and lathered easily. He dried himself with a clean towel taken from the ugly oak tallboy that dominated the room, squirted his antiseptic hand gel onto the wound and gently rubbed it in.

Soon, he was driving up the A3 towards London. Gina's album tucked safely in his Samsonite briefcase on the seat beside him, he was looking forward to a film on the art works of Lucy Glendinning showing at the Saatchi Gallery.

Ties that bind

Guy Fawkes Night had already come and gone with the usual spate of minor burns and hooliganism. Morden Park held a huge firework display that DC Lake took her niece Ally to because her mum, a nurse, was working at St. George's A&E, preparing for the rush of idiots and unfortunates. They had a great night until Helen got home and discovered that some yobs had set fire to the beech hedge outside her block of flats. The youths had doused it in petrol and, not satisfied with just her hedge, torched the whole road.

Helen woke late the following morning, grabbed a banana and a bottle of Evian water, and stumbled down the concrete-and-chrome staircase and out into the front car park. A sopping mist had turned everything sepia-grey, apart from the blackened skeleton of the hedge, which stood like a scar, matching the others on the quiet suburban road. She wondered if the building insurance would cover it or whether it would be another excuse to raid and then increase the sinking fund. She gave up fretting about it, climbed in her Ford Focus, punched Tessa Hayes' postcode into the satnav and eased out into the dregs of the rush hour.

She was hitting eighty by the time she crossed the M25 and when she swung left and then right, back over the A3, she was barely ten minutes late. The Hog's Back hills looked beautiful in the "mistances", a name her father had made up for her when she was a kid. She shook her head, ridding it of the thought that he wouldn't even remember now, and powered down the dual carriageway towards Farnham.

Oakland Avenue was a cul-de-sac of seventies-style detached houses on the outskirts of the town, but looked curiously un-English.

Manicured, open plan front lawns rolled out to meet the path as far as the eye could see, welcoming visitors to the avenue. *No fear of setting fire to these hedges,* Helen thought as she climbed out of her car, *there are none.*

Tessa Hayes opened her oak panelled front door, wearing a chunky cable-knit sweater and cream woollen hat, and beckoned her inside. "Come in. You must be freezing," she said, quickly closing the door on any prying eyes and ushering Helen into the warmth of the sitting room. It was a bit too solidly middle-class for Helen's taste; all Russell Flint watercolours and silk flower arrangements, but immaculately done. And there was a real fire, spitting in the grate.

"Can I get you anything? Tea? Coffee? Soft drink?"

Helen held up her half-eaten banana and bottle of Evian in polite refusal. "Is that a real fire?" she enquired, not having seen one in years.

"Yes. A man delivers the logs. They're still a bit damp but I always think it's nice to have one going. Especially on mornings like this. Please, take a seat," Tessa said, indicating a floral-patterned chair beside the fire.

Helen unzipped her leather jacket, sat, and pulled out her notebook. "So, how are you doing, Tessa? Did your daughter come and stay?"

"She left yesterday… She has these rosters. Anyway, I'm fine now… I get a bit tearful but… It's fine… I'm sleeping a lot."

She looked like shit, but Helen couldn't tell her, or ask why her daughter felt her stewardess job was more important than her mother's welfare. So, she kept up the charade. "Good. Did the counsellor get in touch with you?"

"She phoned. I'm seeing her next week."

"Next week?" echoed Helen, trying to keep the concern out of her voice.

"She's not available until then. She's on a drug awareness course."

Christ, Helen thought, *if she were some junkie social services would be all over her like a rash.*

"Anyway, I'm fine," said Tessa, in that English middle-class way of not wanting to be seen making a fuss. "In some respects, I suppose I've been lucky. I mean, he... well, he could have..." She lowered her voice, as if frightened someone might overhear. "Raped me. And the doctors said he hadn't done... well, anything."

Helen already knew the details of the medical report but let her continue, knowing the more she spoke about her ordeal, rather than lock it away in an emotional cupboard to fester, the better her long-term chances of recovery.

"Apart from my hair," said Tessa, instinctively pulling the woollen hat further down to cover her bare neck. "Why would he do that to me?"

"That's what we need to find out. How is your memory now? Has any of it come back?"

"No. It's weird, I can't remember anything."

"Rohypnol has that effect. You said you remember you were supposed to be meeting a man?"

"And him being late but... the rest is just... gone. There's nothing there. I can't even remember being in the river."

"Well, we know you weren't in it for long, thank God. We found a blanket in the bushes near the bridge. We think he dumped you there. Unfortunately, there's no CCTV on that part of the road."

Helen pulled out a couple of ten-by-eight scene-of-crime photographs, showing a stained brown blanket lying incongruously amongst thick undergrowth.

"What are those... stains?"

"Believe it or not, we think they're bird droppings," Helen replied, holding up a clear plastic evidence bag. "We found these sticking to it. Do these mean anything to you?"

"No. They look like feathers. Were they picked up from the riverbank?"

"Possibly, but they look too small for a swan or a duck."

An image of downy white feather, drifting down towards her, flashed into Tessa's mind and just as quickly was gone. "I can't! I can't remember... Why do you keep asking me?"

"Because, technically, we can't actually prove there's been a crime yet, Tessa."

"I didn't do this to myself!"

"I know that. Okay. Let's start again. Do you remember where you were meeting this online date?"

"Somewhere in Kew… The Gardens, it had something to do with gardens."

"You didn't write it down?"

"In my iPhone. He took it. It had his name and profile and everything."

"You don't have a computer?"

"An iPad. It was in my purse. He took that too. I don't understand. Why would he drug me, not touch me, yet do this to me?" She pulled off her hat, revealing her shaved head, and, despite herself, broke down and began to cry.

* * *

Laura Fell had been sleeping badly, and since she no longer had to get up for work, having posted her formal written notice, she stayed in bed. She was still in her dressing gown at midday when her doorbell started to chime.

She peeked out from behind her first-floor lounge curtain and was surprised to see a steel-haired, athletic-looking older guy in a blue flannel suit standing on the doorstep. He caught a glimpse of her before she had a chance to step back and mimed for her to open the window. Feeling a little foolish, she did.

"Laura Fell," he said, making it sound like a statement rather than a question.

"Yes," she replied. He didn't look like a journalist and they'd pretty much given up on her by now, but she wasn't taking any chances. "Who are you?"

"I'm here on behalf of Mrs Lewis. She'd like to talk to you."

Laura eyed him warily. She'd rung Gina's mother – who she'd met on several occasions – twice over the past week and left messages but had received no reply.

"Now, if that's possible."

This time it sounded ominously like an instruction rather than a question.

"She's in the car," he said, indicating a silver Lexus parked forty metres down the road.

Laura didn't have her lenses in, so she couldn't really see it, which added to her disquiet. "Look, uh, I was just getting in the shower."

"No problem. Mrs Lewis is happy to wait. Shall we say ten minutes?"

He turned and was on his way back to the Lexus before Laura had a chance to refuse.

"Shit. Shit. Shit," she muttered to herself as she raced around the lounge, picking up discarded clothes, dirty mugs and old newspapers – many of which contained reports of Gina's death. She dumped the mugs in the sink and the papers under the clothes in the dirty linen basket. Then closed the door on the mess and hurried into the bedroom to change. The doorbell started up again as she was making the bed.

"Sorry about the mess." Laura apologised as she hauled open the front door. "The refuse people didn't come and you can't leave the bags outside. The foxes get into them."

Celia Lewis smiled serenely, manoeuvred her way around the black bin liners cluttering the tiny, shared hall, and made her way up the creaking stairs.

"Can I get you a tea or coffee?" Laura offered, as she ushered her into the lounge, quickly closing the door behind them.

"No thank you," Celia replied, still smiling, as she perused the room like a polite but slightly disappointed estate agent. "Have you lived here long?"

"Oh... uh, twenty-two years. Actually, I'm just having a new kitchen put in. That's why the place is a bit of a muddle. Sorry."

Celia turned towards Laura, eyeing her quizzically, as if she didn't understand, and said, "You look tired. Have you not been sleeping?"

"I'm okay, Mrs Lewis." Laura never felt comfortable using Celia's Christian name – she'd never been asked to and now, even more so, it seemed to lack respect. "I did try to ring you. Did you not get my messages?"

"Yes. I'm sorry, it's just been…" Celia left the words hanging, everything she said sounded like a cliché, a lie, and she hated herself for having to collude in it. "I'm sorry to just barge in unannounced. I was just passing," she lied again. "I'm on my way to Gina's to start sorting things out. I wondered if you'd come with me? I'm not sure I can face it on my own."

Laura blanched at the thought, but how could she refuse her face to face? Celia waited for her response, hoping that she'd find it impossible.

"Of course. But isn't it a bit early for that?"

"We want to get the house cleared and the legalities sorted out as quickly as possible, to put an end to all these horrendous press stories. You must have seen them?" she said, monitoring Laura's response.

"I've tried not to read anything," Laura lied in return, knowing that the newspapers were full of Celia's troubled relationship with her daughter. Some even questioned whether she was an appropriate person to be heading an enquiry on childhood abuse.

"Nothing at all?" Celia repeated incredulously.

Laura shook her head.

Celia seemed to let it go, and changed tack. "Anyway, I thought it would give us a chance to talk. I know how Gina loved and trusted you."

Laura felt a wave of emotion rolling over her and could only reply, "I loved her too."

"As a friend or something else?"

The question hit her like a low blow. She tried to laugh it off but could see from Celia's implacable face that she was deadly serious.

"I'm sorry. I don't know what you mean."

"Then let me make myself clear. Were you and my daughter having a relationship?"

"You mean... physically?"

"Were you sleeping together? It's a simple question. Yes or no?"

"No!" Laura retorted, finally finding her voice. "How could you think something like that?"

"Because you are evidently the sole benefactor of her estate."

Laura was completely and utterly stunned. She and Gina had promised each other bits of jewellery, as friends do, if either of them suddenly died in car crash or plane crash or something, but nothing like this. She didn't know how to react. Her best friend had hanged herself and now her mother seemed to be accusing her of manipulating her.

"Me?" she mumbled... "I'm sorry, I don't understand. How do you know this?"

"Because Gina changed her will the morning she committed suicide," Celia announced, her eyes never leaving Laura's as she looked for any flicker of recognition. "So, you didn't know that she'd left you the house in Wimbledon?"

***

The journey from Kew to Wimbledon took twenty minutes, but to Laura it felt like a lifetime. Celia retreated into silence the moment they seated themselves in the back of the car, clearly not believing Laura's protestations about knowing nothing of the will. And Laura felt embarrassed and, despite herself, guilty, suspecting that Gina may have changed her will to punish her mother. But also knowing that the house was worth over 650,000 pounds and the money from its sale would change her life.

Laura took a long deep breath as they approached the house. It looked pretty as a picture in the autumn sunshine. A casual passer-by would have no clue to the tragedy that occurred within it only a few days ago. The lounge curtains were closed but apart from that everything appeared perfectly normal. Even the front door, which the surly cop had kicked in, had been replaced.

"I've had the locks changed, for security." Celia produced a set of brass keys from her suit pocket and held them up for Laura.

Laura hesitated and mumbled, "Oh. No. I mean, shouldn't you?"

Celia shrugged and unlocked the door. Then, stood very deliberately aside, allowing the new owner to enter first. Laura, feeling more and more uncomfortable about the situation, which was clearly the intention, eased past her.

"It feels strange, being back here as if nothing happened."

"I'm sure," said Celia, closing the front door firmly behind them and handing her the keys. "What made you come around so late that night?"

The sudden interrogative tone of her question once again threw Laura. "Oh. Well, I don't really know... It was weird."

"In what way? Did she phone you? Had you arranged to meet?"

"I was on my way home from Putney. I'd been seeing some friends. I thought Gina was going to be there... Anyway, I heard these sirens and I stopped and an ambulance came past me, travelling really fast, heading for Wimbledon. And I don't know why, but I suddenly got worried about Gina. So... I followed it." She paused to allow Celia to comment. But she just stared right through her, as if digesting the veracity of the information; forcing her to continue. "Look, I know it sounds a bit weird, the ambulance wasn't even going to Gina's, it turned off, but that's what happened."

"Then why did you carry on?"

It was a logical question and one that Laura had asked herself over and over again, but she couldn't answer because she didn't know herself.

"Had someone said something to you, Laura? Had, Gina?"

She felt trapped. They were both still in the hallway, no more than three feet apart, standing outside the room were Gina had hung herself. She didn't want to lie to Celia but she didn't want to hurt her any more than she obviously had been. "About what?"

"You tell me. If she wasn't in a relationship with you, was she with someone else? A man?"

"I don't know. Gina could be a bit secretive. She said she'd met someone, but she never talked about it."

"I find that a bit hard to believe. I mean, you were supposedly her best friend."

"Mrs Lewis," Laura interjected, "I know you're upset about the will, and I would be if I were in your situation—"

"For Christ sake! I'm not asking for your sympathy! I'm asking you to be honest with me!"

"I am! I can't tell you something I don't know! And it's not my fault Gina changed her will. I didn't ask her to. I wish she hadn't. I wish she hadn't died. I wish I could have stopped her and none of this had happened!"

They stood there in the crushing silence until Celia turned away, fumbling for the comfort of her electronic cigarette. Grateful to find it in the bottom of her Mulberry bag, she took a long hit of nicotine and said in a confessional whisper, "I'm sorry… Gina and I… we were going through a difficult time and… Well, when something like this happens you can't help but blame yourself."

"Gina loved you, Mrs Lewis."

Celia tried to smile, failed and said, "You'd never have thought so from what her friends told the newspapers. I'll make a start on her bedroom. I assume you won't mind me taking any personal items and gifts we may have given her?"

Laura watched Celia, crushed by her guilt, disappear upstairs; disturbing a small white feather that floated momentarily into the air before settling down onto a lower step. Steeling herself, she pushed open the door and entered the lounge. Everything looked perfect, just as Gina had always kept it, except that the chandelier Laura had so carefully chosen as a moving-in present had been replaced by a bare light bulb hanging from a flex.

* * *

The detective's room was situated on the first floor of Wimbledon Police Station, above the front desk, interview rooms and holding cells. It was accessed via its own keypad that could be overridden by a barcoded name tag worn around the neck. Security was tight, since a number of computers containing sensitive information were stolen in 2017 and subsequently discovered at a car-boot sale in Barnet. The incident had been doubly embarrassing for DCI Malcolm Teal, as he'd just gone on record praising his team for successfully targeting burglars in Merton and lowering the crime rate. The journalist he gave the interview to was Pauline Bowe, Everton Bowe's wife. It had soured their professional relationship ever since.

Everton was chatting to Helen at her workstation, a small desk with views of two walls and the men's lavatory. As the latest recruit, she was treated like the runt of the litter and left with only with the scraps – being the only woman in the department didn't help.

"So, you'll knock me up a police insurance report?"

"Yeah, no problem. Email what you want me to say and I'll copy it and send it back." Helen winked.

"Mrs Lewis. How did it go?"

Everton looked up and saw DCI Teal, a bullock of a man, striding out of his office to interrupt them.

"She warned me to stay away from the press." Everton shrugged, aware of the irony.

"Good advice. Helen. A word. My office."

For a big man of over six foot three and 210 pounds, Teal spoke in very short sentences, a habit born out of his dyslexia, which he learnt to cope with in his police exams by writing in short precise sentences. Now it had bled into his work life.

He disappeared back into his room, leaving the door ajar in a gesture indicating "now".

"He loves you really." Helen grinned as she stood up.

Everton, not caring about his career, didn't give a toss what Teal thought of him. He gave her the finger and strolled out.

Teal rolled down his support socks as he waited for Helen. He had angina and was supposed to be on a diet, which he'd ignored until six months ago when he keeled over whilst refereeing his kid's rugby match. Now he ate salads and oily fish five days a week and hated the taste it left in his mouth. He placed an extra-strong mint onto his tongue and barked, "DC Lake."

Helen Lake had the makings of a good copper, but she was one of the new breed of graduates he instinctively mistrusted. She knew a lot about theory but less than she thought about practice.

"DC Lake!"

"Two minutes, guv."

Guv? Even the way she said it, in her confident public-school voice, irked him. It made him feel like a dinosaur, an impostor. Teal had come up through the ranks and never felt entirely comfortable with the PR skills and political nous required of the modern senior police officer.

"Sorry, guv," said Helen, entering and taking a seat, unoffered, opposite Teal's cluttered desk. "You wanted a word with me?"

"Mrs Lewis. What happened?"

"Nothing. I never spoke to her directly myself. I was banished outside to wait with her husband. Why?"

"Bowe. I told you to keep an eye on him."

"I'm not his nursemaid."

"No, but you've had a relationship."

Helen, ignoring the memory of Angus Lewis' ironic remark, replied, "With respect, that's none of your business."

Teal eyed her, crunched and swallowed his palate-cleansing peppermint and got down to the business at hand. "I've had a complaint. Been made aware of one. Mrs Lewis claims Bowe was disrespectful."

"Not when I was there."

"You just said you weren't."

"I was in the room for part of the conversation, during which time PC Bowe handled himself impeccably, then Mrs Lewis ordered me, and I use the word advisedly, to leave the room. Which I did–"

"Okay. Okay. I get the picture."

"With respect" – she was doing it again and didn't care – "wouldn't it just be easier to ask PC Bowe himself?"

"I will – after I ascertain the facts."

Helen shrugged and said no more. As far as she was concerned, it was a dead subject; she had better things to do with her time. Teal did too, but disliked what he perceived, with some justification, as her patronising attitude.

"Do you think you're the only one who has to take bullshit orders?"

Helen was surprised by his sudden change of tack. "No. But–"

"I haven't finished! I have people, important people, people I don't like and as sure as shit don't like me, all over this department like a rash, and not just because some minor politician's daughter goes and tops herself, oh no, I've also got three missing women, whose families fear are dead, and I don't have a damn clue what to tell them, so cut the sarcasm and get on with your job! Okay?"

It was the longest sentence she'd ever heard Teal utter and she knew better than to push him further.

"Sir," she said, and walked out.

Twenty minutes later, Teal walked over to her desk and offered her a conciliatory peppermint. "Okay. Where have you got with the lady in the lake?"

"River."

"Whatever."

Helen accepted the peace offering, handed him the file and began filling him in, explaining that she'd had no luck tracing Tessa's date through Match.com, who were reluctant to release any information on the man, citing client confidentiality, especially since she had no proof that he'd actually committed any crime.

"Frightened of getting sued," grunted Teal.

"Yeah, but they did confirm he'd recently removed his profile."

Teal looked up from the file, interested now. "How recent?"

"The same day Tessa Hayes was found in the river. It's exactly the same MO."

"Maybe, but the other women were all using different sites."

"I think he's changing sites, making himself more difficult to track."

"A lot of people use multiple online dating sites."

Helen said nothing, knowing it was the truth. She'd used them herself a few times and had a couple of interesting one-night stands. Teal sucked on his peppermint and rolled it around his mouth, weighing his limited options.

"What about his credit card payments?"

"They won't release them without a court order."

"And a magistrate won't issue one without us being able to link him to a crime. It's catch twenty-two."

"It won't be in his real name anyway. He's too smart for that."

"Any pattern in the fake profiles? Age? Class? Hobbies?"

"Nothing except the ages. They're all men in their early forties. He's obviously trying to appeal to the age range of the women he's targeting, who are generally a few years older."

"What about the bogus photos?"

"The two we found on the other missing women's laptops were totally different. I was thinking of re-interviewing the families."

"They've already been interviewed by DS Clarke."

"Yeah, but initially he had them down as a low priority."

"There wasn't any pattern."

"Now there is. Come on. It's worth a shot, guv."

"Okay," Teal conceded. "You've got five days. Come up with something or we park it."

"I'm going to need some help – and preferably not DS Clarke. He might feel I'm questioning his judgement."

"You are."

"I'm just following the evidence, guv. I was thinking maybe DC Coyle?"

Teal shot her look that told her the idea was a complete non-starter. "I've got a gang war in Phipps Bridge, and another knifing in Morden."

"Okay. Give me a female PC. I mean, we're dealing with missing women–"

"It was a fourteen-year-old girl who got stabbed. Alright. Alright. Take Bowe. I hear you've doubled up before."

Helen couldn't be sure, but she thought he might have been grinning as he walked back into his office and shut the door firmly behind him.

* * *

Peter Pitt, like the furnishing in the solicitor's waiting room, could best be described as "shabby-chic". Laura returned his welcoming smile, and walked through the door he held open for her.

"Perhaps I should lead," he suggested, performing a smart quickstep past Laura and guiding her through the warren of narrow, musty corridors. "Sorry about the trek. These old buildings are beautiful from the outside but inside… hey ho."

The walls were hung with formally posed photographs of the various partners. Laura's count had reached a dozen, when…

"Most of them are dead," explained Peter. "Here we are."

He opened the door to a spacious, modern office, which was flooded with light from a pair of Georgian windows overlooking the Isleworth towpath and River Thames. Laura was pleasantly surprised.

"I know. It's a bit like the Tardis, isn't it?" He smiled, shutting the door behind them.

"The what?"

"Tardis? Much bigger on the inside… *Doctor Who*?" he said, pulling out one of the Italian chrome and leather chairs for Laura to sit on. "Have you been offered coffee? Tea?"

"I'm fine," Laura replied, waiting as he sat opposite and opened a green cardboard file which lay rather incongruously on the modernist glass desk. "You said on the phone that it was important. I'm assuming it's about Gina's will?"

"Yes. I'm sure this must have come as a shock to you."

Laura wasn't sure if he was talking about the circumstances of Gina's death or the new will, so said nothing.

"I didn't know Miss Lewis well. We'd only looked after her affairs for the past year, but I liked her enormously. She had such life…" He paused, realising his poor choice of words and mumbled, "Very sad."

His respects paid, he reached into the green file, pulled out a letter and handed it to Laura, stating with appropriate gravitas, "This is Miss Lewis' Last Will and Testament."

Laura hesitated; it wasn't a typed document but a handwritten letter.

"As you can see, it's a little unusual but technically quite legal. You are named as the executor and sole beneficiary."

"This is dated the day she died?"

"Yes. I received it two days later. As I say, it's quite legal, but under the circumstances, I must warn you, it may be challenged."

"By her family?" said Laura, feeling swamped by the awful ramifications of her dead friend's decision and suspecting it was why the solicitor had been so keen to meet her personally.

"Yes. Mrs Lewis has already been in contact. I'd strongly advise you to have no further contact with her or her husband."

"Were they the previous benefactors?"

"Sorry. The content of the previous will is strictly confidential."

"I don't understand. If the previous will was confidential, how did Mrs Lewis know it was changed?"

Peter polished his Parker Pen on his sleeve, formulating the correct, non-committal reply and said, finally, "That is a question for her, not me. I can only advise you of the facts I'm legally allowed to."

"You said Mrs Lewis had been in contact with you; surely you must have asked her?"

"I'm afraid any conversations between Mrs Lewis and I are bound to remain–"

"Confidential." Laura was losing patience. "So why exactly did you call me in here?"

"Well… to formally give you the good news about your bequest."

* * *

Angus Lewis was in the eat-in kitchen of his Fulham Palace Road home, talking to his AA sponsor on his mobile. It was a bi-weekly charade that he kept up to placate his wife, Celia, since the car accident that put him in a wheelchair for life and, she believed, led to their daughter's suicide.

"You don't understand," he said. "She needs someone to hate, to blame for ruining the life she's worked so hard to perfect, and with Gina gone it's yours truly."

He picked up his glass of malt and wheeled his way out, across the antique pine hall floor and into the Designers Guild sitting room as he listened to his sponsor's response. Then, said wearily, "My daughter just hanged herself. Wouldn't you be drinking?... We're both self-medicating, hers just comes in a smaller bottle – which reminds me..."

He deftly wheeled himself back out into the hall, down to the cloakroom, and hauled open the pine door. The room was like a miniature gentlemen's club; all mahogany, polished brass and military photographs of Angus's career in the Scots Guards.

"I'm doing the steps but my darling wife keeps pushing me back down them. Just give me a minute, please. I'll put you on loudspeaker... No, as you were. Don't know how the damn thing works." He placed the mobile and tumbler of Scotch on the windowsill, bent down, picked up a glass urine bottle and unzipped himself. "Nearly there – oh, shit."

The rap at the front door made him jerk around, causing him to splash himself and the floor with urine. He groaned and grabbed the mobile.

"Look, I'll have to phone you back... I'm aware that this should be my priority, but there's someone at the door and I've just peed my pants."

The line went dead in his hands.

"Born again bloody puritan," he muttered. Grabbing a magazine to cover his wet trousers, he wheeled himself back out into the hall and yanked open the front door. "If you're the press you can bugger off before I call the police."

It wasn't the press.

"My name is Colin Gould. I was your daughter's fiancé."

Ten minutes later, Colin sat on the edge of the Designer Guild sofa in the sitting room, waiting for Angus to reappear. He'd planned the visit with his usual precision, watching the house from a safe distance as he waited for Celia and her driver to depart. He felt he'd receive a fairer hearing with Mr Lewis, but now he was inside his confidence was evaporating.

He looked around the room again, at the understated but expensive furnishings and baby grand piano that fitted the dimensions of the bay window exactly, and the silver-framed photos arranged in perfect symmetry on the top of it. It was obvious where Gina had got her need for order from. But it was odd that the only thing missing was a picture of her.

"Do you play?" asked Angus as he wheeled himself in, balancing two cups of coffee on a silver-plated tray covering his wet lap.

"No. I'm afraid not. But I love classical music. Brahms and Schubert."

"Can't bear it myself," said Angus, making no attempt to put Colin at ease. "You and Gina were engaged?"

"Oh… Well, yes… unofficially," stumbled Colin, momentarily thrown by the sudden change of subject.

"What does that mean? Either you were or you weren't."

Colin shifted uncomfortably in his seat, surprised by Angus's accusatory tone, and tried to regain his composure. "We were in love, Mr Lewis. We'd talked about moving in together… Maybe eventually getting married–"

"If this has anything to do with her changing her will and the house, you need to take that up with her so-called friend Laura."

"Laura? No. I didn't know anything about–"

"Look," said Angus, realising he may have said too much and moving the conversation on to safer ground. "Gina never said anything to us about you or any of this marriage business."

"She wouldn't have. She wanted to keep it a secret until… well, she was sure. I was…"

"I see. And why do you feel the need to tell me this now?"

"Because… I think she killed herself over us – me…" The words clotted in his throat, and Colin, a man who hadn't cried in forty years since his father walked out, abandoning him and his mother, who despised the crocodile tears of the tax cheats he'd censured, suddenly broke down and wept.

"You see, we broke up a couple of months ago… I don't know why, we hadn't rowed… She just stopped answering my phone calls. I tried over and over again. I wasn't stalking her. I wasn't threatening her. I wouldn't do that. I'm not like that. I'm a good person. I have strong moral values… I just needed to talk to her… To make her understand what she meant to me…"

Angus listened to his confession, knowing that it was a fantasy that his darling, troubled daughter could never have been in love with a man who blabbed like a baby in front of a complete stranger.

"Don Hart caused this, Mr Lewis. He's a liar! A liar and a cheat! He was dating Laura Fell. He was sleeping with her and at the same time he was phoning Gina, turning up at her house at night. I was jealous, I admit it."

Angus, who'd never even heard of Don Hart, had heard enough and cut him short. "Were you spying on them?"

"I had to check him out to protect Gina. The man's a crook. He's being investigated by the Inland Revenue."

"Really? And how do you know that?"

"I used to work for HMRC. I have contacts. He's suspected of making fraudulent benefit claims. He's also been running a dog betting scam. The police are involved."

Angus licked his cracked lips and wondered where he'd left his glass of malt, thinking that as soon as he got rid of Colin, he was going to have to phone his wife and relate the episode, and to do that he was going to need another stiff drink.

Later that night, Colin would need a stiff drink too. Because Celia Lewis' steel-haired driver stood on his doorstep carrying a court order banning him from approaching or contacting the Lewis family again. Furious, he slammed the door in his face and snatched up the phone to vent his anger to Frieda Cole, the only true friend he felt he could now rely on.

And in that moment the spell of the "coven" and its weave of friendships truly began to crumble.

* * *

Megan Howell had resorted to drinking Night Nurse to help her sleep. It worked up to a point, but left her feeling hungover in the morning and did nothing to stop the real cause of her anxiety: the abusive phone calls, sometimes as many as a dozen a night.

She'd contacted British Telecom to try and block them but they came from different mobiles and withheld numbers. Most were silent or just breathing, but some were disgusting, slurping, grunting, orgasmic sounds. She kept a diary, noting down the date and time of each call, gathering evidence that she could never use, because she already knew who was behind them and couldn't go to the police for risk of incriminating herself.

Keeping her secret, living with it every day, was eating away at her from the inside and now she was coughing blood. Her GP had booked her in for an endoscopy but Megan knew her real disease couldn't be cured by medical intervention. She was being punished for her crime and deep in her heart she knew she deserved it.

Three years previously, she was the highly-respected deputy head of Southgate College, a private co-educational school on the outskirts of Swansea; then, in what she called "a moment of madness", she started an affair with a fifteen-year-old pupil. The girl had subsequently taken an overdose when selfies, intended for Megan, were found on her mobile. Fortunately for Megan, she'd refused to press charges and, with no other proof, the police were forced to drop the case. But Megan had been *persuaded* to resign and left the school and Swansea in disgrace.

She'd moved to Putney in South West London because it was an area where she knew no one. She intended to remain anonymous and rebuild her self-esteem and life. Giving up teaching was hard but she found a job in a small language college, for foreign students learning English, on the Lower Richmond Road. Slowly she began to make friends through FrontRow and realised there were a lot of single women of her age looking for companionship. She wasn't interested in them physically; her preference had always been younger women. Teenagers, not children. She wasn't a paedophile; the very thought was repellent to her. But girls on the verge of womanhood, beginning to explore their bodies and sexuality, beguiled her. In her mind, she wasn't predatory. She never touched anyone who didn't want to be touched and *never* made the first move. But after Swansea, she knew she had to stop and, hard as it had been, she had. But then, the disgusting phone calls had started.

She pushed her foam plugs deeper into her ears and tried to ignore the insistent ringing phone. Finally, she was forced to give up. It wasn't her stalker; it was Frieda Cole.

* * *

There was no celebration of Gina's life. Instead, the core members of the group, minus Colin Gould and Laura, who hadn't been invited, gathered to discuss Colin's behaviour and his extraordinary claim that Laura had been left Gina's house in her will.

They met at The Wharf in Teddington. It was still early but the bar area, with its huge deco mirror reflecting the happy punters, was already buzzing.

"Shall we sit at a table? It'll be more private," suggested Frieda, who felt uneasy about attending without Laura.

The group milled around, looking for a suitable table. The maître d' saw them and beckoned them into the conservatory, indicating a table with a river view.

"Enjoy your meal, ladies."

Forced to eat when they only wanted a drink, they ordered from the Early Bird two-course menu and made small talk until the food arrived. Frieda ordered a large glass of Chilean Sauvignon Blanc, but no one else was drinking; either because they were driving or out of deference to the seriousness of the discussion they were about to have.

Megan was the first to broach the subject. "Can I just say, this was supposed to be a celebration of Gina's life and it's sad that Colin's behaviour has tarnished it. Anyway," she said, holding up her glass of water in a toast. "To Gina."

The group reciprocated as one, clinking glasses and waiting for Frieda to speak. She sipped her glass of gooseberry flavoured wine, wishing it were vodka, and said, bereft of anything else, "Colin is a sensitive man, sometimes oversensitive–"

"Sensitive?" Iris interrupted. "He's a βλάκας – an idiot. I'm sorry, I know he's a friend of yours, but what the hell was he thinking? Having a drink with someone, going to the cinema a few times and sharing a pizza, is hardly love. I mean, come on, he's asked us all out at one time or another. He's creepy."

"He says they were sleeping together," said Frieda, more in explanation than in Colin's defence.

"What? When? No way. We'd have known."

"Gina did say she'd met someone else. Remember, in Ibiza? Someone new and special?"

"Someone new couldn't be Colin," corrected Megan. "I mean, I accept that he's upset, Frieda – we all are – but all these accusations about Don Hart… He's completely delusional."

"Okay. Look, he made a mistake, a bad mistake. He knows that and he's embarrassed–"

"He should be." Iris snorted.

"I've asked him to write a letter of apology to the Lewis family."

Megan and Iris said nothing but their exchange of looks spoke volumes. Frieda felt her shoulders and spirits sink. She was tired of trying to defend the indefensible, tired of trying to defend her motives. She just wanted to drink and numb herself to dreamless sleep. She took another hit from her glass of wine and tried again.

"I just think that the least we can do is to try and apologise."

"I'm sorry, but it's not *us* that need to apologise. And I'm certainly not going to do that to a woman who was partially responsible for her daughter's suicide."

"That's an appalling thing to say, Megan, you don't know that–"

"I know she hated her mother–"

"She didn't hate her mother! Their personalities clashed. They were too similar–"

"Gina told me she hadn't spoken to her in over a month."

"Her mother helped her buy her house! Why would she do that if she didn't love her?"

"She was trying to control her. Buy her affection."

"That's ridiculous! How can you say that?" Frieda could feel her throat constricting. She took a calming breath and, choosing her words carefully, continued, "Look, Megan, you don't have children–"

"That was my personal choice! It has nothing to do with this."

"I'm sorry. I didn't mean to offend you. I'm just saying… bringing up kids… it's hard. Despite everything, all the problems, I know Gina's mother loved her."

"So why did she kill herself and make Laura the executor of her will if she wasn't trying to get back at her?" said Iris, siding with Megan.

"We don't know she did. We've only got Colin's word for that and you said yourself he's delusional."

"Actually, I didn't. Megan did."

"Oh, for Christ's sake! Who cares who bloody said it? She's just lost her daughter, Iris, try and show a bit of compassion for once, can't you?"

Heads turned at nearby tables at the sudden outburst. Iris and Megan retreated into silence. A waiter materialised at the bar door. Frieda saw him and downed the rest of her wine in one long deliberate draught, then, with as much dignity as she could muster, stood and walked past him and headed for the sanctuary of the bar.

The waiter approached the table and cleared the plates. Megan and Iris sat in silence, sipping their iced tap water as the table was re-set for a dessert they weren't having, until finally he nodded and, thank God, made his way out.

"I'm surprised Laura didn't mention being made Gina's executor. I mean, we're all supposed to be friends," said Iris, still smarting over the way Frieda had spoken to her.

"She's probably embarrassed. I mean, it looks a bit odd, her being at Gina's for no apparent reason on the night she committed suicide and telling the police that there was someone else inside when there wasn't."

"And being left the house," said Iris. "Which is probably why she split up with Don Hart."

Frieda watched the grisly soap opera reflected in the huge mirror behind the bar, and wondered if Gina could have had any real idea of the devastation her suicide would cause… not only to her family but to her closest friends.

Empathy

Helen's briefing to Everton in the detective's room had overrun. DS Jack Clarke, a man who made sure he publicly shared his superior's views but in private had no problem slagging him off, had insisted on sitting in. Clarke had been the lead on the original investigation, which had found no links between the missing women and would prefer not to be proven wrong, especially by a woman who had a high opinion of herself and her looks, which in his opinion were only mid-range.

Clarke had developed a habit of rating everything on a scale of one to ten. His Philippine wife was a five, their doll-like daughter an eight. DCI Teal an out-of-his-depth four. And know-all Detective Constable Lake – who had a nice arse but knew it – a, being generous, six.

Helen had found her rating, or rather Everton had, on a yellow Post-it note stuck on her back at the end of her first day at the nick. It had been the birth of her and Everton's relationship and conversely set the tone for hers with Clarke. From then on, she referred to Clarke as "Nobby" or, in private to Everton, "the knob".

Today, she was demonstrating her resentment by trying to ignore him, which seemed to Everton a pretty juvenile thing to do. But Clarke was such an arrogant prick he didn't even realise. He sat back from the briefing table, laid out with the photographic evidence, rubbing the toe of his black cowboy boot against the leg of his skinny chinos, calculating whether he needed to get involved or not.

One by one, Helen held up the photos of the missing women and ran briefly through the earlier investigation into their disappearances. And, one by one, Clarke, interjected to question her conclusions.

"The similarities between all the missing women and Tessa Hayes are striking," said Helen. "They're all in their forties, divorced and living alone–"

"I wouldn't call them striking."

"And they were all using online dating sites," Helen persisted.

"One in five relationships start online. There's nothing uncommon in that."

"No, but all of the women disappeared the night they'd arranged to meet their online date. We know this because we found a diary entry on a laptop we recovered from Kate Holmes' flat at the time."

"That's only proof of when *she* disappeared, not the other two women."

"If you let me finish, I'll get to that."

"Be my guest," said Clarke, and stretched out on his seat to wait.

"Thank you." Helen turned back to Everton and caught him checking his watch. "Do you have to be somewhere, PC Bowe? Or am I boring you too?"

"Neither," said Bowe; lying on one count.

"Okay. We know this because the mobile phone records of Francis Cole, missing woman two, and Barbara Crane, missing woman three, both show a number of calls to an 'unknown' mobile number the day they disappeared."

"The same number?" asked Bowe, interested now.

"No. But significantly, both numbers were unavailable the next day."

"Probably pay-as-you-go and he shut them down."

"Exactly. He also removed his profile from the dating sites–"

"Hold on." Clarke could feel the weight of evidence building but wasn't going to give up without a fight. "You only found evidence of that on Holmes' laptop and we found nothing on the other two women."

"They both used iPhones which have never been found, neither have their purses and credit cards."

"Which we checked. In both cases their credit cards were used *after* their disappearance."

"Probably trying to cover his tracks," said Bowe, not buying Clarke's explanation. "How long were they used for?"

"Less than a week. Not long enough for us to trace them, and in different locations. And Tessa Hayes' iPad, purse and credit cards were taken too."

"And never used – and she didn't disappear – so where does that leave your theory? Supposition is not evidence, love."

"Thank you, Nobby, your scepticism has been noted."

Nobby? Everton waited for the shit to hit the fan. It didn't take long. Clarke heaved himself out of his chair and took a menacing step towards Helen.

"I've got your number, Constable. I'd advise you to remember that."

"I know. Six. I've seen it on my little yellow Post-it."

"Once a smartarse, always a smartarse," sneered Clarke. "People don't like that."

"Yeah, well, 'people' better get used to it."

"Ding dong," announced Everton, striking an imaginary bell. "End of round three."

Clarke turned and shot him a withering look.

It bounced right off Everton. "What's in the evidence bag? The one with the little yellow Post-it label?"

Helen allowed herself a small smile, and handed him the clear plastic bag.

"We found this on the riverbank, near where Tessa Hayes was discovered. We think she was dumped out of a car. There's a bridge a hundred metres upstream – and before you ask, there's no CCTV coverage of the road."

"Hmn," said Bowe, placing the shit-encrusted blanket aside and picking up a smaller evidence bag. "What's this?" He emptied the meagre contents onto the table, picking up the solitary, downy white feather. "Is this from a duck or something?"

"No. A dove. We've had it analysed."

None the wiser, Everton placed it back in the evidence bag, resealed it, handed it back to her and said, "Okay. Are we done?"

"Yes. First thing tomorrow you start on the pubs and bars in Kew and the surrounding area and see if anyone recognises Tessa Hayes' photograph. I've made a list. All she remembers is the name had something to do with 'gardens'. I'll start interviewing the families of the other missing women–"

"We did that before. You're wasting your time," interrupted Clarke.

"Fortunately, it's mine to waste."

"For five days. The DCI's asked me to keep him informed of your progress."

Clarke turned and strolled out. Helen pursed her lips in distaste as she stared after him. "He's so far up Teal's arse I'm surprised he can breathe."

"I have a feeling he'd prefer to be up someone else's," Everton grinned, and headed for the door. "I'm late. See you tomorrow."

"Where are you going?"

"To another boxing match."

* * *

Everton was already running when he hit the street and headed for Wimbledon station, and still running when he emerged from the Tube at Fulham Broadway. He bounded up the stairs two at a time, flashed his warrant card at the barrier guard and headed out onto Fulham Road. The offices of Gale Mediation Lawyers were in Farrier Walk, a mile from the station. He tried to hail a taxi, there were none, groaned and began to run.

Two hundred and forty an hour, he chanted to himself, *and the clock is running whether you're there or not. Run.* He was sweating profusely by the time he passed the Chelsea Stadium and he still had eight hundred metres to go. *Two hundred and forty an hour.* He lengthened his stride, calculating that his lateness had already cost him forty pounds.

Pauline Bowe checked her reflection in the lawyer's window. She'd changed out of her perennial leggings and oversize sweaters into more formal navy slacks and cream blouse; which complemented her bob cut, blonde hair. Now, she was wondering why? Who was she trying to impress?

She was sitting in the tiny waiting room of Gales Mediation, reading a copy of the Metro with a headline that declared:

Head of Met Abuse Enquiry under pressure

The door banged open and Everton staggered in, bent double, hands on knees, fighting to catch his breath.

"You're late," Pauline said, folding the paper neatly in her ample lap and waiting for an explanation.

"I know... Sorry... Sorry..."

"Hey. It's your money you're wasting."

She said it, as she always did, without rancour or reproach, as if she were an adult talking to a wayward child. It was one of the things he'd grown to hate about his wife: her innate sense of superiority.

"Believe me, I'm aware of that. I was working. I've been seconded to CID... These missing women..."

A crack appeared in Pauline's studied indifference as she caught scent of a story. "Tessa Hayes?"

Everton saw it immediately, sat and played dumb. "Who?"

"Come on. That Farnham woman who was found in the River Wandle. Is there a connection?"

Everton gave a non-committal shrug and picked up the Metro from her lap, indicating the photograph of Celia Lewis on the front page. "I was the one who found her daughter," he said, fanning himself with the paper.

"Yeah," said Pauline, not overly interested in what she perceived as old news. "Tell me about these missing women."

Everton laughed out loud and said, "Christ. You're never off, are you?"

"It's my job. Like yours is being a cop."

"I hate being a cop."

"Then give it up. Retire."

"And give you half my pension?"

"I'll get it anyway."

"You don't deserve it."

"That's a matter of opinion. It's the law. I'm bringing up your son."

"I'm paying for it."

"He's well by the way, in case you forgot to ask."

Everton stood and looked out of the dusty window, turning his back on his pretty blonde wife and her pain and hiding his. "It's not right, using Adam to punish me."

"I don't. He's fourteen. He's quite capable of doing it himself."

She watched his shoulders slump as the barb hit home and for a second almost felt sorry for him. Then he gave a little shuffle sideways, tottered and fell against the window.

Everton could hear Pauline's worried voice through the static rushing through his head, but he couldn't respond. The floor had turned to sponge beneath his feet. The last thing he remembered was falling to his knees and looking up to into the concerned eyes of Fiona Gale, their mediation lawyer.

"Mr Bowe? Everton… Are you alright?"

He vomited in response. Looking down at the sour pool of stew on the Persian rug, he wondered how much more the consultation was going to cost him.

Pauline insisted on giving him a lift home despite his protests that it was just his vertigo playing up. She joked about him playing for the sympathy vote, but he could see how concerned she was, and was surprised how much comfort it gave him, knowing that part of her still cared for him. She caught his smile and asked him what he was thinking about.

"Nothing," he replied, not wanting to ruin the moment. "Don't tell Adam about what happened. Okay? I don't want him to worry."

She smiled and nodded. He looked back out of the passenger-seat window, knowing – and happy – that she undoubtedly would.

Later, in his flat, whilst reading the copy of the Metro he'd filched from Pauline, who'd insisted he keep it on his lap in case he threw up in her car, another wave of vertigo swept over him. This time he was ready for it. He lit a spliff, lay flat on his back and began rolling his head from side to side as he focused on a laminate card, printed with the letter W, stuck on the ceiling.

* * *

Frieda phoned Laura to fill her in about the meeting at The Wharf. She'd subsequently heard from an irate Colin Gould that he received an email stating that he was no longer welcome at the Chill Out. And that when he phoned Megan for an explanation, she put the receiver down on him.

Laura could hear from the burr in her voice that she'd been drinking and suggested they meet for a coffee, but Frieda cried off. She just wanted to let her know that she was resigning from the club and that, as a friend, she was disappointed Laura hadn't shared the news of Gina's will with her, rather than her having to hear it second-hand from Colin.

It was a gentle rebuke, but hurt Laura nevertheless, because it was true. Floundering in her own confusion, she'd told no one, reasoning that it was no one's business but her own – except now it was. And it wasn't just the Lewis family who felt betrayed by their daughter, but now seemingly her own friends.

She felt bereft and the summons from Merton Council that arrived the following morning was the last straw. It was from the Traffic Enforcement Centre and contained a grainy black-and-white still downloaded from a CCTV camera on Putney Hill, showing her car jumping the red light on the night of Gina's suicide. It warned her that she had thirty days to pay the hundred-pound fine unless there were any mitigating circumstances.

"Mitigating bloody circumstances!" she exploded, ripping the summons to pieces and throwing it into the wicker basket.

Everton was rudely awoken by Laura's phone call. He listened patiently to her complaint because, in truth, he had a stinking hangover and he couldn't think of anything to say. But then, he surprised himself by promising to intervene to get the ticket rescinded and suggested they meet for a coffee.

Cutting the connection, he wondered what the hell he'd just done. Being the first cop on the scene of the suicide made him technically the lead officer, but with no suspicious circumstances it was a relatively simple case, despite Mrs Lewis' involvement. He'd therefore mentally put it on the back-burner until the inquest, which would be weeks away and well out of the press spotlight if the Lewis family and their high-ranking friends had any influence. So why was he involving himself now? He already knew the answer, even if he couldn't admit it to himself. For the first time since he discovered his wife's affair and his trust was shattered, he actually felt something for someone. And it wasn't sex, unlike with Helen Lake who, at first, he'd slept with to punish his wife for her betrayal. It was something deeper than that and ultimately more dangerous, especially for a cop. Empathy.

* * *

Laura had been a Friend of Kew Gardens for over ten years. Having no outside space of her own, she used it as her back garden. And since it was barely a five-minute stroll away from her flat, it was perfect for her. She preferred it out of season, when there weren't too many tourists and you could walk the far-flung corners without seeing another soul. Especially on weekdays when people were at work. It gave her time to think, and today she had a lot to think about.

Only five weeks ago, she invited a group of friends to the September Kew Music Festival, one of a series of open-air concerts held every year in the grounds. The lead act was a Brazilian samba band, whose vocalist – an extraordinary woman who sounded like a man – must have been in her eighties. They queued for an hour to get in and ran to claim their picnic spot, laying out various blankets, plastic plates and glasses; along with barbecued chicken, numerous salads, French bread and wine.

Don Hart loved it and insisted on teaching Laura to samba, which he knew nothing about. Everyone fell about laughing at his inept attempts until Gina pushed him aside and grabbed Laura's arm, and the pair performed a brilliant duet, Gina taking the male role. Everyone stood and clapped and toasted them with Prosecco. Don claimed it was the sexiest dance he'd seen since "a bird with a snake in *From Dusk Till Dawn*" – a film no one had ever heard of, let alone seen. Still, it was terrific fun and everyone "oohed" along with the firework finale and vowed to do it again next year.

Now, as she wandered past the towering spikes of echiums and silver agaves in the Princess of Wales Conservatory, killing time before she met Everton, she wondered where it had all gone. How easily their friendships fractured, exposing the petty jealousies concealed beneath. She'd done nothing, yet events conspired to portray her as greedy and manipulative and her erstwhile friends had so readily accepted it. Her mind was reeling. She wanted to phone Megan, who she knew was the ringleader, but was too angry. Christ, she wasn't the one who'd been betrayed – *she* was by Megan Howell. And the others had just followed like lemmings.

"Excuse me, please."

A lone Japanese tourist smiled at her and held up his camera, miming to ask if she'd take his photograph beside the Princess of Wales plaque. She walked straight past him, seeing nothing but her own pain. *Lemmings.* Don Hart was right, she thought, when he'd called them that. He may have had his own selfish reasons – he may even be a crook as Colin Gould claimed – but he was still right about them. Her supposed friend Iris and her (not so) secret phone calls to Don. Frieda, who had initially defended her but felt obliged to "share" her disappointment at her behaviour. They'd all appointed themselves judge and jury. She shook her head, irritated at her frailty. What would her father think of her? Had she forgotten everything he taught her about having the courage of her convictions and doing the right thing no matter what the personal cost? She dabbed her eyes with a tissue and blew her nose hard into it, ridding herself of her doubts, and strode out to meet PC Bowe.

* * *

Everton Bowe was having a rough morning too. True to his word, he phoned Merton Traffic Department on the direct police line and explained the extenuating circumstances of Laura's ticket, but he got short shrift. Whilst the supervisor sympathised with her position, he pointed out to Bowe that she'd had no knowledge of her friend's suicide at the time of the offence and was therefore still culpable. Everton thanked him for nothing and slammed the receiver down. Then promptly picked it up again, redialled the automatic payment line, entered Laura's ticket number and paid the fine himself.

So, when he exited Rock and Rose, the fourth on the list of garden-related bars and pubs in Kew, in which absolutely no one recognised Tessa Hayes' photograph – he was not pleased to discover a traffic warden issuing him a ticket.

"Whoa. Hold on. I'm a copper," he said, flashing his warrant card.

The warden, a benign-looking Indian chap in his fifties, was nothing of the sort. "Then you should know better than to park in a restricted zone," he said, pointing to an UNLOADING ONLY sign.

"I'm on duty."

"And I'm doing mine, mate," he replied, tapping Everton's car registration details into his handheld computer.

Everton pulled out his notebook, gave his pencil a theatrical lick and said, "Name?"

The warden was not going to be intimidated and pointed to his ID badge. "Ravi Gupta. My number is below it. Please use it in all communications with the traffic department."

"Ravi Gupta. I'm arresting you on suspicion of aggravated vehicle-taking, under Section 12 of the Theft Act–"

"What…?"

"You do not have to say anything but anything you do say–"

"No! You can't… What are you doing?"

"My job, *mate*. You match the description of a car thief we've been looking for. Hold out your hands," ordered Everton, producing a pair of handcuffs and flicking them open.

The warden faltered momentarily, but stood his ground. "No! This is harassment. I'll complain."

"Be my guest. My number is 3339. You can fill out a complaint form down at the nick."

"Alright! Okay. Alright… Look, I'll let you off with a warning this time," said the warden, cancelling the input on his computer and beating a hasty retreat.

"Ditto," replied Everton. "Have a nice day."

He pulled out a packet of Rothmans and lit one up in celebration of a job well done. Then he perched on the bonnet of his Ford Focus, ignoring the rain, determined to enjoy the ritual. He placed the cigarette lightly between his lips, rid his lungs of air, and slowly sucked the delicious smoke back in, holding it to cool in his mouth, letting it wash across his tongue, savouring the taste before finally taking it down into his lungs.

Helen's phone call rudely interrupted him. "Where are you?"

"Where you sent me. Kew."

"Any luck?"

"Not yet. But you missed some off your list. The Glasshouse, The Cricketers, The Rose and Crown–"

"I don't need an inventory. Did you ask about their CCTV?"

"Those that have it – a lot don't – usually wipe it after seven days."

"Shit. Okay. Get anything they still have."

"I already have. But it's going to be a slog, just you and me going through them."

"I know. Let's hope we can pin it down or we're in for some long nights."

Everton toyed with the idea of making a crack, thought better of it and said, "And no overtime. Terrific."

* * *

She was standing outside the Victoria Gate entrance to the Gardens, sheltering from the rain under a green National Trust golf umbrella. Everton didn't recognise her at first. For a cop, he had a poor memory for faces, but curiously almost a photographic one for facts, which somewhat compensated for it.

His mother, Eileen, first noticed it when he was eight years old and he wrote his homework essay backwards. Not just from right to left on the page, but with each word backwards and correctly spelt. His primary teacher was stunned and suggested that he might need to see a child behavioural psychologist. Eileen, who would defend her sons, right or wrong and to the death, was affronted and categorically refused. But when, five weeks later, it happened again in a history class, she finally relented. The psychologist, a twitchy guy who looked like he needed therapy himself, diagnosed Everton with Development Co-ordination Disorder. Eileen, who'd never heard of dyspraxia, was warned that it was a lifelong condition and that her son would need long-term rehabilitation classes – neither of which, it transpired, were true, since Everton never had an episode again. Eileen's mother called it the "Lord's work". But Eileen had seen too much suffering to put her faith in the Lord, so she put her faith in herself and her two boys.

Everton pulled his unmarked police car to a halt thirty metres past the gate on a single yellow line and tooted his horn. Laura briefly looked up from beneath her umbrella and, not recognising the car, ignored him. He tried again and carefully reversed past a black cab, which had stopped on the double yellow lines, mistaking Laura for a punter. The cabbie, then mistaking Everton for a minicab driver, began hurling abuse and honking his horn in complaint. Everton, who'd had enough aggravation for one day, ignored him. He pulled up beside Laura and powered the passenger window down.

"Miss Fell? It's me. PC Bowe."

Laura didn't recognise him for a moment. He looked different out of uniform; less imposing. Ordinary. "Oh, sorry. I thought you were a minicab."

"Yeah, so does Mr Angry." Everton grinned as the black cab U-turned past them, the cabbie giving him the finger, and disappeared in search of more willing prey. "Climb in."

Laura collapsed her sopping umbrella and eased herself into the passenger seat, propping it in the footwell. "You're not in a uniform. Are you not on duty?"

"I've been seconded to CID."

"Ah," she said, not really knowing what it meant. Realising she must look a mess, she dabbed her face with a tissue and said rather obviously, "It's horrible out there… The rain…"

"Tell me about it," said Everton. "I've been traipsing all over Kew looking for a pub or a bar with a name related to the Gardens."

"You mean Kew Gardens?"

"Yeah. You know, like The Rose and Crown, The Plough, The Magpie…"

"What about The Botanist? It's a bar on the corner of Kew Green. Near the main entrance."

Everton rechecked Helen's list. The Botanist was not on it. He slewed the car round, in a tight U-turn and headed for Kew Green.

Laura sat on the faux-leather window seat, watching Everton, who was deep in conversation with the bar's garrulous Australian manager, wondering what on earth she was doing? She'd phoned Everton not about the traffic ticket but because she needed someone to vent her anger to, and there was no one else. She wasn't a bitter person by nature and had been thrown by the depths of the resentment she felt. And now she'd agreed to meet him for a coffee. The surly cop who trampled all over her dead friend's flowers and didn't believe a word she said about seeing someone in Gina's house. *Christ*, she thought, *I can't be that lonely*.

Everton returned to the table carrying two large cups of cappuccino.

"Sorry it's taking so long. They're just checking through their CCTV. Would you like a cupcake? They're evidently home-made, but not on the premises."

The tiny joke was lost on her. She shook her head and pushed an unruly lock of blonde hair behind her ear, allowing herself to lift the cup to her lips. Everton watched her, for a moment, her long slender fingers cradling the cup, and long slender neck arching down like an antelope to drink. Then, catching himself, he turned abruptly back towards the manager, who was waiting behind the wrap-around bar.

Laura, who'd seen him watching her, killed the time by destroying the cocoa-powder B, sprinkled onto the frothy milk of her coffee, with her spoon.

"Sorry."

She looked up. Everton was seating himself opposite her, carrying a clear plastic bag containing a small memory card, which he placed in a folder alongside a number of others, and Tessa Hayes' photograph.

"Is she on there?"

"I don't know yet. It's the right date but we'll need to check it out properly back at the station. None of the staff recognised her photo."

Laura gave an involuntary shiver and whispered, "It gives me the creeps."

"Sorry," said Everton. "I didn't mean to frighten you. I shouldn't really have told you."

"No. I meant… I've actually met guys here myself."

"You mean on blind dates?"

"From online dating sites."

"Surely you don't need – sorry… I meant that as a compliment, not…"

Laura managed a small smile and said quietly, "London is full of lonely people."

Everton wasn't sure if it was an observation or if she was speaking from personal experience. He'd lived in London all his life and he'd never felt really lonely. Even after the break-up of his marriage, he'd regrouped, taken stock and got on with his life. He suspected he never really felt strongly about anything, apart from his guilt over the death of his brother and the estrangement of his son.

"Were you... ever married?"

"It nearly happened a couple of times," she replied, non-committal.

"I didn't mean to be personal. Sorry."

"You don't need to keep apologising. I'm not ashamed of being single, if that's what you're thinking?"

"Christ, no. My marriage could hardly be described as a thing of beauty, I can tell you."

She brushed off his attempt at levity and said baldly, "I take it you're divorced?"

"In the process of getting one... The end of fifteen years of hard labour for the both of us, and our son. Fortunately, she had the courage to do something about it."

Laura turned aside and began fishing around in her handbag. She took out a small tortoiseshell comb and dragged it through her damp hair. Avoiding his eyes, she said, "It's the one thing I regret. Not having a family... children."

"So do I now," he said, and continued in response to her quizzical look, "My son won't speak to me. But I've got no one to blame for that but myself."

They sat in silence, sipping their tepid coffee, surprised and a little embarrassed by the sudden intimacy of their conversation.

"Oh," said Everton, clearing his throat and trying to move their discussion on to more comfortable ground. "Some good news. They've cancelled your ticket."

"I know. I phoned to complain and they told me that it had already been paid?"

Everton flushed in embarrassment. "Yeah," he lied. "The way it works is you have to pay it in full and then get it cancelled... Petty bureaucracy... I used my card, it was easier. They'll reimburse me."

Laura gave the briefest of smiles, and shook her head; she'd met a lot of men and a lot of them, to their regret, thought they could lie to her. "Is this some sort of weird guilt trip or something?"

"What? No–"

"Because if you're trying to come on to me...?"

Everton could sense the frailty behind her attack. He'd felt it himself the days after his brother had been found dead in a crashed stolen car with a syringe full of ketamine in his pocket. "Look, you're upset. Who wouldn't be? And... I don't know, I just thought it might help if I explained where we were with everything. As you can see, I was in the area."

"That was rude of me... I'm sorry," she said, fighting to regain her composure.

"Hey, I'm a cop. I've heard a lot worse, believe me. Look, how about we start again and you tell me what's been upsetting you?"

"You mean apart from the obvious?" she said, with a crooked smile, and began to cry.

Everton handed her his clean handkerchief and listened in silence as she poured out her heart. It reminded him of watching his mother sob over his brother in the morgue, blaming herself for his wasted life, rather than the true culprit – him. Sympathy welled like a tide inside him. He reached out, gently took her hand and said, "Listen to me. None of this is your fault. You couldn't have done anything to save your friend. She was already dead by the time you arrived at her house. The autopsy confirmed it."

"What?"

"We've had the initial coroner's report. She died at approximately nine forty-five, almost an hour before you got there, Laura. So, you see, you have nothing to reproach yourself for."

A light went on in her tear-filled eyes. "If it wasn't Gina, who did I see?"

"No one. A shadow. You were panicking. The mind can play tricks–"

"No! There was someone there–"

"Trust me, there wasn't–"

"There was!" She pulled her hand from Everton's and began twisting his handkerchief around her finger in an ever-tightening knot. "Did you find her mobile?"

"No. But she may have lost it or had it stolen, or left it at work or something."

"I heard it ringing! He must have taken it."

"Laura. There was no 'he'. There was no one there. No sign of a break-in. No disturbance. Nothing missing. I checked with the neighbours. No one saw anything–"

"I did!"

"You *think* you did. We have forensic proof that Gina hung herself. She took her own life, Laura. It's a tragedy, and it's awful, but even her family have accepted it."

"But not that she changed her will."

"What?" Everton hadn't got a clue what she was talking about. "I'm sorry. I don't see the significance–"

"On the day she committed suicide, she changed her will and left everything to me. She left nothing to her family, not a penny. She left it all to me."

He stopped in his tracks. It was the missing piece of the jigsaw she'd left out of her story and made sense of her despair. Everton could see it clearly now. She felt guilty.

"And now her parents hate me."

"Okay… Okay. That's a shame. But you've done nothing illegal. Nothing underhand. You didn't persuade her to change her will."

"My ex-friends think that I did." She placed Everton's handkerchief on the table and stood, saying politely, "I've sent a cheque to you, care of the Wimbledon Police Station. Thank you for the coffee and for listening."

She picked up her umbrella and coat and walked quickly out. Everton watched her through the window, disappearing into the sepia rain, thinking how similar they were. Both scarred by guilt – she for something she hadn't done and he for something he had, when he saw the needle marks on his younger brother's arm and said nothing to their mother. And now he was dead.

Traps

Romford Stadium was extremely good value for money. The food may be basic – fish and chips and mushy peas, burgers and chips and mushy peas, saveloy and chips and mushy peas – but the drinks were cheap and the greyhound racing exciting. Especially if you were winning.

Iris Costa and Don Hart were in the Laurie Panthers Bar, watching through the trackside windows as the dogs were paraded for race five. Iris had a feeling about Greek God, but Don persuaded her against it and since he was the expert she'd gone along with his suggestion, as she'd done all night.

The traps sprung open and the six dogs surged out. For a few moments, they seemed to be running in symmetry, but as they rounded the second bend dog number three lengthened his stride and eased away from the chasing pack.

"Oh my God! I'm winning!" Iris screamed. "Come on, number three!"

Don smiled in satisfaction as his chosen dog powered down the home straight and won by a length. Iris was ecstatic. It was her first time at a greyhound meeting and they'd won on almost every race. Don congratulated her but warned her against over-confidence, suggesting she collect the winnings whilst they were still ahead and head off home. Iris was disappointed but he already had her by the arm, leading her towards the Tote.

"Romford's a long way from Twickenham," he said, as if in explanation.

"I know, but aren't we going to celebrate?"

"Yeah. In bed."

Iris smiled compliantly and let him lead her away.

The Fraud Squad raided Don's Tooting home at 10.30pm after a tip-off from the track. It took three swings of the tubular steel battering ram to shatter the multiple locks and allow the bellicose police to pile in.

His son, Ritchie, heard them, leapt naked out of bed, grabbed his stash from beneath it, hauled open the window and hurled the bag of dope into the next-door neighbour's garden. A futile exercise, since there were three coppers guarding his back door, watching him.

"Police! On the floor! Now!"

Ritchie wheeled to face a wall of riot shields. Behind it, a phalanx of men in black riot gear bellowed orders.

"We have a dog! Move and you will be bitten!"

A whippet-thin, brown-haired guy sporting a wispy beard and battered leather jacket pushed his way between the shields to confront Richie.

"DS Tann, Fraud Squad. Where's your father? Speak, you little shit, or I'm going let this dog go."

Having nothing in his hands but his genitalia, and with a German Shepherd snarling six feet from him, Richie hesitated. It was his second mistake. Tann nodded to the handler. He released the dog. It sprang forward and sank its teeth deep into Ritchie's hairless thigh.

* * *

Don was otherwise engaged, so ignored his son's panicky call. Iris Costa lay beneath him, groaning as he pushed deeper inside her. She reached her mouth up towards his, but he turned aside and pushed her probing hands from beneath his shirt. It was as if he couldn't bear her touching him. He could touch her, do what he wanted with her, but she had to be compliant. She wondered if he'd been like that with Laura. If he refused to take his clothes off with her too.

Ten minutes later, he opened his voice message from Richie and, muttering an apology, raced back home, leaving a hundred pounds, Iris's share of the winnings, on her kitchen table. She was appalled. She wasn't some whore he could just screw and pay off! But in Don's mind that was exactly what she was. Besides, he had more pressing problems.

Arriving home, he discovered that not only had the police smashed his front door in, they'd boarded it up, padlocked it and left with the key! And they'd done exactly the same with the back door! He was forced to break into his own house through the kitchen window.

The place was a mess. The shattered front door was propped against the hall stairs and had an invoice for boarding and securing the house taped to it – another sick joke from the boys in blue. He ignored it. Pulled some latex gloves and a Swiss Army Knife from his pocket and started up the stairs.

He already knew they'd found Ritchie's stash but was praying they'd not found *his*. Six steps up he stopped, knelt and unscrewed the carpet runner. He teased out the grey carpet, which had been neatly sliced across – the cut hidden behind the runner – to reveal the wooden riser. Two cross-thread screws held it in place. He unscrewed them and placed them on the carpeted tread above, then levered out the wooden plank. Inside the stair void, his magic box of instruments was still there, thank God, including his Safeway bag of prescription drugs: Propranolol, Bisoprolol, Viagra, Stanozolol and Rohypnol. He removed them all, placed them on the step and replaced the riser.

* * *

Early next morning, he sat opposite DS Philip Tann in interview room two – a battleship-grey windowless room in the bowels of Catford Police Station. His solicitor, William Shelby, a man in two-tone wingtips which seemed out of sync with the rest of his solidly middle-class persona, sat slightly back from the table. On it, amongst the detritus of empty paper cups and ashtrays, was a red plastic folder and beside it a voice-activated recording machine.

"Your son was observed throwing a bag containing 106 grams of skunk from his bedroom window and you want me to believe you know nothing about it?"

"Mr Hart has already said he has no knowledge of any drugs in his house, Sergeant. I suggest you ask his son these questions if you have evidence of his wrongdoing."

"When I want advice, Mr Shelby, I'll ask for it," interrupted Tann, who knew and distrusted the solicitor of old. "Anyway, I'm not interested in a bit of puff his son may have been dealing."

"Then why assault him?"

"He wasn't assaulted. He was resisting arrest."

"With what, his dick?" retorted Don. "He was stark bollock naked. He didn't have a weapon, nothing."

"He refused to surrender." Tann shrugged. "Appropriate force was used to subdue him."

"Is this your idea of appropriate force?" Shelby produced a micro video recorder and held it up for Tann to view the gory close-up of Ritchie's thigh, where pools of black blood seeped from puncture wounds. "Two thousand seven hundred and twenty-five, Sergeant. That's the number of claims currently being pursued against the Met directly related to police dog attacks."

"People make malicious claims. It goes with the territory."

"One hundred and ninety-five of those came from your own colleagues."

Tann fixed Shelby with his baleful, unblinking eyes and said quietly, "Are you threatening me?"

"Informing you that my client's intention is to sue you and the Met."

"Good luck with that," sneered Tann, irritated by Shelby's holier-than-thou attitude.

"And I strongly object to your dismissive tone. Ritchie Hart has suffered serious injuries that may well require further surgery."

Tann saw the RECORD light flashing on the device and was stunned. "Turn that off! Now!"

Shelby feigned a look of apology and switched it off. Tann, realising that he'd been set up, bit down hard on his anger and turned his attention back to Don. "Do the figures: 7/2, 4/1, 5/2, mean anything to you?"

Don knew where the interrogation was heading but resisted the urge to turn to Shelby for advice, knowing it would be read as suspicious. "I'm assuming they're betting odds."

"Give the man a bone."

Tann produced a ten-by-eight print from the red folder in front of him and handed it to Don, saying clearly, "For the recording. Mr Hart is being shown a photograph of himself and an unknown blonde woman taken at Catford dog track on the twelfth of October 2015, at 7.45pm."

Don examined the photograph carefully, buying himself time to think, reasoning that the cops must have had him under surveillance, and wary about what else they knew. Seated beside him, Shelby was thinking the same thing.

"I trust you obtained a court order permitting this surveillance, Sergeant. Otherwise it could be construed–"

"I did. It won't. This must have been taken on one of those rare visits, Mr Hart? Can you tell me the name of the blonde woman you are handing cash to?"

"Laura something. I only met her once. It was one of them online dating things."

"Then can I ask you who this is? For the record, I am now showing Mr Hart a photograph of himself and the *same* blonde woman taken at eight fifteen on the night of the twenty-fourth of October at Wimbledon Stadium dog track."

Don knew he'd stumbled into a trap but didn't hesitate. "Okay. Her name is Laura Fell. We dated a few times and broke up."

"So you lied?"

"I was trying to keep her out of this. She's been having a rough time. Her best friend just committed suicide."

"Yeah, and what was her name?"

"Gina Lewis. You can check it out. It's the truth."

"Laura Fell's address?"

"Okay. Alright. It's 17 Brentwood Avenue, Kew. I don't know the postcode."

Tann began scribbling some tiny, illegible notes in his book, and said without looking up, "Why were you giving Miss Fell what appears to be a considerable amount of money?"

"She didn't have enough cash and she wanted to bet."

"And she won on every race she bet on?"

"Beginner's luck."

"Who chose the dogs she bet on?"

"She did. I'm not allowed to, as you well know."

"Exactly. You have an injunction against being involved in any form of dog racing after a previous doping conviction. And now, hey presto, you're suddenly on the scene again with this grieving blonde, who a cynic might construe as an accomplice."

"My client's injunction does not bar him from attending greyhound racing, only betting on the outcome. He's committed no offence, and you have no evidence to the contrary apart from some photographs, which he has explained. Now, if you have no further questions, Sergeant, he would like to check on the medical condition of his son."

Tann scratched at his wispy beard, quietly seething as he pondered his limited options. Don's story was bullshit, but if the blonde substantiated it, which she'd undoubtedly do if she was working with him, Shelby was right, he had nothing.

"Interview terminated at 9.54 am, November 16," he said, leaning in and whispering as he turned off the voice-activated recorder, "You're filth, Hart, you and your skanky son, and I'm going to have you."

Shelby switched on his camera and aimed it directly at Tann. "Are you threatening my client, Sergeant Tann?"

Tann leapt out of his chair and snatched it, snarling, "You point that camera at me again and I'm gonna ram it so far up your arse even Jimmy Savile couldn't find it."

* * *

The Met divided the thirty-two boroughs of London into four links, each covering eight boroughs: the north-east, north-west, south-east and south-west. Each borough's forensic manager had a team of Crime Scene Examiners working under them. These examiners provided a 24/7 service and on average investigated over eleven thousand crimes a month, including murder.

Teddy Baldwin, the Forensic Manager of the south-west, had therefore seen a lot of homicides in his thirty-year career. Some committed in the marital home by so-called loving couples, others on the streets by complete strangers. A glut of shootings, stabbings and bludgeoning's, carried out by terrorists, racists, homophobes, psychopaths and, more recently, fourteen-year-old kids stealing mountain bikes. It gave him a somewhat jaundiced view of humanity which he expressed through his epic comic book, Murderopolis. He worked on it every night. Sitting alone at his kitchen table with his bleed-proof paper and Forest Choice pencils neatly laid out in front of him, and a bottle of Wild Turkey bourbon at his right hand. Since the death of his wife he found he didn't need much sleep and now his real work consumed and sustained him, though it was a pity that no one would ever see it but him.

He was seated between Everton and Helen in a large open-plan office that looked more like a call centre – all computers, bleached wood and neutral colours – than a forensic lab specialising in video image enhancement.

Helen thought they'd struck gold when she spotted Tessa Hayes on the footage that Everton sequestered from The Botanist. But her male companion had his back to the camera, either by chance or planning, and was seated in a dark alcove. From what they could tell, he appeared to be wearing a dark coat and glasses and had thick brown hair. But when they tried to blow up the image on a laptop, it pixelated and became unreadable. So, they brought the hard drive to Teddy, an old acquaintance of Everton's, to see if he could help.

"Some digital recorder hard drives, like the one you have here, aren't designed to be portable. They work with a different codec system, which makes copying the files onto another computer system to allow enhancement difficult. I've improved it marginally but blowing it up any further will only cause you to lose image definition."

"What about the timing?" said Everton, keen to find something positive, since the visit was his suggestion in the first place.

"Well, I've made some progress there," replied Teddy, dragging his cursor along the timeline at the bottom of the video and freezing it to reveal the shadowy figure of a man entering The Botanist. "Your suspect arrived at 19.45, half an hour before your victim. Notice he keeps his head down and away from the CCTV camera even when he sits. He doesn't look around, doesn't order a drink, just sits and waits."

"You reckon he knew it was there, the camera?"

"Yes. Which would indicate to me that he's been there before. That he meticulously plans his abductions, cases appropriate bars before suggesting them as meeting places."

"If he's so meticulous, how come he let Tessa Hayes go? It doesn't fit the profile," said Helen, giving voice to a problem that still puzzled her.

"Maybe he didn't? Maybe she escaped?"

"After he'd drugged, abducted, stripped and shaved her body hair? I don't buy that."

"Okay," said Everton. "If we've got nothing inside the bar, what about outside?"

Teddy dragged the timeline cursor forward on the video image and stopped it at 21.09.

"They left together, as you can see, just after nine o'clock. If you look carefully, you'll see she's just a little unsteady on her feet. Notice him guiding her through the door. The Rohypnol, if that's what it was, was probably put in her drink around thirty minutes earlier. There's a shot of him at the bar ordering two glasses of wine, but nothing conclusive."

"He needed to get her out of there before it really took effect?"

"Yes. Or he might have drawn unwanted attention to himself. Now look at this. These are taken from exterior CCTV and traffic cameras in the area."

He opened another window on the screen. Helen and Everton leaned forward to get a better look. There were a series of uploaded thumbnails of Tessa Hayes and her assailant exiting the bar and making their way over the road to the far side of Kew Green, displayed in a sequential timeline.

"These aren't going to help you physically identify the man – it's too dark and he's still wary, keeping to the shadows – but I trawled through all the local cameras and found this." He pointed to the final thumbnail, double-clicked on it and enlarged the image.

"It's them. That's his car!" exclaimed Helen, pointing to a grainy image of Tessa Hayes being helped into the passenger seat of a midnight-blue Mercedes Estate on the VDU screen. "Can you read the number plate? What does it say?"

"P767 XWR. But don't get too excited. The plates are false. They belong to a Fiat Uno that was written off in an accident in 2012."

"Bollocks."

"My sentiments entirely. But all is not totally lost. We now know that he's using a Series C Mercedes Estate. It might be possible to track the car's direction of travel using other traffic cameras in the vicinity."

"And how long will that take?" said Helen, fearing she already knew the answer.

"Well, if they're all in working order – and that's a big if – two to three days."

Helen groaned to herself – DS Clark was going to love this – and turned to answer her mobile. It was more bad news.

* * *

It looked like an IRA "dirty protest". Excrement was smeared on the walls, floors, furnishings and bedding. And it stank.

"Where is he now?" Helen stood in the doorway of the geriatric ward of Wilson Hospital with the ward manager, Nora, a middle-aged overweight woman who believed in the sanctity of the NHS and her own authority.

"Your sister is giving him a bath."

"Delia? When did she get here?"

"Twenty minutes before you. I suggested she look after your father whilst we get the room cleaned and disinfected. As I explained to her, we'll have to discuss arrangements for your father if this continues. She said that you might be able to take him?"

"Me?"

Helen was shocked by her sister's nerve but in retrospect not surprised; suspecting that the suggestion was not made in the best interest of their father but to make a point to *her*. Delia had always felt Helen put her career before her family – an accusation that Helen resented because deep down she knew it was right.

It wasn't that she didn't love her father. Beneath all his patriarchal, head-of-the-family bullshit, she knew that Frank was a sensitive man. A man broken by his illness and his wife's refusal to stand by him until his inevitable end. A man of contradictions, who worked in a garage and yet loved listening to Stockhausen. Who read the Daily Mail *and* Dickens. Who hated pubs but on Friday nights always offered his "fledglings" tiny nips of his home-made marrow rum as a treat before bedtime.

She stood in the doorway, staring at the shit crusting on the walls, and remembered the first time she thought that something was wrong, that his mind was going walkabout. She was nineteen. They were living in a nice three-bedroom terraced house in Croydon. Her mother was teaching her aerobics class and was late, as usual. He came fumbling out of the bathroom, after his ritual of scrubbing the ingrained oil from his hands and forearms, and had forgotten to zip his flies up. Not only that, but there was a large wet patch where he'd obviously peed his pants. Of course, she never said anything to him and a few minutes later he changed into fresh clothes, and back to his old self.

But later, when she broached the subject with her sister, Delia, she dismissed it in the crude way she always did when she didn't want to confront bad news. "The poor old sod was probably having a wank."

"Delia. That's disgusting."

"Why? You think because he's old he doesn't get the urge? And he's not going to get any from Mum, is he? She shut up shop years ago."

And that was the last conversation they had about it. Helen went off to Leeds University to do a degree in Criminal Psychology and Delia got pregnant, married and had two kids. And now she had another on the way and resented Helen for her success and freedom – and Helen knew it. So, her suggestion that Helen should care for their father because she had other family commitments stuck in Helen's craw. Where was Delia when their mother went off to her aerobics class and never came back? In Disneyland Paris, celebrating her wedding anniversary to a guy she wished she'd never married! And had she flown home? Had she hell. Helen was left to deal with it alone.

Helen stepped out of her dark thoughts and into the room. She pulled out her iPhone, knelt and began photographing the shit-smeared scrawl on the wall.

"Excuse me. What are you doing? You can't take photographs in here."

"I'm a police officer," snapped Helen, "and this could be a crime scene."

The scrawl read:

hElp

Later, Helen and Delia stood arguing in the echoing Victorian hallway. Frank sat in a wheelchair between them like an umpire refereeing a match. Except that he wasn't seeing or hearing anything; at least nothing his warring daughters would recognise.

He was remembering, in a series of seemingly unrelated images, his Morris Minor Traveller. The desire he felt, seeing it as a junkyard wreck. Him, dismembering it, piece by rusty piece.

Its refurbishment, bolt by bolt, into a gleaming thing of beauty. The radiant smile on his wife's face, reflected in the gleaming new paintwork, as he proudly unveiled his restoration for the first time. Its inaugural seaside trip. His beautiful young daughters laughing excitedly from the back seat…

His smile faded as he wondered who the two unhappy women were standing above him, and why they were arguing about someone he'd never heard of.

"He hasn't been abused. There isn't a mark on him."

"There are different types of abuse. There was no water in his room."

"If he doesn't want to eat or drink they can't force him."

"Someone needs to sit with him, even if it's only for a few minutes, to persuade him."

"This is the NHS, not Harley Street. You get what you pay for and we don't pay anything. That's why *we* have to do it."

"By we you mean *me*. You're living in his house, Delia."

"I've got two kids and I'm five months pregnant, in case you hadn't noticed."

"And I'm investigating the abduction and possible murder of three women."

"Shame one of them isn't our mother… *What?* Fuck her. You hate her as much as I do, Helen."

"I'm not talking about her, I'm talking about him. What if he heard?"

"He's away with the fairies. He's in gaga land. Now, are you going to have him or not?"

"How can I unless I give up my job?"

"Get a nurse in."

"Have you any idea how much that costs? Do you want to sell the house to pay for it?"

"I'll help out with the cost if that's what's worrying you."

It wasn't. It was putting her life, her career and her future on hold. Giving the best years of her life away to a man who now didn't even recognise her.

Delia shrugged, took out a wet wipe from her purse and, like Pontius Pilate, washed her hands of the problem.

* * *

The house was morgue-cold. Laura stood in the hallway, her back against the front door, allowing her eyes to slowly accustom to the dark, wondering why she'd come. What evidence she hoped to find. She contemplated turning the lights on to ease her fear but decided against it, not wanting to draw attention to herself. *Why?* She wasn't doing anything illegal. It was her house. She owned it; she was free to come and go as she pleased. She was being irrational.

She pulled a torch from her tweed overcoat pocket, switched it on and immediately off, worrying that if anyone saw it she'd look even more suspicious, then gasped as her mobile started up in her pocket. Memories of the night of Gina's suicide came flooding back, of someone on the stairs hearing *her* phone call. The panic in his footsteps as he ran for it, passing inches from her face. *Jesus,* she thought, *it could be him outside now.* Or he could be *inside.* She inched the mobile from her other pocket, took a deep breath and checked the Caller ID: Don Hart. She blew in relief, tapped in BLOCK CALLER and turned on the hall light.

She found nothing in the kitchen, but in an effort to calm her nerves made herself a cup of coffee. The milk was off in the fridge so she poured it down the sink and rinsed the container, then placed it in Gina's recycling bin. Fortified by the scalding caffeine, she made her way into the sitting room.

The heavy brocade curtains were still closed but the room felt ten degrees colder than the kitchen. Or was it just her imagination? Ignoring the ceiling light, she turned on the table lamps that book-ended the sofa and surveyed the room like an appraiser, not calculating the value of the fittings, but calculating what was missing. At first sight there was nothing. She began a methodical search. Starting at the sideboard, she emptied, searched and replaced the contents drawer by drawer, then the shelving unit, from top to bottom, removing the books and ornaments to allow her to check behind them. She removed the leather sofa cushions, squeezed her hand down the void at the back. She did the same with the armchair. There was no sign of Gina's missing mobile phone.

Her coffee was cold by the time she finished and made her way back into the hall. Unopened post littered the floor. Most were junk, but there were a few bills – gas and Three Mobile – and some handwritten letters of condolence. *To a dead person*, she thought grimly to herself as she tossed them onto the hall table and made her way up the stairs.

She was in Gina's spare bedroom-cum-study when she found the power connector for the iMac still plugged in under the bed. But where was the laptop? She went through every wardrobe, cupboard and drawer. It wasn't there and neither was her mobile. It made no sense. She slumped onto the bed amongst the flotsam and jetsam that had once been her friend's life and a sudden thought hit her like a blow – Gina's phone bill! She stumbled out of the room and down the stairs, snatched up the Three Mobile envelope and ripped it open.

* * *

Nephilim was retouching his installation. It needed constant attention to keep his "angels," in pristine condition. Completely thrown, hearing the skylark call again, he stupidly answered his mobile. She said her name was Laura and that she was a friend of Gina's. He knew immediately who she was. He dropped the phone, stamped it to pieces, picked up the SIM card and destroyed it. But now he was panicking. How had she known the number? Only Gina knew his private number and she was dead. He shivered at the thought of it and felt the tell-tale tug of his scar. He was getting cold and it wasn't good for his condition. He warmed his hands over the Calor Gas heater, placed them over his mother's "gift" and tried to collect himself and his thoughts.

The air temperature in his studio needed to be a constant three degrees. Any lower and he risked the surface of the meat freezing. Any higher and the model's mummified flesh beneath the feathers would begin to attract microorganisms and parasites and rot, forming a fungus-like bloom on the feathers. He'd installed a dehumidifier, which helped, but the wooden structure and corrugated iron roof, even though it was partially insulated, were not ideal. Still, they would have to do for now. He couldn't risk drawing any more attention to himself.

He hadn't visited the farm in over a week; taking too much time off work would appear suspicious. At first, he was so distraught that he actually contemplated suicide himself. He even bought a length of nylon clothes line – a romantic gesture in honour of his fallen dove's wishes – but hadn't had the courage to go through with it. It had made him sick reading her so-called mother's statement in the newspaper. He knew the real truth about her and her self-inflicted cripple of a husband. But that would have to wait until he solved the problem of Laura Fell. *Christ*, he thought. *How did she get my personal number? Why couldn't the stupid bitch leave well alone?*

He walked slowly around the installation, minutely adjusting the tableaux as he circled it, tightening or loosening the fishing lines that held his female "angels" upright and suspended in position so they appeared to float above the floor. They were wingless, because in his mind they were "fallen" and waiting for His redemption. But every inch of their bodies was covered in beautiful white plumage, even their eyelids and lips, making them appear half-human, half-angel. Like him. There were only two now. One had become infected by parasites and he'd been forced to dismantle and burn her in the chicken pit, under the fowl. The smell of paraffin and barbecued flesh was disgusting but there was no other alternative. He couldn't risk the body of Kate Holmes being discovered and he comforted himself with the thought that, with his help, she'd found redemption.

Finally satisfied, he repacked his instruments, turned off the light, unlocked the dividing door and walked through into the dovecot. The birds were roosting and barely noticed his intrusion.

He re-locked the door from the outside, lifted the wooden plank from the floor and laid his tools carefully in the void. Then, replaced the plank, made his way outside, padlocked the door behind him and trotted up to the farmhouse.

He was late – a failing he'd shared with Gina and they'd both chastised each other about – so he only had time for a quick strip-wash at the sink. He remembered watching her standing naked at another sink, washing herself in preparation for their lovemaking. How pale her skin was in contrast to her black, unruly pubic hair. And how it glistened like dew and dripped as she walked towards him. And how she opened her legs to allow him to dry her there. And how she lay on the bed, smiling and submissive, as he picked up his shears and made her even more beautiful. The memory was both exquisite and agonising.

He moaned and dried his stiffening penis. He pulled on his clothes, put his brown contact lenses in, and headed for the door.

* * *

Everton had trawled through the CCTV traffic footage and found absolutely nothing. He'd done two hours unpaid overtime and hadn't heard a damn thing from Helen, who'd rushed off to deal with some family issue. So, when Laura Fell rang, he put aside his scepticism and agreed to meet her at Gina Lewis's house in Caxton Road.

It was less than a five-minute drive from the nick and she was waiting for him in the doorway when he pulled up. He smiled, thinking how different she looked from the last time he'd seen her, still beautiful but somehow less defeated and more energised.

"Would you like a coffee?" she offered, shutting the front door behind him and ushering him into the sitting room.

"No thank you. I'm caffeined out. It's been a long day, one way and another."

"Oh. I'm sorry. I didn't think–"

"Don't apologise. I didn't mean you. You, I like…" If Laura heard his Freudian slip she said nothing. He hastily changed the subject. "You said that you discovered something about Gina's missing mobile?"

"Yes. Take a look at this." She handed him a sheaf of mobile phone bills and stood so close to his shoulder as he examined them that he could smell her perfume. *Concentrate*, he said to himself.

"What am I supposed to be looking for?"

"Okay. This is Gina's last mobile bill. You can see it shows no more outgoing calls after the night she died."

"Which is what you'd expect."

"Right. But look at the last incoming calls. They're nearly all from me. This one," she said, pointing to a call marked 10.34 pm, "is when I was standing outside the house. Which proves I phoned her. Now, look at the next day. See?" she said, jabbing a finger at the numbers. "Those are more calls from me, which means her phone was still live."

"Yeah, but the same would be true if someone stole it."

"I heard it ringing. *In here*. I heard it and someone turned it off."

"Okay. But—"

"And now not only is her mobile missing but her laptop is too. *Someone was in here*." She said it with such utter conviction that for the first time Everton felt a creeping inclination to believe her. But he was still a copper.

"Okay. That's interesting. I didn't know that. But let's look at the facts—"

"I haven't finished yet," she said, taking the bills from his hand and pointing to another set of telephone numbers. "These are all Gina's outgoing calls for the last month. Look how many of them are to the same number. Thirty-seven. More than one a day."

"Yeah, okay, that's a lot. But it's probably to one of her friends."

"I know all her friends. And I don't recognise that number."

"You're sure? I mean—"

"I've already checked the contact numbers on my phone. It's not there," she said, offering him her mobile. "See for yourself if you don't believe me."

Impressed by her tenacity, he shook his head.

"I phoned it," she said, as if to reinforce her point. "A man answered."

"Who was it?"

"I don't know. He asked who I was and when I told him he cut me off."

"Okay," said Everton, taking out his mobile. "Let me have a go. What's the number?"

Laura gave it to him and watched him dial. "You won't get anything. He's switched it off."

She was right. And cynical as Everton was, he had to admit that it was odd. "Have you got anything else to drink?" he said. "Apart from coffee."

"There's Scotch in the kitchen. But there's no ice. The fridge is switched off."

"Neat is fine by me," he replied, and followed her out towards the kitchen, deep in thought.

As he did so, something caught his eye; something that would later, although he didn't know it, threaten both their lives. It was a downy white feather drifting like a warning cloud across the hall floor in front of him.

* * *

Members of Parliament had eight subsidised bars in which to toast their successes or drown their failures. Celia Lewis was meeting Conrad Lester, the mayor's chief of staff, in the Smoking Room, which no longer allowed smoking and had therefore lost some of its appeal. But as such, it was a discreet venue for their meeting.

Celia, who preferred intimate dinner parties rather than the Commons restaurants and bars, was not a frequent visitor but had been personally invited by Conrad Lester, a quietly spoken Old Etonian, and since he was the voice of the mayor she could hardly refuse.

Drinks were ordered and small talk and canapés shared – pistachios for her, roasted salted almonds for him. Celia watched and waited as Lester put the monogrammed bowl aside, brushed his hands clean and finally came to the point.

"As you know, Celia, the mayor's office has issued a number of statements refuting these awful allegations made by the gutter press about your relationship with your daughter, asking them to respect you and your husband's privacy, in what we appreciate must be a terrible time for you both."

"Thank you," said Celia. "It's not been easy but we are coping."

"That's good to hear." He held up his Tanqueray and tonic in a small toast and took a sip, savouring the citrus flavour.

Celia watched him, mentally framing the appropriate words; the real reason for his invite. They duly came. "But the mayor feels that we still have a problem. We're heading into the local by-elections…"

"I know. I'm defending a marginal seat myself."

"A number of us are, unfortunately. And these child abuse scandals are becoming a real issue. Not just in Rotherham and Oxford but even closer to home, so to speak."

"Are you talking about Lambeth, and the rumours that MPs were involved?"

"There are people sitting within fifty feet of us now who are implicated; powerful people with connections. And we're not just talking about here, we're talking about people from the 'other place' too."

"If they're involved they need to be exposed. If we don't do it, Conrad, the press will and we'll be vilified for being involved in another cover-up."

"Absolutely, not to do so would be morally reprehensible. But we can't run the risk of being accused of double standards."

There it was; the dagger was out of its sheaf. Celia took a sip of her orange juice and said as calmly as she could, "Are you asking for my resignation? Because if you are, that would imply that we really do have something to hide."

"We're aware of that."

"I have explained my relationship with my daughter and family, in detail, to the Ethics Committee. I was under no parliamentary obligation to do so."

"Celia. No one has more admiration for you and your qualities than the mayor. Why do you think he appointed you chair of the committee in the first place? This is merely cosmetic; a way to kill off, if you'll forgive me putting it that way, any further speculation."

"I'm sorry… I don't understand," said Celia, aware that her fingers were drumming on the table and that she was finding it difficult to control them.

"All the mayor is asking is that you hold a press conference to—"

"No!" The venom in her refusal surprised both Lester and herself. "I'm sorry. You asked me to release a statement and I did."

"And we're extremely grateful. We all appreciate how difficult this has been for you."

"No, you don't! How could you? It's not your child who hung herself. It's not you the press is hounding, that her friends are blaming. It's *me*!" She could feel her voice rising and her tears welling. She bit them both back and continued, "She left nothing. Not even a note of explanation. Nothing! Do you know what that feels like to a mother?"

"Celia—"

"No! I haven't finished! I loved my daughter – I still do despite everything – and I shouldn't have to prove it to you or some grubby little shit of a journalist or *anyone*!"

"Celia. No one, least of all the mayor, wants you to resign."

"Of course he bloody doesn't." She was on her feet now, her face flushed with anger, her hands trembling as she snatched up her bag. "It would reflect badly on his choice, wouldn't it?"

Lester stood and said evenly, "It is, of course, your decision." Then, turned on his polished heel and walked purposefully out.

Celia watched him go, loathing him and his practised concern, and her desperate need to please him.

* * *

Everton relit his spliff and stretched out on his sofa to think.

Laura was right. Something didn't add up – not least Celia Lewis' attitude. She and Laura were the only two people who'd had access to Gina's house since the night of her suicide. One of them must have taken the laptop – and it wasn't Laura. Or could someone else have been there? The mystery man on the telephone perhaps? But why was Celia so uninterested? Surely as a mother she'd have some concerns? And then there was the strange white feather.

He took an envelope from his pocket and shook it out onto his palm. It was tiny, like down, and to his untrained eye looked like it came from the breast of a white bird. It appeared identical to the ones they'd found by the river.

Could it just be a coincidence? Maybe it came from a different type of bird? Or from a pillow or a duvet or something? But Laura reckoned Gina had suffered from allergies and never used feather bedding and when he'd checked everything was foam – *Whoa*, he said to himself, *I'm trying to build a link between a suicide, a bald woman in a river, and three women missing, presumed dead; because of a missing laptop and a feather! Shit. I have got to be stoned.*

He hauled himself up and headed for the bathroom. It wasn't his favourite room. For a start, it didn't have a bath, which he always thought was something of a prerequisite considering its title. Plus, the white tiling gave it too much of an institutional feel, even for a man with his Spartan tastes.

Helen used to joke that he'd be happiest living in a place that he could hose down. Which was only partly true. He'd pared down his life like he'd pared down his emotional commitments, whether it was to the job or people, after the death of his marriage. The contrast between his flat and his comfortably shambolic marital home could not have been starker. And he liked it that way, or to be more precise, chose to live it that way.

He pulled off his sweat pants and hoodie, stepped into the shower and groaned as his mobile and doorbell rang in unison. It could only be Helen. He pulled on his sweatpants, strode into the lounge, peered through the spyhole and yanked open the door. "Do you know what time it is?"

"Do you want me to leave?"

"What?"

"Do you want me to go?" she repeated, brushing past him and inside.

"You just walked in."

"I've had a shitty day," she replied, as if no further explanation was needed.

"And?"

"Do you have any vodka?" she said, ignoring his question and opening the fridge to retrieve a bottle of Corona. "No. I forgot, you think it's 'girly'."

"Helen. Do you want to tell me what's wrong?"

"Everything. Where's the opener?"

"On the fridge door."

She prised the 'Stay Calm Drink Beer' magnet from the fridge door, pulling a face at the irony of it, and yanked off the bottle top. "Why are you always half-naked when I come around?"

"Because I didn't know you were coming around. I was in the shower. Now do you want to tell me what you want?"

"I needed some company. Don't worry, not like that – well, not unless you want to. Have you got any gear? I know you have, I can smell it."

"Yeah, but not when you're driving. I'll be back in a second."

He made his way back into the bathroom, wondering what had happened to upset her so much. Assuming that it must be something to do with her family, a subject that she rarely spoke about – like him. He turned off the shower, pulled on his hoodie and walked back into the lounge to ask her. She was laid out on the sofa, her eyes closed, cradling her beer. He watched her, remembering the comfort he'd found in her, the only woman he'd slept with since the end of his marriage, and her generosity, demanding nothing from him but respect.

"Why are you staring at me?" she said without opening her eyes.

"I'm not."

"Liar. I know I look a mess. Do I look a mess?"

She did, and she hadn't even bothered with her make-up.

"You look a bit…vulnerable… It makes a pleasant change."

She opened her eyes, surprised by the cack-handed compliment, and smiled. "It wouldn't really work, would it?"

"Hey. A fuck is just a fuck. A friend is for life."

"Wow. That is possibly the nicest thing a man has ever said to me."

"Yeah?" Everton grinned. "I think it's a lyric from a Jay-Z song."

Helen laughed and put her beer on the coffee table, right on top of the feather. She took a moment to register it, eased herself into a sitting position and plucked it off with her thumb and forefinger.

"What's this? It looks like one of our pieces of evidence."

"I know. You're not going to believe this, but I found it in Gina Lewis' house."

"Who?"

"The woman who committed suicide."

"Seriously? It looks identical to the ones we found with Tessa Hayes. Hold on. What were you doing at Gina Lewis' place?"

"I'm the lead investigating officer. I got a call from one of her friends; she thinks there might have been someone else in the house with her when she died."

"Was there?"

"Not that we know of. But her mobile and laptop are missing."

"Hm. Interesting."

"Yeah. And I didn't tell Laura — her friend — but the autopsy report mentions that she had no pubic hair."

"She'd been shaved?"

"Or she'd done it herself. Anyway, I thought it was worth checking out."

"Yeah," said Helen, slumping wearily back on the sofa. "So today wasn't all bad news."

Everton made his way over to the kitchen, opened a cupboard and pulled out a bottle of Mount Gay Rum. Poured a finger into a couple of shot glasses and handed her one.

"Okay. Let's hear it. Warts and all."

She pulled her mobile from the pocket of her jeans, hit the photo icon and handed it to Everton. "The family album. Enjoy."

Everton flipped through the bleak photos of her father and his hospital room in silence, knowing there was nothing he could say that would make her feel any better.

* * *

He woke at 4am with a raging headache and a torrent of white noise in his head – the consequence of a spliff and half a bottle of Mount Gay. Helen lay naked beside him, wisps of her tangled hair covering her face like a veil and moving in rhythm with her boozy breath. He gently eased her arm from across his chest and turned his guilty face away from her, knowing that, despite his best intentions, he'd capitulated and taken advantage of the situation. That he'd failed again.

Five hours later they were sipping cappuccinos, minus any froth, from a vending machine in the reception of the forensic lab, a cheerless room enlivened by red plastic chairs and a view of a red-brick wall.

Helen, wolfing a Kit Kat, having missed breakfast to dash home and change before their appointment, shrugged away Everton's apology. "Relax. I had a shitty day. I needed to get laid and you obliged. It's no big deal. If anyone should be apologising it's me not you. Anyway, it won't happen again. I'm dating someone."

The revelation hit Everton like a slap. He wasn't in love with Helen but still...

"Don't look so shocked. I haven't slept with him yet and I didn't want to last night, just because I was angry."

"Is that supposed to be a compliment?"

"Oh, come on. I needed a bit of a cuddle. That's what friends are for."

Everton surrendered and made his way into the gents to splash his face. He felt bilious and slightly unsteady on his feet, and keeling over in the laboratory was not a great option. He popped a couple of Nurofen and scooped some metallic-tasting tap water into his mouth to help them down. Then stood staring at his dripping face in the mirror, not liking what he saw. Why did he still feel so guilty? Helen didn't and she was dating. He knew the answer but was too scared to admit it to himself. He ripped a couple of paper towels from the dispenser and dried his face. Even his skin hurt. *Christ*, he thought. *What's wrong with me? I've had no relationship with Laura Fell apart from on a professional level. Why should I feel I've betrayed her?* It was pathetic.

"You okay?" enquired Helen; who was standing waiting for him as he made his way out, alongside Teddy and a shaven-headed guy with Bowie incisors and a Morrissey T-shirt that matched his personality.

"Yeah. No problem," lied Everton.

"This is James Noonan," said Teddy. "Our bird man."

"Sorry," apologised Noonan, wafting a bloody, surgically gloved hand in welcome. "Dismembering a contaminated liver."

"Cirrhosis?" offered Helen.

"Knife wound," said Noonan. "Right. Shall I show you what I've found?"

He dumped his gloves into a surgical waste bin and led them towards a pair of double doors at the rear of the room.

"You're lucky," said Teddy. "James is a rare breed of forensic pathologist in that one of his fields of excellence, ornithology, is also his hobby and his sport."

"You actually train pigeons?" Helen asked incredulously, as Noonan swiped his ID card and led them into a large custard-coloured room filled with a dizzying array of equipment and attendant technicians. "Forgive my ignorance, but why would you do that?"

"You have to train them before you can race them," he replied, as if talking to a child. "Otherwise they wouldn't come back."

Helen, suitably chastised, said no more.

Noonan, satisfied that his status was still intact, gestured them towards a tall, futuristic, chimney-like metal structure standing on top of one of the laboratory desks. "This is an electron microscope. I won't bore you with the technical details; suffice to say it is very powerful indeed, allowing magnifications upwards of ten million times. Now, let me show you what you have here."

He lent down and peered into one of the viewfinders, talking as his pale hands deftly manipulated the various controls. "Okay. I examined four feathers in total; three from the blanket and this one from the house. In my opinion, this is the chest plumage of a rock dove. It's been plucked from the bird, which is good news, because it's likely to still contain traces of its DNA and, all being well, we can compare it to the ones on the blanket, by feather-sexing."

"It's possible to tell all that just from a single feather?" asked Helen sceptically.

Noonan didn't dignify her with an answer.

Teddy took pity on her and explained, "Biotechnology doesn't just allow us to map the human genome but in theory the genome of every single living organism on the planet. It has huge potential, not just in forensic investigations but in medicine and–"

"Can you confirm that these feathers are all from the same bird?" interrupted Everton, badly in need of fresh air, not a science lecture.

"I can confirm that the plumage you previously sent me and this one are all from the same *genus* of bird, a rock dove, but the three I've tested are all from different individuals."

"That's the end of that theory then," sighed Helen.

"Not necessarily," said Noonan, removing the feather from under the electron microscope with a pair of small plastic tweezers. "What colour would you call this?"

"White," said Helen, wishing he'd get to the point.

"Wrong," said Noonan, placing the feather back under the microscope. "Try again."

Helen, irritated by Noonan's patronising attitude, shot Everton a look and peered through the viewing lens again. "Oh, my God. It's pink, not white."

Everton elbowed in to have a look. She was right. The feather under the bright light and magnification was the palest pink.

"Just like the other three samples," said Teddy, producing a set of ten-by-eight blow-ups of the feathers found on the blanket by the river.

Helen was still confused. "And that's significant?"

"Possibly. This feather comes from the underwing plumage of quite a rare breed of dove, a Steinbach."

Everton's hangover was forgotten. Maybe they were actually on to something. "So, what you're saying is that finding these matching feathers is not likely to be just a coincidence?"

"It's unlikely. I wouldn't go farther than that. If I feather-sex them all, we may get lucky and get a DNA match. Then you'll know for sure."

"How long will that take?"

"A couple of days. We have to use a PCR enzyme to break it down and then set it into an electrophoretic gel before–"

"Basically, it's easy to get false readings," Teddy cut in, realising Noonan was losing them again. "We'll need to double-test our findings."

"Okay. Let's do it."

Teddy nodded and moved off. Noonan started to follow him. Everton stopped him with a touch to his elbow.

Noonan reacted like Everton was contagious and drew his arm aside. "If you need any further information, I suggest you contact the Professional Breeders Association or, failing that, the homing and racing pigeon clubs. Some people use them for racing. They're larger than the common dove and have good homing instincts. But they're also used in displays or at weddings and funerals; they're similar to the ones you see released as symbols of peace and purity."

Everton pursed his lips, suspecting the donkey work was going to be all down to him. Noonan saw it and, cracking a smile, appeared to relent a little. "I'll make a couple of phone calls. But I can't promise anything."

* * *

Daniella, or Dani as she called herself, had the face of an angel and the mind of a whore. She professed to be nineteen and had come over from Brazil to study English at Megan Howell's college on a student visa. Megan suspected she was older than she claimed and the moment she left the room to freshen-up, Megan took the opportunity to check her passport, which she'd seen poking out of her woollen tote bag.

DANIELLA CORTEZ 25-05-95.

She was right. She was twenty-four; she had lied to get the visa. Megan photographed the page on her mobile and quickly replaced the passport. Then settled herself, primed if she needed to be, to wait for her reward.

She flicked through the selfies of her and her ex-students on her mobile, wondering why she found them so attractive. It wasn't just physical. It ran deeper than that; it had to do with respect. As deputy head of the school she had a given status but she listened to their problems and, in doing so, earned their trust and respect. They felt comfortable opening up to her emotionally and physically. In her mind that wasn't exploitation.

"Megan! You come *now*."

She smiled, hitched up her pencil skirt, pulled down her panties, tossed them onto the sofa and walked into the bedroom. It was a surprisingly feminine room, full of antique lace and bedside lamps draped in silk. Dani stood naked at the French windows, staring out over the balcony. Megan walked up behind her and bit the back of her neck.

Dani screamed and pushed her away, pointing in horror out to the balcony. Where Gabriel Oak, Megan's Spaniel, lay dead; his swollen black tongue lolling like he was drinking from a pool of his own bloody vomit.

* * *

Tessa Hayes took a lot of persuading before agreeing to take part in the reconstruction. Only agreeing after Helen explained that if it unlocked something in her memory, it would not only benefit her but possibly three other missing women.

They showed her the bar's CCTV footage, which Helen had uploaded onto her iPad. Then, seated her in the same seat, at exactly the same time she'd arrived at The Botanist. Everton sat in the alcove where her dark-haired abductor had. Nothing. They walked through the scenario after they left the bar. Her being shepherded across Kew Green by her attacker towards a blue Mercedes, parked in the same position. Nothing. Tessa Hayes went through the reconstruction in mute horror, because although she'd seen the evidence of what had happened and her body still bore witness to it, she had absolutely no recollection of meeting her attacker or what he'd subsequently done to her.

She grew more and more distressed, feeling she was letting them down. Helen assured her that she wasn't but found it hard to hide her disappointment. Finally, she suggested that Everton drive Tessa home, explaining she had an appointment with the manager of the Wilson Hospital about her father.

Everton shot her an old-fashioned look. "At eight thirty at night?"

The journey back to Farnham passed largely in silence. Everton suspected it was the longest time Tessa had ever spent alone with a black man who wasn't an employee of some sort. He was surprised when she insisted he stay for a cup of tea and a sandwich, as a thank you for driving her home. He declined but thanked her for her help and her courage. Leaving, he felt embarrassed about how easily, and crudely, he'd stereotyped her.

* * *

Helen hadn't totally lied. She wasn't at the Wilson Hospital but at a soulless pub, The Greenkeeper, next door to it.

Nora, the ward manager, had texted her to ask if they could meet off the hospital premises, unofficially, to find a solution to her father's care problems. She arrived accompanied by a bearded man in his forties, who was wearing an expensive three-piece suit, a yellow tie and black brogues.

"Thomas Bayne," he said, offering his manicured hand and seating himself in one smooth movement. "But please call me Thomas."

"Detective Constable Lake," replied Helen, sticking to her formal title. "You're joining us?"

"I'm sorry. This is my trust manager," said Nora, by way of explanation. "He is aware of the situation."

If the explanation was supposed to reassure Helen, it didn't. But she held her tongue and waited to see what would unfold. Bayne laid his calf-skin briefcase on the table and reached inside for his matching wallet. "Can I get you a drink?"

"No thank you. I'm driving."

"Of course. Nora, would you mind? I'll just have a Red Bull."

Nora took her cue and the wallet and made her way over to the bar.

Bayne smiled, held up his hands in a gesture of openness and said, "I should explain. Nora and I are a couple. I'm telling you that because I want you to be reassured that my involvement in this is completely open and above board."

Helen nodded but thought, *Then, why are we meeting in a pub?*

"I understand that you have an issue regarding your father's care whilst he's been a patient at the Wilson?"

"Lack of care would be a more accurate description."

"And that you have photographic evidence of this," continued Bayne, unwilling to get mired in semantics.

Helen took out her mobile and showed him the photographs.

"Do you mind?" he said, taking the mobile and slowly flicking through them; totally ignoring Nora, who stood behind him holding the drinks, obviously under instructions not to interfere. "I'm sorry. This must have been very distressing for you and your sister."

"And my father."

"Of course. But these photographs are hardly evidence of maltreatment and certainly not enough to justify a full-scale police investigation."

"That's a matter of opinion."

"Constable Lake," he said, leaning forward and clasping his delicate hands together as if to emphasise the importance of what he was saying. "Please don't let the press turn this into another care scandal when there isn't one. It's taken us years to get this hospital reopened. We still struggle for Trust recognition and finance. Something like this could be extremely damaging."

He smelt of breath freshener and cologne. Like an expensive brief. But Helen wasn't buying any of it, or him. "That's your responsibility. Mine is my father's welfare."

"As it should be. Look, Nora will confirm that I've ordered an enquiry and a full review of our geriatric care. And I can assure you that the wellbeing of your father, as with all our patients, is our top priority."

Either they have something to hide, thought Helen, *or they genuinely want to make amends.* Either way, she knew they wanted to make a deal. She did the selfish but pragmatic thing and offered them one: "Nora said my father may have to be moved."

"Your father's care is secure at the Wilson Hospital for as long as it's required," said Bayne with conviction, offering Helen his firm, open hand as proof.

Helen weighed up her options and took it.

* * *

The team were grouped around one of the wipe boards in the detective's room, sipping anaemic tea and devouring slabs of bacon sandwiches, as they waited for the DCI's briefing to start.

It was always the worst part of Teal's day, because in his mind the pleasure of the crisp bacon, fresh white bread and salty butter was like sex, but its pleasure was now denied to him by his furring arteries. He blew the smell of it from his nose into one of the paper napkins on the desk, and said, "The Merc. You got nowhere tracking it."

Helen wondered how he knew, and then realised it must have come from DS Clarke, which meant that he must have been accessing her case notes, trying to cover his arse. She fixed him with a knowing look. Clarke ignored her and continued to work his way methodically through his plank of a sandwich.

"That's true, guv, but we've come up with something else—"

"First things first. The reconstruction. Negative?"

"Unfortunately, yes. I don't think we're going to get any further with Tessa Hayes. She's suffering from post-traumatic shock."

"Which makes a successful prosecution all but impossible. Even if you find the guy in the bar, the CPS will never go for it," interrupted Clarke.

"I'm aware of that. But if we can tie him in to the other three murders—"

"How are you going to do that without bodies?"

"If you let me finish, I'll tell you. And you might want to wipe your chin. You've got ketchup all over it."

Clarke tossed the rest of his sandwich into the metal bin and wiped his mouth with the back of his hand.

"Continue," growled Teal.

Helen did, laying out everything that they'd discovered, first about the feather Everton had found at Gina Lewis' and then Noonan's subsequent blank enquiries with the Breeders Association and pigeon clubs.

Clarke interrupted again, "I'm sorry. You've tried – and failed – to tie in the Tessa Hayes abduction to three other missing women. And now you're trying to suggest that Gina Lewis' suicide could be connected to her as well?"

"I'm aware it sounds implausible–"

"Implausible? It sounds bloody ridiculous."

"Jack. Let's hear her out–"

"Oh, come on. This is all just circumstantial bullshit–"

"Sergeant!"

Clarke held up his hands theatrically and sat back down on the edge of his desk. Teal turned his attention back to Helen. "This better be good."

Everton stole a glance at Helen, fearing she'd already given them everything they had. He was wrong. He detected the glimmer of a smile as she picked up a large buff-coloured envelope stamped FORENSIC and handed it to Teal.

"As ridiculous as it may seem, the feather found in Gina Lewis' house is a perfect DNA match to one that we found on the blanket with Tessa Hayes at the River Wandle."

The stunned silence that followed was finally broken by the crack of Teal's peppermint. "Are you saying that Gina Lewis was murdered by the same man?"

"No. The autopsy confirms that she committed suicide."

"Then what the hell are you saying?"

"I'm saying that whoever attacked Tessa Hayes was also in Gina Lewis' home and was therefore probably known to her."

"You don't know that. It could have been there for months, been brought in by anyone–"

"Unlikely. Miss Lewis was extremely house proud. The place was pristine."

"Interesting," said Teal. "But Jack's right. It's still just supposition."

"But worth further investigation, considering that Gina Lewis' body hair was also shaved. And that Laura Fell insists she saw someone else in the house. We know from Gina's mobile records that she made dozens of phone calls to an unknown number in the days prior to her death."

"Have you checked it out?"

"Laura Fell phoned it. A man answered and immediately hung up. It's now dead. Everton checked the number; it's a pay-as-you-go phone. And we haven't been able to find her mobile or laptop. It's the same MO for Tessa Hayes and the other missing women, guv. Their mobiles and iPads are missing too."

"Okay. I agree it can't be just coincidental. So, what's next?"

"Start interviewing Gina Lewis' family and friends. But that's going to take time."

"Fair enough. Jack. You'll be overseeing but Helen will head the team. And I stress the word *team*."

Helen was elated. It was as close to a compliment as she'd ever received from Teal and, better still, it was a nail in the coffin of DS Knobby Clarke's ambitions.

* * *

When Everton phoned Laura with the news, she was elated too, feeling vindicated that she'd been proved right and that someone at last believed in her. The feeling was so overwhelming that almost immediately after replacing the receiver, she fell into a deep dreamless sleep on the sofa. It was 9.20am.

An hour later, she was woken by the harmonic *ping-pong* of her doorbell and a man's voice calling her. In her confusion, she thought it must be the police arriving to interview her. She stumbled to her stockinged feet and down the stairs, checked her puffy reflection in the less-than-flattering hall mirror, gave her tangled hair a finger-comb and opened the door. It wasn't the police; it was Don Hart.

He was standing at the front door, shoulders stooped against the cold, wearing a blue windcheater with its hood pulled over a black baseball cap and sunglasses, even though the sky was weepy and grey. Laura lied and told him that she was expecting visitors but he begged her for just a few minutes of her time. Eventually she relented, feeling guilty that she'd just dumped him without an explanation, and invited him up for a coffee.

They sat like strangers on separate seats; a sign of the demise of their intimacy. Don stared down into the dregs of his instant coffee like a clairvoyant looking for an answer to his problems. Laura sipped her peppermint tea and wondered why he was still wearing his coat and gloves inside but decided against mentioning it for fear it would look like an invitation for him to stay longer. Finally, he spoke in a voice so hesitant and low that she could barely hear him, apologising for letting her down and not being there on the night of Gina's suicide, and confessing that he felt dreadful about her having to cope with it all on her own. But Laura was past being angry and told him simply and directly that she had no hard feelings, she just needed to move on. Don minutely adjusted the seams on his brown leather gloves as he listened and seemed genuinely upset.

"Look, I know I've made some mistakes… and some of your friends think I'm not trustworthy–"

"It's not that."

"No. They do. It's okay. And sometimes I think you do – or have. I just want you know I'm sorry if I made you feel like that… and that it's got to end like this… You've been an important part of my life, Laura. The only real friend I have apart from my son and he's a complete mess. Do you know the real reason I wasn't with you that night?"

"Don. It doesn't matter–"

"Please. It does to me. He got involved in a fight. A guy tried to mug him. He had a knife. Richie ran into a shop and phoned me."

"God," said Laura, momentarily thrown. "I mean, that must have been frightening."

"He was terrified. The guy was hanging around outside waiting for him."

"Why didn't he just phone the police?"

"He did. A cop turned up and let the guy go."

"Why would he do that?"

"He'd thrown the knife away, claimed that Richie tried to mug him."

"Why would the police believe him?"

"Richie's got form with the police. He doesn't like them and they don't like him."

Laura, who'd never heard this before, said, trying not to appear shocked, "Was he hurt?"

"His face was a mess. I had to take him to A&E," Don lied, "and now, would you believe, he's in there again. The police raided my house, I was staying with my mum – she's had a hip replacement. Anyway, they kicked the front door in and went in mob-handed with a dog. Richie got bitten on his legs."

"I don't understand. Why would they raid your house?"

"They said it was drugs. But when my solicitor started making noises about suing them over Richie's injuries, they changed their tune. Started saying they were investigating a betting scam. The whole thing's a farce. They've even got pictures of you and me at Walthamstow."

"Us? What have I got to do with anything?" said Laura, appalled at her sudden involvement.

"Nothing. I told them that. Nor have I. They're just trying to scare me into dropping the complaint."

"The police wouldn't do that–"

"Laura. I know this is hard for you to understand. But where I was brought up, they do shit like this every day. Read the papers. Some cops are as corrupt as the criminals."

Laura was lost for words. The whole concept of any corrupt authority figure seemed completely alien to her after her upbringing. But she remembered her first bruising encounter with Everton and how he'd subsequently changed.

"Anyway," said Don. "I just wanted to let you know personally and... well, apologise for all this... and any hurt I may have caused you. You're a sweet person, Laura. You deserve better."

He appeared very vulnerable and Laura felt for him. But she was still her father's daughter and instinctively wary of any criticism of the law. "What am I supposed to say if they call me?"

"The truth. That we went out on a date and you won on a couple of bets. Look, honestly, I doubt they will. My solicitor reckons it'll all blow over. You can phone him if you like."

"No. I don't want to be involved," she said with a finality that signalled the end of the discussion and their relationship.

Don shrugged another helpless apology and picked up his cap. Laura caught the tell-tale glimpse of a freckled scalp beneath the thinning hair and wondered why she'd never noticed it before. He caught her looking, quickly jammed the cap back in place and turned away. Laura followed him out of the flat, down the complaining stairs and into the shared hall, eased past him and opened the front door.

"I'm sure your son will be okay," she said, putting a metaphorical full stop on their relationship.

"He's going to be permanently scarred," he replied, hovering on the doorstep. "I feel bad for him... Actually, I feel bad about everything... especially us."

He waited for her to reply but Laura had run out of words and sympathy. She had her own problems and couldn't – wouldn't – take responsibility for anyone else's. Don knew better than to press her any further. He kissed her lightly on the cheek and, to her relief, turned and pulled the hood of his windcheater over his cap and walked away.

He was fifty metres up the road when he looked back. He knew she wouldn't still be there. Which was just as well, because she'd have seen him climb into the passenger seat of a black BMW driven by Harry the Hat, a notorious Walthamstow bookie.

"She gonna play ball?"

"Dunno," growled Don. "She may need some more persuading."

Dark secrets

The sudden death of her mother from a brain aneurism stunned Amy Tann and changed her life. Not just because of the love she felt for her, but the dark secret that her death revealed.

She was sorting through her belongings when she made a shattering discovery that would redefine her whole life, past and present. It was a letter to her parents, Tim and Sheila Sale, from an adoption agency, and contained a photo of a three-year old, red-haired girl: Amy Sale, their new daughter. Her. She was dumbfounded. She appeared to have been adopted, and by another member of her birth parent's family.

Tim explained that her mother had been married to his cousin, Bernard, a violent drunk, who'd abandoned her with a young baby, and that Tim subsequently fell in love with her, married her and adopted Amy as his own. He'd begged her not to reopen old wounds, insisting he knew nothing of Bernard's whereabouts. Besides, he was her father now and he loved her. Surely that should be enough?

Amy desperately wanted it to be, but it wasn't. Unbeknown to him, she'd begun searching Internet adoption sites and tracing agencies, looking for her birth father. Her obsession had begun to affect her personal life. She lost her teaching job. Postponed her IVF treatments to save money, angering her husband, Philip, a Fraud Squad Detective in the Met.

When she finally found her birth father, Bernard, she felt only contempt for him. But he swore that he hadn't abandoned Amy, insisting he'd been in hospital with pneumonia and they'd just disappeared. That he only later discovered Sheila had been having an affair with his cousin, Tim. Amy accused him of lying. If that were true, why hadn't he tried to contact her? Bernard pulled out a faded wad of unopened letters, marked 'return to sender'. He had tried. They'd all been returned. And he'd kept every single one.

Five years on, Amy still bore the emotional scars: abandoned IVF, a broken marriage, drink, casual sex, prescription drugs. Philip sneered in one of their rows that a person would have to be "fucking desperate" to ask for her help. Amy sneered back that "a lot of fucking people are."

She was sitting in a tiny office in the West London Holistic Centre, a rather grand name for a red-brick building behind a supermarket, watching her therapist, Simon, tug at his salt-and-pepper eyebrows as he listened to her relaying the story. She suspected he plucked them – although he denied it – and enjoyed teasing him about his obvious vanity. She'd been coming to see him for over a year and was attracted to his casually manicured good looks and brutal honesty, even if she didn't always agree with it.

"You want to know the real reason you set up this tracing agency business?"

"It's called Lost and Found, Simon."

"Whatever. You're still in denial about your feelings of betrayal over your stepfather."

"I'm not in denial. I know what he did and I made a conscious decision to cut him out of my life."

"That's not what I'm talking about and you know it. You're not seeing your birth father either. The truth is, whether you admit it or not, you blame men for ruining your life."

"That's rubbish."

"Is it? Why do you think you never had children?"

"I had fibroids. I couldn't–"

"You could. You stopped your IVF treatment. Not only that, but you didn't tell your husband you had. And you're upset because he's angry with you. No, the truth is, you don't want kids, Amy, because deep down, you don't trust men. You're frightened of being betrayed again. That's why you always need to be in control – even sexually."

A smile parted Amy's crimson lips like a wound. "Have you finished?"

"No. You're forgoing your own personal life in the vain pursuit of making other victims, like yourself, whole. Why? You're not God. Sort out your own life and marriage before you start interfering in other people's."

"Shit. Talk about calling the kettle black."

"What's that supposed to mean?"

"You're telling me that *you* don't live through your patient's triumphs and tragedies vicariously? Christ, it's the only thing that gives your sad life a purpose."

"We're here to talk about you. I don't want to talk about me–"

"Of course you don't. Why don't you sort out your own marriage and 2.4 perfect children, Simon? Rather than lecture and fuck me."

Simon's aquiline features creased in a smile. "Touché." Easing himself forward on his chair, he took Amy's bird-like hand, as if to emphasise the point he was making. "Except *I'm* not the one drinking. *I'm* not the one self-medicating to numb my anger and bolster my low self-esteem."

"I am not an alcoholic! So I have a couple of drinks. It relaxes me. Makes me feel more attractive – okay, *wanted*; is that what you want me to say?" She took his hand, placed two fingers in her mouth and said, "So does sex."

He could smell her boozy cigarette breath. Feel her tongue working up and down his fingers. He pulled them roughly from her mouth and pushed them up her skirt.

After it was over, Simon went home to his perfect family, whilst Amy went to meet Kieron Allen in The Black Cat, a recently renovated pub on the edge of Catford Market. There, she toyed with a second vodka and tonic and the attentions of a Ryanair pilot from Belfast as she waited for Kieron to arrive.

Kieron, who'd been held up in traffic on the South Circular, arrived half an hour late, by which time the pilot, who felt he'd paid for Amy's attention for the evening, took exception to him trying to share it.

Kieron, a quietly spoken, reserved man, tried to defuse the situation. "Honestly, I'm not trying to… muscle in… Look, my sister died… rather tragically… and, well, tonight is the first chance we've had to talk about it."

The guy deflated, muttering, "Oh. Right. Well… that's different… Right, well… I'll say goodnight."

"Thank you, Ryan," said Amy, confusing his name with the company he worked for.

The pilot let it go and strode off with his dignity more or less intact. Kieron suggested that they sit at a table away from the bar. Amy found them an alcove beside the spluttering gas log fire and Kieron bought a bottle of Prosecco so that they could toast Gina's memory. They sat there quietly on the worn oak pews, sipping their wine and grieving her loss.

"Are you going to the funeral?" Kieron asked. "I read in *The Standard* that it's on Friday."

"I don't know. Why? Would you like us to go together?"

He shook his head and said softly, "I'm not going. I don't want to cause any more trouble."

"Kieron. You're her brother. You have every right."

"Her step-parents don't want me there."

"Gina would have."

"I know. But I don't want to make it worse. I got a message from Mrs Lewis stating that I wasn't welcome. She said there was stuff missing from Gina's house. Her laptop. She accused me of taking it, threatened me with the police."

"That's ridiculous."

"They haven't spoken to you, then?"

"No, and neither have the police.

He nodded in relief and took a sip of his wine as if to celebrate a small victory. "She may have just been trying to scare me off. I wouldn't put it past her."

"You mustn't let them do that, Kieron. You've done nothing wrong."

"I know. Would you like some water? I think I need some water," he said, changing the subject and quickly removing himself from the distressing conversation.

Amy drained the last of her Prosecco and poured herself another glass. She sipped it as she watched him at the bar, thinking that even from the back he looked crushed. Haunted. She felt for him. After years of searching, he'd finally been reunited with his sister and Amy had had to phone him with the news that Gina had committed suicide. Worse, her step-parents, the real culprits, who'd put every obstacle in the way of their reunion, were now blaming him. It was so unfair. Why didn't they blame *her*? She'd been the person Gina had come to asking for help to trace her birth mother. She'd been the one to set the train of events in motion. How could she have known the tragic consequences? She'd warned Gina about the risk of being rejected by her biological mother, but hadn't foreseen the malicious reaction of her adopted parents. The Lewis' response to Kieron was inexplicable. The poor man had done nothing but want to find his long-lost sister and they seemed to hate him for it – just like her own lying shit of a stepfather had with her.

She hid her concern behind a smile as he turned back to the table, carrying two glasses of water and an array of bar snacks on a metal tray displaying a faded print of a cockerel.

"I'm sorry," he said apologetically as he placed packets of crisps and peanuts on the table. "I thought it would be good to have something to line our stomachs, what with us driving, but this is all they have unless we have a full meal."

"It's fine. Thank you," she replied.

He ripped open the individual packets one by one and laid them flat on the oak table like little silver picnic plates. She took the gentle hint and picked at a few of the crisps. The combination of cheese and onion and cheap fizzy wine was horrible but she made sure she ate enough to satisfy his concern.

Kieron picked up a dry-roasted peanut between his finger and thumb and held it up to his face as if forensically examining it.

"Aren't you going to eat that?" she said rather lamely, struggling to fill the silence.

"No," he said. "I'm allergic to them. So was Gina. Isn't that weird? Someone you'd never met, that you didn't even know existed, and you finally meet and find you've both got the same allergy."

"They reckon that some twins have a sort of sixth sense between them."

"I know. But I was over fifteen years older than her."

Amy said nothing, but thought that he looked every day of it. His jacket hung loose on his concave shoulders, giving him a hollowed-out appearance. And the boyish enthusiasm and hope she'd first seen in him had been eroded by a deadening, misplaced belief that Gina would still be alive if they'd never met.

"Kieron," she said, suddenly stone-cold sober. "Meeting you, knowing she had a brother, was one of the happiest days of Gina's life. She told me that."

Kieron's grave face lit up, and for a moment he allowed himself to believe it.

* * *

Arriving home, Amy felt good about herself for the first time in weeks. But she should have changed the locks on her front door. She thought that, being a detective, her husband would have obeyed the restraining order she'd taken out against him. She was wrong. Philip was waiting for her in the hall when she fumbled her way in, dropping her handbag and keys on the coir entrance mat and muttering a stream of expletives.

Out of the darkness a disembodied voice said, "They're by your feet."

She staggered back and switched on the light. Philip was sitting midway up the stairs, tugging at his wispy beard, watching her.

"How did you get in here?"

"With a key. This is my house–"

"You don't live here anymore. You can't just let yourself in."

"I'm still paying the mortgage."

"Get out! Now! Before I call the police."

"I am the fucking police! What d'you think they're going to do, Amy? Nothing."

She knelt and searched through the spilt contents of her handbag for her mobile. He watched her, pursing his thin lips in disgust, as she scrabbled around on the expensive oak floor that he'd laid himself.

"And what do you think they're going to say when they arrive and find you pissed after driving home?"

She pulled herself to her feet, her hand resting on the wall to steady herself, and said with as much dignity as she could muster, "I am not pissed, thank you very much."

"You are! I can smell it from here," he said as he stood and made his way towards her. "You stink of it. Who've you been screwing tonight? One of your saddo clients?"

The riposte spat from her mouth before she could stop herself. "No. My saddo therapist and he's a better fuck than you'll ever be!"

He didn't hit her hard; it was more of an open-handed cuff than a punch. But it knocked her back – *smack* – against the door, cracking the frosted-glass panel. He was as surprised as she was to see the blood, her blood, spattering onto the engineered wood floor.

"You bastard," she said, and pulled out a pepper spray from her bag and sprayed him full in the face.

He screamed and launched himself, fists and feet, blindly at her… until her screams drowned out his own.

* * *

Everton and Helen spent the morning with Laura Fell, compiling a list of Gina's friends and associates. DS Clarke insisted he should accompany them to get a feel for the case, but Helen bullshitted him about not wanting to go in mob-handed and risk unsettling

Laura. Instead, she tasked him with tracing all the other numbers that Gina had called from her mobile in the week before she died. Everton reminded her that they were supposed to be working as a team and that she couldn't just ostracise him. But she was unrepentant, arguing that Clarke wasn't interested in getting a feel for the case; he was interested in burying it.

Helen was keen to pin down the exact timings of Laura and her Chill Out friends movements on the night of the suicide. She'd already pulled the CCTV traffic camera image of Laura's car jumping the red light on Putney Hill, which had helped narrow it down, but was keen to learn the events leading up to her decision to visit Gina. Laura was reluctant to say too much, especially about Don Hart, and the meeting ended inconclusively.

Everton drove them back to Wimbledon. He decided to take a shortcut through Richmond Park, but the twenty-mile-an-hour speed limit meant that he had to drive slower to accommodate the perennial "Lycra louts", as he called the cyclists.

"I've just realised something," said Helen, opening her pad to check her notes. "Gould and Hart are the only male regulars of this Chill Out thing. And both of them were absent on the night of Gina Lewis' death when they'd both been expected."

"Hart phoned to apologise."

"But only later that night, when Laura Fell was outside the house."

"Yeah, that's true. And Laura reckons that Gould had a real thing about Gina Lewis."

"It could be nothing, but we have to start somewhere, so let's put them first on the list. I'll get Nobby to run a background check on them and we'll do the interviews."

"What about Mrs Lewis?"

"She can wait. We don't need any more flak."

"Okay. But she's hiding something – and I don't just mean about the laptop. Gina Lewis changed her will the day she died and made Laura the sole beneficiary. And Mrs Lewis knew she'd done it *before* Laura saw the will."

"What? How do you know that?"

"Laura told me."

Helen mentally noted the repeated use of her first name, stored it for later and said, "Does she know why she changed it?"

"No, but Mrs Lewis clearly does."

"And how do you know that?"

"Because she'd already contacted her daughter's solicitor contesting the will."

"Which means, she must have known what and who was in it previously."

"Exactly. Odd, considering that Gina Lewis evidently loathed her mother."

"Why didn't you tell me this before?"

"Because it was told to me in confidence and I didn't know if it was relevant."

She shot him a quizzical look. Everton steadfastly tried to ignore it. But, momentarily distracted, he clipped one of the small wooden bollards that bordered the road. The front offside tyre punctured with a spectacular bang, sending the car slewing off road and towards a herd of grazing fallow deer. Barking in alarm, they stampeded past the car and across the tarmac, like a scene from *Jurassic Park*, decimating a peloton of cyclists.

"Shit!" exclaimed Helen as the car finally slid to rest. "What happened? Are you okay?"

Everton nodded and climbed out of the car to assess the carnage, lost his balance and fell flat on his face.

* * *

Everton's hastily arranged appointment at the ENT department of St. George's Hospital turned into a microcosm of all that was good and bad in the NHS.

He spent ten minutes playing musical cars in the packed car park – bad – before a departing Indian guy waved him into his spot – good. He arrived ten minutes early for his 9.15am appointment and found a free seat in the heaving waiting room in front of the television – good. Waited only twenty minutes to be seen by the triage nurse – surprisingly good – then two hours to be seen by the Consultant – unsurprisingly bad.

And it only got worse. The oddly attractive Austrian consultant, Mrs Bauer, sporting fiercely back-combed sixties hair and extravagant lip gloss, reprimanded him for missing his last two appointments and potentially making his condition worse. Everton was adamant that he hadn't and was proved right when she discovered that the department actually had two files under his name and had been sending his appointment letters to his old marital home.

"Ah," she said, without a hint of apology. "Mystery solved. When did this last episode start, Mr Bowe?"

"About a week ago."

"And have you noticed any change in your tinnitus?"

"No. It's still the same."

"And where were you when the vertigo started? Were you doing anything that you think might have sparked it off?"

"No. I was actually – without being overly graphic – about to use the lavatory. I pulled down my trousers and just keeled over."

"Did you hurt yourself?"

"Only my pride," he answered ruefully.

"Well, what is that saying? Pride always comes before a fall."

"This time it came after. And yesterday I crashed a police car in Richmond Park and some deer stampeded into some cyclists. Fortunately, they weren't hurt – the deer."

She gave a throaty smoker's chuckle, picked up her otoscope and began cleaning the plastic cone with an antiseptic wipe. She had big hands for a small woman, and knuckles like walnuts, which made her coral gloss nail polish look oddly out of place.

"Well, I'm glad you haven't lost your sense of humour, Mr Bowe."

"I have my moments, Doctor," he said, surprised at how easy he found it to speak so openly to her, a complete stranger, and yet struggled with the people close to him.

She pulled down his left earlobe, gently inserted the nozzle and said, "I'm sure. Tinnitus is an unpleasant condition even without the vertigo. I've known some of my patients to become suicidal over it."

"Yes, well, on the list of things I could become suicidal over it's probably about third."

She laughed again and switched to his other ear. "Is that what you police call gallows humour?"

"Something like that. You have a good memory."

"How do you mean?"

"About me being a policeman. You must see hundreds of people."

"Actually, I'm dyspraxic. I have to do these mental exercises. It helps my memory."

Everton laughed out loud.

"Did I say something funny?"

"No. Sorry. It's just weird. They thought I was too as a kid."

"So, we have something in common. Right. I'm going to smuggle you in for a videonystagmograph and caloric test. Let's see if there's been any change."

Everton should have been pleased to have been jumping the NHS queue, but he'd had both procedures before and knew they weren't pleasant. He was mildly claustrophobic. So, to be strapped into a dentist-like chair in a blacked-out room the size of a wardrobe was bad enough, but to have heavy goggles fitted – with a video camera attached to record his eye movements as the chair spun clockwise and then anticlockwise – filled him with dread. It wasn't as bad as he remembered, but it was bad enough.

The West Indian technician unstrapped him, smiling broadly, and said, "One down, bra. Only the caloric to go." He helped Everton out of the chamber and led him over to the other side of the room. "Take a seat," he said, indicating another dentist like chair. "You need another bag?"

Everton shook his head. He barely listened to the technician's instructions as he placed the vomit bag aside and began fastening another pair of goggles over his eyes. Taking a deep, deep breath, he gritted his teeth and waited for the cold, then warm, water to be alternatively syringed deep into his ear canals. He didn't throw up but came close to it.

The results were, yet again, inconclusive, but he lied to Helen that it was a middle ear infection. He didn't want to risk being forcibly retired from the job – or the case, which was beginning to occupy his thoughts more and more.

* * *

The interview with Celia Lewis did not go well. After numerous phone calls, she finally agreed to meet Helen and Everton at her London constituency office, a converted Victorian building overlooking Putney Heath. She could give them an hour, no more, before she drove down to Oxfordshire to check the final arrangements for the private funeral service.

The impeccably coiffured secretary ushered them into the constituency manager's drably furnished office. Celia sat at a teak-style desk in front of her steel-haired driver, who stood, like a character out of a Tarantino movie, silhouetted against the winter light flooding in through the sash window behind him.

"You wanted to see me?" said Celia brusquely, forgoing any of the formalities.

"Yes. I'm sorry if it's an inconvenient time."

"It is. If you can please get to the point."

Helen felt her hackles rise; she was willing to cut Celia some slack for being under tremendous stress but did not take kindly to her dismissive attitude. "I'll endeavour to do that," she said, nodding to Everton, who dutifully took out his notebook and pen. "Do you mind if my colleague takes some notes?"

Celia ignored the question. Everton took it as a sign of her acceptance. "If this is about the laptop, I already told your colleague that I have absolutely no knowledge of its whereabouts or, for that matter, why it should be so important."

"It may not be. But we have reason to believe that someone who was in contact with your daughter is also responsible for the abduction and possible murder of three missing women."

Hard as she tried to conceal it, Everton saw a hairline crack appear in Celia's icy composure. "I don't understand."

The driver saw it too and immediately interjected, "Excuse me. Mrs Lewis agreed to this meeting on the understanding that it concerned her daughter's missing belongings."

"We think they may be connected in some way."

"Why would you think that?"

If Helen didn't like Celia's patronising tone, she liked his and his silhouette even less. "Sorry, we haven't been introduced. Who are you, sir?"

The tall man took a calculated step forward, revealing himself, and said, "Brian Hoffman. I look after Mrs Lewis' personal security. And you are?"

"DC Lake, PC Bowe, Metropolitan Police Missing Persons Unit, South West Division."

He nodded his acknowledgement to them in turn and said, "May I ask why you think Mrs Lewis would have any useful information about these missing women?"

Behind the studied politeness, the Savile Rowe suit and club tie, Everton smelt ex-Old Bill and weighed in on Helen's side. "We have no idea if she has or not. That's why we need to ask her these questions. To help us eliminate her from our enquiries."

Hoffman slipped a leather notebook and Mont Blanc ballpoint from his chalk-stripe jacket and asked, "Who is your lead officer on the investigation?"

"I am, sir," Helen replied evenly, knowing the reaction it would get.

"*You?*"

"Yes. Do you mind if we sit, Mrs Lewis? My colleague has an ear infection; it can upset his balance."

"What? No. Just get on with it. Please."

Everton was surprised by Helen's sudden concern and wondered if it was a delaying tactic to prolong the interview and questioning. He took the seat and waited to see. He didn't have to wait long.

"I understand that your daughter changed her will on the actual morning of her death. Have you any idea why she would have done that?"

Helen's question came so far out of left field that it threw Celia completely. "I don't understand... How do you know that?"

"How I know is unimportant, Mrs Lewis. My concern is how you knew. Had you seen the will previously?"

"No."

"Had Gina told you about it previously? I ask because, and forgive me for saying, my understanding is that you weren't on the best of terms with your daughter."

"That's rubbish. Total lies, and press fabrication."

"My information didn't come from the press, Mrs Lewis."

"If you're accusing Mrs Lewis of lying, she has a right to have her lawyer present," cautioned Hoffman, studiously recording his version of the conversation in his notebook.

"I'm not accusing her of anything, sir. I have the utmost sympathy for her and her loss. But you must understand this is a possible murder investigation."

Everton was impressed. Helen was like an impeccably polite dog with a bone.

"And I'm obliged to find answers to some difficult questions. It's my job–"

"No!" Celia snapped, trembling with emotion. "I won't be bullied into answering insulting questions about myself and my daughter's private affairs – especially the day before I bury her!" She snatched up her Prada handbag and stalked out of the room. "And stay away from my husband too!"

Hoffman took an embossed card from his wallet and tossed it on the table in front of Everton. "Mrs Lewis' lawyers, Harbottle and Lewis. I assume you've heard of them? They represent the royals."

Everton shrugged. "No, but I'll google them."

Helen stood and headed for the door. Everton picked up the card and followed her. Hoffman stepped in front of them, blocking the exit.

"A friendly word of advice. You two are well above your pay scale. Tread carefully."

"And what was yours?" said Everton, "And don't tell me you're not ex-Met."

"Detective Superintendent. But I like this job a lot more and intend to keep it."

"Well, bully for you," grunted Helen, pushing past him and out.

"She's going to get you into trouble, mate," said Hoffman, easing back in front of Everton to prevent him following. "And I don't mean just on the job."

It was said lightly but Everton immediately got the message – Hoffman had been watching them. He leaned in menacingly close to him and whispered, "I like trouble, Mr Hoffman. And if you don't mind your own business and step aside, you're going to find out just how much."

Everton and Helen decamped to the window seats of Caffé Nero on Putney High Street, staring morosely out at the traffic crawling past the window as they mulled over the problem.

"Let him do his worst," grunted Helen, sipping her mocha latte. "I've got nothing to hide, nor have you."

"Really? We were stoned out of our trees and screwing on the carpet last week," replied Everton, dunking his Danish pastry into his double espresso and taking a sloppy bite.

"So what? It was a bit of weed. I know a guy on the drug squad dealing smack."

"That's not the point. He was letting us know he's been checking us out. It was a warning from his employer."

"And she wouldn't be trying to warn us off if she didn't have something to hide, would she? I mean, did you see her reaction when I brought up her daughter's will?"

"Yeah. But the only other person who is going to know what was in it is Gina's solicitor and he's not going to tell us because of client confidentiality."

"Unless we get a disclosure order."

"A magistrate is going to need some serious proof of wrongdoing before they'll agree to that and we don't have any."

Helen shrugged; she knew Everton was right but she wasn't going to admit it. She picked up her skinny blueberry muffin and began idly nibbling at the crust.

"It looks like we're back to the two guys."

"Not necessarily," corrected Helen. "I mean, think about it. Out of Gina's family and friends, who gained the most from her death?"

Everton could see where her train of thought was leading and didn't like it. "No way. Laura had no idea she'd been left everything until Gina's mother told her."

"That's what she says. And before you jump to the lovely Laura's defence, I'm just playing devil's advocate."

Everton caught her teasing smile and felt himself flush.

"You're blushing."

"I am not blushing – and I do not have a thing for Laura Fell."

"Okay. Fair enough. It's just that I know from personal experience that you do have a bit of a thing for us whitey women."

Everton grabbed her muffin, shoved it whole in his mouth and said, "Not anymore, and that's racist."

* * *

Amy Tann missed her therapy session, and when she didn't answer her therapist's calls, Simon dropped by to check on her, concerned, he said later, that she'd been going through a "bit of a bad patch".

After getting no response to his knocks, he lifted the flap of the brass letter box to call inside – and smelt her. She was lying in a foetal position on the hall floor. For a second he thought she might be in a drunken stupor and called her name again. Then he saw the flies and the black clotted blood matting her hair.

Her husband Philip and a police colleague kicked the front door down. Philip fell to his knees in shock at finding his wife, weeping real tears on seeing what some "monster" had done to her. But the bruises on his knuckles and the front door key in his wallet ended his desperate charade. He was arrested on suspicion of murder and eight hours later formally charged.

Borough Commander Walsh, who thought he'd seen just about every act of senseless brutality in his twenty-odd year career as a copper, was appalled. Tann had battered his wife beyond recognition. Beneath the spongy mess that had once been her face, her jaw, nose and left eye socket had been fractured and several of her teeth were missing. The pathologist reckoned that she must have died slowly and in agony.

Acutely aware that he would be expected to hold a press conference to explain how a senior Met officer could cold-bloodedly murder his wife, Walsh swallowed his disgust and paid DS Tann a visit in his cell.

Philip looked up from pacing the bare box of a room, belligerent and unrepentant, snarling, "I don't need any lectures. She was a lying, drunken bitch and she got what she deserved."

Walsh listened to his echoing tirade from the doorway, wondering how so much hate could be contained in one man, and how the hell he was going to explain it to the press.

"What, you got nothing to say?"

"What would be the point? You're screwed up, Tann. In here," Walsh replied, tapping the side of his head.

Philip exploded, banging his chest like an ape and screaming, "If I'm fucked up it's because my whore of a wife fucked me up! And now she's fucked up herself! I call that justice!"

Walsh, lost for words, just stared at him. Philip held out his arms, like the Messiah, challenging him to disagree.

"Well, enjoy it while you can," said, Walsh, "Because inside they're going to show you another kind of justice and you will not enjoy that."

* * *

Laura skipped over the front-page story of the murder in the *Metro* and was therefore unaware that Amy Tann's husband's arrest had forced the suspension of the doping investigation, involving her.

She was scanning the inside pages for a report on Gina's funeral. She finally found one. A brief article headed: MP's SUICIDE DAUGHTER buried. That was it. No photograph. No eulogy. Her friend's life and death was now just old, page-four news.

It was only just five o'clock – too early for a drink – but she didn't care. She opened a bottle of Australian Shiraz, Gina's favourite wine, and curled up on the sofa with her laptop, clicking through their shared Facebook photos, creating her own personal eulogy.

She was woken by her mobile at nine-thirty. She hoped that it might be Frieda phoning to talk to her about the funeral. But it wasn't, it was Everton.

"I'm sorry to phone you so late. I just wanted to check you're okay? I know today can't have been easy for you."

She was touched by his interest but couldn't help feeling a growing unease about their relationship. Was he merely showing concern as a friend, because she barely knew him, and not at all socially, or was there something else? Because as much as she liked him, that was not going to happen. No matter how lonely she felt.

"I'm fine," she lied. "But I've got someone with me. Can I ring you in the morning?"

"Oh. Of course."

She thought she could she hear his disappointment, but it may have just been her imagination. She waited for him to hang-up but suddenly remembered. "Oh! Wait! Did you go to the funeral?"

"No. I had a difficult meeting with Mrs Lewis yesterday and under the circumstances I thought it was best not to."

"I didn't go either. Gina's solicitor rang to warn me that the Lewis's intend on going to court to freeze her assets in lieu of contesting the will."

"On what grounds?"

"Diminished responsibility or something. The whole thing is a nightmare."

"Don't worry about it. I'm going to get to the bottom of all this, Laura. I promise you."

Later, she wondered why he'd said "I", like it was his own personal crusade.

Everton wasn't even aware that he had. And the moment Laura cleared the line he immediately redialled. A male voice answered his wife's mobile.

"Hello?"

He hesitated, thinking that she could be out with a date or even something worse…

"Hello. Is anyone there? Hello? Mum! They're not answering."

"No. No. It's okay," spluttered Everton, embarrassed that he hadn't recognised his own son's voice. "It's me, Adam. Your dad."

The voice at the other end of the line went quiet. Everton had a vision of him holding the mobile up to his mother and rolling his eyes.

"Listen, how's the team doing? Your mum said they'd made you captain? Adam? Are you still there? Adam…?"

"Mum! It's him."

Then he was gone. Not even a goodbye. Just a dull thud as the mobile was tossed onto the sofa or something. Everton wasn't sure if he'd been cut off, until Pauline's self-assured voice cut in.

"I can't talk now. I'm helping Adam with his homework."

"At ten o'clock?"

"He's fifteen, Everton. He's doing his GCSEs. They get lots of homework." She was tired and didn't deliberately intend it as a criticism of his ignorance but it still hurt. He tried not to show it.

"So how many is he doing? Six, isn't it?"

"Eight."

"Oh. Great. How are they going?"

"Why don't you ask him yourself?"

"He won't speak to me."

"You're his father," she said, lowering her voice for privacy. "Make an effort."

"I am. I went to see him play the other day."

"He didn't say."

"No... He didn't know I was there. I didn't want to upset him."

"It's obviously not working."

They were off again, pounding the same treadmill and getting nowhere. Pauline knew it herself and changed the subject. "How's your balance?"

"They're doing some more tests. Can we meet?"

"To talk about what? The settlement?"

"No. I need some help."

"Christ, Everton, let it go. Just give him some time. Please."

"It's not that. The woman we found in the river, the one who interested you..."

"Tessa Hayes?" He could hear the sudden spike of curiosity in her voice and made her wait for a moment to whet her appetite. "Well, go on then."

"We think the attack on her may be linked to three other missing women. Meet me and I'll tell you why."

* * *

Pauline knew that if Everton had something for her he'd want something in return. The gifts between them had dried up long ago. She was huddled on a bench near the windmill on Wimbledon Common, waiting for him; something she seemed to have spent most of her married life doing. A dog was haring in loony patterns in front of her in forlorn pursuit of the bored crows that effortlessly flapped up into the blustery wind whenever it got within striking distance. *My God*, she thought. *It has got to be male. Only a male could be that stupid.*

Despite her caustic commentary, Pauline wasn't a feminist. On the contrary, feminism bored her almost as much as politics, which was interesting considering she thought of herself as a serious journalist. She'd never vehemently campaigned for or against anything in the whole of her eighteen-year career. She viewed her work with the emotional detachment of a surgeon, looking for the narrative rather than the emotional structure of the stories she covered. They were always meticulously researched and concisely written, but a critic might observe that they lacked heart, almost as if the writer distrusted themselves emotionally. Which, in a sense, Pauline did.

It started the night that she lost her virginity. She was on a sixth-form camping trip to the Lake District and told the boy as he came, "At this moment, I love you." And the next morning as they struck camp she heard him sniggering about it to his mates.

Strange, she thought, as she watched Everton drive up the access road towards the car park, how a simple, naive, expression of love could be turned into something ugly and stay with you like an invisible birthmark. How the smallest things in the distant past stained the future. She wished she'd told Everton to help him understand her need for some emotional separation, but it was too late now. Now she was dating again and she'd probably make the same demands and mistakes all over again.

After their separation, she signed up to a few dating sites, even went out on a couple of dates, but what could she do with a fifteen-year-old son waiting for her at home and constantly phoning to check on her? Have sex in the back of a car? No, she was too old for that. It would have been easier if Adam had agreed to spend the weekends with Everton but he'd refused. He blamed Everton and his job for the break-up and was determined to punish him, which wasn't entirely fair; it was a mutual decision but actually prompted by her. She felt she'd outgrown Everton. He was only ever going to be what he was: a solid beat copper, a "plod". He'd lost what little ambition he had and she hadn't. She was still hungry for more, like the dog chasing the crows – only she'd catch whatever she was chasing.

"That dog has lost its marbles," Everton hollered as he trudged up the gravel drive behind her. "He'll never catch them."

She called back, "So must I be, agreeing to meet here." She stood and negotiated her way across the shallow ditch separating them, grumbling, "It's freezing."

"Yeah, sorry. I needed somewhere private."

She looked around at the joggers and dog walkers traversing the windswept common. "This is private?"

"Here, if anyone's watching us, I can see them doing it."

She grunted, not entirely getting the logic, but let it go and said, "So why the secrecy?"

He unzipped his parka and indicated a sheaf of papers inside. "These are copies of the case notes on Tessa Hayes and the other three missing women."

"You think they're dead?"

"Yes, and probably murdered by the same man. The man that abducted Tessa Hayes and – here's the kicker – also knew Gina Lewis."

"That MP's daughter who committed suicide?"

"If it was."

"Wow. And you're going to give them to me?"

"Yes…"

She felt the "but" coming and she was right.

"But I need something from you first," he said, re-zipping the parka like he was closing a safe. "Some confidential information that I can't be seen to be looking for, but you can."

"Because it's illegal?"

"Because I'm a cop and I'm being leant on. Do you want them or not?"

Pauline stared at Everton, thinking she could have seriously underestimated him, and nodded her acceptance.

* * *

Iris Costa's round-robin email about the Friday film night had largely gone unanswered. Frieda hoped to make it, being a fan of French films, but Rust and Bone would not have been her choice. She'd have preferred something with a little more Gallic flare and a little less brutality.

Iris was relieved when she did eventually turn up because no other member of the group had arrived at the Richmond Curzon. It was disappointing because she'd arranged the evening in the hopes of reuniting the friends, and with Don Hart finally out of the picture she felt more comfortable about meeting Laura again. But Laura, like the others, hadn't even bothered to answer her email.

Colin Gould saw the earlier five o'clock screening and then watched Iris and Frieda's arrival from the window seat in the Watermans Arms opposite, noting that both his tormentors, Don Hart and Megan, hadn't turned up. After they were safely inside he made his way to Vestry House on Paradise Road and spent a desultory hour and a half killing time by looking at an exhibition of tepid watercolours by local artists. Ninety minutes later, he hot-footed it back to the Curzon to wait for Iris and Frieda to emerge from the cinema.

They were as surprised to see him as he claimed to be them. And barely hesitated before accepting his offer of a drink. They sat upstairs in the perennially empty dining room of the Watermans, away from the crush downstairs. Colin insisted on buying a bottle of house Chardonnay and some Thai hors d'oeuvres to nibble as they talked. He seemed much more like his old self and was keen to get their reaction to the film; lying that he'd never seen it, but that it was high on his bucket list.

They spent a pleasant hour critiquing the movie, and French films in general, and when last orders were called Colin insisted on giving them both a lift home. Frieda had her car but Iris accepted, knowing that it would give the two of them the chance to talk more openly. They took the shortcut to the car park, turning right down Water Lane and right again, walking with their heads down against the blustery wind and along the Thames towpath.

"I want to apologise for what I did. Not for what I said, because I *did* love Gina and we *did* have a relationship… a special relationship."

The vehemence of Colin's outburst took Iris by surprise and it took her a moment to compose her response. "The 'special man' she met… that was you?"

He gave an almost imperceptible nod and said, as much to himself as her, "She made me promise to keep it secret… until she was sure… and then this happened. I don't understand why she would do this to me. That's why I went to talk to her parents… to try and make sense of it… but I shouldn't have done that, just turn up like that, without them knowing, and upset them even more. They had every right to be angry… You all did… especially you, because, well, you and me, we've been more than close."

"Colin. There was never anything between us; you may have wanted it but there wasn't."

He remembered her over-eager tongue when she invited him to a "traditional Greek meal" at her cottage and thought, *Christ, what a hypocrite.* But accusing her now would not serve his purpose. That could wait. He merely repeated his hollow apology. "Anyway, I'm sorry about what happened… and I hope we can be friends again."

He waited for her to reply but she merely smiled. They walked on in silence and turned right onto Friars Lane. He could feel her watching him, judging him, out of the corner of her eye and, as they entered the car park, knew he was running out of time.

"I would never intentionally hurt you, Iris. I hope you know that."

"Well, I'm disappointed you weren't more honest with me, but I accept your apology."

"Thank you," he said, opening the passenger door for her. "I'd like to try and apologise to Megan too. I phoned and left a message but she didn't ring back."

"That's Megan, I'm afraid. She's not as forgiving as me. She's not speaking to Frieda either."

"That's a shame. Is that why she didn't come tonight?"

"Actually," said Iris. "I haven't heard from her for days. I was getting a bit concerned."

She was right to be. Because when she finally visited Megan's Lower Richmond Road flat two days later, Iris found the lights on but got no response to her knocks at the door. Concerned, she made her way to the back of the mansion block, up the rusting cast-iron fire escape and onto the second-floor balcony.

She didn't find Megan. But her dog lay dead under a cloud of voracious flies.

The local police were called and forced entry into the flat. But they found nothing apart from empty wardrobes and a pair of women's panties on the sofa.

* * *

Don Hart read about the arrest of Philip Tann and felt a huge sense of relief. His son's complaint against the detective now looked even more plausible, which meant the Met would in all probability quietly drop the doping case against him. So, he was doubly frustrated to find Everton and Helen rapping on the newly repaired front door of his Tooting semi.

"You want to see me, phone and make an appointment. Don't just turn up here and expect me to start answering bullshit questions about something I know nothing about."

He stood in a white velour dressing gown and matching monogrammed Hilton open-toed slippers, like he'd just crawled out of bed. Helen smiled to herself, wondering if he'd stolen it directly from the hotel or it had fallen off the back of a lorry. Either way, he didn't look as good as he thought he did in it.

"We did try and phone, Mr Hart. But the mobile number Miss Fell gave us was unavailable?"

"Yeah," said Don, more watchful now on hearing where they'd got his details from. "I stood on it. Had to get a new one."

"Maybe you could give us your new number, in case we need to contact you again?"

"Leave me your card. I'll text it to you."

"You can't remember it?"

"It's new."

Helen knew he was being obstructive but had no other option than to hand him her card. He barely gave it a glance before pocketing it in his dressing gown.

"You want to tell me what this is about? I was told that Gina Lewis committed suicide?"

"We're investigating some articles that appear to have gone missing from her Wimbledon home," said Everton, avoiding a direct answer. "Her mobile and laptop."

"Well, I haven't got them," declared Don, suspecting he wasn't being told the whole story, because in his experience it didn't take two coppers to investigate a bit of thieving. "I don't think I've ever been to her house. Who told you I had? Laura?"

"We asked her to compile a list of Gina's friends who were at the Chill Out on the night of her suicide. You were evidently expected but didn't make it. Where were you?"

Don ignored the question and slouched into the kitchen, calling over his shoulder as he went, "I'm assuming you don't want tea."

Undeterred, Helen tracked him into the small but surprisingly tidy room, which looked like it had rarely, if ever, been cooked in. "I ask because Laura Fell said that she tried to ring you repeatedly but your mobile was off."

"Like I said, it's knackered. I phoned her back later to apologise."

"Why? Were you dating?"

"We had a thing for a while. She used to call me her 'bit of rough'," he said with a barely concealed smirk. "Some women like that."

"Really? Do you enjoy being rough with women, Mr Hart?"

"It was a figure of speech, and not mine."

"I see. Was there any reason you changed your mind about going to the Chill Out that night?"

"I didn't change my mind. I was going but my son got mugged."

Everton appeared in the doorway beside Helen, echoing, "Mugged?"

"Yeah. Some black bastard jacked his mobile."

Everton ignored the dig and said, "Where was this?"

"South Wimbledon. I was on my way to The Telegraph when I got his call."

"You were lucky."

"My son had just got mugged, mate. I don't call that lucky."

"I mean that your mobile was working again."

"You don't believe me, check with him. He'll confirm everything I just told you."

"Of course he will. You whistle and he barks."

Helen couldn't believe the aggressive change of tone in Everton. He seemed to have taken a genuine dislike to Don. She assumed it was because of his sexist remarks about Laura Fell.

"If you're going to be a smartarse, mate, you can piss off out of it. Okay?"

"My pleasure, mate. Give my best to Richie. Be seeing you."

Helen watched Everton go, wondering what in God's name had got into him.

Driving back to the nick, she found out.

"He's lying," growled Everton.

"Yeah, and you weren't exactly subtle about letting him know it."

"Guys like that, you need to rattle their cage a bit."

"Just as long as that's all it was."

"What do you mean by that?"

"Nothing. Do you want to tell me how you know he was lying?"

Everton pulled out a photograph from his inside pocket and said, "I borrowed this from the lounge. It's Hart and his son, Richie."

"So?"

"I know him. Richie didn't get jacked in South Wimbledon. He and his junkie girlfriend were trying to mug a Rasta guy on Wimbledon Ridgway."

"How do you know that?"

"Because I took the shout. The guy fought back and beat the shit out of them. They tried to stitch him up, called us and claimed he attacked them."

"So why would Hart lie about it?"

"I don't know. But he wasn't there. And wherever he was, he wasn't on his way to The Telegraph either."

Lost and found

The number of officers working on the case had grown to nine, and the investigation had been given a formal name: Riverbank. The team – six men and three women – were gathered around Helen, who was updating them on the latest developments.

"We've run a CRO check on Don Hart and he's got form. In 2014 he was involved in a doping ring, targeting dog tracks in the Midlands. He was accused of supplying and administering the drugs used on the greyhounds."

"He was acquitted," corrected Clarke, keen to establish his status in front of the new team.

"Yeah, on a technicality, but he was subsequently banned by the GBOG from any connection with the sport. He's now under investigation again by the Fraud Squad."

"I've spoken to Catford nick. That case is on hold. One of the investigating team battered his wife to death."

"Not a great career move," grunted Teal.

"Yeah. Hart, for the foreseeable future, is unlikely to be charged with anything."

This was unwelcome news to Helen and further proof that Clarke was intent on undermining the missing-women enquiry.

"Don't you think it might have been useful to share that information?"

"I'm sharing it now," replied Clarke, turning towards Teal and directing the rest of his comments to him. "And I've got to be honest, guv, I still don't see how any of this connects Hart to Gina Lewis and the other missing women."

"I'm getting to that," interrupted Helen. "We know that Hart lied about his son being mugged but also, critically, about the time. He maintains that he received a distress call from Richie whilst he was travelling to The Telegraph pub. But if he was travelling at ten thirty he'd have been far too late to meet Laura Fell or any of the others."

Teal turned to Everton, demanding, "You sure of the time?"

"Positive. It was just prior to me getting the shout about Gina Lewis' suicide. I went from the incident on the Ridgway straight there."

"You're suggesting Hart could have been at Gina Lewis' house?"

"It's possible."

"Let me get this straight. You're saying she was murdered and it was made to look like a suicide?" scoffed Clarke. "Because forensics found no sign of a struggle, no bruising or scratches on her body, and the pathologist is one hundred per cent sure that it was suicide."

"I'm aware of that."

"What are you saying? That Hart was there watching her hang herself?"

"I don't know what he was doing there. But what we do know is that Gina Lewis was already dead. The pathologist puts the time of death between nine and nine-thirty pm. And Laura Fell made her 999 call at ten forty-seven, an hour and a quarter later, claiming to have seen someone in the house."

"*Claiming* being the operative word; there was no sign of a break-in or forced entry."

"And we now know why," interjected Helen, holding up an evidence bag containing a silver Chubb key. "We subsequently found this hidden underneath an ornamental boot brush outside the back door. Whoever was in there had no need to break in because he knew there was a key."

"Prints?" said Teal, turning to Teddy, cutting to the chase.

"It's been wiped clean. Like the house. We didn't find a single print apart from hers. In fact, we've found absolutely nothing apart from PC Bowe's feather and we came up blank on that too."

"Okay. Let's assume someone – for the sake of argument, Don Hart – was there *after* Gina Lewis committed suicide. What was he doing?"

"Maybe they were in a relationship?" suggested Jerry Coyle, a boyishly good-looking young DC who'd recently been seconded to the case and was keen to make his mark. "I mean, we know that Hart likes to play the field and it would explain him knowing about the key."

Teal turned a bleak eye on him and said, "I might be old-fashioned, Jerry, but in my day, you didn't invite your lover round and then top yourself before they got there."

The room broke up in laughter.

Teal held up his hand for silence. "Anyone else got any bright ideas?"

No one was willing to risk another theory.

Teal turned back to Helen. "You're the graduate. Enlighten us."

"We think he was looking for something. Gina's laptop and mobile are missing. And we know the mobile was in the house at ten forty-three, because Laura Fell phoned it and she heard it ringing inside."

"That doesn't make sense," countered Clarke. "Hart phoned her fifteen minutes later to apologise for not making the Telegraph meeting."

"He could have done it from inside the house or just after he got out, creating an alibi for himself. He told us he'd broken his mobile, which means, conveniently for him, we can't check."

"Okay," said Teal. "Just for the hell of it, let's go with the theory that Hart took the mobile and the laptop. Why would he do that?"

"Because they both contained incriminating evidence of his and Gina's affair," said Jerry, sticking doggedly to his previous theory.

This time Teal didn't shoot him down. "She topped herself because she was screwing her best friend's boyfriend behind her back and felt guilty. A bit Mills & Boon, but not impossible."

"It would explain why she changed her will and left Laura Fell her house. It was her way of apologising."

"Why didn't she leave a letter explaining it?" Helen challenged. "Hart's not the type of guy to go to all the trouble of stealing a laptop and mobile just to hide the fact he's screwing someone. Especially when his relationship with Laura Fell was on the wane. There's got to be more to it than that."

"Jesus. We're going around in circles," groaned Clarke. "Forget the theories and look at the facts. One: you've got no definitive proof that Hart was actually in the house. Two: therefore, you've got no proof that he actually took anything. Three: and I'm sorry to hark back to my original problem – none of this links in any way to Tessa Hayes or the other missing women."

"Not directly–"

"Exactly," said Clarke, holding up his hands as if resting his case.

"But *one*," retorted Helen. "Hart lied and he knows Gina Lewis. Two: we found a rare feather in Gina's house that's a perfect DNA match for the one found on the blanket with Tessa Hayes. Three: one of the drugs mentioned in Hart's dog-doping trial was Rohypnol, the same drug that was used to incapacitate Tessa Hayes. Four: her mobile and laptop were taken, as were all the other missing women's – including Gina Lewis'."

"It's still all circumstantial."

"*Wait*. There's more. Hart uses online dating sites; he met Laura Fell on one. Hart's changed his mobile number; Tessa Hayes' attacker did the same. Hart has brown hair and wears glasses; the CCTV image we have of the attacker shows him – guess what – with glasses and dark hair. Now you may think that's all just random bullshit but, in my manual, that adds up to something a lot more than circumstantial."

Clarke's challenge had been answered and the group waited in loaded silence for DCI Teal's judgement.

"I'm inclined to agree with her, Jack."

Clarke shrugged and said no more, knowing better than to go publicly against his DCI. Teal turned his attention back to the troop.

"Okay. Let's see if we can join up some of the dots. Get a warrant to search Hart's place and sequester his laptop and mobile phone records."

"Guv. Come on. He was only busted last week by the Fraud Squad."

"Bust him again. Constable Bowe. My office. A word."

Everton, thrown by the sudden change of topic, shot a quizzical look at Helen. She turned aside, pretending not to see it.

"Now please, Bowe."

Everton hauled himself to his feet and trailed after Teal, into his office.

"Close the door. Take a seat."

Everton did as he was ordered.

Teal unwrapped a roll of peppermints and offered Everton one like it was a cigar. "Okay. This is not personal. You're back in uniform."

Everton had sensed that something was coming when Helen had turned away from him in the detective's room. But it still hurt. "Isn't it? Tell me why."

"You and DC Lake have been ruffling the wrong feathers."

"You're talking about Celia Lewis. Oh, come on. This could be a murder investigation and she's hiding something. What was I supposed to do?"

"Use a bit of diplomacy."

"I'm a copper, not a diplomat. I thought you were too."

"You don't like the answer, don't ask the question."

"Christ. You're even beginning to sound like a politician."

"You want to criticise me? Sit on this side of the desk. See how much you like it."

"Be honest. Are you telling me that you wouldn't have done the same thing?"

"No. I'd have done exactly what you did and got shafted too." Everton was taken aback by the weary resignation in his voice as he continued. "Look, putting aside the fact that I don't like you, my hands are tied. I need a fall guy. Someone to appease the powers that be. Or they're going to shut down this investigation."

"Celia Lewis isn't powerful enough to do that."

"Isn't she? The assistant commissioner got a call from the mayor's office. He phoned Borough Commander Walsh. He had a chat with my superintendent. He called me. Had a word in my ear. Now I'm having one in yours – as ordered."

"What about DC Lake? She was there too."

"It was either her or you, and, frankly, she's better than you."

Everton cracked a rueful smile. No matter how much he hated it, he had to admit that there was an inexorable logic to Teal's thinking. "You allow them to bury this case and it will come back and bury you."

"No one's burying anything on my watch."

"DS Clarke will, to save his skin. You'd better not let him."

Teal watched Everton turn and walk out of the door, knowing that it was not an idle threat.

Everton chewed on the cud of his anger and strode out of the detective's office without a backward glance. He was done. Done with the case. Done with the job. Done with being rejected by people he didn't respect. And done with friends who chose their careers over him.

Helen was waiting for him in the corridor. She heard the truculent rhythm of his footsteps before he steamed around the corner.

"Everton. Listen…"

He walked straight past her. Shoved open the swing door to the stairwell and started down the concrete steps two at a time.

Helen followed him, her voice and footsteps echoing as she struggled to catch up. "Everton. Wait–"

"You should have told me."

"He ordered me not to."

"So you're suddenly following orders now, are you? Working with Nobby?"

"Hey! I fought to keep you on board. Okay?"

"Clearly not hard enough."

"Look, they know about me and you. They know about you and Laura Fell."

"They don't know anything about me and Laura, because there's nothing to know."

"Oh, come on. You're too close to her."

"Fuck you, Helen! I was close to you, and look what it got me!"

He banged out of the stairwell through the charge area, hit the exit button, yanked open the door and stalked out into the prisoner's holding cage in the yard.

Helen, doggedly following his footsteps, called after him, "Listen to me! Hoffman has got files on both of us! About me doing a deal to keep my father in care. Your medical condition – that you lied to me about. You crashing our car in Richmond Park and us not reporting it. Teal's trying to protect you."

"No. He's trying to protect *you*. I don't need protecting because I care more about the truth than my career."

It was another low blow, intended to hurt.

It did. Helen took a moment to regain her composure and said simply, "No. You care more about justice. And justice and the law isn't always the same thing, Everton."

It was the truth, but he couldn't admit it. He turned, punched in the exit code for the mesh metal door and watched it grind slowly open. "Good luck with your career, Detective. You've earned it."

He walked out of the cage that had been metaphorically holding him for years, to start the first day of the rest of his life.

* * *

One hundred and ninety-four miles away, Megan Howell was attempting to do the same thing.

The Morgan family were sitting at the window table of the Sticks'n'Sushi restaurant in Swansea, laughing and joking like they hadn't a care in the world. Like one of them hadn't poisoned her dog. Sian was eating sashimi sea bass, her favourite dish, with chopsticks. Megan watched her from her car, parked on the other side of the street, deftly placing the pieces of fish into her mouth; remembering their laughter when she'd first taught her how to use them.

There were four of them at the table. Her perma-tanned, cruise-loving mother and father, who picked at the delicate food with forks and would have preferred a smarter venue to celebrate their daughter's eighteenth birthday if the circumstances were different. Her barrel-chested rugby-prop brother, Idris, who Megan knew of old - she'd seen him pissing on her front lawn, and mooning at her when she complained.

Sian knew nothing of the abuse, of course, and Megan hadn't told her. She was just an innocent, unwittingly caught up in it and now its consequence. Megan knew she'd never have hurt Gabriel Oak. Sian loved him and Bathsheba. She'd taken them for walks in Victoria Park and let them sleep in bed with them on their stolen afternoons in her parent's home.

No, she knew the guilty party, and whether he was being encouraged by his parents didn't matter; he was going to pay for them all. Not content with driving her out of Swansea, they'd now killed her dog and driven her out of London. Well, enough was enough. She was tired of being punished. Tired of being afraid to answer her phone or open her emails. Sick of the blood-speckled bile that she hacked from her stomach every morning. She would show them that there were consequences to their actions.

She'd cleared her rented flat of everything she could carry. Made three journeys by cab to the Yellow Box storage facility is New Malden and deposited her belongings. Closed her NatWest bank account and transferred the money into an online Instant Cash ISA. Telling no one, she caught the overnight National Express coach from Victoria to Swansea. It was a long, three-and-a-half-hour journey down the M4 corridor and across the Severn Estuary into Wales, but it gave her time to think, to formulate a plan.

She booked into the Travelodge on Princess Way and slept fitfully, Bathsheba on the bed beside her, until lunchtime. She spent an hour haggling before buying a second-hand Polo for cash from a backstreet dealership. She didn't have time for lunch, so she bought a tasteless tuna sandwich, water, dog food, barbecue fluid and a Zippo lighter from a Tesco Express.

It was almost three thirty when she parked up a discreet distance from the fancy wrought-iron gates of her old school to wait for the end-of-day bell. The caretaker opened Abigail's Gate – named after a former pupil and gifted to the school by her bereaved parents – and the Day Girls filed out. They spilled noisily out into the road and disappeared into the Range Rovers and SUVs that waited impatiently, engines running, to make their escapes.

Megan eased down in her seat and wrapped her scarf around her face, so as not to be recognised. She hoped that Sian, prompted by her parents, had reverted into a Day Girl after the abuse scandal. She was right. Sian's mother, Bethan, cruised past in her BMW X6 and double-honked at Sian as she appeared through the gates. Megan thought that Sian looked thin, but she appeared happy enough, joking with her classmates before she manoeuvred through the convoy of SUVs to climb in beside her mother and kiss her on her proffered cheek.

Megan groaned to herself as she remembered a different kind of kissing, of wet tongues and slippery saliva, and warm flesh and soft curves that opened... She watched them drive away through the expensive traffic.

She knew where they'd be going. She once spent a weekend in Sian's palatial home in East Cliff when her parents were away watching her brother's rugby tour. She and Sian swam naked in the pool and drank expensive bottles of Barolo from her father's spiral wine cellar, hidden underneath the Italian marble floor of the kitchen.

She watched Sian disappear behind the electronic gates of the red-brick mansion and settled down with Bathsheba and the other half of her tuna sandwich to wait. Three hours later the family reappeared in a black Mini Cooper, driven by an excited Sian. It had a red ribbon tied in a bow around the roof aerial.

And now, she sat opposite it and them, waiting, as they celebrated. Forty minutes later, still laughing and joking, the family made their way out. Idris shook hands with his father, gave his mother and sister dutiful pecks on the cheek and set off – she imagined to meet up with his drinking buddies. She waited for Sian's Mini to disappear, clipped a leather lead to Bathsheba's collar, picked up her Tesco bag and climbed out of her car to follow him.

The windswept street was dark and empty. But Idris walked confidently, secure in his physical presence. She followed him, observing him from a safe distance, hoping that he wouldn't disappoint her. He picked up his pace as she crossed the road. She did the same but stayed on her side, walking parallel to him, twenty metres behind. Bathsheba dragged against the lead, complaining about not being allowed to loiter and mark her new-found territory. Megan ignored her. She couldn't afford to lose sight of her prey, not now she was so close.

"He's looking for change," she muttered to Bathsheba as she watched Idris pause mid-step and begin rifling through his khaki chino pockets. "He's going to do it."

Almost as if he'd heard her, Idris turned and checked the street behind him. She slipped into a shop doorway and waited for him to move off again. She could see where he was going now. The red public phone box drew him inexorably to it. And to his fate.

Idris hauled open the heavy door and stepped inside. It smelt of stale urine and curry. He placed a pile of twenty-pence pieces on the graffiti-scarred plastic shelf beside the phone. He fed in the coins one by one. Satisfied he had enough credit for his purpose, he punched in the London code. He knew the number by heart and knew she wouldn't answer even if she was in. What he didn't know was that she was standing five feet behind him with a plastic bottle of barbecue fluid and a lighter in her hands.

She was surprised that the flames took so quickly. The lighter lit up the barbecue fluid like he was a straw guy on a bonfire. She wondered if the confined space held the vapour in place, adding to its efficacy, but she didn't hold the door shut long – he was too strong and his shrill screams would draw attention. Just long enough to enjoy the look on his face when he realised who she was.

Then, she turned and walked briskly away with Bathsheba at her heels, content in the knowledge that her tormentor's rugby-playing days were over.

* * *

Everton Bowe groaned, stepped out of the shower, relit a spliff that was resting on the side of the sink and took another hit from the half-bottle of Mount Gay beside it. His mind was reeling and he needed something to take the edge off.

Why did the rejection hurt so much? He'd been rejected before. Christ, his whole career had been one long rejection; he should have been used to it by now. And why did he feel so disappointed in Helen? She was a realist. She'd done the pragmatic thing and saved her career. He'd sacrificed his, like the idiot he'd always been, for his ideals. So what if Laura Fell had been involved with a scumbag like Hart? She wasn't perfect. Why had he put her on a pedestal and been so disappointed when she'd fallen off? She didn't owe him anything and he wasn't her moral guardian. Helen was right. He'd allowed himself to get too close to her, to feel for her, and he wasn't good with feelings. Like his mother used to say, "You make your decisions and you don't bleat about the consequences."

He took a last toke on the spliff and flushed it down the lavatory, watching it swirl around the bowl like a tiny canoe caught in a whirlpool, disappearing to God knows where. It reminded him of watching Richie Hart's blood dripping down the drain, like a bad metaphor for his career. How long ago was that? It seemed like years but it couldn't have been more than a couple of weeks.

He was getting cold and reached for a towel on the chrome radiator. As he did so, the room shifted ninety degrees on its axis and he tipped forward, cracking his head on the edge of the sink. He came around moments later with warm rivulets of blood running across his face and onto the white-cotton bath mat. *Shit*, he thought. *That's going to stain.* He groaned and got gingerly to his feet, easing the blood-soaked mat into the shower with his foot and turning the faucet on to soak it. For a second, he debated getting back under to wash the blood from himself, then realised he'd be staining the rug again. *Fuck*, he thought. *I'm going to...*

He awoke on the floor, took a deep breath, reached slowly up and grabbed the edge of the sink. Hauling himself up, he leant over the bowl and turned on the cold-water tap, letting it run across his face to clean the gaping wound bridging his nose. The pressure wasn't great with the shower on, but it was still enough to make him wince. He glanced up into the mirror but his eyes refused to focus and the more he tried the more the room began to swim. Even in his confused state, he knew that his nose was broken and that he'd need stitches. But there was no way he could get to the front door, let alone drive. And there was absolutely no way that he was calling an ambulance, Helen or – God forbid – his wife. He fumbled for the bottle of Mount Gay, staggered into his bedroom and collapsed onto the bed.

He finally came to in the Brodie ward of St. George's Hospital after being in and out of consciousness for three hours.

He'd been found by his downstairs neighbour, a truculent Polish guy he'd barely ever spoken to; who had found water cascading through his ceiling and raced upstairs to remonstrate with Everton. Getting no response, he raced downstairs again to phone Thames Water for advice – a futile gesture – and found half his ceiling on his kitchen floor. One kick from his steel-capped boot had smashed Everton's front door clean off its hinges. He found the shower still running on the bath mat, which was blocking the plug hole and flooding the floor, and Everton sprawled comatose on the blood-soaked bed, the bottle of Mount Gay rum beside him. Thinking he was drunk, he tried to shake him awake but finally realised that he was unconscious and called an ambulance.

The medics sent him for bloods and a CT scan. The scan revealed nothing but the bloods showed high levels of HTC and alcohol in his system. They therefore deduced that his injuries – a fractured nose and a zygomatic hairline fracture to his left cheekbone – were most likely caused by a fall whilst he was under the influence of drugs and/or alcohol. But when they checked his medical records they found the extenuating cause: he was suffering from Meniere's Disease, a disorder of the inner ear that affected both hearing and balance.

He learnt from a baby-faced Filipino nurse that his wife and son had been to see him whilst he was unconscious. The nurse promised Pauline not to tell him, but she thought Everton ought to know. After she left the room, he groaned, remembering how much love he'd let go from his life, especially Adam's. How, as a child, his son taught him what unconditional love was - the joy of giving and receiving it - and as a teenager had withdrawn it and in doing so hurt himself as much as Everton. Everton wanted to believe that his visit was a sign of better things to come.

He had another visitor too. DCI Teal arrived with a cacti and jokey card from Helen that read: *from one prickly customer to another*; which he knew was her attempt at an apology. Teal didn't stay long but ordered him to take a week's sick leave and informed him that he'd be backing his claim for early retirement on health grounds. Everton bit his tongue, aware that Teal would have been informed about his incriminating blood tests.

He heard nothing from Laura Fell and assumed she hadn't been told of his accident.

That wasn't the case. Helen had phoned her, ostensibly to let her know Everton would no longer be working on the investigation, but also to gauge her reaction to the news that he was in hospital and might be taking early retirement. Laura asked her to pass on her best wishes, but nothing more. A relief for Helen, since it confirmed her suspicion that Everton's feelings weren't reciprocated and vindicated her axing him from the investigation.

* * *

Laura's apparent lack of concern wasn't born out of indifference but the fact that her own life had skewed on its axis.

She was walking up to the door of Pitt Hancock Solicitors in Isleworth and quite literally bumped into Kieron Allen, who had evidently been delivering some legal documents about proof of his identity. He recognised her immediately and introduced himself as Gina's brother. Laura was stunned. She'd known Gina nearly twenty years yet had never heard her or her family speak of a brother. Kieron told her that there was a reason for that and if she had time he'd like to explain.

They walked the couple of hundred metres to the London Apprentice, a Georgian pub overlooking the Thames. Kieron insisted on buying a pot of tea and rock cakes. They sat outside under one of the heated awnings, Kieron feeding the swans and mallard ducks with crumbs as he tentatively told his and Gina's story.

"Eighteen months ago, I saw an advert placed by a woman called Amy Tann in my local newspaper. Actually, you may have read about her in the *Evening Standard* recently…?"

Laura shook her head, not realising that she'd skipped over the sensational headline, whilst searching for news of Gina's funeral:

Met detective MURDERER

"Well, anyway, that's another sad story," Kieron continued. "She runs – ran – a tracing agency which finds and reconnects estranged families."

"You mean like adopted children looking for their real parents?"

"Their birth parents, yes. The ad said she was seeking information about Jennifer Allen, my mother, and her daughter, Gina."

"Are you saying that Gina was adopted?"

"Yes, when she was a few days old. My mother had split up from my father. She couldn't cope."

"But… she never said anything to me or anyone."

"She didn't know until recently. And when she found out, Mrs Lewis swore her to secrecy before she would give her the name of her real mother. She'd never told her and didn't want it to come out."

"But why?"

"I don't know. I only met them a couple of times. The family didn't want anything to do with me. I think Mrs Lewis was concerned about her career and the press. Gina and I had to meet in secret."

"How did Gina find out about being adopted?"

"Her father, Gordon, had a car accident. He lost control and crashed into a parked car."

"I know, said Laura. "He's been in a wheelchair ever since."

"What you don't know is that he was drunk. He was breathalysed but it got hushed up. He never even went to court."

"How?"

"Mrs Lewis has powerful connections. Gina was in the front with her so-called father…" Laura was confused, *what was he implying,* but before she could interrupt Kieron continued, "and they both needed blood transfusions. But when the blood labelled G Lewis arrived, meant for him – Gordon – it was given to Gina by mistake."

"Wouldn't that have been dangerous?"

"It could have been. Fortunately, the registrar realised the mistake and stopped the transfusion. But later Gina noticed that something else seemed to be bothering him. He was reluctant to explain, probably frightened about getting sued, but eventually told her that there must have been a mistake with her blood typing. Because her blood was AB rhesus negative, which is extremely rare, but her fathers was an O+DD type and quite common."

"I don't understand. What does that mean?"

"That genetically, Gordon couldn't have been her real father."

"God. But that must have been devastating for Gina."

"She said she felt like she'd been living a lie for thirty-eight years."

"What about you? Did you know that you had a sister?"

"I only found out the truth three years ago; my mother told me before she died. She said it was the biggest regret of her life, giving Gina up."

"And you eventually found her. How lucky was that?"

"Yes. I'd been made redundant. If I hadn't been looking through the job adverts that day, I would never have known."

He took out his wallet and carefully extracted a neatly folded piece of newspaper with an ad highlighted in yellow. It read:

Lost and Found

"Is this the name of the tracing agency? Lost and Found?"

"Yes. Ironic, don't you think? She was lost and found and now she's lost again, forever." He picked up the remains of his cake, lobbed it into the river and watched it slowly sink below the brown water. "No wonder they call it a rock cake."

Neither of them smiled at his bleak joke. Laura refilled their cups with the tepid tea and they sat in silence, watching the tiny dace voraciously attacking the cake, now suspended three inches beneath the surface. Laura finally broke the silence.

"Do you know why... she did it?"

"No. Amy, the tracing agent, said she suffered from depression. But I never saw it. She always seemed so happy whenever we were together."

"She was taking lithium," said Laura, as if in explanation.

"Lithium? No way."

"She was. She said she shouldn't have been prescribed it and was going to come off it."

Kieron appeared genuinely shocked, and said, fighting to hold back his anger, "Lithium is what they give schizophrenics. My sister was *not* a schizophrenic!"

"I'm not saying she was," said Laura, touched by his defence of his sister but needing to make him understand the truth. "But I think she may have been borderline bipolar. She was prone to mood swings... Maybe she was depressed that night and–"

"It's because of me, is that what you're saying?"

"No. No, she was obviously desperate to find her real parents – and you. I think it was more likely to have been caused by her " mother's" reaction. Mrs Lewis, you know yourself, isn't an easy woman. She can be controlling. Gina fought against it all her life."

Kieron took a blister pack of Nurofen from his pocket and popped a couple into the palm of his hand, washing them down with the dregs of his tea. "Sorry. I shouldn't have snapped at you like that. I know you're upset too."

"The Lewis' are threatening to sue me."

"What? Why would they do that?"

"Gina changed her will the day that she died. She left everything to me. The house, her car, everything. Now her parents are contesting the will and the police are investigating."

"The police? What have they got to do with it?"

"I was outside Gina's house the night that... she died. I thought I saw someone inside and phoned the police."

"Inside? Did you recognise them?"

"No. It was just a shadow. A man, I think. We discovered that some things were missing from the house: Gina's laptop and mobile."

"Have they found them?"

"No. But the thing is, I kept ringing Gina's mobile and a man answered and then the line went dead."

"Are you saying that this man might have had something to do with Gina's death?"

"No – I don't know. None of it makes any sense. The police are sure she took her own life but now they think there could be some connection to some other cases."

Kieron looked totally nonplussed. "I'm sorry. I don't understand."

"Neither do I. Any of it… I just want it to be over. It's been a nightmare. I've lost my job, my friends and worst of all Gina."

Laura missed her appointment at the solicitors. She phoned and apologised, explaining that she hadn't been well, which was a lie. She spent the rest of the afternoon with Kieron in the nearby grounds of Syon House, a two hundred-acre oasis of lakes and parkland created by Capability Brown in the eighteenth century. Wandering amongst the ancient oaks in the arboretum, they shared their memories of Gina. Kieron was a good listener, something he told her that he'd learnt from experience as a care worker and prided himself upon, and for the first time in weeks Laura felt comfortable about openly sharing her fears.

They were in the Butterfly House, marvelling at the myriads of species that floated like delicate aimless angels and then homed in on any new splash of colour. Laura's blonde hair and cherry nails were covered in them, much to the delight of Kieron who insisted on taking a video on his mobile.

"Do you know why they're called butterflies?"

"Is it something to do with what they eat?"

"No. But interestingly, they actually taste with their feet."

Laura pulled a face, not sure she liked the sound of something tasting her hair, and brushed one gently away from the vermillion balm on her lips. "This one's getting a bit too friendly."

"It's the bright colours. It thinks you're a flower."

It took her a moment to realise that he wasn't just relaying information; he was paying her a compliment. She wasn't sure how to respond so merely smiled. Kieron looked abashed and changed the subject. "It's looking for nectar. So, the name. Believe it or not they were actually known as Flutterbys until someone got the words mixed up. Flutterby became butterfly and it stuck."

Laura laughed out loud and said, "That's a lovely story, but I'm not sure it's true."

"Who knows." He shrugged. "But I like it. Actually, and this is true, some psychics call them 'angel calling cards'."

"You can see why, looking at them."

"You know my favourite? The Clouded August Thorn. Isn't that a beautiful name?"

"Yes. What does it look like?"

"Like it sounds. Gorgeous. We used to have them in our garden. Clouded Augusts, Clouded Yellows."

Laura felt a slight but unmistakable pang at hearing *we*, signifying that there was someone else in his life, and immediately felt embarrassed by her insensitivity. He seemed to sense something was amiss and felt obliged to explain. "I'm divorced. She liked gardening. I like wildlife. You?"

"Oh," said Laura, momentarily thrown by the directness of his question. "Proudly single. But like Gina used to say, I'm willing to be convinced otherwise – and now I come to think of it, she loved butterflies too."

Kieron smiled and held his mobile up for her to view the video. She stood close to him, shielding the screen from the light as she watched it. He caught the scent of spring flowers from her White Linen perfume and pushed the thought of anything more intimate from his mind.

"If you put in your number I'll send it to you."

"Great," she replied, happy that he'd asked, and typed it into his mobile.

* * *

DS Clarke wasn't overly concerned about Megan Howell's apparent disappearance. There was no sign of foul play and nothing out of place in the flat apart from a pair of women's panties on the sofa. It looked to him like Megan had removed any personal items, including her clothes, and just locked up and left. Possibly prompted by the death of her dog, which had clearly eaten something poisonous.

DCI Teal ordered him to run a check with Megan's bank and informed him that from now on he'd personally be overseeing the missing-women case. And that he expected Clarke's total support, whatever they uncovered. Clarke knew that he'd been shown a yellow card and that he would have to tread softly.

He intercepted Helen on her way out of the detective's room and asked if he could buy her a coffee and have a chat to clear the air. Helen was reluctant but Clarke seemed to genuinely want to build bridges and she was smart enough to realise she'd be better off, him working with her rather than against her. She decided to give him the benefit of her very large doubt.

Clarke knew the manager of Maison St. Cassien, a tiny cafe on the corner of Church Road in the heart of Wimbledon Village that served a spectacular brunch, and suggested they walk up for some exercise. Helen was surprised to learn that he was in training for the London marathon, having once toyed with the idea of entering it herself, and agreed.

On the trek up Wimbledon Hill they made small talk about his training regime and the charity he was running for, the Alzheimer's Society, in honour of his mother who'd died from it, which struck a chord with Helen because of her father's condition. For the first time, she saw Clarke as a real person, with genuine fears and feelings, rather than an obstacle to her career, so much so that she even offered to sponsor him.

She had no idea that Clarke was lying. Not about running the marathon, but who he was running for. He signed up for Guide Dogs for the Blind but learnt from his ex-detective mate Brian Hoffman about her father's illness so decided to use it to his advantage.

They sat at the rear of the cafe and ate tortilla melts and salad, Clarke's favourite dish, whilst they chatted about the case. He admitted he'd been defensive, concerned about being made a fall guy, but insisted he'd had a change of heart, realising now that the only way to stop it happening to another woman was to help solve the case. Helen agreed to wipe the slate clean as long as he accepted her absolute authority when it came to running the investigation and the team. Clarke conceded and began filling her in on the circumstances concerning Megan Howell's disappearance, informing her that any connection between Megan, Gina Lewis and the other missing women was probably coincidental. Helen wasn't entirely convinced but agreed they should put it on the back-burner and concentrate on the investigation into Don Hart. The second search of his house had revealed absolutely nothing. Not even a trace of weed – which was odd considering the previous drug-related convictions of his son. Plus, they'd drawn a blank on his phone records and his brief was demanding his release and making threatening noises about police harassment.

* * *

With only six hours remaining in which to either charge or release him, Helen finally bit the bullet and agreed to let Clarke sit in on her interview with Don Hart; reminding him that she was taking the lead.

"You gave us a false alibi for the night of Gina Lewis' death."

"I refute that."

"My client has an independent witness that will confirm his alibi, Detective."

"I'd hardly call his son independent, Mr. Shelby."

"Not just his son, Kelly Holland, who was also a victim of the mugging."

Helen, knowing that another witness, albeit an unreliable one, spelt trouble, altered her line of attack. "Not forgetting that Miss Holland has convictions for petty theft and aggravated robbery, let's move on. Do you recognise this woman?"

She nodded to Clarke, who produced a photograph of Tessa Hayes from a manila folder and placed it on the table in front of Don.

"No."

Helen nodded to Clarke again. He produced a second photograph from the folder and placed it alongside the first.

"No."

Another photograph appeared and, with Don's negative response, another. Don barely glanced at them but Helen could see from the tiny tell-tale movement of his Adam's apple that he was nervous.

"Aren't you interested in who they are?" she queried, leaning forward, her elbows on the table as she scrutinized Don's implacable face.

"Not particularly. I'm sure you're going to tell me eventually."

Helen held up the photos one by one as she went methodically through the list. "This is Kate Holmes. She's forty-four years old and was first reported missing on 6 September 2016; now presumed dead. This is Francis Cole, forty-six, reported missing 11 December 2017; now presumed dead. Barbara Crane, also forty-six, missing since 21 May 2018 and also now presumed dead. And this last lady, Tessa Hayes, is not missing but she was drugged, abducted, assaulted and dumped in a river, on 8 November. The night you have no alibi for."

"I have no idea who these women are or what you're talking about."

"You're going to have to do better than that, mate," interjected Clarke.

"My client has provided you with an alibi, Sergeant. Badgering him will not alter the fact."

Clarke ignored Shelby and leant in next to Helen, physically forming a united front to further pressurise Don, and said bluntly, "Do you use online dating sites?"

"No," replied Don, unconsciously shifting back in his seat and away from the pressure.

"That's odd. Because Laura Fell told my colleague that you met her on one. Are you saying she's lying?"

Don swallowed the bile rising in his throat and said nothing.

"Playing dumb is not going to help you," said Clarke. "Forensics have been going through your laptop."

Shelby, keeping his head and mouth away from the prying eyes of the police, whispered to Don, "Do not say another word."

Clarke waited patiently for the interplay to finish and said, "Well?"

"Sergeant," interrupted Shelby. "Bearing in mind the seriousness of these new allegations, I'd like to request a short recess so that I can confer with my client in private?"

Clarke turned obediently toward Helen for her approval. She thought about it, cracked a crooked smile and said, "Confer away. But let me make myself clear, 'no comment' is not going to cut it. We're looking for a serial killer and your client's in the frame. He's not going anywhere until I get some straight answers."

Don was allowed out into the prisoner yard for a comfort break. Something of a misnomer, considering his mood as he paced the perimeter walls like a caged animal. Shelby watched him with growing disquiet. He was a man with no moral qualms about representing drug dealers, thieves or fraudsters. He wasn't concerned with whether his clients were guilty or innocent. He wasn't naive – he knew that the majority of them were compulsive liars who preyed on their victim's weaknesses – but they were entitled to a defence in a court of law and, for a price, he provided it. The jury was the final arbiter of their guilt or innocence. Besides, since he privately reviled his clients, it didn't much matter to him whether they won or lost. However, he drew a deep line in the legal sand when it came to attacks on women. His own daughter had been beaten senseless by her junkie husband and lost the child she was carrying. He walked away with a two-year suspended sentence on the proviso that he attended a residential addiction centre. Three weeks later he disappeared to Kerala in southern India. It had cost Shelby three grand for justice to be finally served by three men with bamboo canes who administered a dozen lashes to his genitals. It gave him some comfort to think that he would never abuse another woman, but it wouldn't bring his grandson back or ease his daughter's grief. So, listening to Don Hart vent about "DC cock-sucker Lake" filled him with grave misgivings.

"I need to know where you were when this Tessa Hayes got attacked, and it better be the truth or I'm walking out of here right now."

"Fuck off. You can't walk out on me. I'm your client."

"I choose who I represent and I don't choose to represent men who murder women. Now, I want the truth – and don't give me that bullshit about being with your son either."

"Okay. Look," he said, lowering his voice and gesturing Shelby aside from the inquisitive eye of the CCTV camera. "It wasn't me. I was with Harry Bellows, busting a bookie in Tottenham. One of the cashiers got hurt."

"How badly?"

"Bad. Harry shot him with a taser. The guy went into convulsions and had a heart attack."

"What the hell was he doing with a taser?"

"He thought it would be safer than a gun."

"I do not believe this."

"It gets worse. It was Harry's own shop we were turning over."

"It was an insurance scam and he shot his own cashier?"

"He wanted to make it look authentic. We've done three in the last six months, all owned by Harry. The idea was to make it look like a rival bookie was muscling in on his turf."

"If that cashier dies, he's going to be facing a murder charge and you're an accessory."

"I know."

"So, you're going to risk getting charged with multiple homicides, crimes you say you didn't commit, to conceal a crime you did?"

"What else can I do? Anyway, they're not going to be able to prove I touched any of those women, because I didn't. I was nowhere near them."

"Yeah, the only trouble is, you can't prove that, can you?"

* * *

Later that day, DS Clarke received a breakdown from forensics on what they'd found on Hart's laptop hard drive. Its history revealed hits on some desultory porn sites and a number on a dating site called PlentyMoreFish.com. Helen's hopes were momentarily raised but a closer investigation of the user profile that Hart had uploaded revealed a photograph of himself and his real contact details. An hour later, she was forced to release him from custody.

The following day, Shelby received a DHS delivery from Don. It was a presentation box containing a twelve-year-old bottle of Scotch and a card saying that his services were no longer required. Shelby was relieved that at least they'd parted on good terms and later opened the bottle to toast a successful outcome.

It was not a twelve-year-old malt but urine.

* * *

Colin Gould had taken a few days off from St. Mary's on compassionate leave and spent the time trawling through Facebook, hacking into the private messages of Iris Costa and Freida Cole about Megan's sudden disappearance and the death of her dog. Theories had been offered and discounted, but ultimately only one person knew the real truth: Colin himself.

His strategy worked more perfectly than he could have imagined. He intended to hurt Megan, the way she'd done when she ridiculed him and banned him from the meetings. He wanted to make her experience the deep sense of loss that he had felt over Gina. But, coward that she was, she'd packed her bags and run at the first sign of trouble. Well, good riddance. The group was now free of her domineering arrogance and would be the better for it.

He phoned Iris, the font of all gossip, and professed his shock when she told him the news. Colin was stunned to learn that the police had arrested Don Hart. Surely, they couldn't believe there was any connection between the poisoning of Megan's dog and him? That would be too fortuitous. *God*, he thought. *I'd have loved to have seen the supercilious smile wiped off his smug face as they dragged him out still protesting his innocence.*

He lowered himself into his captain's chair, his forty-fifth birthday present to himself, and opened the iPad lying beside the diary on his mahogany desk. He powered it up, tapped the photo icon, typed in a password and opened a folder labelled

"Friends", then began flipping through the images: Gina and himself, Hart and Laura, Hart and Gina, Megan and her naked Brazilian girlfriend, and finally the body of Gabriel Oak. The dog he'd poisoned.

It reminded him of his "warm kills" at the tax office, but this time it had been for real, and it filled him with a warm and profound pleasure.

* * *

DC Jerry Coyle, being the newest recruit to the missing women case, was tasked with collecting the breakfast orders. He'd made the trek to the canteen on the third floor, struggled back with a precariously balanced tray of teas, coffees and rolls and was doling them out when DCI Teal strode out of his office.

"Give me one of them."

Heads turned. Everyone on the unit knew that Teal's heart condition prohibited him from eating anything fatty or fried.

"What about the diet, guv?" chided Clarke, wary of getting his head bitten off.

"It went AWOL with Don Hart."

"Guv–"

"Alright! Bugger it. Take the bacon out and just give me the roll."

Coyle removed the bacon from his roll and handed it over.

Teal held it to his nose, savouring the lard aroma like it was a fine wine, and bit into the bread. "Okay," he said, through a mouthful of crust. "Who was tailing Hart?"

KR, a bearded copper who looked a bit like Kenny Rogers, hence the moniker, placed his pork sausage sandwich aside and held up his hand. "Me and Tony, guv. He got a cab back to his house on Seeley Road and never moved for the rest of the day."

"You reckon he clocked you?"

"Could have. He's pretty cute. I stayed on until 2am and Tony subbed me. He's there now. There's been no comings or goings apart from Hart's son, Richie."

"And there won't be," said Clarke. "If it's him, he's just going to go to ground and wait us out."

"You got a better idea, Jack? Let's hear it."

"Helen reckons we should bring in a forensic profiler."

"We're coppers, not psychologists – and before you start, Helen, I know you've got some sort of degree in it or something."

"Guv," said Helen, dropped into the fray by Clarke and now forced to defend herself. "The attack on Tessa Hayes was peculiar. Not just the shaving of her body hair but because we still don't know why or if he let her go. If we had some sort of offender profile it might be possible to compare it to Hart."

"No way. We don't need another Rachel Nickell. The press will crucify us and it'll never stand up in court."

"No, but it would stop us wasting valuable man hours on Hart if we don't have to," said Clarke.

"Well, well, what happened to Mr Sceptical?"

Clarke grinned ruefully and held up his hands in mock surrender.

Helen, sensing a weakening in Teal's opposition, pressed home her advantage. "Jack's right. We know nothing about the missing women apart from that they're all of similar ages and that they were all using online dating sites. But Tessa Hayes we do know something about–"

"Except she can't remember a bloody thing."

"Yeah, but we know he drugged her and shaved her, guv. A profiler may be able to compare the MO to people who have committed similar crimes. Also, Tessa Hayes wasn't raped, which is odd…"

"Okay. Okay. Do it. But I don't want to read a word about this in the press. Understand? Moving on. Any other good news?"

"I've contacted all of Harts' potential matches on the PlentyMoreFish website. He appears to have only met one woman so far and she reckons that she had a pleasant evening," said a muscular-looking female PC standing at the rear, eating a fat-free yoghurt.

"That would seem to indicate that it's not him," moaned Teal.

"Why would he lie about his whereabouts on the night of Gina Lewis' death?" countered Helen.

"Exactly," agreed Clarke. "He's got to be hiding something, guv."

Helen pulled out a sheaf of printed papers and began handing them around as she explained, "We know he was playing the field. We also found a number of suggestive emails on the laptop. You'll see that these are between Hart and Iris Costa, another member of the group."

"You reckon he might have been sleeping with her too?"

"It would appear so."

"Okay. Have a word with her."

"Also, if you check sheets four and five you'll see there's a number of unflattering references to a Colin Gould. I've highlighted them."

"Who the hell is Colin Gould?"

"He's the only other regular male member of the group. And, interestingly, he was missing on the night in question too."

"Did you run a PCR check on him?"

"Yeah, he's clean," replied Helen. "But Hart clearly has a problem with him. You can see he refers to him as 'creepy'."

* * *

Everton's wife, Pauline, was waiting for him at the top of the stairs with the keys to his newly installed front door.

"Welcome home," she said as she ceremoniously handed them over.

Everton was a bit thrown. He'd only been out of hospital for forty minutes and was still wearing a plastic nose guard, with two strips of micropore tape holding it in place, across his swollen face, which made the whole episode feel slightly surreal.

"Thank you," he said, mumbling through a nose full of wadding. "It looks great... Sorry you had all the hassle."

"I've left some groceries for you on the kitchen table."

"Oh. Right… Money… Let me give you some money."

"Do it later. The receipt's in the bag."

Everton opened the front door and Pauline followed him inside. The flat was pristine; she'd obviously cleaned up. He walked into the bedroom. The bed linen had been freshly laundered and the bed remade.

"Thanks for doing the laundry."

"I didn't. It was covered in blood and puke. I threw it out and bought you some new sheets. The invoice is in the grocery bag."

Everton smiled ruefully and made his way back into the lounge, calling to Pauline, who was now busying herself and unpacking the groceries in the kitchen, "You don't have to do that."

"I know. I'm trying to be nice. Most people are if you give them a chance."

There it was again, the thorn on the rose. She couldn't help herself.

"I meant you've done enough already."

"I know what you meant."

Shit, he thought. *Even after all these years she doesn't miss a thing.*

"*I* was merely pointing out that cops, unfortunately, don't get to see the best in people."

"And journalists do?"

"Occasionally, but they make less interesting stories. Speaking of which, the Lewis family…"

She walked back in, picked up her shoulder bag, opened it, took out sheaf of official-looking printed papers and said, "You may want to sit down."

Everton made himself comfortable on the sofa. Pauline sat beside him and began laying out the documentary evidence one by one as she spoke. "Mrs Lewis evidently contracted an STD, chlamydia, and it affected her fertility. Gina was not their birth daughter. She was adopted as a baby–"

"Whoa. Wait a minute. How do you know that?"

"I bribed a guy to hack into the hospital records department. There was evidently a mix-up with some blood samples after a car accident involving Gina and her father. He was driving drunk. It looks like it got hushed up."

"Gina found out after the crash that she was adopted?"

"Yes. Her real mother was a woman called Jennifer Allen. Gina was born 4 September 1980 in Southampton and almost immediately given up for adoption. The birth certificate doesn't have the father's name."

"Interesting."

"I know. Anyway, it looks like Gina was trying to find her birth mother."

"And it really screwed up her relationship with her adoptive mother."

"Yes. Celia was desperate to keep it quiet – and before you ask, I know because both of them were seeing psychiatrists and it's in the hacked transcripts of their meetings."

"Isn't that unethical?"

"Totally. Do you want me to stop?"

Everton said nothing.

"They were both on medication. Gina was on lithium for the last sixteen years."

"Why didn't it show up in the post-mortem results?"

"Ask the pathologist, not me. She'd been weaning herself off, against her psychiatrist's advice, for the last four months. My guess is that it tipped her over the edge – another reason for Celia Lewis to try and keep a lid on it. Plus, she's on anti-depressant's herself: Seroxat and Valium."

"Jesus. The accident really fucked up their lives."

"Yeah, and not just the two of them. Gordon Lewis now has an AA sponsor, not that he ever appears to attend meetings."

"Wow. The newspapers would die for a story like this."

"I know. I'm writing it."

"Not yet." Everton picked up the hacked files, knelt and began laying them out on the floor, like a screenwriter trying to find the narrative thread in his story. "This gives us a motive for the Lewis' taking Gina's laptop and mobile. There may have been something incriminating on them – photos or texts – but we still don't know who was actually in the house on the night Gina died."

"You said it was a man, so it would have had to have been her father."

"It couldn't have been Gordon Lewis. He's wheelchair bound." He began rifling in Pauline's bag and pulled out a pen.

"Feel free. Help yourself."

Everton wasn't listening. The investigation was opening up, he could feel it. He just didn't know how to slot into place the pieces of information yet. "I need you to find out everything you can about this man," he said, scribbling a name onto a scrap of paper ripped from one of the files and handing it to Pauline. "His name's Brian Hoffman. He's ex-Met, a DCI. He now works as security for Celia Lewis. But be careful, he's still very connected."

"Hey. I've done my bit. You're the cop, do it yourself."

"I can't. I may not be a cop for much longer."

Pauline was stopped in her tracks. "Don't tell me they're going to offer you early retirement on medical grounds?"

"It's more of an ultimatum than an offer. I've got seven days to accept it or it's a disciplinary hearing and dismissal."

"What? Why?"

"My blood tests revealed drugs in my system. Someone informed DCI Teal."

"Detective Constable Helen Lake?"

"Who knows? Anyway, as you're aware, I'm not his favourite person."

"Everton. For once in your life, don't be stupid. Forget the case. Forget the lousy job. Take early retirement and the cash and get on with the rest of your life."

"Are you making tea?"

"Is that a way of telling me to mind my own business?"

"We're getting divorced, Pauline."

"You're right. It's your life. Ruin it." She disappeared into the kitchen, biting back her frustration.

Everton eased off his jacket and sat on the floor, lost in thought, as he perused the innocuous-looking printed papers that charted the wreckage of three other lives.

Epiphany

Colin Gould's first day back at St. Mary's University turned out to be eventful. The Victorian central-heating system had grumbled to a halt and he was forced to hold his lectures in an overcoat and gloves, whilst his students huddled around two industrial blow-heaters for warmth.

Colin hated the cold. He suffered from pneumonia as a child, the result of an ex-army father who never settled into civilian life and expected his family to embrace his military values, which included having the windows wide open even in the winter. He'd subsequently got a job as a prison officer in a Young Offender Institution which allowed him to express his beliefs even more rigorously and with impunity. But, on the plus side, it meant he worked long hours and was seldom at home.

They were forty minutes into the class and Colin was finding it hard to make himself heard above the roar of the heaters. "Alright. Can anyone give me the classic definition of mise en scène? Anyone? Come on, you should know this."

A hand went up from amongst the huddled throng. "Is it a scene that's missing? Like, you know, been edited out?"

Colin fixed the youth with a baleful stare and said, "No. And if that's intended to be a joke, it's not funny."

Since no one was laughing, he assumed that it wasn't and turned away to the wipe board.

"Mise en scène, from the French, refers to everything that appears in the camera lens. That is not only the sets, props and actors but also includes the lighting, cinematography and editing…"

He was finding it difficult to write in his woollen gloves so gave up and turned back towards the class. He caught sight of one of the faculty secretaries beckoning to him from the doorway, mouthing, "The police. For you."

There was barely enough room for Helen, Clarke and Colin in his freezing shoebox of an office. He offered them a "warming cup of tea" from a vending machine in the hallway, but Helen refused, obliging Clarke to do likewise.

"So how can I help you, Detective?"

"We're investigating the circumstances surrounding the death of Gina Lewis. I'm told you were engaged to be married?"

"Not formally, but we'd talked about it."

"But you were in a physical relationship?"

Colin paused, uncomfortable with being questioned about his sex life, especially by an attractive young woman. "Look, I think I'm owed the courtesy of being told what this is all about. I mean, am I some sort of suspect in something?"

"And why would you feel that, Mr Gould?" interjected Clarke.

"Because it's the natural conclusion to draw from the tone of your questioning," Colin bridled, resenting being patronised by someone he felt of inferior intellect.

Helen nodded to Clarke, who removed a number of photographs from an envelope he was carrying, made a space on Colin's cluttered desk, and laid them out in front of him.

"These are all missing women that we presume are dead, Mr Gould," said Helen. "My colleague, Sergeant Clarke, is going to run through a list of their names, addresses and the dates they disappeared. I'd like you to tell him where you were on each of the dates."

Echoes of his times at Her Majesty's Revenue and Customs stirred in Colin, only he knew that now he was the one being hunted. And not just for poisoning Megan Howell's dog. This was potentially much more dangerous.

"Look, I have no idea who these women are. I've never met them–"

"I ask," interrupted Helen, tapping one of the photos, "because Tessa Hayes was abducted and assaulted on the eighth of November – the night your fiancée committed suicide – and you were supposed to be meeting Gina Lewis at The Telegraph Pub that evening but didn't turn up. Can you tell me why?"

"I had a flu bug. I picked it up from one of my students."

"You were at home? Can anyone confirm that?" said Clarke, very deliberately taking out a pad and pen and laying them on the desk.

"No. I watched television and had an early night."

"Can you remember what you saw?"

"No, can you?" Colin snapped… "Look, I wasn't feeling well–"

"Yet you went to work the next morning as usual."

Colin was unnerved, realising that Clarke must have been checking on his movements. "I view my teaching as a vocation. I take it very seriously."

"You must do, considering your fiancée had just died."

"I didn't know she'd just died!" Colin barked, rising to his feet. "And I resent your condescending tone. Now, if you've quite finished…"

"I'm afraid I haven't, sir. Have you ever used online dating sites?"

"What? No. They're just cattle markets."

"Yet you were happy to join Chill Out, a group of predominantly middle-aged women looking for companionship?"

"That's hardly a dating club. It's an offshoot of FrontRow, a group of mature people who meet to share and discuss their interest in the cinema, theatre and the arts."

"And you never met Tessa Hayes online or at any dating club?"

It took Colin a moment to readjust to Helen's abrupt segue. "I told you. I don't know who she is. I've never seen her before."

"Have you ever been to Gina Lewis' Wimbledon house?"

Colin could feel himself beginning to wilt under the barrage of questions. He poured himself some water from a litre bottle on the windowsill, into the plastic cup on the desk.

"You've already got tea in that one, sir."

He wanted to slap Helen. Shove her smartarse comments back down her throat. "Thank you. I have a habit of doing that." But he merely emptied the plastic cup into the brown metal bin below the desk and refilled it.

* * *

Helen's interview of Iris Costa should have been more straightforward, since she was primarily just gathering background information on Don Hart. It wasn't.

They were sitting in Iris's office, a tiny room full of Greek memorabilia, that doubled as her occasional dining room. But today there was no fire in the Victorian grate and little cheer to be had around the pine table. Helen quickly began to suspect from her evasive answers that Iris may have had affairs with not only Hart but also Colin Gould. She fervently denied it, but was eventually forced to come clean, explaining that she was concerned about her friend's reaction if it became public knowledge. Helen told her bluntly that she could care less about her problems, she was investigating the possible murder of three women and needed some honest answers.

Iris admitted to having a "liaison" with Colin Gould and sleeping with Don Hart on a few occasions. But she claimed to have no knowledge of either of their whereabouts on the night of Gina's suicide, and insisted she knew nothing about their relationships with other women. Apart, of course, from Laura Fell, who she now deeply regretted letting down.

Back at the station, after comparing notes with DCI Teal, Helen asked Clarke to run an APNR (automatic number plate recognition) check on both Hart and Gould's cars on the eighth of November, the date of Tessa Hayes' abduction, but also going back chronologically to check their whereabouts on the dates the other missing women had disappeared. Clarke groaned, knowing it was going to be a long and tedious process, which didn't guarantee success, but he couldn't refuse.

Later, when he bemoaned the fact to Helen, she scraped her nails across his hairless chest in response and said, "You want to moan, go home to your wife. You want to fuck me, stop whingeing and get on with it."

He knew he should get out of her bed there and then, and leave, demanding her respect, but he suspected that it would make no difference to her. He pulled her down to him and kissed her hard. Helen ground her hips into him and kissed him back even harder.

* * *

A thought came into Nephilim's head. A thought so radical, yet so beautiful in its simplicity, that at first, he dismissed it as too macabre. But each night as he slept, it rose again like a bubble to the surface of his REM sleep and burst into his limbic system and memory.

It came to him during his evening class. He was working on the same bench as a wild-haired young guy who called himself, rather pretentiously, Ludo. He had a Masters degree in Twentieth-Century Interior Design from Westminster University and was setting up his own boutique company specialising in rare stuffed animals. Ludo prided himself on knowing the market price of each piece he'd ever worked on since, in his words, "Damien Hurst made dead animals fashionable".

Nephilim disliked him immediately. Ludo was a talented taxidermist and brilliant with his hands, able to remove the skin of a rabbit with a dexterity that he didn't yet possess, but there was a calculated detachment to his works. Ultimately, there was no art in them because there was no art, no compulsion, no *love* inside him. He possessed all the accoutrements of an artist – the look, the unapologetic language – but beneath it all he was as hollow as the carcasses they worked on. He didn't cherish his subject or the process. He cherished only the end product and the success it would bring him. He was a charlatan, an accountant pretending to be an artist, and Nephilim hated him for demeaning the purity of his own beliefs.

But ironically it was Ludo's very cynicism that sparked Nephilim's idea, his epiphany.

It was during their Wednesday evening class. The lecturer, who dressed like a farmer in baggy cords and Viyella check shirt, yet lived in Islington, was explaining the religious rituals that accompanied Egyptian mummification. Ludo couldn't have cared less. He was simply there to hone his technique and had no interest in the religious, mythical or historical contexts of taxidermy.

"The thing is, in its so-called purest form, it's a dead art – no pun intended. We don't need to mummify our loved ones to preserve their memory. We have HD video for that. The cloud is the twentieth-century version of heaven, mate. You got to move with the times, create new art forms, like Damien. Like him or loathe him, the man sells."

Nephilim loathed Damien Hurst, but he'd stopped listening anyway. An idea had exploded like shrapnel into his mind, a thought so pure it actually frightened him. He tossed his scalpel onto the brushed steel table and, without a word, walked out of the emergency door into the empty school playground. The clear winter sky was ablaze with stars. So was his mind. He'd received a message. Sent by Him. He should have seen it before; he'd been doing His work, prosecuting and purifying the diseased, setting them free and honouring their release. But ironically his calling had cost him the most beautiful and purest love of all, and no photograph or HD video could ever compensate for that.

Unless…

* * *

It was not in the nature of Laura Fell to bear grudges, but she hadn't spoken to any of the group in over a week. Even though Iris had been leaving messages, clearly holding out an olive branch, Laura knew there would still be questions about Gina's house and the will and that the Chinese whispers would only start again. She turned off her laptop, screened her calls and went for longer and longer walks in Kew Gardens whilst she waited for something to change.

She even contemplated refusing Gina's bequest. But Kieron, who sweetly phoned every couple of days to check she was okay, advised her against it, insisting that she'd done nothing wrong and she should honour Gina's wishes. Besides, if she stood aside it might be read as guilt and make her look even more complicit to her friends.

As the days dragged by, she found herself musing about him more and more, and was embarrassed by the intimate nature of her thoughts. She remembered taking notes at a child protection conference regarding a mother and her son. He'd been abandoned as a child and they'd met again twenty-five years later and started a sexual relationship. The psychologist had called it something like "genetic sexual attraction" and said it wasn't uncommon for people to experience such feelings when they shared a deep emotional bond. Laura reasoned that it was what she must be feeling, because she and Kieron had both shared and loved someone they'd lost. She suspected he felt it too, even if he was too shy to openly admit it, otherwise why all the phone calls? *God*, she thought. *I sound like a character out of a Barbara Cartland novel.*

She was wandering around the Queen's Garden, situated at the rear of Kew Palace, the smallest of all the royal palaces and a place she never tired of visiting since its reopening in 2006. She'd spent the previous hour exploring the nearby Georgian kitchens of the house, marvelling at its original two hundred-year-old features. One of the guides, a middle-aged guy possessing an extraordinary amount of enthusiasm and knowledge, had trapped her for half an hour, explaining the intricacies of the four preparation rooms. Delighting in showing her the lead-lined sinks in which the scullery boys – girls not being allowed in the king's kitchen – laboured for hours, scouring pots with a mixture of soap and sand, eventually tearing the flesh from their adolescent fingers.

It was a relief to escape from his encyclopaedic zeal into the peace of the Queen's Garden, with its formal arcades, sculptures and beds full of plants used for medicinal purposes in the seventeenth century. She sat on the large curved bench at the end of the parterre, eating an exorbitantly priced sandwich she'd brought from the White Peaks Cafe, whilst she admired a statue of a boy with a dolphin and wondered what its significance was.

"Laura?"

She wheeled around and saw Everton Bowe looking down at her from beside the gazebo. For a moment, she didn't recognise him; his right eye was bruised, an ugly wound ran across the bridge of his swollen nose and his cheeks looked raw and inflamed. Hardly surprising, since an hour earlier it had taken him ten excruciating minutes to peel the micropore tape from his face and remove the plaster cast from his nose.

"It looks worse than it is," he said, seeing the startled look on her face and making his way down the steps towards her.

Laura slid the remains of her sandwich into her shoulder bag and stood to greet him, wondering what he was doing there.

"That was a stroke of luck," he said, sensing her concern. "I was about to give up. Have you got a minute?"

"How did you know I was here?"

"You weren't answering your phone and you told me you liked to walk here. That day in The Botanist, remember?"

Laura did, but still felt uncomfortable, embarrassed that she hadn't contacted him after his accident, which from the look of his face appeared serious. "I'm sorry. I'm actually supposed to be meeting someone," she lied.

"It'll only take a few minutes. It's about the case."

"DC Lake said you weren't on it anymore. That you're retiring... for medical reasons?"

Everton smiled grimly to himself, thinking how quickly Helen had written him off. "DC Lake may be a bit premature. Can I buy you a coffee?"

"I'm sorry. I really don't have the time."

"That's okay. We can chat on the way out."

Laura could hardly refuse so merely nodded her head in acceptance. Everton fell into step beside her as they walked out of the garden and across the dew-soaked grass, the pair of them leaving tell-tale footprints in their wake.

"I'm sorry. I didn't get a chance to come to the hospital," Laura said, attempting to bridge the silence until he told her what he really wanted.

"Don't worry about it. You've had a lot on your plate."

"Actually, things are a bit clearer now."

"Good. Well, I've dug up some information that should help make it even clearer…"

Laura listened patiently as Everton relayed the story of Gordon Lewis' drunken crash and the subsequent discovery by Gina that she'd been adopted. And when he finally finished, she said simply, "I know."

Everton, bewildered by the news, stopped in his dewy tracks. "What? I mean… How? Who told you?"

"I met Gina's brother, Kieron, at the solicitors."

"She had a brother?"

"Yes. She was evidently trying to find her birth mother. She was using an agency."

"You mean a tracing agency?"

"Yes. They're called Lost and Found or something. Anyway, Mrs Lewis categorically denied that Gina was adopted but Gina found her adoption certificate and gave it to the tracer. It said that she was born in 1980 and that her mother's name was Jennifer Allen. She contacted the local council and adoption agencies but they don't keep records going back that far. In desperation, Gina placed an ad in the local paper and Kieron, her brother, saw it."

"And who told you all this? I'm assuming this Kieron. Right?"

"Yes. Why do you say it like that?"

"It's all a bit fortuitous, don't you think?"

Laura started off again, quickening her pace, and replied without looking at him, "Hardly. His sister just killed herself."

Everton mentally kicked himself, knowing that his comment was born more out of jealousy than fact and immediately apologised. "Once a cop… Sorry."

"He's not a suspect. Why on earth would he lie?"

"I know. I'm just saying–"

"If you don't believe him, ask the Lewis's . They tried to stop them seeing each other. Mrs Lewis even threatened to disown Gina."

Everton couldn't stop himself playing devil's advocate. "I understand what you're saying, that she wanted to keep the news of the adoption secret, but if she did that she'd risk losing Gina anyway."

"She did!" Laura snapped. "That's why Gina committed suicide! She was driven to it."

"I know you want to believe that, Laura, but that's not proof."

"How much more proof do you need? Christ, you said it yourself. You said that if it came out there'd be a risk Mr Lewis' drink-driving accident and the cover-up would also. It would have ruined Mrs Lewis' precious career. That's why they took Gina's laptop and mobile to get rid of anything that could possibly incriminate them."

"And how did they get in?"

"Mrs Lewis had a key. She let me in with it, the day she told me Gina had changed her will."

"Okay. The only problem with that is you said you saw a man on the stairs and Gordon Lewis is wheelchair bound."

"Well maybe they got someone else to do it for them? Maybe that security guy they have working for them?"

It was a thought that had crossed Everton's own mind before Don Hart had lied about his alibi for the night and put himself firmly in the frame. "Brian Hoffman's an ex-cop. He wouldn't risk burgling a house with a body in it."

"Maybe he didn't know? Either way, I'm sorry, as far as I'm concerned, it's over. I'm done with it."

"Laura. They're still threatening to sue you."

"They're not going to sue me. Kieron's right, they won't want to risk having all their dirty laundry aired in court."

"Look, I appreciate you've had your fill of all this – you wouldn't be human if it didn't affect you – but what about the feather we found?"

"I don't know anything about that and I don't want to. I just want to get on with my life! I'm sorry, I know that sounds selfish and I know it's not what you want to hear, but that's what I want. To be left alone."

Everton knew she wasn't just talking about the case, she was talking about him. She couldn't have been clearer and it was the end of any romantic notions he'd naively harboured. Helen had been right – he'd grown too close to Laura and his stupidity looked likely to have cost him his job. But for now, at least, he was still a cop.

"Okay. But let me give you some advice. You withheld information about Don Hart being investigated for running a betting scam."

"He said he'd been set up… I didn't want to get involved."

"Well, you are. Your misplaced loyalty may have been protecting a serial killer."

Laura took a step back as if retreating from the shock of what she'd been told.

"Hart's in the frame for the suspected murder of three women and the abduction of another on the night of Gina's suicide." It was said with brutal finality and he didn't care. He was doing what *she* wanted: burning the bridges between them and putting an end to their friendship. "Stay away from him. And if he tries to contact you, call DC Lake immediately."

He turned and walked briskly away down the adjoining gravel path. Laura's heart was beating faster than his diminishing footsteps as she watched him, fearing that she was in danger of becoming a victim again.

* * *

Helen was on her way to Basingstoke to meet Sheila Moriarty, a forensic profiler, and was already regretting her one-night stand with DS Clark, who now seemed to regard her as his private property, stroking her arm as she drove like she was some cherished pet. Since they were passing, she decided to stop off briefly at the forensic lab to get an update from Teddy Baldwin and Dr Noonan on their findings.

She was bent over a laptop examining a series of electron microscopic images that had been blown up using the latest Buena

Vista software and transferred on to Teddy's iMac. "Yeah, well, they're definitely not the same feathers."

"Yeah, but these weren't actually found on the blanket, they were beside it," cautioned Clarke, crouching down beside her for a closer look and placing his hand dangerously low on her back.

A gesture not missed by Teddy, who remarked cryptically, "Ever seen a chicken nesting by a river?"

Clarke casually moved his hand away and looked up into Teddy's implacable eyes, waiting for him to explain the non-sequitur. He didn't. He'd heard that Everton Bowe had been side lined from the case and took a dim view of it, especially since he'd found the dove's feather and given Helen's moribund investigation a new lease of life.

Helen could sense his displeasure in the abrupt tone of his answers but chose to ignore it. She didn't care about Teddy's opinion of her – or anyone else's for that matter. She only cared about his results because they directly impacted *her*. It was why she'd slept with Clarke, to control him. It was a strategy she'd developed working as a woman in a predominantly male environment, to protect herself and her career. She'd slept with a lot of men but Everton was the closest thing she had to a friend, male or female, and she'd cut him adrift. Whilst some might accuse her of being selfish, she regarded it as a strength.

"I'm assuming these chicken feathers have traces of blanket fibres on them as well, like the dove's feather?" she said.

"Ergo, they were all on the same the blanket at some point. Give the lady a coconut," Noonan replied with a smile that barely reached his eyes.

"Anything else?"

"Like what?"

"Like what it might have been doing there?"

Noonan picked up a file from the desk, handed it to Helen and said, "Page three, highlighted yellow."

She opened it and began to read through the comprehensive findings. Noonan turned back to his desk and began eating his lunch, an M&S chargrilled vegetable salad in a plastic container.

"What's the difference between a chicken bred for eggs and a meat chicken or breeder chicken, apart from the obvious?" said Helen, as she scanned the document.

"Chickens live up to ten years but factory farm birds, like those, are killed after six weeks. They're selectively bred overfed and kept in tiny cages so that they grow unnaturally quickly and disproportionately. Their breasts grow huge – Joe Public likes white meat – but their skeletons and organs lag behind, which mean they often suffer things like heart failure," said Noonan, picking up his lunch and exiting. "I'll be in my office, Teddy, if you need me."

"Christ," said Clarke sceptically. "Did he get all that from a couple of feathers?"

"And Wikipedia. He reckons these particular feathers came from a breeder bird."

"And how does he know that?"

"Because he's a scientist who races pigeons," said Helen, without a trace of irony. "Go on, Teddy."

"Parent chickens – breeders – have their diets restricted to keep them from gaining weight. This helps them live longer and breed more chicks that in turn grow rapidly into meat chickens, that in turn…"

"I'm assuming there's a conclusion to this natural history lesson?"

"Yes. Do you want to hear it or not?"

Helen smiled, said nothing and waited for him to continue.

"The man you're looking for either works in or has access to a factory farm."

"They don't exist. Factory farming's illegal," interjected Clark.

"Only if you're caught," retorted Teddy. "Which reminds me – where's Everton? I thought you were working with him?"

Helen ignored the question, knowing full well that Teddy already knew and was simply being inflammatory, but Clarke weighed in with the answer and his two pennies' worth. "Back in uniform. What can you do? He's not a bad copper, but he could never really cut it."

"Jack. Leave it. Okay?"

"It's the truth. The guy can't hack it anymore. His body's given up on him."

"Really?" said Teddy, pulling his thin lips back in a knowing smile. "Have you told him that to his face, Sergeant?"

"Hey. Come on. I like the guy but everyone knows he's been self-medicating."

Teddy gave a derisory snort. "So does half the Met. It's the only way to make the job bearable. That and screwing around behind your partner's back. Are you married, Sergeant?"

Clarke hesitated, sensing something was amiss but not quite knowing what, held up his left hand, revealing his platinum wedding ring, and said, "For my sins."

"How long?"

Helen glanced up from the file, but decided to let Clarke dig himself out of his own hole.

"Six years."

"A couple more and you'll be self-medicating like the rest of us, son – if you're not already."

"I didn't know you partook," Helen said, handing Clarke the file and attempting to move the conversation on. "What's your vice, Teddy?"

"I was faithful to my wife for twenty years."

"Was?"

"She died of a brain haemorrhage. Now I'm just faithful to a bottle of bourbon."

It was said with such devastating honesty that it cut straight through Helen's suggestive banter and caught her off-balance. "Oh… I didn't know… I'm sorry."

"Yes. So am I, every day. Any more questions or are we done?"

"What about Gould's laptop?" said Clarke, slipping back into professional mode. "Have you got anywhere with that?"

"The hard drive is encrypted. We're still working on it."

"How long will it take?"

"Twenty-four hours. It's not shop-bought software. Whatever is on there, he clearly wants to keep it to himself."

"Okay," said Helen.

With a brief smile of thanks, she was gone. Clarke picked up the forensic file and strolled out after her, calling back over his shoulder, "Sooner would be better."

Teddy grunted to himself and called through his office door, "You can come out now. Your ex-partner and her new buddy just left."

The door opened and Everton Bowe walked out into the laboratory.

"You were a bit hard on them, Teddy."

"Screw them. He's a plank and she stabbed you in the back."

"You can't knock her for having ambitions."

"So has he. He had his hand all over her arse."

Everton smiled grimly to himself, not entirely surprised, and said, "DC Lake always works on the principle of 'better the enemy you know'."

"You should take a leaf out of her book. Are you jacking it in or not?"

"If I was jacking the job in, would I be here?"

"Good man. How long have you got?"

"A week at most, before they pull the plug on me."

"In that case, take a look at this." Teddy opened his desk drawer, pulled out a USB stick and plugged it into the dock on his laptop. The screen glowed, revealing row upon row of thumbnails of photographs, each one with a digital date in the bottom right-hand corner.

"Where did you get these?"

"They were downloaded from the encrypted hard drive on Gould's laptop."

"I thought you told them you hadn't been able to access it?"

"I lied. I wanted to give you the heads-up first. I'll send them over to them this evening."

Everton scrolled through the thumbnails, which all appeared to have been taken on a long lens without the subject's knowledge. "Christ. He's taken hundreds. He's got them all. Gina Lewis, Iris Costa, Laura – whoa! What the hell is this?" He double-clicked on a thumbnail and brought up an enlarged image of Megan Howell and her naked Brazilian girlfriend standing at the window of Megan's apartment. "What is he, a peeping Tom?"

"No. He's more dangerous than that. The older woman is called Megan Howell. She was part of Gina Lewis' close circle of friends. It appears he didn't get along with her."

"So why is he taking photographs of her?"

"Open the next one."

Everton double-clicked again and brought up a closer image of Megan's poisoned dog. "Shit. Do you think he did this?"

"It looks that way. Megan Howell disappeared the next day. No one's seen her or heard from her since."

"You think he could have killed her? That he's our man?"

"Possibly. But there are some shots here taken on November first, the day that Tessa Hayes was abducted, but none of them are of her, which is odd if it is him."

"Show me."

Teddy scrolled through the thumbnails, looking for the appropriate date, and brought up a number of images of Don Hart sitting in a car with a heavy-set man wearing a fedora.

"Who's the guy with Hart?"

"No idea. Even after enhancing them I still can't get a clean image of his face. The hat is casting a shadow."

"What about the vehicle's number plate?"

"It's not visible in any of the shots. But it's not Hart's car; he drives a Passat."

"Hold on. Go back to that last photograph."

Teddy moved the cursor back and double-clicked.

"There! The guy in the hat. In his right hand – is that what I think it is?"

"Shit. I must be getting old. I never saw it."

The man sitting beside Don Hart was holding a blue stun gun.

* * *

Bramshill House was a Victorian mansion surrounded by woodland on the outskirts of Basingstoke. It was the home of the National Policing Improvement Agency and employed a number of behavioural investigative advisers – profiler being a dirty word after Paul Britton's disastrous involvement in the 1992 Iris Nickell murder investigation.

The head of the department, Sheila Moriarty, a pocket battleship of a woman, stood with Helen and Clarke in front of the leaded windows of a large room. In front of them, fourteen researchers sat, heads bowed, poring over VDU screens.

"Pretty grim viewing," said Helen.

Each researcher's desk supported two screens, one replaying harrowing video testimonies of rape victims, the second displaying matching CCTV footage of the actual attacks.

"But necessary," replied Sheila. "Every bit of knowledge, however tiny, is fed back into our database, allowing us to cross-reference and minutely compare the information."

"Excuse me. But what has all that got to do with our guy?" interrupted Clarke, who had no genuine belief in the merit of profiling.

"If you let me finish, I'll explain," replied Sheila with a steely smile. "Profiling used to be based on pseudoscience, now it's based on statistics. For instance, the database contains a file we call the Unusual Activities Box, a reference to any irregularity or inconsistency – an uncommon element of an attack or rape that occurs in less than five per cent of our documented cases."

"Such as shaving the body hair of a victim?" suggested Helen.

"Exactly. There was a case in Glasgow where four adolescent boys disappeared. A convicted paedophile finally admitted to their abduction and murder. When the bodies were found, they'd been shaved of all their body hair. He wanted to make them appear more childlike and innocent, therefore adding to his pleasure when he abused them."

"Our guy's not gay and he's targeting women." Clarke smiled, stating the obvious.

"There are still similarities in the attacks. I'd suggest that you're looking for someone who is unmarried, who was abused either sexually or physically by a woman, most probably his mother. He lives alone. He's intelligent, artistic. Probably has a white-collar job. He's meticulous. Particular in his tastes and dislikes. There's also an outside chance he could be bisexual or impotent. Shaving the body hair can be a way of making the victim look more innocent but also a way of desexualising the victim. Objectifying them."

"What about the feather?"

"That's more difficult. We don't have sufficient data to cross-reference it with. However, the dove is often seen as a symbol of purity, which would fit with his need to recreate a more innocent or pure image of women."

Clarke shot Helen a cautionary look and said, "It doesn't explain why he let her go."

"I suspect he didn't. She either escaped, which seems unlikely considering she was drugged, or something major happened to panic him and made him change his plan and release her."

"Like Gina Lewis' suicide?"

"It's a possibility."

* * *

The car park of St. Mary's University was rammed. Everton cruised around it once and dumped his Vauxhall Corsa in the disabled bay and trotted inside the reception.

He made his way over to the comely receptionist and asked for Colin Gould. She gave his bruised face and crumpled uniform a cursory once over and told him to take a seat whilst she called Colin. Everton sat on the banquette opposite her desk, nursing the foolscap envelope Teddy had given him, and waited, ignoring the quizzical glances of the students as they passed. Barely five minutes later, Colin appeared at the end of the corridor and beckoned him impatiently towards him. Everton got to his feet and ambled down. By the time he arrived Colin was quietly seething.

"Who are you and what do you want?"

"PC Bowe, Wimbledon Police. I need to talk to you in private."

"Not now. I can't. I'm working…"

"I can arrest you and take you down the nick if that helps?"

"You can't arrest me. I haven't done anything."

"Really?" said Everton, indicating the envelope in his hand. "These photographs we found on your laptop say different. You want me to show you–?"

"No! No, not here."

They made an incongruous couple: a muscular black copper and an anxious middle-aged white man sitting on a bench overlooking the bowling green in Radnor Gardens.

Everton watched Colin leafing through the damning evidence, making no attempt to hide his revulsion. "I like the ones with the naked girl. Very artistic."

"I'm saying nothing without speaking to my lawyer," Colin spat in reply, and pulled out his mobile.

Everton grabbed his wrist, bent it backwards and prised the mobile from his hand. "That is not going to happen."

"Let go of me! I have rights–"

"So do these people, mate, and you abused every one of them."

"I didn't abuse anyone. I'm not a pervert–"

"You're worse. You don't like people, do you, Colin? People who you think have hurt or offended you? You like to get your own back, don't you? To punish them."

"I was trying to protect Gina!"

"By killing Megan Howell's dog and then killing her?"

"What? No! For Christ's sake, I'd never do something like that."

"Then where is she?"

"I don't know! Look, okay, I admit I killed the dog. But I was only trying to teach her a lesson. To hurt her like she'd hurt me."

He broke down and began to cry like a baby. Everton took out his clean handkerchief and then thought, *screw him*, and shoved it back in his pocket.

"You don't understand. She was a hypocrite. She ridiculed me for being jealous of Don Hart, said I should know better at my age, and yet she was having affairs with schoolgirls."

"What are you talking about?"

"It's true. She was thrown out of a school in Wales for abusing a girl. That's why she moved to London, to hide it. But I wouldn't let her. I phoned her – she didn't know it was me – and let her know that her dirty little secret hadn't been forgotten."

"Wow. You, mate, are seriously screwed up." Everton took the photographs from Colin's hand and shuffled the one's containing Don Hart to the top. "Okay. Forget Megan Howell. Where was this one taken?"

"I don't know… I don't remember–"

"Do not bullshit me, or I swear to God, I'll pick you up by your scrawny fucking neck and drown you in the river!"

"Okay! Okay…"

"This was taken on the night of Gina Lewis' suicide. The same night a woman called Tessa Hayes was attacked. *Where were you?*"

"In Walthamstow."

"Walthamstow? What the fuck were you doing in Walthamstow?"

"Following Hart."

"You were stalking him too?"

"I was trying to protect Gina. Hart is a crook. The police are investigating him. He was involved in a betting scam. The man wearing the hat, with the gun thing, is a bookmaker–"

"What's his name?"

"Harry Bellows."

"What was he doing with a taser?"

"I don't know. It's the truth! I got scared when I saw it and left."

Everton was already dialling his mobile as he left, dodging through the traffic, and hurried back into the university car park.

"Teddy. The guy with the taser is a bookie called Harry Bellows. Run a PNC check on him and ring me straight back."

The car park attendant circling Everton's Corsa, looking for a disabled sticker, was confused seeing a copper in uniform approaching the battered hatchback, and even more so when Everton homed in on him, demanding to know if it was his car.

"*Mine?...* No."

"Lucky for you, mate. It's illegally parked. I'm seizing it."

He unlocked the car, climbed in and fired up the engine. As he did so, his mobile started up. He answered it as he reversed out into Waldegrave Road, past the bemused attendant. "That was quick. What have you got?"

He listened in stunned silence. Then, slewing the car into a tight U-turn, warned Teddy to expect an imminent call from DC Lake. To give her the information but play dumb about absolutely everything else.

* * *

Helen and Clarke were crawling back up the M3 towards London and she wasn't enjoying the heavy traffic or his company. Clarke clearly thought the trip had been a total waste of time, which was a red flag to Helen since it had been his idea in the first place. Worse, he had his arm draped around the back of her shoulder, idly playing with her hair as she drove.

"You can't deny that there are similarities in the attacks," she said, swapping lanes for the umpteenth time.

"A couple, but most of it is way off. I mean, she said we're looking for a white-collar worker, so where do the chicken feathers and the factory farming fit in?"

"Maybe he owns a farm?"

"We've got two prime suspects and neither are farmers, Helen. No, my money is on Gould. He doesn't have an alibi and he actually fits the white-collar part of the profile."

Everton's phone call could not have come at a less inopportune time. Helen checked the Caller ID and debated whether to take it, having not spoken to him since their row at the nick, but felt she had to front it out, knowing Clarke would start asking questions if she ignored it.

"Hello. Look, I can't speak now… You did *what*?"

Clarke's antenna was immediately up. "What's going on?"

"How do you know this? Hello? *Hello*? Shit!"

The line cut dead in her hand. She tossed it into the centre console, turned to Clarke and said, "Phone the nick. Gould's hard drive – see if forensics have sent over anything."

"Why?"

"Because if what I've just been told is true neither he nor Don Hart can be the killer."

* * *

Harry Bellows and Don Hart were arrested for armed robbery in simultaneous dawn raids the following morning. Colin Gould was charged with stalking involving fear and violence, in front of his students – they rated it the best class he'd taught all term.

It was, however, a pyrrhic victory for Helen. Because although both arrests were ostensibly down to her, they were also a tacit admission that neither man could have been responsible for Tessa Hayes' abduction. Even so, Clarke was content to play devil's advocate and offer his support, confident that DCI Teal was never going to buy it.

He was right. Teal slumped in his office chair, tapping Gould's photos on his desk with a rolled-up newspaper, his temper ticking in time with the beat.

"Helen could be right, guv. If Gould left Walthamstow immediately after taking the photographs, it's feasible he could have got over to Kew."

"That's bullshit, Jack, and you know it."

"It is theoretically possible, guv," said Helen, more in hope than judgement.

"But hardly bloody probable! Gould stalks Hart, then rushes over to Kew to keep a date with Tessa Hayes so he can drug and abduct her, is that what you're telling me?"

"I know it's a long shot. We're checking the CCTV around The Botanist to see if he's on it."

"He better be," growled Teal, tossing the newspaper onto the desk to reveal the headline:

MERTON POLICE employ PROFILER

"Because *this* is the last straw! I want to know who leaked this."

"I don't know," replied Helen. "I wish I did."

"You're supposed to be leading this investigation. *Find out!* This is a shambles! You have no suspects, no motive, you haven't been able to connect Tessa Hayes to any of the missing women *or* Gina Lewis, and now the whole debacle has been leaked to the sodding press!"

"Guv, be fair. Busting Hart for the bookie robbery was down to me."

"No, it wasn't, it was down to luck! Luck and some scrote informant who grassed them up - and whose identity you refuse to divulge."

There it was. The way out. All Helen had to do was to inform Teal that Everton was the informant. Rightly or wrongly, Teal would assume he'd leaked it to the press and she'd be off the hook. But for some reason she couldn't do it. Everton was way out of line, yes. He'd ignored her repeated calls and texts, yes. But the bottom line was that he'd tried to help. She couldn't betray him again, even for the sake of her career.

DS Clarke finally excused himself, explaining he had a meeting with a snout of his own, leaving Helen to take the heat. He made his way out of the nick and over to his car feeling as good as he had in weeks. It was now only a matter of time before the missing women enquiry was eased onto the Met's back burner, which would be seen as a vindication of his prior investigation. He rated the success of his strategy a seven out of ten. It would have been higher but for the fact that Helen would no longer be fucking him after their Basingstoke row. Still, he thought, she was a seriously good lay – a nine – whilst it lasted.

* * *

The Hurricane was a snooker hall close to Tooting Bec. Recently refurbished in the style of a gentlemen's club, its clientele was an eclectic mixture of lowlifes and city boys. Brian Hoffman felt an immediate affinity with its shady light and even shadier characters. He used it as his unofficial office, and a refuge from his humdrum home life. Which with three teenage daughters was loud and emotional, something he'd never fully appreciated until his early retirement from the Met. A fact his wife delighted in reminding him, ad infinitum. So, The Hurricane, a four-minute walk from his front door, was ideal. It had a late-night license, sixteen good tables and a pneumatic redhead behind the bar who remembered his name and brand of Irish, Bushmills.

The place was almost empty, pre-the lunchtime rush. A quartet of taxi drivers were playing a fiver a frame at one end of the room and an ample blonde in a LA baseball cap was bent over a card table playing Whist as she sipped diet coke through a straw.

Hoffman was idling the time away waiting for Clarke, watching an Indian guy who was dressed from head to toe in black practising on a nearby table. The guy's play was as smooth as his dress; even his matt-black cue and case matched his cashmere roll-neck. But these were not Hoffman's primary interest. The guy was wearing silk gloves, hiding the fact that his bridge hand was false, a detail that only became clear when he unscrewed it and positioned it back in its case, replacing it with his "day" hand, which was similarly gloved.

"Set them up. Smartarse DC Lake's on her way out," called Clarke as he breezed in through the double doors.

Hoffman grinned and ordered a couple of pints of Stella and Irish chasers from the redhead and followed him over to a table in the corner. The blonde in the cap, Pauline Bowe, put down her cards, switched her HTC mobile to video-recording mode and zoomed in on them and their conversation.

Ninety minutes later, Everton followed Hoffman from The Hurricane back to his semi-detached Edwardian house in Manville Gardens, a stone's throw from Tooting Common. The area, once a hunting ground for prostitutes and their punters, was now only patrolled by young mums and nannies driving Chelsea tractors. Hoffman paused to fold back the wing mirror of his Range Rover Discovery, a precautionary measure he took whenever the school run was imminent. He made his way through the gate up to the black lacquered front door and let himself in.

Everton counted to ten and crossed the road and strolled up to the car. It was immaculate inside and out, its lustrous shine matching that of the front door. He checked the road was clear, walked around to the driver's side, grabbed the folded wing mirror in both hands and wrenched it backwards until it snapped from its mounting. Leaving it dangling from its power lead, Everton made his way over to the front door and pressed the bell. He checked his reflection in its mirror finish – unshaven, jeans, T-shirt and Nikes – as he waited for it to be answered.

An overweight woman with defiantly short cropped hair yanked it open and looked him up and down like he was a *Big Issue* seller. "Read the sign," she said, as if he'd committed some sort of criminal offence. She pointed towards a metal plate that was screwed above the bell:

NO HAWKERS

"I'm not a hawker. I'm a police officer. Is your husband in, Mrs Hoffman?"

He couldn't make out if she were simply ill-tempered or racist or both, because his explanation cut absolutely no ice. "Warrant card."

He ignored the demand and said, "Someone's just ripped the wing mirror off your Range Rover."

"What? Brian!" she bellowed without pausing for breath. "*Brian!*"

Hoffman came running out of the kitchen and did an emergency stop on seeing Everton in the doorway. "What the hell are you doing here?"

"He's a police officer. He said someone's just smashed up our car."

Hoffman pushed past them both and out. Everton stepped aside to allow Mrs Hoffman to barrel after him.

"It's on the driver's side," he called helpfully as he ambled out to join them.

They stood in a tight semi-circle, staring down at the broken mirror.

"Shit!" said Hoffman. "Did you see who did it?"

"Yeah. A black guy, about my height, my age, my build…"

Hoffman fixed him with a baleful stare. Everton carried on regardless. "I think I took a video on my mobile," he said, handing it to him and adjusting the volume. "There's sound too."

Hoffman stared down at the screen and was stunned. He was watching a recording of his meeting with DS Clarke in The Hurricane club an hour previously. "Go inside, Ruth. I won't be long."

"No. Not without some sort of an explanation–"

"Just do it! Christ, why is everything a bloody debate with you?"

Ruth took a small step towards Everton, attempting to cower him with a look, but he was way past caring. "Nice to meet you too, Mrs Hoffman."

She shouldered past him, trampled back up the path and into the house, slamming the door behind her for good measure.

"Is she a bit short on the social graces, Bri, or is it just me?"

"What the fuck do you want? And it better be good or I'm going to wipe the floor with you and what's left of your poxy career."

Everton's ankle-tap was delivered with the toe of his size-eleven Dr. Martens, a trick he'd learnt in his semi-pro football days.

"Jesus! What did you do that for?" groaned Hoffman as he staggered back and slumped against the Range Rover.

"To make a point. You can't scare me, personally or professionally, because my poxy career that you and DS Clarke so kindly helped me fuck up is over. But you attempt to hurt DC Lake and this wing mirror is not the only thing that's going to get broken."

"Are you threatening me?"

"Yes. And you better start giving me some straight answers or this recording is going straight to the press and you can say goodbye to your precious security job."

They decamped to the Tooting Bec Lido and sat on a couple of deckchairs, watching some hardy member of the South London Swimming Club plough length after length of the icy waters. Everton was surprised to discover that Hoffman was a member and even more so by the scale of the magnificent open-air pool.

"How big is it?"

"One hundred metres long, thirty-three wide," grunted Hoffman.

"Thirty-three. My lucky number."

"Really? Did you ever win anything with that number? No…"

"You want to cut the snide and get to the point?"

"You just *think* it's lucky. You've got no proof. Just like you *think* you've been stitched up by me. You've got no evidence, no hard facts, just an out-of-focus video that you illegally recorded in a snooker club."

"I didn't record anything. It was a journalist."

The word hit Hoffman like a slap and momentarily rocked his composure. "I don't have anything to hide."

"DS Clark does. He's been leaking sensitive information to you about the Lewis case and this," Everton said, holding up his mobile, "confirms it."

Hoffman opened his mouth to riposte, thought better of it, affected a shrug and said, "I'm not a grass."

"Okay. How about this? You don't have to speak, I'll just assume I'm right until you tell me I'm wrong. How's that?"

Hoffman said nothing.

"Okay. Mrs Lewis paid you to undermine, through DS Clarke, our investigation – which included her daughter's suicide – because she was desperate to hide something."

Hoffman said nothing.

"Mrs Lewis contracted a sexually transmitted disease and consequently become infertile, which would have become public if the press started asking questions about Gina's subsequent adoption."

"There were other reasons."

"I know about the drink-driving cover-up. What I want to know is who was in Gina Lewis' house on the night of her suicide and why they stole her laptop and phone."

"Not me. I was at an all-female version of *The Merchant of Venice* at my daughter's school. An extremely long evening, as 150 other bored shitless parents can testify."

"Does Celia Lewis have them?"

"Not to my knowledge. It's possible Kieron Allen could have."

"You knew Gina had a brother?"

"Mrs Lewis had me check him out. She didn't trust him."

"Why?"

"I couldn't find anything about his past. Nothing. No NHS number, PNC record, nothing. The guy is like a ghost."

Everton's tinnitus suddenly rang in his ears like an alarm bell. "Gina found him through a tracing agency. Surely they must have run checks?"

"If they did they weren't telling me. Client confidentiality and all that."

"Who runs it?"

"A woman called Amy Tann. But you're wasting your time."

"I can be very persuasive."

"You'll need to be. She was murdered ten days ago."

Christmas common

Kieron's offer took Laura by surprise. He wanted to visit Gina's grave and wondered if she'd like to drive up to Wheatley with him to pay her last respects. He thought it might give them both some closure. She was wary at first, but the more they talked about it the more attractive the idea became. Besides, Kieron was right, the press would have long gone and Mrs Lewis wouldn't even know that they'd been there, so what harm could it do?

At 11.40am, she zipped up her Mountain Warehouse quilted jacket and walked the few hundred metres to the florist in Kew Village. She bought a spray of Lily of the Valley, Gina's favourite flowers, which she jokingly used to describe as being like her: sweet but deadly. Then sat sipping a latte on the pretty terrace of The Tap on the Line – a handsomely restored railway pub that served all-day breakfasts and seriously good coffee – as she waited for Kieron to pick her up. She was blissfully unaware that two of her Chill Out friends were sitting in police cells after being arrested twenty-four hours earlier.

Laura had suggested that, being new to South West London, Kieron might find the pub an easier place to meet. In truth, she was embarrassed about the condition of her flat, having cancelled the installation of her kitchen, feeling unable to face the upheaval on top of everything else. Jay, the B&Q designer, who looked nothing like his boyband name, warned her, as per script, that the offer would expire. But when she decided to cancel the contract rather than mess them around he'd, as per script, relented and offered to extend the deal.

Blustery clouds scurried across the watery sun like moths across a low-wattage bulb. Laura closed her eyes and let the pale sunlight warm her face. When she opened them again, she saw Kieron watching her from his car on the other side of the street.

"You looked like you were asleep," he said, as they headed up the on-ramp at Brentford and eased into the West Way traffic.

"No. I was just resting my eyes and thinking."

"About what?"

"My kitchen, actually," she said with a rueful smile. "And what a mess my flat is."

"Is that why you wanted me to pick you up at the pub?"

"No – yes," she said, hastily correcting her white lie. "How did you know that?"

"Because I'd have done the same thing."

They both laughed and it seemed to reaffirm the bond they'd felt on their first meeting.

"You know, my wife accused me of being obsessive, because I was so proud of my house and garden."

"Gina definitely was."

"There you go – the same genes. But the odd thing is, the minute she left… I just seemed to lose heart… I should really sell the place. It's too big for me on my own."

"Where is it?"

"Oh, uh, near a place called Goodwood."

"I know it. It's near Chichester; I've been to the races there. It's great."

"I've never been."

"Horse racing? How come?"

"I hate gambling." He left the words hanging, like it was a dark secret that he preferred not to reveal. Laura, whose good manners would have usually prevented her from enquiring any further, was intrigued.

"Not even a flutter on the Grand National or the lottery?"

Kieron shook his head.

"Why? I mean, it's just a bit of fun. It doesn't harm anyone."

"Doesn't it? My father gambled away pretty much everything we ever had. Every Thursday he'd pick up his pay packet and go straight down the bookies and piss it away. And when the bailiffs were knocking on the door, he just packed a suitcase and disappeared… like we were just another bet he could renege on. It took my mother years to get over the shock and even longer to pay back his losses."

Blessed with an idyllic childhood, Laura felt emotionally out of her depth and thought it best to say nothing. Kieron lapsed into silence and went back to driving. They headed out past Heathrow and took the M25 towards Oxford. Laura passed the time by checking her emails, hoping there would be one from Frieda, who she'd heard nothing from in over two weeks. Finding nothing, she texted her and was about to replace the mobile in her bag when it started up in her hand.

"Ha," she said. "That was quick."

But when saw the Caller ID, it didn't read Frieda but PC Bowe. She switched it off and placed it back inside the zip pocket of her handbag.

"Who was that?"

"Oh, uh, no one."

"An admirer?"

"No – well, maybe…"

Kieron laughed and said, "You don't seem very sure."

"He's the policeman who's been investigating Gina's death… He's become a sort of friend."

"Sort of?"

"He's started getting a bit… overprotective… He even tried to warn me off you."

"Me? I don't understand. How does he know about me?"

"I just told him how we'd met, and he started implying that it could have all somehow been set up and that I shouldn't trust you. It's just silly."

Kieron muttered something under his breath and went back to driving. Laura could see from the way he gripped the wheel that he was annoyed and sensed that it was with her rather than Everton. She felt obliged to apologise.

"I'm sorry. Would you have preferred me not to have mentioned you?"

"Yes."

His curt response and the silence that followed took her by surprise. Finally, he said, "I'm sorry. It's just... what happened between Gina and myself was precious and I hate to think of the police getting involved and trampling all over the memory of it."

An image of Everton traipsing over the flower beds outside Gina's house on the night of her death flashed into Laura's mind and she instantly understood his concerns. "I don't want that either, Kieron. That's why I've stopped answering his calls."

Her response was so genuine that he felt fleetingly ashamed of his anger, and said, "Maybe he's jealous of me? I know I would be if I were him."

Laura returned his diffident smile and said, "Thank you."

She leant across and kissed him on the cheek. And at that moment, Kieron felt what he'd desperately been fighting to suppress: the unmistakable tug of sexual attraction.

They parked the car in Garsington Lane and walked up the path towards the twelfth–century Norman church that stood on top of a hill on the outskirts of Wheatley village. The views were spectacular. Sweeping vistas of the Thames Valley were laid out like an offering before them and in the distance the huge cooling towers of the Didcot power station stood sentinel-like over the Vale.

Kieron opened the wooden gate for Laura and followed her inside. The graveyard wasn't huge but the irregular layout and trees made it difficult to get a clear view of it. Neither of them spoke as they set about searching for the newly tilled earth that would signify the position of Gina's grave. They found it in a far corner, in the shadow of a drystone wall.

"They hid her away," whispered Kieron. "They were frightened of the press and their dirty little secrets, so they hid her away. Their own daughter."

He dropped to his knees beside the plain headstone that read simply:

GINA LEWIS
25.05.1978 – 07.01.2017

Kieron clasped his hands and bowed his head in prayer. Laura watched, surprised by his overt display of devotion, but when he held out his hand to her she took it and knelt beside him. She thought she could hear him praying and realised he was crying. She laid her posy of flowers on the bare earth and allowed herself to join him in his grief.

Kieron smiled, as if in thanks, and helped Laura to her feet and they walked hand in hand out of the graveyard and down the hill to the car. He was still holding her hand when he opened the passenger door for her, and for the first time she registered the large weal in the shape of a bite on the back of his hand.

"Oh, did you hurt yourself?"

"No. It's a birthmark," he lied, knowing that soon Laura would see much more of it and that he, Nephilim, would hurt *her*.

* * *

Helen had chopped and mashed her father Frank's fish fingers into a soggy mush and was now spooning it into his gaping mouth as if she were feeding a baby. Which in a sense she was because he was no longer able to do anything for himself: eat, drink, wash or, worst of all, use a commode. It sat in the corner of his room below the family photos that leavened the bare walls, like a salutary reminder to any visitor of the indignity of old age. Lately the staff had resorted to using disposable incontinence nappies to stop any "accidents", but removing them and cleaning up the mess left behind was still horrible. Helen hated it, feeling it demeaned them both. She had no idea that her father's mind had regressed to a time when being fed with a spoon and shitting his pants was perfectly normal.

She and her sister, Delia, had finally agreed that, in lieu of any decision about who should look after their father, Helen would visit the Wilson Hospital twice a week to check on his well-being. But with her investigation having stalled and the interviews with Colin Gould proving unproductive, Helen was under serious pressure. She was not best pleased to discover a dishevelled looking Everton standing in full uniform beside her car in the visitor car park.

"What are you doing?"

"I need your help."

"No way. Absolutely not. Who told you I was here?"

"DC Coyle. Just five minutes. Please."

"I don't have five minutes. My father doesn't know me. And my sister insists on me wiping his arse, whilst my case goes down the pan – along with my career. So, if you'll excuse me."

"I want to help."

"By intimidating witnesses?"

"I didn't–"

"You threatened to drown Colin Gould! You're out of control, Everton. I mean, look at you, you're a mess. You shouldn't even be in uniform. You're suspended from duty. Do you want to lose your pension?"

"Do you want to lose this case?"

"What's that supposed to mean?"

Everton held up his mobile and pressed PLAY on the video. Helen watched the playback slack-jawed in astonishment.

"DS Clarke has been leaking information to Hoffman to kill the investigation."

"But… why?"

"Hoffman's protecting the Lewis'. And Clarke, as you suspected, his career."

Helen's mind was working overtime, replaying the recent events. Clarke's apology and offer to clear the air, sleeping with her, his suggestion to use a profiler, his lukewarm defence of her in front of Teal; it had all been a sham. For a woman that prided herself on being in control the realisation was a devastating blow to her self-esteem.

"You thought you were using him, Helen, and all the time he was playing *you*."

She glanced up at Everton and her eyes were like flint. "Are you enjoying this?"

"A bit. But, as you say, I have a lot to lose. I'm assuming you'd like this?" he said, holding up the mobile like a prize.

"Too bloody right, I do."

"I need something in return."

"Go on."

"I need access to a murder scene. A woman called Amy Tann. She ran a tracing agency…"

Helen let out a derisive snort, unlocked her door, climbed in and fired the engine. Everton jumped in front of the car, attempting to block her exit.

"Get out of my way!"

"Colin Gould is not the killer! Ask Hoffman about Kieron Allen, Gina's brother. They'd been seeing each other secretly for months. Yet there's no record of him on any birth certificate and no record of Gina's birth father on hers either. And now he's been in contact with Laura Fell."

"Oh, Christ," groaned Helen. "You're infatuated, Everton. Let it go."

She slammed the car into reverse and powered away from him. Everton bellowed after her, "He could have been in the original will, Helen! Check him out!"

* * *

They were heading out on the M40 towards London when Kieron suggested to Laura that they take the scenic route back through Henley and stop off for lunch. He'd heard of a pub called The Fox and Hounds near Watlington which TripAdvisor praised for its delicious food and thought they could go for a walk afterwards on Christmas Common, an area of natural beauty nearby that offered stunning views from the top of the Chilterns.

The pub was full of rustic charm and well-heeled locals. They squeezed in beside the huge inglenook fireplace, toasting themselves whilst they waited for their ciabatta sandwiches to arrive. Brie and caramelised onion chutney for Laura and steak, onion and honey mustard for him. Kieron ordered two halves of Brakspear real ale to wash them down and "fortify" themselves for their walk.

"Cheers," he said. "To us."

"Cheers," she responded in kind and winced as she took a sip of the tart, fizzy beer.

"It's a bit of an acquired taste. Would you prefer wine?"

"No, honestly, I like it," she lied. "Gina and I got drunk on scrumpy once. I hated the first glass – it tasted nothing like cider – but after the second I absolutely loved it. We had to get a cab home and the next day I couldn't even remember where I'd left my car."

Kieron smiled and fell silent, waiting for the Rohypnol he'd surreptitiously dropped into her beer at the bar to do its work. He'd been hoping to use her in his tableaux – she looked like she had a good body and he would have enjoyed playing with her a little before starting the serious preparation – but that wouldn't be possible now. The black cop she'd obviously been screwing was getting too close and he couldn't risk contaminating the evidence further. Not if his plan was to work.

Laura watched him as she sipped her beer, wondering why she found him so attractive. It couldn't just be the bond they shared over Gina; it had to be more than that. He was the antithesis of her usual, extroverted type of guy. Kieron was shy, almost guarded, and despite his efforts to hide it, wore his hurt in the deep frown lines etched onto his boyish face. Perhaps that was it; his pain brought out her nurturing side, her long-suppressed maternal instinct.

He caught her looking at him and said, "Sorry. I was thinking about what you said about Gina and what a shame it was that I'd missed her growing up."

"I've got some photos on my mobile if you'd like to see them?" she said and, without waiting for his answer, took her iPhone from her bag and opened the photo app. "These only go back a couple of years but I've got albums full of our earlier stuff at home. Look, these were taken on a walking holiday in Ibiza. We had a brilliant time. That's a pension we all stayed in. Six of us went. That's mine and Gina's room, which as you can see wasn't big enough to swing a cat in… Formentera, which is beautiful but most of the beaches are full of nude Germans and hippies. And this is Club Lio, which was frighteningly expensive but a riot – oops, you don't want to see those."

"Why not?" he said, grabbing the mobile and admiring the photo of Laura taken as she climbed out of the club's pool in her bra and pants, which the water had turned transparent.

"I should have deleted that."

"Or posted it online." He grinned, expanding the picture so that the shadowy triangle of her pubic hair was just visible through her panties. "You'd get a lot of hits. You look like Ursula Andress in that Bond film."

Laura smiled sheepishly and said, "I don't think her costume turned see-through."

"No. Are there more?"

Laura rolled her eyes and reached for the mobile. As if by magic, it started up in her hand. Kieron saw the Caller ID – PC Bowe – and smiled wryly.

"Your friend is very persistent."

Laura took the phone, switched it off and said, "He's not my friend, Kieron. You are."

As if to prove it, she leant across and kissed him lightly on the lips. Kieron flushed in embarrassment and she thought she'd offended him.

He smiled and said simply, "Do you think we should make a move?"

"Okay," she replied. "I'll just pop to the ladies before we set off."

Kieron watched her go, muttering, "Slut," under his breath. Then, he deftly unzipped her handbag, took out her mobile and removed the battery before replacing the handset in its original place inside the zip-pocket. When Laura returned a couple of minutes later he'd already paid the bill, in cash, and was waiting for her by the door holding her bag and coat.

* * *

Everton ambushed Peter Pitt outside his Isleworth office on his way back from lunch. The solicitor was polite but wary; Everton's uniform was as creased as his unshaven face and he appeared slightly unsteady on his feet.

"Vertigo. Do you mind if we sit?" said Everton by way of explanation as he slumped down onto the top step and patted the space beside him.

Peter stayed firmly on his feet. Everton looked more like a guy in stag-night fancy dress than a police officer and, cautious man that Peter was, he wasn't taking any chances.

"I assume you have some form of identification?"

Everton fumbled in his pocket, held up his warrant card and sighed. "Constable Everton Bowe. Lead investigating officer on Gina Lewis' suicide."

"I see… Look, don't you think you'd be more comfortable in my office?"

"Probably not. I'm here unofficially. I'm on sick leave. I'm telling you that because you will undoubtedly check. You represent the estate of Miss Lewis and Laura Fell – and before you start quoting 'client confidentiality' I already know that you do…"

Peter, who was about to do just that, took a precautionary step backward and said nothing.

"I'm not asking you to disclose anything about the contents of the will; if needs be I'll subpoena you for that. But I urgently need to know the contact details of Kieron Allen."

"I'm sorry. I'm afraid I can't help you with that."

Everton groaned, grabbed the wrought-iron handrail and hauled himself wearily to his feet. "Look, mate, I don't care about your code of bloody conduct, Allen is the prime suspect in three possible murders! If you're withholding information–"

"I'm not withholding information. I've never heard of anyone called Kieron Allen."

"Bullshit. Laura Fell met him here. He told her he had an appointment with you."

"Not with me he didn't."

"She met him coming out of this office, mate."

"That's impossible. For security reasons, access to this building is strictly by appointment only. And I have never had an appointment with anyone called Kieron Allen. Check with my secretary if you don't believe me."

A blizzard of white noise threatened to overwhelm Everton, as he realised that the solicitor was speaking the truth, and that Laura Fell could be Kieron Allen's next victim.

* * *

Kieron left the car in the Watlington Hill car park and they walked to the top of the eight hundred-foot escarpment. The view of the vale below them was spectacular and above them red kites freewheeled in the darkening sky.

Laura was surprised how tired she felt. She was an avid walker and had often hiked the eight-mile perimeter of Richmond Park with Gina and Iris before meeting Frieda in Pembroke Lodge for coffee and well-earned carrot cake. But now her legs felt heavy and the biting wind chafed at her skin. It was embarrassing; she didn't want to ask Kieron, who was clearly in his element, if they could turn back, but she was beginning to feel queasy.

"Don't you think it's beautiful?" he said. "It reminds me of the Sussex Downs. It's beautiful up there, Laura. It's weird. After she left – my wife – I was on my own for months. I couldn't really face anyone but up there on the hills with only the skylarks for company I never really felt lonely. They were like my guardian angels. I would walk for hours and never see another soul and yet I never felt alone. Nature can do that. Transport you… Take you out of yourself and make you forget your problems."

"I go… to Kewww…" The words congealed in her parchment-dry mouth. Her limbs felt heavy, like she was walking through treacle, like gravity was pressing down on her. "Gaaarrrrdensss…"

Kieron smiled, content that the Rohypnol was doing its work, and helped her out, "You know why that is, Laura? When you're looking at something really beautiful, like a flower or a perfect sunset or a view with no people to spoil it, there's a sort of purity to it, an honesty, and it makes you forget how shitty life and the human race really is."

For some inexplicable reason, Laura wanted to laugh. What was he going on about? Flowers and perfect sunsets and purity? She stifled the desire, lost her footing and stumbled. Kieron reached out his hand and, taking her firmly by the arm, steadied her.

"Oops. Careful. It's like the Grand Canyon. Have you been there?"

"Whaaat? Uh… No–"

"You're tired. We'll sit." He helped her down onto the tufted grass and sat beside her, draping his arm protectively around her shoulder as he continued, "The Grand Canyon, Laura, is honestly mind-blowing. Only a god or one of his angels could have made it. But the thing is, you have to see it properly. Actually, I went there with Gina."

"I dooon't… understaaaand?" Her voice echoed in her ears and seemed to mingle with the distant calls of the red kites, forming a weird duet.

"It was our secret. I treated her. It was on one of those fly-drive holidays. We drove from Los Angeles to San Francisco, all the way up the coast along Big Sur. It's one of the most scenic drives in the world. Then headed to Yosemite, which was amazing; waterfalls falling thousands of feet. And then on to Las Vegas, which was amazing for different reasons – I booked the honeymoon suite at the Marriott – and finally on to the Grand Canyon."

"Honeymoooon… suiiite?" Laura couldn't understand what he was talking about. "Sorry… dooon't feeeel well."

"You won't. I've drugged you. Anyway, this receptionist in the hotel told us that the only way to see the Canyon properly was to cover your eyes an hour before you get there."

"Kieeeeron…?"

"*Shut up!* For Christ's sake, woman, I'm trying to share something important!"

Laura couldn't believe the savagery with which he'd turned on her. Her glassy eyes brimmed with tears that began to run down her cheeks.

"And stop snivelling!" He pulled his arm from around her shoulder and let her flop sideways onto the grass. "Imagine that… You have to keep the hood on for a whole hour because the Canyon is that big; it stretches for over 250 miles. Its twenty miles wide and almost a mile deep. Of course, she didn't get to see any of it until she got to the rim. I walked her right up to the very edge and whipped off her blindfold and she went "wow". I put the blindfold straight back on and told her she should never look at it again… She told me afterwards that's what she imagined love at first sight must feel like."

He looked down at Laura, hoping for some response, but she was barely conscious. "Have you ever felt something like that, Laura? Probably not. No, you're too busy looking for Mr Right in all the wrong places. It's a shame, you have a nice figure, but women of your age shouldn't dye their hair blonde…" He lifted up the hem of her skirt, exposing her thighs and panties to check. "It doesn't look natural."

Laura opened her mouth to scream but her voice wouldn't work anymore.

She awoke five hours later and in her confusion thought that she'd been having a nightmare about dying. She was lying on her side and her mouth was sealed with gaffer tape. When she tried to remove it, she realised that her wrists and ankles were bound too. She tried desperately to focus but it was impossible – something was covering her, shutting out any light. She thrashed from side to side in an attempt to wriggle free, then froze as she realised that she was not alone. Something was behind her, lying against her back. Something cold and waxy that smelt of soil. She eased her head around and looked directly into the cloudy lifeless eyes of her best friend, Gina, and screamed.

Kieron yanked open the boot and slapped her into silence. The moon, haloed behind him, told Laura that it was night, but she had no idea how long she'd been unconscious. He ripped the tape from her mouth, pinched her nose and, as she gasped for air, squirted the contents of a syringe into her throat. Then, he re-taped her mouth and slammed the boot shut.

* * *

After a number of unanswered calls and a fruitless trip to Laura's Kew flat, Everton downed a Zolpidem with a glass of five-year-old rum and fell into a dreamless sleep. He barely heard the insistent ping of his mobile, only reluctantly rolling over on the sofa and fumbling for it on the floor.

"Hello?" he said, and groaned as he realised it was not a call but a text. He blinked himself awake and tried to focus on the Caller ID. *Thank God*, he said to himself as he saw the name Laura Fell and quickly opened the text. It simply read "OX49 5HG". He pressed redial but the number was unavailable. Hauling himself to his feet, he stumbled over to the sink and, shoving the dirty pile of plates aside, splashed his face with water from the cold tap. Grabbing his ASP baton, he headed for the door.

It was beginning to rain and he hadn't brought a coat but it was too late to go back for it. Besides, he reasoned, the cold would help keep him awake. He climbed into the Corsa and as the engine grumbled to life entered the postcode into Google Maps on his mobile, mumbling to himself, "Where the fuck is Christmas Common?"

Thirty minutes later, windows wide open and eyes streaming, he was hitting a hundred as he headed west on the M25 towards the M40 turn-off to Oxford. And less than twenty minutes later, he was wide awake and turning left onto the A40 towards Stokenchurch.

A sopping drizzle hung in the air over the National Trust car park like a grey blanket, obscuring the corners where the encroaching trees seemed to cast shadows even in the darkness. Everton switched his headlights to full beam and eased the Corsa around the muddy potholes, scanning the area for any sign of Laura. Suddenly he saw it. A dark Mercedes Estate, half-hidden underneath the overhanging branches. The hairs on the back of his hands began to prickle as he drew closer and saw the colour. Midnight blue. The same colour and model as the one used to abduct Tessa Hayes. He cut the engine, reached over for his baton and stepped cautiously out of the car.

"Laura," he called. "Laura! It's me. Everton Bowe."

His voice echoed and dissolved into the darkness. He flicked open his telescopic baton and felt the reassuring heft of the twenty-one inches of steel in his hand. Slowly, he approached the Mercedes. Someone – or something – appeared to be sitting in the front seat. It looked like a shop-window dummy. He inched closer, his eyes focused on the figure, checking for any sign of movement. He was barely five feet from the car when he stopped in his tracks, realising that it wasn't a dummy. It was Laura Fell.

"Oh, Jesus."

He ran forward and yanked open the door. Laura toppled sideways into his arms. She was naked and her body had been completely shaved of hair, which was in two clear plastic evidence bags on the seat behind her. He laid her gently back across the seat and checked for a pulse in her neck, and let out a sigh of relief as he felt warmth and a faint beat beneath his fingertips.

"You're alright, Laura. It's me, Everton," he whispered. "Laura. Can you hear me?"

Her eyes popped open, revealing hugely distended pupils. Everton eased the tape from her mouth and she began babbling incoherently, repeating the same word over and over again. He couldn't understand what she was trying to say. It sounded like gibberish. Like she'd been drugged and was hallucinating.

"Ronkier! Ronkier!" she screamed. "Ronkier... Ronkier... Ronkier..." Her eyes widening in panic. "Ronkier, Ronkier..."

"Shh. It's okay, Laura. You're safe now," he reassured her.

"No no no – Ronkier, Ronkier!" she shrieked, desperately trying to warn him. But it was too late. Ron (Kieron) rose like a ghost from the rear of the Mercedes and struck Everton a sickening blow with a tyre wrench.

Kieron laid the unconscious Everton and Laura beside the body of Gina in the trunk of the Mercedes. Then took Everton's hand and scraped the nails across the inside of Laura's thigh. Rifling in his pockets, he found Everton's mobile and deleted his own earlier postcode text. He switched it to camera mode, pulled Laura into position and took a number of nude photographs of her. Finally, he replaced the mobile, took a second syringe from his kit and administered a dose of Rohypnol to Everton before easing him out of the trunk and dragging him over to the passenger seat of the Corsa. Satisfied with his work, he re-covered Laura and Gina with the tarpaulin, picked up his medical kit, locked the Mercedes and climbed into the driver's seat; for the car, and Everton's, final journey.

Stokenchurch Gap was less than a mile away. He'd decided on the location two days before when he formulated his plan, and knew it was ideal because its elevated position offered an uninterrupted view of the headlamps of any approaching vehicles for miles.

He parked in a lay-by on the brow of the hill and turned off his headlights, climbed out of the Corsa and hauled Everton into the driver's seat. He took the clippers, scissors, shaving foam and razor that he'd used on Laura from the medical bag, wrapped them in a towel and placed them into the passenger footwell. He took a half-bottle of vodka from his pocket and poured a large slug into Everton's mouth before placing it in the glovebox. He removed his surgical gloves, replaced them with a fresh pair and dropped the soiled ones into the driver's footwell, alongside the other "proof". Finally, he took Everton's head in his hands, twisted it into the correct position, and smashed the wound against the steering wheel.

Satisfied that he'd left no incriminating evidence of himself, he switched the ignition and headlights on, shoved the car into Drive and steered it out onto the brow of the hill. There was nothing but darkness and the slippery incline receding beneath him, but he knew from his recce that two hundred metres down the road turned sharply left, and a sign warned "DANGER". He slammed the door shut and released the car. He watched it gather speed down the hill, smash through the retaining barrier and launch itself into the gulley below.

It took him another hour to reach the farm. He was dog-tired and every muscle in his body ached. Removing Gina's body from the grave and reinstating the earth had taken two back-breaking hours, even though the soil was still relatively fresh, and he wasn't prepared for the shock of seeing how they'd butchered his beautiful dove. His only comfort was that her post-mortem scar almost perfectly matched his own and that the pathologist had unwittingly made his preliminary work much easier. Now all he had to do was make her beautiful again. And Laura Fell, her closest friend, would witness the transformation and eventually become a part of it herself.

He gently removed the bugs from Gina's hair and sponged the mud from her alabaster skin. Then he scrupulously washed her body with CHG, a powerful anti-bacterial liquid soap that he'd used at work and found very effective. He lifted her out of the bath, laid her onto a clean sheet and patted her dry with a towel. Then dusted her with perfumed talcum powder before wrapping her in a fresh sheet and carrying her downstairs. Manoeuvring into the boot room, he prised open the lid of an industrial-size freezer that took up most of the space with his knee. He laid her inside and adjusted the temperature to three degrees above freezing. He toyed with the idea of putting Laura in with her but, attractive as the idea was, he didn't have the energy; so, he emptied the bath, wrapped her in a blanket and dumped her in the bottom, ready for an early start in the morning.

He hated sleeping in his mother's brass bed; the memories of her leery smile as she patted the empty space beside her still haunted and humiliated him even in his dreams. She'd given her "bastard son" nothing in his life but loathing and a genetic mutation in his MLH1 gene – the Lynch syndrome – that carried a high risk of stomach and colon cancer. And like all good curses it had come true and he'd been forced to have most of his lower intestine removed. He had little choice but to use her bed since he'd used all the other bedroom furniture as fuel for the chicken pit, and he was too tired to drive back to London.

He peeled off his wig, shook it clean and draped it over the bedside lampshade, prised out his Instant Smile cosmetic teeth and placed them in their Tupperware container. He pulled the eyelid of his left eye open and, leaning close to the silver dressing-table mirror, eased the russet-coloured contact lens to the outer corner of his eye before lifting it out with his finger and thumb. He did the same with his right eye, placed both lenses into their individual plastic containers, added cleaning solution and shook them clean.

Satisfied, he sat on the edge of the bed and unlaced his desert boots. He stood and removed his chinos, precisely folding them before placing them on the end of the bed. The room was freezing and he couldn't risk getting a chill, so he was forced to keep his shirt and socks on before sliding under the musty merino-wool counterpane. He pulled it up around his chin and said a silent prayer of atonement to Gina; the same one he'd said every night since her death. Then Nephilim rolled over to sleep, content that the body of the interfering black copper would soon be found and allow him time to complete his sacred work without interruption.

He had no idea that Everton's body had already been found by a sixteen-year-old student called Pauline. Who, by a strange quirk of fate, not only shared his estranged wife's name but had also just lost her virginity to a fellow student. They were interrupted in their shared sleeping bag, like young lovers in a low-budget horror movie, by the sound of something crashing through the trees towards them. Pauline pulled on her tracksuit bottoms and peeked out the tent flap to be confronted by a scene of utter carnage. Everton's Corsa came to a metal screeching halt barely ten feet from the Duke of Edinburgh Award hiker's campsite, wedged on its side between two silver birches. Behind it lay a trail of devastation, as if a tornado had ripped through the coppice, and in front of it Everton sprawled in a bloody heap, as if spat from the wreckage. Without a second thought, Pauline ran towards him and called for help.

Her tutor, Lionel, who'd taken a Valium and zipped his sleeping bag above his head to help him sleep, hadn't heard a thing in his tent. He was staggered when he eventually answered his student's panicky calls and saw the drama being played out in front of his tent.

"What the hell are you doing?" he demanded of Pauline, who was kneeling beside Everton, pounding his chest.

"Giving him CPR. He's not breathing. There's been an accident."

"Pauline," Lionel said, asserting his authority. "Are you sure you know what you're doing?"

"I did first aid for my Silver Award. I need blankets and clean towels. He's bleeding."

"Alright! Someone get Pauline some blankets and towels!" Lionel shouted to no one in particular. "And call an ambulance! If you can't get a signal go to the top of the hill!"

"Done that, sir," said Pauline's boyfriend, who was standing amongst the half a dozen students gathered in an awed semi-circle, watching Pauline working on the black man.

"Right. Good. Phone the police."

"Done that too."

"Well, don't just stand there, move back and give her some room! And keep away from the car; it could be leaking fuel. Do not light anything. It could explode."

The Corsa didn't explode and soon after a fire crew and two medics arrived to take over from Pauline.

They were thirty-two minutes into the "golden hour" for trauma survival when Everton was winched up into an air ambulance as it hovered precariously above the rotor-battered tree tops. And the vital hour had come and gone by the time the chopper finally arrived at the John Radcliffe Trauma Unit in Oxford. The triage team were already working on Everton as they rushed the gurney from the car park landing zone and into A&E, where six medics lifted him onto an operating table and the critical battle to save his life began.

It took four hours and five pints of blood to stabilise him. At 3.12am he was transferred to the intensive care unit on the first floor. His injuries included multiple blunt-force traumas to the head, including three missing teeth and sixteen stitches to his scalp; a fractured collarbone, left arm and wrist; a punctured lung; and a bruised spleen. Cannula and multiple large bore lines were inserted into his arm and connected to infusion pumps. He was attached to a ventilator and put into a pentobarbitone-induced coma to allow his body and brain time to recover from the massive trauma.

The coop

Kieron – or Nephilim as he called himself on the farm – was awoken before dawn by a cacophony of crowing as the alpha birds of the Battery engaged in their daily battle for supremacy. He hated the sound and looked forward to putting an end to it once and for all. He should have done so earlier but there was something about their stupid bravery that he admired. They protected their flock from threats at all costs, even at the expense of their own lives. On killing days, as the piles of dead hen birds grew, he saw them launch suicide attacks on his mother, and her laugh as she kicked them like feather footballs into the wire-mesh netting of the coop. But, battered and bleeding like him, they'd still come back for more.

Even when she told him that she'd never loved him, that he was the "bastard progeny" of a hospital psychiatrist she was sectioned under, he never blamed her. He blamed *himself.* But it made no difference; she punished him for it all the same, banishing him to the coop. On his long nights alone with only the birds for company he learnt how to lie dead still and allow them to roost on him and keep him warm. It was a tiny symbiotic act of kindness and the only time in his life that he'd truly felt accepted – until Gina, his dove.

His first act of real defiance was at the age of ten, when he tried to intervene to protect his favourite cockerel from his mother's garrotte. She pushed him aside, grabbed the bird by its legs and clubbed him across the head with it until it was dead. She hadn't said a word but later as she tended the gash on his face with TCP, she told him that he'd learnt his first lesson about the cost of love… and by the time he watched her dying slowly of stomach cancer, he'd become a master of it.

Laura Fell seemed different though; she'd shown him respect and kindness and he was uneasy about abusing her trust, although he reasoned that it would only be a matter of time before she failed him. She'd already made advances, kissed him, showed him half-naked photos of herself whilst she was supposedly grieving. No, he was doing the right thing. But he had to be vigilant and control his craving. Nephilim could touch her but not purge her like the others. He wanted her conscious so she could experience first-hand his ultimate creation.

Groaning against the ache in his back and arms, he hauled himself out of bed and stood shivering on the worn lino. The room was arctic and icy draughts whistled through the rotten window frames. He'd been forced to get up in the night and put on his mother's old fleece dressing gown for warmth, but waking with the smell of her on his skin disgusted him, so he doused it and himself with talcum powder and made his way into the bathroom.

For a moment he panicked, seeing Laura lying motionless in the bottom of the bath, thinking that she was dead. But then he saw the soft swell of her white belly rising and falling in time with her shallow breathing. She looked beautiful and would look even better when he'd finished with her. He pulled off his dressing gown, covered her with it, turned and walked out of the bathroom, closing the door quietly behind him.

The chicken pit was an inferno. He was concerned that the smoke might be seen – he usually only burnt at night – but he had little choice but to get rid of the old installation to make room for his masterwork. He looked down into the pit, shielding his face against the furnace's heat. Francis Cole was burning well, but Barbara Crane's plumage had barely caught alight. He doused her again with petrol and stood back as she ignited into a fireball, intoning, "I am Nephilim… My spirit shall not abide in mortals… for they are flesh."

Rubbing the smoke and soot from his eyes, he trotted over to the mini-digger in preparation of refilling the pit.

Soon his work was nearly done. He scrubbed the coop clean and placed Laura inside. He eased the tape from her mouth and placed a bottle of water – with a few added drops of Rohypnol – and four slices of gluten-free fruit loaf beside her in case she woke. Finally, he exited, locking both doors behind him, secure in the knowledge that there was no one to hear her or find her.

He was standing at the kitchen sink, washing with some water that he'd boiled from the kettle, when he heard the news on Radio Jackie that a Met police officer had been found under suspicious circumstances in a crashed car near Stokenchurch. He smiled at a job well done and began to towel his face dry. Until he heard that Everton was still alive and had been airlifted to the John Radcliffe Hospital in Oxford.

"Fuck!" he exploded, gnawing at the back of his hand until he drew blood.

DCI Teal was prowling Stokenchurch Gap watching the Fire Crew in the gulley below laboriously fix steel cables to the Corsa and winch it, inch by inch, up to the road. Above him, the morose clouds rumbled ominously, as if reflecting his mood.

"It doesn't make sense. There are no skid marks, nothing," he called to Helen and Clarke as they trudged from the crash site back up the hill towards him.

"He was drunk," Clarke called back, pulling the collar of his donkey jacket up to shield him from the biting wind. "The medics reckon he stank of booze."

"He'd have still tried to brake," retorted Helen, who was still in a state of shock after being woken by a terse 4am phone call from Teal.

"He suffers from vertigo, maybe he blacked out?"

"And maybe it was a suicide attempt?" said Teal, stopping the discussion mid-flow.

"You're not serious, guv?"

"Of course I'm not bloody serious! But I'm going to have to tell the press something and nothing I've heard so far makes any more sense," he said, staring grimly down at the numerous evidence bags containing clippers, scissors, a razor, hair and a mobile; that were laid out on his car bonnet as if it were a car-boot sale. "Jesus. I can see the headlines now. 'Second Met COP KILLER."

"There's no way he murdered Laura Fell."

"She's missing and his mobile's full of naked photographs of her – bound and shaved," snapped Clarke. "Christ, Helen, how much more proof do you need?"

"In case you hadn't noticed, he's black. Our suspect is white."

"Keep it down," whispered Teal, who was in no mood to referee a shouting match between two of his detectives whilst the greedy-eared members of the press were corralled behind a barrier barely fifty metres away.

Clarke gave a disgruntled shrug and said, "Okay. But in my book, if it looks like shit and it smells like shit…"

Teal shoved his hands deep into the pockets of his Crombie overcoat, fishing for the comfort of his peppermints as he mused out loud, "Maybe Bowe was trying to make it look like it was our killer?"

"They could even have been working as a team, guv. Bowe was the first person to enter Gina Lewis' house after her suicide; he could easily have taken her mobile and laptop."

Helen feared she was losing Teal to Clarke's twisted logic and desperately needed to undermine his credibility. There was nothing else for it; she was forced to come clean and reveal Everton's information. "If he was in league with the killer, why would he give our two prime suspects an alibi?"

"He didn't," Clarke said dismissively.

"He did. He was the grass who told me Hart was robbing a bookmaker in Walthamstow at the time Tessa Hayes was attacked. And that Colin Gould was there too, stalking him."

"I was in the car when you got that call. You never said it was from Bowe."

"Because I didn't trust you! You've been leaking information about this enquiry from day one–"

"DC Lake–"

"It's the truth, guv, I can prove it–"

"Oh, this is bullshit," snorted Clarke. "Stop trying to protect him, Helen. Stop mixing up your professional and personal life. It doesn't work."

"Really? It didn't stop *you* sleeping with me, did it?"

Clark reacted like he'd been slapped in the face and spluttered, "You're a bloody liar."

"And you're a lousy fuck! You want proof, guv, check Everton's mobile. He showed me a video of the sergeant here secretly meeting an ex-cop called Brian Hoffman, who just happens to work as Celia Lewis' head of security. That's why you've been getting so much heat from above."

Teal fixed her with a look as dark as the overhead clouds and said, "I hope for your sake you can prove that."

"I can. It's all there. In the mobile–"

"Guv–"

"No! Not another word, Jack. Not a word." Teal pulled a pair of latex gloves from his pocket, deftly manoeuvred his huge hands inside and removed the mobile from the bag. Helen never took her eyes off Clarke, determined to savour the moment that the axe finally fell on him and his self-serving career.

"There's nothing here." Teal held up the mobile, revealing the empty video folder. Helen felt physically sick, realising that Clarke must have deleted the incriminating video when he'd first found the mobile.

"Sorry, Jack," said Teal, offering his hand to Clarke. "I wouldn't be doing my job if I hadn't checked."

"Hey, no problem, guv."

"Okay. Get these bags over to the lab. I want a full DNA profile on any blood or hair they find, ASAP. And tell them not to assume it's all from Laura Fell. I want to see if any of it matches Tessa Hayes."

Clarke nodded, collected the bags and made his way back over to his car. Helen watched him drive away.

Clarke could see her through his rear-view mirror and waited until she was out of sight before dialling Brian Hoffman to give him the news that they were in the clear.

Back on the hill, DCI Teal slipped another peppermint into his mouth and savoured the peppery heat before turning wearily to Helen. "For a woman with a first-class honours degree, you seriously fucked up – twice."

"It was there, I swear to God. Why would I ask you to look if it wasn't?"

"I have no idea. Who's supposed to have shot this mystery video? Not Bowe himself?"

"No. I think it was his wife. She's a journalist."

"I know," groaned Teal, remembering how she'd stitched him up after an interview two years previously. "Where is she now?"

"On her way to the hospital. DC Coyle's driving her and her son."

"Get in the car."

"Where are we going?"

"To the John Radcliffe Hospital – and I warn you, if Pauline Bowe doesn't corroborate what you're saying, you and your degree are going to be history."

* * *

Relaying the news of the accident had been bad enough, but having to explain the circumstances was a nightmare for Jerry Coyle. The young detective had been forced to field a barrage of awkward questions from Pauline Bowe on the journey from London. Questions that he didn't have answers to, or if he did he wasn't at liberty to divulge. To make matters worse, her son, Adam, broke down and sobbed. Coyle had tried his best to ignore it, but it was acutely embarrassing.

He was relieved to finally arrive at the John Radcliffe, even if it took him four laps of the car park to find a space. He followed

Pauline and Adam towards the reception, but as they entered the double doors she froze, seeing a crush of press and TV camera crews clustered to one side. A duo of Thames Valley cops was holding a press conference and it was clear from their taciturn replies to the questions that the story had already leaked. It felt like an out-of-body experience for Pauline. Her natural habitat had always been amongst the baying pack, but now she was isolated and felt vulnerable, knowing that if they saw her they'd attack. She covered her face, turned and walked quickly back out of the double doors.

Coyle found another entrance into the building through A&E, avoiding the press. They made their way through the battlefield of the walking wounded, heads down, and out into the main wing of the hospital. Coyle checked the confusing floor plan on the wall beside the lifts and finally pressed two for the intensive care unit.

As the lift doors gasped open, they were faced by another set of double doors leading to the ward. A sign below an orange bell on the wall read "Use antiseptic scrub" and "PRESS FOR ENTRY". They followed the instructions and one side of the double doors clicked open.

They walked into another world. The ward was like a set from a science-fiction movie. Eight identical beds, four on either side of the bare hangar-like room, contained patients, lying like statues, connected by various IV drips and feeding tubes to blinking monitors. Some were old, sunken-chested husks, whose parchment skin was bruised and punctured by catheters. Others were young; Adam had to avert his eyes as they passed the teenage victim of a hit-and-run accident, who'd had both her legs amputated below the knees. Accompanying the horror, like a movie soundtrack, was the constant low hum and harmonic beeps of the life-support machines. The ward's heartbeat.

"Excuse me. Can I help you?" offered the eager young sister, who'd materialized from behind the curtain of the only bay screened-off from the ward.

"DC Coyle. I'm looking for Everton Bowe. This is his wife and son."

The nurse nodded, disappeared behind the curtain and immediately reappeared with a constable, who looked incongruously out of place in a mask, with a hospital gown over his uniform.

"Hello. I'm PC Hope, Thames Valley Police."

"Is he alive?" The abruptness of the question took the young cop by surprise, especially since it came not from Pauline, but the intense-looking youth loitering behind her.

"Yes. Uh, he's critical but stable. Would you like me to get a doctor?"

"And a strong cup of black coffee, no sugar," added Pauline.

"Let me do that," said Coyle, eager for a break from what had been the longest two hours of his life.

Pauline and Adam were gowned and masked-up and led into Everton's cubicle by a no-nonsense IC nurse, who'd developed a habit of treating all visitors to the unit as if they were an encumbrance to her work.

"Please do not touch him or any of the monitoring equipment," she warned, as if it was a common occurrence.

"How long has he been unconscious like this?"

"He's not unconscious. He's in an induced coma. He's quite stable."

"Stable?" replied Pauline, horrified by the state of Everton. "This is stable?"

Everton heard the brittle female voice and something deep inside his limbic system, a somatic marker, stirred and awoke, allowing a memory to rise like a bubble to the surface of his brain.

And it was at that precise moment that he knew he was still alive.

* * *

The Real Bean Cafe was more McDonald's than Costa Coffee but not priced accordingly. Even so, it was packed at 7.55am with staff refuelling after their night shifts and outpatients who'd arrived for their early clinics. DCI Teal and Helen were sitting with Pauline at a quiet corner table, watching Adam, who was morosely checking the meagre display of Danish pastries on the burnt-sienna counter. It was the first time Teal had spoken to Pauline since she wrote the damning article about his failed burglary initiative and he felt obliged to clear the air before questioning her. Especially considering the circumstances.

"Look, Mrs Bowe, I know we've had some issues in the past…"

"Issues? I wrote an article which was the truth and you blamed my husband for setting you up. And then, despite the fact that you couldn't prove he had, you penalized him for doing it anyway. Well, you want to know something, Inspector? He didn't stitch you up. It was *me*. I did it. I used Everton to get to you and expose you and your inept department. He was actually appalled when he discovered what I'd done and begged me to shelve the interview. But I wouldn't, because I'm a journalist and it's my job." She took a tissue from her handbag, blew her nose, tossed it onto the table and shrugged as if to say "so now you know". "Actually, it was the thing that finally broke up our marriage. That and his blind, naive, faith in doing the right thing. And what did it get him, Inspector? You tell me?" She paused and waited for his response. But like all good coppers Teal knew when to stay silent.

Helen unfortunately didn't. "Pauline–"

"Mrs Bowe."

"Look… I know this must have come as a terrible shock for you, but–"

"For you as well. You and he are an item, aren't you?"

It was said without obvious malice but it stung like a nettle and Helen for all her bravado suddenly felt out of her depth. "That was a long time ago."

"Of course. I should have said 'were'. You shagged him and dumped him, didn't you? You know something, you're worse than he is," she said, nodding to the tight-lipped Teal. "You don't care about anything but your career."

"Helen," said Teal, placing a twenty-pound note onto the table. "Do you think you could get us all some coffee?"

"I like mine black," said Pauline.

Teal ignored the barb and continued, "And I'll have a bacon sandwich. I'm starving."

Helen hesitated, then rose and made her way slowly over to the counter. Pauline watched her go, bleakly amused. "Looks like *she's* got a problem with you too."

"No," lied Teal. "I have a heart condition. I shouldn't eat bacon, but on days like this you think fuck it, there are worse ways to die. Are you okay?"

"You mean considering my husband's a serial killer?"

The flak just kept coming; she had an arsenal of the stuff. "Is that a rhetorical question or do you want me to answer?"

"No," she said, allowing herself a wintry smile. "I have a tendency to switch to attack mode whenever I feel threatened. It's not my most endearing trait."

"In the circumstances, I can hardly blame you."

"About the article – it was a cheap shot. A headline for a quiet week. Sorry." Teal smiled ruefully in return but said nothing. "If it's any consolation to you, my over-eager colleagues outside are going to do the same to me and my family."

"How is he doing, your son?"

"He's not sure whether to hate his father or love him. I've always had that problem too."

"He doesn't make it easy for people. Speaking of which, I need to ask you a couple of questions. Did you record a meeting between one of my officers, DS Clarke, and a man called Brian Hoffman?"

Pauline, impressed by how deftly he'd manoeuvred the conversation, cracked a grin and said, "That was very smooth, Inspector. Yes, I did."

"Did you by any chance make a copy of it?"

"No. Everton didn't trust me not to use it. Once bitten, you know?"

Teal groaned. The ray of hope that had flickered briefly had as quickly been extinguished, and without it he knew that it wouldn't be DS Clarke's career that was over but DC Helen Lake's.

The journey back to London was punctuated by a series of prolonged phone calls to Teal. First from his superintendent, demanding to know what the hell was going on and why he'd been informed about Bowe by Commander Walsh, who'd heard the news from a "bloody journalist" rather than from Teal. Then from the borough commander himself, demanding to know exactly the same thing, and ordering an urgent meeting of all the heads of department to discuss the "disastrous management of the investigation" and how to limit the fallout. Then from Teddy, the forensic manager of the lab, confirming that he'd prioritised the case and even called in Dr Noonan, who was on sick leave, to help. He hoped that they'd have some preliminary results from the photographs later that day. But he felt it incumbent to voice his concern that DS Clarke seemed more concerned with convicting Bowe than waiting for any corroborating evidence.

Helen listened second-hand to the phone calls with a mounting sense of dread. Teal had already warned her that without hard evidence there was no way he could support the word of a police constable suspected of murder against a senior serving officer. His superiors would hang him out to dry. Helen argued in vain that there was no evidence to link Everton directly to the other missing women. But Teal told her she was being naive. The Met needed a result to get the press off their backs and charging Bowe would give them one. Plus, it would allow them to slip the moribund missing women enquiry quietly onto the back burner.

"Hold on. Are you saying you're pulling me from the case?"

"You've had a prior relationship with our prime suspect and made serious unfounded accusations against a fellow officer. What do you expect me to do?"

"Unfounded? I'd hardly call them unfounded."

"That's what DS Clarke will say, and you can't prove different. If he makes a formal complaint, I can't protect you"

"Or yourself."

"I'm not going to martyr myself for you."

"What about Hoffman?"

"He's an ex-cop, he knows the score. He'll deny everything. I'm re-assigning you to the Phipps Bridge stabbings."

"Guv, no. Please. I've been working on this missing women case for over a year."

"What you do in your spare time, DC Lake, is entirely up to you."

"What's that supposed to mean?"

Teal looked her squarely in the eyes and offered her a peppermint.

* * *

The briefing room on the second floor of the Wimbledon nick was full. Commander Walsh, Superintendent Cross, DCI Teal, DS Clarke, DCs Rogers and Coyle and PC Sugarman sat on one side of the Formica conference table with various files laid out in from of them. Forensics occupied the other side, along with two representatives from media and communications, who said little but took copious notes. The only absentee was the lead officer on the case, DC Helen Lake.

Teddy Baldwin was referring to a series of images uploaded from Everton's mobile that were being projected onto a whiteboard. "All of the photographs were taken at the same time, but you'll notice the body seems to have been moved into different positions, which would indicate that she'd been posed. Which suggests he was doing it for his own sexual gratification. I think he gets pleasure from dominating his subjects, terrifying them whilst they're still conscious."

"Hold on. How do we even know that she's even alive in these photos?"

"There'd be no need for him to tape her mouth if she was already dead," said James Noonan, as if patiently stating the obvious to a dim student.

The commander cleared his throat and moved the discussion briskly on. "Do we know anything about the car she was photographed in or the location?"

Noonan nodded to Teddy and allowed him to pick up the baton again. Teddy scanned the table for an ally, someone who was willing to support a fellow copper. There was no one. Not even Noonan. A decision had been made, and they were no longer looking for the truth, merely corroborating evidence to convict Bowe.

He ploughed on regardless. "Nothing, sir, except that the photographs appear to have been taken outside and at night."

"She was seen leaving her flat by a neighbour at around 11am. It's doesn't get dark until after five. Someone must have seen her in between," suggested PC Sugarman.

"She didn't take her car. We're assuming she either travelled to meet someone or was picked up locally," replied Coyle.

"We do know that Bowe placed a number of unanswered calls to her in the days prior to her disappearance," added Noonan. "Teddy logged seven I think."

"Six," corrected Teddy. "But if she was meeting Bowe surely she'd have answered his calls."

"Not if he was harassing her," interrupted Clarke.

"Why would she agree to meet him?"

"Maybe she didn't. He could have just lost it and abducted her."

"In broad daylight? Bowe's not stupid, Sergeant, he wouldn't take the risk."

"He was drunk. He reeked of alcohol. He didn't even attempt to brake when he crashed through that barrier on Stokenchurch Gap."

The commander glanced over at his PR team, smelling a potential problem, and said, "Did Bowe have a history of alcohol abuse?"

Teal, who could feel the noose tightening, and not just on Everton, formulated his response, saying finally, "He had some medical issues, sir. He was on gardening leave and I recommended that he apply for early retirement on health grounds."

"What type of health grounds specifically, Inspector?"

"High blood pressure. He also suffered from Meniere's Disease – vertigo. And he was diagnosed as suffering from chronic tinnitus in both ears."

"We're going to need a copy his medical records," interrupted one of the PR guys, leaning forward animatedly, intent on making a contribution. "To prepare a response before it leaks."

"It won't leak," interjected Teal, staring hard at Clarke. "Or heads will roll."

"For the record, sir," said Clarke, ignoring Teal and addressing the commander, "although I suspected PC Bowe was drinking, he never gave any indication of being under the influence of drugs whilst on duty. It wasn't until DC Coyle and I searched his flat that we found quantities of cannabis resin openly on display."

Superintendent Cross turned balefully towards Teal for confirmation. "He was using drugs too?"

Teal hesitated and took the only course left open to him: to side with Clarke and cut Bowe adrift. He said, "It appears that Bowe was self-medicating, sir. Using the drugs to treat his anxiety and ease his symptoms."

"Terrific," snorted the commander. "The press is going to love this. Alright. What about the car she was photographed in? Have we any idea what make it was?"

Teddy clicked through to another image, an extreme close-up of a chrome tailgate locking mechanism, and said, "It's a soft-close design, probably a Mercedes, sir."

"The same model used in the abduction of Tessa Hayes," added Noonan.

"Well, that's something at least. What about the colour?"

"From the trim, I would say it was either black or dark blue."

"Midnight blue. It's the same colour," said Clarke, ramming home the point. "It's him, sir. It's too much of a coincidence for it not to be."

"Except Bowe doesn't own a Mercedes," countered Teddy, doggedly determined to add a note of caution.

"That we're aware of," replied the commander. "I suggest we make tracing the car a priority. What about the scratches on the victim's leg?"

Noonan held out his hand, forcing Teddy to relinquish the clicker and his authority. He moved the images rapidly on to another close-up, this time of a series of small scratches on the inside of Laura's left thigh.

"The marks are consistent with those made with human fingernails."

A close-up of Everton's bloody fingernails was projected onto the screen.

"Significantly, the blood type of the sample retrieved from under PC Bowe's nails, seen here, matches that of the victim's, found in her medical records."

The room fell silent, realising the significance of the damning piece of evidence.

"Thank you, Mr Noonan. Alright, that's all for now, ladies and gentlemen," said the commander.

The team filed out of the room. The commander watched them go, leaned over to Teal and said, "Find her or her body. Then charge Bowe. Bury the bastard."

* * *

Celia Lewis was overseeing the preparations for her dinner party. The mayor was guest of honour and she'd invited five other influencers, none of whom were politicians, to balance the table. The Admirable Crichton were catering, which was expensive, but the dinner signalled her rehabilitation into the party so the investment was worthwhile. She was in the dining room checking the Wedgewood crockery whilst Angus decanted the Côte de Beaune in the kitchen. Under strict instructions not to sample it, he'd sneaked a sharpener earlier so was happy for now just to savour its heady perfume. Both of them heard the front door but left it for the other to answer. Since the debacle over Colin Gould, they'd barely been on speaking terms but had been forced to call a truce for the dinner. A waiter finally answered the door and ushered Helen into the hallway. Angus saw her and, mistaking her for the chef, wheeled himself out to welcome her. His greeting turned distinctly cool when Helen reintroduced herself as Detective Constable Lake.

"I suggest you speak to my wife. Celia!" he called, reversing back into the kitchen. "It's the police again!"

She was already dialling on her mobile as she powered into the hall.

"Mrs Lewis. I apologise for–"

Celia held her hand up for silence and barked into the handset, "Celia Lewis for Commander Walsh... Tell him it concerns our discussion and to ring me ASAP. Thank you." She turned with a face like bleached stone to Helen. "You do not come to my home without a prior appointment."

"If you'll just let me explain–"

"No. No more explanations. No more harassment. Leave. Now, please."

"Laura Fell has been abducted."

Celia took barely a moment to compose herself and replied in a voice that remained frighteningly detached, "I'm sorry, what has this got to do with me?"

Helen couldn't believe her indifference. It was as if they were talking about a complete stranger, not the closest friend of her daughter. "Mrs Lewis, it's possible that she could have been murdered. Don't you care?"

"Of course, I care. But it's your job to find her, Detective, not mine–"

"For God's sake, Celia!" snapped Angus from the kitchen doorway. "That's what she's trying to do, her bloody job."

Celia turned witheringly towards him. "She's not doing her job! She's been removed from the case! This has nothing to do with her. Now, will you please go back into the kitchen, pour yourself another whiskey or whatever it is you're drinking tonight, and leave this to me?"

Angus visibly wilted under her anger and, head down in humiliation, wheeled himself away. Helen was stunned, not by his capitulation but that Celia already knew about her demotion. Surely the information couldn't have come from commander Walsh?

"You're very well informed, Mrs Lewis."

"I make it my business to be. Now, I advise you to leave before I make a formal complaint and you find yourself in even more serious trouble."

Helen's confidence faltered. Until now she'd always put herself first, been ruthlessly pragmatic, but caring for somebody other than herself made her feel vulnerable. Celia sensed it, took the initiative and, reaching out, took her firmly by the arm and steered her towards the door.

"Goodbye, Detective."

It was the utter confidence in her voice that stopped Helen. "I'd think very carefully before you start complaining, Mrs Lewis. Otherwise the story of your infertility and Gina's adoption is going to be all over the newspapers. Not to mention your part in your husband's drink-driving cover-up."

Celia removed her hand and said icily, "You can't blackmail me."

"Watch me." Helen pulled out her mobile and pressed speed dial. "The news desk, please. Pauline Bowe… Pauline, it's me… Yeah, the Lewis cover-up story, go ahead and print it."

"No! Wait, damn you… Alright. Alright… What do you want to know?"

* * *

Teddy Baldwin tried to ring Helen back after her bizarre phone call, but found that her phone had been switched off.

Not long after, she walked through doors of the forensic reception and demanded an urgent meeting with him. He made no attempt to hide his animosity as he beckoned her to follow him inside the laboratory. "I'm busy. Make it brief."

"Of course," she replied, not rising to the bait.

She knew that Teddy had been the source of Everton's information regarding the bookie robbery. The question was whether she could persuade him to put aside his dislike of her to help his friend again.

"Look, you don't like me, Teddy, and that's fine," she said, keeping her voice low so as not to attract the attention of James Noonan, who glanced up at her as she entered from a nearby workstation. "But we both know that Everton Bowe is incapable of hurting a woman."

"It doesn't matter what you or I think, the evidence doesn't lie."

"Everton would never drive if he were stoned."

"How can you be sure of that?"

"Because his younger brother was killed in a crash whilst he was out of it on Ketamine and Everton never forgave himself for turning his back on him."

This was news to Teddy and he took a moment to assimilate it. "Okay. But he was found smelling of booze with a half-bottle of vodka in his car."

"Yeah, and that doesn't make sense either. He hates vodka, calls it 'girly giggle water'. He won't touch it. He only drinks rum."

Teddy caught the eye of Noonan, who was looking up from his bench, having overheard part of the conversation. Noonan shook his head and mouthed "stay out of it".

Teddy knew he should take his advice, that as a scientist he should adhere to the principles of the probability theory, but friendship and love weren't quantifiable like physics. He'd already lost a wife; he couldn't turn away and lose a friend too. "I'm assuming you told all this to DCI Teal?"

"I'm off the case."

"I know, I was at the briefing. As far as the Met is concerned you never existed."

"They need a scapegoat and I'm it."

"Now you know how Everton felt."

"Then help me clear his name."

"And get you your job back?"

"The two things aren't mutually exclusive, I admit. Are you going to help me or not?"

Teddy looked her slowly up and down and said, "Not you. Everton."

"Okay. Celia Lewis confirmed that her daughter Gina was adopted and that she'd traced her brother, a man called Kieron Allen. But she swears she knows nothing else about him. The thing is, Everton couldn't find anything about Allen either. He said it was weird, like the guy doesn't exist."

"The tracer must have found him."

"Exactly. She ran a company called Lost and Found. The thing is, I need access to her files to find him."

"So, phone her up."

"I can't. Her husband battered her to death ten days ago."

Helen left the lab with a folder containing the latest forensic data, and a warning that if she intended to remove evidence from a murder scene, Teddy didn't want to know. Noonan watched her exit and homed in on Teddy like an Exocet.

"Are you mad? Bowe did it—"

"Don't." Teddy held up his hands like a boxer on the ropes, knowing what was coming. "And you didn't see or hear any of that."

Noonan stared bleakly at him, then turned and stalked off, muttering, "Be it on your own head."

* * *

Everton hated eavesdropping on his family's grief but, hard as he tried to fight against the pentobarbitone, the words of reassurance wouldn't come. Worse still, he had no recollection of how he'd even got there, let alone the monstrous things he appeared to have done.

Adam was watching the Chelsea v Roma European Cup match on his iPad whilst he and his mum sat vigil beside the bed, but when Pauline slipped out for a coffee, he took one of the headphones from his ear and gently placed it inside Everton's.

"There you go, Dad," he whispered. "Up the blues, eh?"

It was a tiny gesture but the first act of kindness that his son had shown him in over two years, and if he could Everton would have cried with joy. Instead, he sank into the warmth of the feeling and let himself be swallowed by the drama of the big match. And as he did so, the face of his attacker, the man who had abducted Laura Fell, formed like a video camera pulling focus deep in his subconscious…

His name was *not* Kieron Allen.

All of a sudden, the dove's feather made perfect sense. It had been staring him right in the face. Why hadn't he seen it before? *He'd* known every move they'd made. *He'd* been playing with them. Christ, he had to warn Helen. She was the only one who could save Laura now. But how? He couldn't move. Not a finger. Not a muscle.

Adam stood and gently inserted the other headphone in Everton's ear, whispering, "Half-time. I'm going to check on Mum. Enjoy."

He turned and left the cubicle. Everton was alone. Beneath the numbing anaesthetic, panic began to gnaw at him. For the first time in his life, he felt fear, *real* fear. Not the nervous adrenaline rush of facing a drunk brandishing a bottle or a mouthy kid with a blade in his pocket and a braying gang behind him. But the certainty that an innocent person was going to die in a horrific way and he no longer had the power to stop it. It would be his ultimate failure. Worse than the loss of his job. Worse even than the self-inflicted loss of his son and his marriage. Then something extraordinary happened. His rage reached deep down into the barbiturate void, found him and began to haul him towards the surface. He lay there mute, in agony, ears howling with tinnitus, waiting, willing, praying for something to move.

Finally, the index finger of his left hand did.

* * *

Helen was wary of tripping a security light, but the floodlight over the white uPVC back door remained puzzlingly dormant. She tried the handle. It was locked. She drew a set of brass knuckles – illegal but useful – from her jeans pocket. She removed her scarf and wrapped it around her fist to deaden the sound when she punched out the kitchen window – but stopped as she saw the buckled frame.

Someone had already been there, jemmied their way in. Probably some scrote thief who'd been checking the newspaper obituaries and read about Amy Tann's murder. She blew in disgust, pulled the window open and climbed inside. The house was cold and smelt of bleach and pine disinfectant; disturbingly like the police morgue. And although Amy's body had been removed there were still faint blood spatters on the hall walls that the crime scene cleaners hadn't been able to remove.

Concerned about being seen, she shielded the glow from her iPhone light from the window, as she crept into the modernist through-lounge. Nothing appeared to have been disturbed, which was strange, but it was immediately obvious that the room was not being used as an office. She backed out, into the hall, and started slowly up the oak stairs.

Nephilim stood motionless in the gloom, waiting with mounting excitement as he listened to her footsteps approaching, knowing that she would soon be helpless under his knife and that he would finally purge himself of her. She was getting closer now. He could almost taste her.

Helen scanned the landing. Every door was open, apart from the front bedroom. She inched towards it, reached out and tested the chrome handle.

Nephilim watched the tiny, almost imperceptible movement of the handle. It was time. Checking Amy's laptop was secure under his sweater, he lifted the sliver of a blade above his head as if he were about to make a sacrifice, which in his mind he was. The door swung lazily open. He leapt forward to strike.

"I am Nephilim the…!"

The blade sliced through thin air. She wasn't there! He couldn't believe it. She had to be; he'd heard her on the stairs, seen her light. *Where the fuck was she?*

Helen was crouching in the bathroom behind him. She stepped out and aimed a chopping punch at his forearm. He screamed like a stuck pig and dropped the Stanley knife, clattering onto the floor.

Helen grabbed him by the back of his hair, snarling, "Move and I'll fucking brain you."

But as she dragged him around to get a view of his face, his hair literally came away in her hand. She stared down at the wig, stunned. Nephilim launched himself over the wooden banister, crashing down into the hallway below. Helen leapt down the stairs after him. But she was too late. He was already climbing out of the shattered window and by the time she got out and around to the front of the house he was nowhere to be seen.

She stood in the middle of the road, staring down at the chestnut-brown wig. It was made of real hair and was clearly expensive. She never heard the grey VW Golf powering up the road behind her until it was twenty metres away. Turning into the blinding headlights, she thought she caught a glimpse of the implacable face of the driver, before she was forced to dive aside. She lay on the cold tarmac, catching her breath, staring up at the starless sky, trying to place the features of her bald attacker. A face that was both similar but somehow different.

* * *

The sound of breaking glass reverberated around the ward like a gunshot. Hearing it, the IC nurse came running towards Everton's bed and was confronted by a scene of carnage. A tangle of weeping intravenous lines lay beside their shattered monitors, and beneath them sprawled Everton, face down in a slurry of saline, IV drugs and his own blood. She hit the crash team button and began yelling for help. The ward sister and the emergency resus team came racing onto the ward, struggling to digest what they found. How could a patient in a medically induced coma haul himself to the edge of the bed and fall/throw himself off?

Pauline panicked, seeing the curtains drawn around Everton's bed. The IC nurse tried in vain to keep her outside but she was having none of it and pushed her aside. Everton was back in his bed, re-medicated, eyes taped shut, as if nothing had happened.

The sister reassured Pauline that he was fine, that one of the monitors had come loose from a faulty stand, toppled over and broken an IV lead. But the shards of glass and blood on the floor indicated a different story. Sensing Pauline's disquiet, she grabbed a handful of paper towels and began to mop the floor. Pauline reluctantly stepped aside to allow her to work and was stunned – beneath her feet she appeared to be standing on the remains of a word written in Everton's blood. It read:

Ki noOna

Before she could question the sister further, the lino and Everton's message had been mopped clean.

* * *

James Noonan was in agony. Not just physically – he could barely grip the steering wheel – but mentally, wondering if Helen had seen his face. If she had, would she even recognise him, from the forensic lab, without his wig? He'd no way of knowing but knew he had to plan for the worst and that would mean disappearing. But in doing so he'd immediately draw attention to himself?

His mind was reeling with the possible ramifications as he pulled in and parked on the forecourt of the Tesco Express on the Upper Richmond Road. Biting down on the back of his hand sent shards of pain searing up his injured forearm, but finally his head began to clear.

Nursing his arm, he made his way inside the gaudily lit shop and bought a packet of Nurofen and a half-bottle of Bells using a twenty-pound note. Head down, away from the security camera, he hurried into the unisex lavatory. The fluorescent light flared on automatically and he caught sight of his stark reflection in the mirror above the moulded plastic washbasin. He looked haunted, furtive, nothing like Nephilim, a demigod. *More like a fox caught in a chicken coop*, he thought, bleakly.

It took three Nurofen and a couple of huge belts of Scotch to stop him screaming as he eased off his jacket and – worse – his sweater. A four-centimetre bruise puckered his left forearm and purple swelling flowered around it. He feared his radial bone was fractured but he knew he couldn't risk going to A&E. If the police were looking for him it would be the first place they'd check. He fashioned a sling out of his sweater by tying the two arms together and slipped the loop over his head. He took another hit of the Scotch and gingerly eased his left arm inside the crude woollen cradle.

"Hello… Hello?"

Someone began rattling at the lavatory door.

"Hello? There are other people waiting, you know. Hello?"

"Sorry. I won't be a minute," he replied through gritted teeth.

He slipped his jacket over his shoulders, hiding the sling, pocketed the Scotch and tablets and slid the bolt open. The paunchy guy threw him a dirty look and hurried his kid inside. Nephilim wanted to kick the door down and smash him and his mewling progeny to a pulp. But Noonan was forced to swallow his anger like a piece of rancid meat and walk out.

Forty minutes later he'd cleared his rented studio flat of anything compromising and was on his way down the A3 to the coop and his dove. The pain in his arm was easing and he'd regained some mobility in his fingers, which thankfully meant that it hadn't been broken. But he knew he could still be in danger.

He calculated it would take twenty-four hours at least for anyone to connect him to the farm. If he worked through the night he should have more than enough time to complete his angels. Even if he had to leave Gina behind, she would be his legacy and Laura, her best friend, his gift to her.

* * *

Helen was driving back to her flat and debating whether she should report the break-in and attack at the house. But how could she explain what she was doing there when she'd been removed from the case? The Met were looking for another scapegoat and would throw the book at her. Pauline's phone call interrupted her gloomy deliberations. She pulled over, fearing it was more bad news, but Pauline informed her curtly that Everton was not dead; on the contrary he seemed to be trying to communicate with someone. She assumed it must be her, since she had no idea who "Ki" or "Noona" was.

Helen listened in awed silence as Pauline relayed the story of the name Everton had written in his blood. *Ki = Noona...?* Ki could be Kieron. Kieron Allen. But who or what was Noon...? It sounded like Noonan, the forensic scientist. Surely Everton couldn't mean James Noonan?

She wracked her brain, trying to picture the hit-and-run driver. She'd only caught a glimpse of him, but she remembered thinking he seemed somehow familiar. Could Noonan be the killer she'd been hunting? Not just having changed his name and appearance when trawling the online dating sites, but in real life too? It was bizarre, but it would explain why Kieron Allen had been impossible to trace – he didn't exist.

She thanked Pauline for her help, cut the connection and picked up the brown wig from the passenger seat. Turning it over to examine it more closely, she noticed as small label stitched on the seam beneath it: RayRee M628. Could it be the name of the owner? Or maybe the manufacturer code? She began googling RayRee on her mobile.

Reece Holloway had taken Raye, his over-glamorous wife, to dinner to celebrate the return of her driving license after her second drink-driving ban. It meant he no longer had to do the school run, which he dreaded because at his age he got some odd looks at the school gates. So, the wig-maker was not entirely happy to have his crab linguine interrupted by a phone call from some police woman he'd never heard of. Helen apologised and explained that she'd got his contact number from the RayRee website. He was adamant that he couldn't meet until the following morning until she informed him bluntly that a woman might have been murdered by one of his clients.

Half an hour later, she was waiting outside his office on the Upper Richmond Road when Reece and Raye emerged from a taxi clutching a doggy bag of linguine and the remains of an expensive bottle of Rioja. Reece unlocked the warehouse door and ushered Helen inside.

The ground floor was the size of a tennis court. Eight equally spaced workstations were centrally situated, each with its own inbuilt sewing machine and extendable electric magnifier. Numerous bits of wig-making equipment littered the desks and one wall was taken up by a huge wooden filing cabinet with numbered drawers.

"Each drawer has a three-digit code which breaks down the hair into the colour, ethnicity and style of the sample," explained Reece. "The drawers are lined with linen and the samples individually wrapped in parchment paper and renumbered with the client's ID code."

"So my wig can be traced back to its owner?" said Helen, cutting to the chase.

"Yes. I'm assuming you have it with you?"

Helen unzipped her leather jacket and dug the hairpiece out.

"That's one of mine," said Raye, without evening check the code.

"You made it?"

"God, no, I wouldn't have the patience. I'm a hair stylist. Once the wig's been made, I cut and style it on the client. All our wigs are bespoke."

"Do you remember the client's name? It's very important."

"Not offhand. But it would be in our records. Reece, be a doll and bring down the laptop and a couple of glasses," she said, deftly removing the bottle of Rioja from his hand.

Reece did as he was ordered and laboured up the steel staircase and into the glass-fronted office that overlooked the workspace like a giant aquarium.

"Can you remember anything about the man?"

"I think Reece made a number of wigs of different colours and styles for him, which was unusual."

Helen felt her excitement rising; everything pointed to it being the same man.

"His name was Moon. Joshua Moon," Reece called from the office door. "I think I've still got his fitting photographs on my Nexus."

Helen met him at the bottom of the stairs and swiped through the series of photographs on his tablet. They were of the forensic scientist, James Noonan, trying out an assortment of wigs. Helen was stunned.

"You're sure that was his name? Moon not James Noonan?"

"Yes. I remember, because he was weird around women. Didn't like being touched."

"Do you have any contact details for him?"

Reece handed over a card with an Earlsfield address.

She was risking everything to nail Noonan personally, but Helen calculated that DCI Teal would be reluctant to believe that the forensic officer had attacked her and tried to run her over. Besides, if she didn't do something urgently he'd disappear and, in all probability, Laura Fell with him.

"If he hasn't already," she muttered to herself as she pulled up outside a brutally ugly block of flats on Burntwood Lane in Earlsfield.

Jake Oliver was in the habit of ignoring the caretaker's buzzer after dark. The block had been plagued by local kids playing knock-knock and he was tired of being taken for a mug, especially when he was concentrating on his miniatures. He only reluctantly placed his sable brush aside, switched off his fluorescent magnifier and hauled himself over to the video entryphone. He was intrigued to see an attractive young woman holding up a warrant card to the security camera.

Helen was right. She was too late. Apart from the furniture and a few prints on the walls, Noonan's studio flat was virtually empty. There were no personal photographs, letters or bills in the drawers and few clothes in the wardrobe. Even the kitchen bin was minus its inner bag.

Jake was impressed. "He's very neat."

"Not neat. Careful," corrected Helen. "When does your rubbish get collected?"

"Tomorrow. Around 6am. Why?"

The bin shed was dark and stank of fox, sour milk and soiled nappies. Worse, some of the bin liners had overflowed from the enormous containers and spilt onto the cement floor, making it unpleasantly sticky to walk on.

"If there's anything here it'll be in a landfill bag. He'll have tried to hide it."

Jake switched on his Magalite, hissed at a couple of truculent rats, forcing them to scurry for cover, and began sifting through the mush. Helen spotted a copy of *Racing Pigeon UK* jutting from a ripped bag and told Jake to dump the contents onto floor. Amongst the detritus were some scraps of a photograph. She began to reassemble them like a jigsaw and gasped as an image emerged of Gina Lewis standing beside a silver Golf – the same car that had earlier tried to run her down.

"Can you make out the number plate?"

"No. But that's not a problem." Jake grinned. "Follow me."

Helen stared in awe at the scale of the work. The whole lounge floor had been turned into a battlefield, a miniature version of

Waterloo with the British, German, Belgian, Prussian and Dutch armies lined up in formation against Napoleon's French Grande Armée.

"Still got to do the French infantry and the Little Corporal. I'm saving him until last," Jake explained as he scrutinised the reassembled segments under his magnifier. "Bingo. C102 LYT."

Helen almost decimated the Prussian army in her haste to retrieve the photo.

Trotting back to her car, she called in requesting an urgent PNC check on the silver Golf and plate. But it was not Joshua Moon, James Noonan or Kieron Allen who came back as the registered owner. It was a woman. Her name was Penny Croft and she lived seventy miles away, in Winchester, Hampshire.

The doves

Laura screamed herself hoarse. But as the hours went by, slowly, inexorably, she began to realise that there was no one to hear her cries.

She was lying in a large wooden shed with a metal workbench at one end, covered in anatomy and religious textbooks, and a small Calor Gas heater at the other. Her left wrist was shackled by a chain to a large iron ring on the wall. She had no idea where she was or how she'd got there or what time it was. The last thing she remembered clearly was having lunch with Kieron. Everything afterwards was just a montage of horrors; of ripping clothes, falling hair and dripping blood.

She reached for the bottle of water and lifted it to her lips. But as she did so another flashback stopped her. An image of her gagging as someone squirted liquid into her mouth. She'd been drugged! That would explain how he'd got her here without a struggle and her nausea and her blinding headache. She sniffed the water. It smelt of nothing and she was desperately thirsty, but she knew she couldn't trust it. She emptied the bottle between the wooden planks of the floor and began to weep, dabbing her parched lips with her own salty tears.

It was three hours later when she woke again needing to pee. There was just enough play in the chain to allow her to find a suitable gap in the planks where she could squat and relieve herself. She remembered her father's warnings on their Maasai Mara safaris about burying any trace of yourself so as not to attract animals and *never running when faced by a predator*. Even in her panic she knew he was right and that her only hope now was to find the courage to do the same.

She eased herself to her feet, shuffled along the wooden wall and peered through a gap in the planking into the adjoining room. It seemed to be some sort of aviary. She could hear birds cooing and occasionally something white fluttered past. *Oh, my God*, she thought. *They're doves.* Had Kieron been the man who abducted the woman in the river? Had he been the person she stumbled upon in Gina's house?

She staggered back and checked the room, looking for clues. The wall opposite was covered by posters of Hieronymus Bosch paintings; *The Fall of the Rebel Angels* and *Paradise and Hell.* Scrawled across the metal ceiling were the words:

the CHILDREN of HEAVEN LUSTED AFTER THEM

Her mind was reeling. She tested the ring that she was padlocked to, but much as she tried there was no way she could loosen it without some sort of tool. The slightest effort made her feel weak, and the room pitched and rotated, forcing her to grab for the wall to steady herself. Thankfully, after a few seconds it subsided, but she still felt nauseous and let herself slide slowly down until she came to rest on the floor. Something sharp dug into her thigh. She felt inside the dressing-gown pocket and amongst the detritus found the cause of her discomfort. A metal hairpin without a safety tip. She fished around in the other pocket and found an old handkerchief and three more hairpins

One by one she started to pull them apart. It was painstaking work and as her fingers tired she resorted to holding one end of the rigid metal between her teeth and slowly prising the other leg open until it straightened out. The metal was stiff and the sharp ends cut her lips and gums. She had nothing to rinse her mouth with, so every few minutes she had to tear off a piece of currant loaf and suck on it to soak up the blood and metallic taste.

An hour later, totally exhausted, she'd plaited the thin iron strips into a crude fifteen-centimetre shank. Now she had a tool – and a potential weapon.

When she woke again the room was dark but for the orange blush of the gas heater. She crawled over to the iron ring again and dug at the planking around the edge of it. The wood was soft but the planks were thick and the ring had been tightly screwed into the surface.

She was still burrowing the wood when she heard the sound of his car approaching. She swept up the wood splinters and, chewing them into a rough paste, desperately moulded them into the trench she'd scored in the wood. She did the same with the current bread to approximately match the wall colour. It was a crude disguise, but in the half-light passable. She still had to find somewhere to hide the shank so it could be retrieved at a moment's notice. She pulled the embroidered hanky from the dressing-gown pocket and wrapped it around the shank. Then she took a deep breath and reached down between her legs.

* * *

Joshua Moon, a.k.a. James Noonan, a.k.a. Kieron Allen, took a shot of his mother's morphine. He re-strapped his forearm and, gritting his teeth against the pain, lifted Gina from the freezer and laid her on a clean sheet on the pine kitchen table. He applied foundation to the scar that haloed her neck, disguising his shame, before using a hairdryer to gently bring her body up to room temperature, in preparation for cutting her hair.

It was a time-consuming process but necessary. He still needed to inject the body with a precise solution of water and formaldehyde to keep it plastic and sterile. He needed the flesh malleable enough to allow him to hook in the wire loops, which the nylon monofilament would be threaded through to keep her and the finished tableau fixed in position, but not so soft that her flesh would tear – a problem he'd encountered with some of his earlier models. Fortunately, he didn't need to bleed and gut Gina, and any signs of rigor had long left her body which would make moving her considerably easier.

Once in the coop, he would apply the Duo surgical adhesive and, one by one, the poultry flight feathers until he'd covered her whole body and face. Then he would start on the meticulous over-dressing of the dove plumage, until only her beautiful agate prosthetic eyes, framed in chaste, white down, would be visible. Gina would be resurrected as an angel, but not like the others, she would be *Nephilim's bride*.

The thought filled him with pure joy.

* * *

Forty-six miles away, Helen was in the lounge of Penny Croft's Winchester semi, a room that looked as worn its owner. Helen guessed she was probably in her forties but bitterness had aged her beyond her years.

"Joshua Moon or whatever he calls himself now is a lying piece of shit," she said as she paced the rug in front of Helen.

"How did you originally meet him?"

"I'm an oncology nurse. He was referred to the unit for post-operative chemo."

"He had cancer?"

"A genetic abnormality. The Lynch syndrome. He inherited it from his mother. He had to have his colon removed. They should have taken his balls too; it would have saved me a lot of grief. Three years we were together. Three years I nursed and cared for him. Then he got some job in London and everything changed. He started not coming home at night, saying he had to work late, help his mother at her farm on the weekends."

"Was it a poultry farm?" Helen interjected, already knowing the answer.

"Yes, but it was just an excuse. I checked his mobile and found out he'd been using sex lines and online dating sites. He went mad when I confronted him. Accused me of spying on him and betraying his trust. Acted like he was the victim not me. I came home from work the next day and found he'd packed his stuff and left. No note. Nothing. He just took the car and pissed off."

"Did he leave anything behind? Anything at all?"

"He didn't have anything to leave. He said it was all in storage until he moved into the farm. Some letters came for him. He texted, asking me to forward them to some PO box."

"And did you?"

"No! Screw him. If he wants them he can come and face me like a man."

"You mean you still have them? The letters?"

Penny shook her head. Helen sensed that she was embarrassed, that by admitting it she'd look as if she still harboured some naive hope of him returning. Which was probably why she never reported the car missing.

"If you want to punish him, Penny, help me find him and I promise you I will."

Penny nodded for Helen to follow her into the kitchen. Ten minutes later, sitting at the cluttered pine table, reading through Noonan's letters, Helen pumped her fist in triumph. The document she held in her hand was an invoice for poultry pellets and was addressed to:

Mr Joshua Moon. Dark Water Farm, Bignor, West Sussex.

* * *

Hoare frost flowered like a rash on the corrugated roof of the coop. Joshua Moon checked his pockets for his gloves and felt the reassuring handle of the electric cattle prod – an eBay present to himself that had come in useful on occasion. He'd made a cursory check on Laura on his return but, finding her still unconscious with the empty bottle of drugged water beside her, simply turned up the dial on the gas heater and left her to concentrate on his love, Gina. But by now Laura should be conscious.

He let himself in, switched on the strip light and held out his arms in welcome to the birds. None of them moved. He looked down at the floor and saw why. Two doves lay dead on the shit-encrusted floor. He couldn't understand what had killed them. Checking the water trough, it became clear. It was bone-dry. Consumed by his problems, he'd forgotten to replenish it and the birds had died of thirst. He stood over their limp white bodies, ashamed of his selfish cruelty. They'd been his friends and he'd abandoned them. Just as he'd been abandoned in the past.

Laura heard him agonising over his loss. The connecting door swung open and she saw him through half-closed eyes looming above her. In each hand, he cradled the body of a dead bird like an offering. He knelt beside her and held them close to her face as if somehow comparing or matching the colour to her skin tone. He eased open her dressing gown, pulled out a red felt-tip pen from his pocket and began to draw on her stomach. She hardly dared breathe, praying he would look away for the split second it would take to reach her weapon. He didn't. Finally satisfied, he laid the dead birds on her belly, mouthed a silent prayer, bent and kissed them and made his way back out.

She wanted to scream but she suspected that he was listening next door, testing whether she was really unconscious. After an eternity, she heard the outer door bang shut and his feet on the gravel walking away. Only then did she look down at her stomach – and it wasn't the dead birds that horrified her but the plan for the incisions he intended to make.

* * *

Helen got lost in the warren of country lanes south of Petsworth and only stumbled upon the sign to Dark Water by luck.

The lake seemed to suck the light from the cloud-swept moon, leaving the track beside it ominously dark. She parked on a grass verge and checked her iPhone. No signal. Calling for back-up was not an option. She should have done it earlier but she'd been preoccupied in reaching the farm and now she was on her own. She smiled ruefully to herself; perhaps she'd wanted it that way all along?

She climbed out of the car and scanned the rutted track that branched at an acute angle from the road. Three hundred metres ahead it was swallowed by a pine forest. She shivered, zipped her leather jacket tighter under her chin and opened the car boot. Reaching inside a sports bag, she pulled out a can of pepper spray and an ASP baton. She slid the baton inside her knee-length boot, the spray into her jacket pocket and her brass knuckles onto the fingers of her right hand. She closed the trunk, took a deep, deep breath, and started up the track.

* * *

Laura cursed as the shank caught the bottom of the iron ring and dug into her palm. She re-wrapped the handkerchief around her hand and laboriously scraped at the wood again. She was making progress but the deeper she dug the harder it became and she was reluctant to widen the cut, fearing it would make it more likely to be seen.

"Hello, Laura," a voice called from outside.

She froze. It was him. Why hadn't she heard him approaching? Had he been watching her through the wall? Christ, did he know she had a weapon?

"How do you like my studio?"

She could hear him walking around the perimeter of the coop, his footsteps crunching on the frosty grass. She began desperately ramming the splinters of wood back into place. But she knew she wouldn't have time. She heard the outer door open and the scraping sound of something being dragged along the wooden planking. *Shit* – the splinters kept falling from the cut. She spat on them, desperately trying to knead them back into position – *shit* – he was unlocking the interconnecting door – *shit* – she had to get rid of the shank, do something to distract him.

"I have a surprise for you." The door swung open and Joshua entered, dragging a black body bag behind him. "Can you guess who this is?"

She took a step backwards, horrified of the thought of who might be inside, but still had the presence of mind to block his view from the gouge she'd made in the wall.

"Don't be frightened. I am Nephilim, and I'm going to make her beautiful again," he said as he hauled the body bag onto the workbench and unzipped it with his good hand. "And you're going to help me."

Laura was horror-struck, unable to move or speak. Gina's whole body had been shorn of hair and she lay amongst a bed of chicken feathers and pure white dove down.

"And in return I'm going to do the same for you."

He watched her reaction and leant down and kissed Gina full on the lips. Laura felt physically sick but she knew that he would only feed off her fear. She swallowed her revulsion and somehow found her courage and her voice.

"Did you kill her?"

"No," he said, full of righteous indignation. "I loved Gina. She taught me the true nature of love and devotion. Something you'll never understand."

"This isn't love. This is disgusting! You're insane–"

"Don't!" he warned, drawing the cattle prod like a pistol. "Or I will teach you the meaning of sin and atonement…"

He switched on the baton and, smiling, moved slowly towards her. She could hear the hum from the electrodes protruding out of the fibreglass tip, but stood her ground, repeating her father's words like a mantra in her head. *Never run… Never run…*

"And you, Laura, will lament in tears."

Something snapped in Laura; she stepped forward, ripped off her dressing gown and stood, nakedly defiant, in front of him, challenging him, "Come on. This is what you want. Come and take it. Or aren't you man enough to do it with a woman without drugging her first?"

Joshua hesitated. Apart from his mother and Gina, the only other women he'd ever seen naked were the victims of his attacks. And now Laura stood in front of him, like his mother had, mocking his masculinity. He jabbed the electric wand against the metal roof above her head, watching the electrodes crackle and spit, and sneered, "I don't do sluts and I don't do whores. But if you don't put your clothes on, I will do you with this and it will burn and hurt. Do you want that, Laura? Do you want to fry?"

Never run... Never run... Never run...

"If I'm a whore your perfect sister was too," taunted Laura, inching closer to the smoking terminals. "Do you want me to tell you about Gina? The men she fucked – that we fucked together?" She could see Joshua's hand trembling. "The times we fucked each other?"

The confusion in his eyes, as she smiled and inched even closer. "What's the matter? Don't you like it when I talk dirty?" Licking her fingers one by one, she reached slowly down between her legs and smiled, "Gina did."

He couldn't take his eyes off her and her fingers working between her legs.

"She said I was better than any man."

He was transfixed. Laura could feel the shank at her fingertips. She inched forward to within striking distance, gritted her teeth and – *whaa-whaa! whaa-whaa!* – a piecing alarm wailed a warning, sending Joshua scurrying from the room. She groaned, staring down at the home-made shank in her hand, knowing that the chance she'd waited and worked so hard for had gone. She dropped slowly to her knees and wept. Not just for herself but for her best friend Gina.

* * *

"Fuck," Helen cursed her stupidity. She'd assumed the house wasn't alarmed and had inadvertently triggered a PIR sensor whilst searching for evidence.

She was cowering in the bedroom, watching Joshua through the window as he knelt on the frozen grass examining the neat set of her footprints that led directly up to the cottage. He looked up and saw her, and for a moment she actually thought he smiled. Then he stood and ran.

She snapped his Samsonite briefcase shut, shoved it under her arm and started for the stairs. But she could already hear him banging through the front door. She backtracked up onto the landing, desperately looking for another escape route. The bathroom door was open and she ducked inside and slipped the bolt. She could hear him pounding up after her. The door wouldn't hold him for long and there was no way out apart from the window. But it was a twelve-foot drop onto a concrete patio. She swung the briefcase and smashed the window to pieces.

Joshua heard the breaking glass and knew immediately what was happening. He raced back down the stairs, ripped open the front door and, howling like a wolf, loped around to the rear of the cottage. She wasn't there. Only his open briefcase lay on the concrete floor. It was empty. His secret was gone. The bitch had tricked him.

"I'll gut you!" he bellowed as he kicked the back door off its hinges. But she was gone too. The bathroom door was open and this time there were no footprints leading away from the house for him to track. He let out a howl of frustration, "I am Nephilim. You cannot hide from me!" He began to search.

Laura could hear him raging and screamed for help.

Thank God, thought Helen, as she slipped through the sliding metal door of Battery 1, *she's still alive*. But she daren't reply for fear of revealing her own hiding place. She switched off the fluorescent lights and crept into the ominous void, squeezing herself deep between the narrow avenues of cages, watched only by the beady eyes of the occupants.

Joshua knew she was inside. There was no sign of her on the track out of the farm and no other way out. Besides, who else would have shut off the 24/7 lighting? He hauled open the heavy doors, threw the switch and powered the fluorescent tubes back on. Hollering and howling and clattering the cages as he passed, he started to hunt. The chickens screeched in panic and threw themselves against the cages. Still he couldn't find her. He ripped open the cage doors. The birds spewed out and surged through the aisles like a tide. He waded through them like a demented shepherd, thrashing them into a frenzy. The air was full of dust and shrieking and feathers. In the middle of the mayhem Joshua found comfort in his hand. Biting it until the taste of his own blood satisfied his lust and he regained his composure.

It was a vision from hell and Helen could only crouch in the shadows, clutching her baton and pepper spray, transfixed and terrified.

Joshua strode out into the central aisle so he could be clearly seen, unbuttoned his jacket and shirt and smeared the blood across the vertical scar on his belly to form a crucifix. He held out his arms like a prophet and proclaimed, "I am Nephilim. A giant. A son of God. A hunter… and I will purge you."

Then he turned abruptly on his heel and was gone. Helen was staggered. It was the closest she'd ever been to true madness and it had shaken her to the core. Her knuckles were white from gripping the baton and she realised she'd been holding her breath. She sucked in a huge, shuddering lungful of air but the awful sense of dread still clung to her.

"Get a grip," she whispered to herself.

She stood and plotted her way through the maze of empty cages towards the exit – and was hit by 2.3 million volts of electricity.

Joshua switched off his cattle prod, kicked her baton and pepper spray aside, knelt and removed the brass knuckles from Helen's twitching fingers. Then he grabbed her by her hair and dragged her out into the central corridor, towards the door.

The sea of chickens parted in silence to allow the prophet to pass.

* * *

Laura kept her head down, not daring to look as he staggered in with Helen and dumped her onto the studio floor like a carcass.

"Crisis over, and she didn't bring any back-up," he grinned, tossing Helen's mobile beside the cattle prod on the bench. "She hasn't used her phone in the last two hours."

He removed some plastic cable ties and a pair of pinking shears from his metal toolbox on the bench, hauled Helen onto her back and sat astride her, chuckling as he fastened her wrists to the iron rings on the floor. "I'm going to enjoy giving you whores absolution."

He turned to check on Laura's reaction. But she said nothing, simply remained curled in a foetal position beneath the dressing gown with only the back of her bald head visible. He reached over and gave her a slap on the rump.

"Not so cocky now, are we?" He picked up the pinking shears and began to scissor through Helen's leather jacket. "Don't think that will save you. It will be your turn next."

Reaching inside the jacket, he pulled out a faded newspaper. "Ah, here it is," he said and tossed it beside Helen's mobile on the bench. "Now let's see what other secrets you've got hidden in here," he said, ripping open Helen's blouse and sliding the blade of the shears under her bra.

"Leave her alone!" Laura's interjection took him completely by surprise. He pivoted around to confront her. But something was wrong. She hadn't moved. She was still lying inert in the corner. "Move and I'll kill you."

He was bewildered. It was Laura's voice but it didn't seem to be coming from her body.

It wasn't. He was staring at the body of *Gina*. Laura was stepping out of the black body bag *behind him*. He turned quizzically towards her.

She lifted her home-made shank like the sword of an avenging angel, saying, "I told you not to move," and stabbed him in the neck, puncturing his carotid artery.

Joshua flapped like a wounded bird, attempting to stem the fountain of blood. Then slowly toppled off Helen and rolled onto his back on the floor.

"I warned you."

His eyes brimmed with tears as he stared up at Laura in disbelief. Her naked body was spattered in his blood and white down. He watched in awe as a tiny feather fell from her hand and floated slowly down to land on the bloody cross on his chest.

"I thought you were my Gina," he whispered. "Risen again."

Then with a smile of infinite sadness he closed his eyes and died.

A cockerel still heralded the new day at Dark Water Farm, but now its flock ranged free, scavenging around the police vehicles and the tent that had been erected to shield the chicken pit and its precious human remains. Helen watched the SOCOs going about their grim work, clutching Joshua's faded newspaper and its final secret to her chest. She'd refused to leave with Laura in the ambulance, insisting that it was *her* case, she'd cracked it and she would see it through to the end – and *nobody* apart from PC Everton Bowe was going to take any credit for it.

* * *

Three days later, Everton was woken from his induced coma with the news that he should make a full recovery. A week later he was moved out of intensive care onto a general ward.

He was sipping his lunch, a watery banana smoothie, through a straw when the sister interrupted him to ask if he felt well enough to have a visitor. It wasn't his wife who entered the ward, nor Laura Fell, but Acting Detective Sergeant Helen Lake.

He was delighted by the news of her pending promotion and told her it was fully deserved, but he still didn't understand Joshua Moon's obsession with his sister. It had to be more than just genetic sexual attraction. He seemed to genuinely care for Gina and blamed himself for her suicide.

"That's because she wasn't his sister. Joshua wasn't Gina's brother. He was her father."

Everton was stunned.

"Her *father?*"

He watched in silence as Helen pulled out an evidence bag containing the faded newspaper she'd found at the farm.

"Yes. And there's more. I found this in his briefcase," she said, handing it to him, "along with an MMS selfie Gina took of her suicide."

The newspaper was dated 1979. The headline read:

15-year-old Boy accused of Rape

"Joshua Moon raped her mother. A woman called Jennifer Allen. She had an illegitimate child. A girl called Gina. She gave her up for adoption."

"Christ. That's why he was so obsessed with Gina. She was his own *daughter*. He slept with his own daughter."

"Yes. And when Gina found out who he really was, and what he'd done, she was horrified; she couldn't live with it. She hung herself, filmed it and sent him the video."

"It was an act of retribution. She wanted to punish him."

They talked for over an hour, replaying the elements of the case and reviewing the mistakes they'd made. It felt good to Everton to be included as an equal. But he knew that Helen would have to leave.

She was almost out of the ward when he noticed the Warrant Card and tube of peppermints on his bedside table, and called after her, "Hey. What's this?"

"They're for you, from DCI Teal, if you want them."

Then, with a smile that lit up her face, she was gone.

* * *

Everton jerked awake at 3am. He'd been replaying the tragic story of Gina Lewis in a dream and had felt the crushing blow that Joshua Moon had delivered to his head again. He groaned and tried to wipe the thought from his mind, and something remarkable happened. He realised that his tinnitus had disappeared, that the mosquito inside his head had gone.

Mrs Bauer, his ENT consultant, explained that the blow to his head had probably reversed the damage of an earlier trauma. Everton couldn't remember having suffered one but was happy to accept what she said.

Being free of the perpetual whine took some getting used to. For years, he'd never experienced true silence, even in his sleep or moments of deep concentration or relaxation, and now the sudden realisation of the empty space in his head startled him.

Like his body, his mind would take some time to heal, but he was content. He'd found himself and, hopefully, his family again.